BLOODLINE LEGACY

Deirdre Jonker

Prepublication Data Service
P.O. Box 159, Calwell, ACT Australia 2905
Email: publishaspg@gmail.com
http://www.inspiringpublishers.com

A catalogue record for this book is available from the National Library of Australia

National Library of Australia The Prepublication Data Service

Author: Deirdre Jonker
Title: Bloodline Legacy
Genre: Fiction

Paperback ISBN: 978-1-923250-39-0
ePub2 ISBN: 978-1-923250-40-6

Prologue

"And who are you?" Amy asked as she held Gabrielle facing ahead. Viviana smiled.

"My name is Viviana, and I hope to become a new nanny for this family." Vivianna said with a smile that would have melted Gabriel's dead heart. Amy looked over, confused, at Viviana.

"Hm," Amy said. "I do not recall that I needed a nanny. I have my mother, sister, and an extended aunt that help me with the children," Amy said. Viviana smiled and nodded.

"Your father invited me to be a new nanny. Give you, your mother, sister, and aunt some time to take some time for yourselves," Viviana said. Amy rolled her eyes, wondering if her father was telling the truth or if he had no faith in Amy being a good mother.

Amy sighed and nodded. "Okay. Excuse me for a moment, Viviana, was it?" Amy asked. Viviana nodded. Amy gave a small smile before she turned around and headed for her father, who was sitting on one of the steps halfway up the staircase.

"Father, what is going on? Who is this girl, and why did she suddenly show up at our home?" Amy snapped. Gabriel groaned as both his hands remained on his head. Then the pain seemed to have subsided. Gabriel smiled unexpectedly.

"Oh, Viviana. Yes. She would like to help out with the family. The fact that she was able to find her fiancé, Larry, back, she wanted to see the family some more," Gabriel said.

Amy burrowed her brows. "What?" Amy snapped. "Fiancé of that monster?" Amy ran back toward Viviana, who remained in the same area of the kitchen. Suddenly, Amy felt a strong, sharp sensation in her head, which caused her to fall to her knees while clutching her head. "What are you doing to us?" Amy asked. Viviana shook her head.

"What are you talking about, Amy? I just wanted to become a new nanny for the family," Viviana said as she looked down at Amy. Amy started to grit her teeth till Viviana relaxed her body, which allowed Amy some time to recover.

"What did you do to me, Viviana?" Amy asked as she got to her feet slowly. "What are you?"

Viviana scoffed and rolled her eyes. "Your father never mentioned me, has he?" Viviana said. "Of course not. Why should he?" Amy focused her attention on Viviana.

"What does that mean, Viviana? Are we somehow related?" Amy asked. Viviana glared at Amy before she walked over to the sliding doors that looked out at the courtyard. Amy crossed her arms, looking around to see if there was anyone else in the area.

"Your father turned me into this weird monster, Amy," Vivian said with sadness in her voice. "I was engaged to my beloved Lawrence Harrison, the love of my life, and your father destroyed our lives with his impulsive behavior of having us near killed rather than leaving us alone," Viviana said. "Your father is the actual monster in this world, not Larry and not me. We are both victims of this life; we are focused on living," Viviana said.

Amy relaxed her body and mind as she kept listening to Viviana's sad story. "I was ready to have children and live the life of a housewife and mother, but your father took that dream away from me. I ended up in some woodsy area, all alone, with this extreme thirst and burning sensation in my body. Water did not help. Soda beverages did not help either; as a matter of fact, that stuff made me sick. Then I started hearing distant pounding, which was driving me nuts for a while, till I realized I heard heartbeats," Viviana said.

Amy rolled her eyes. "Yes, I understand where you are going, Viviana, but to make a long story short, why are you here?" Amy asked. Vivina rolled her eyes before turning around to face Amy.

"I wanted to meet Gabriel's offspring. There is another one, is there not?" Viviana asked. Amy did not respond. "I believe it was Jennifer, Jasmine," Viviana said as she kept trying to find the name that sounded similar. Amy sighed.

"Ginger?" Amy snapped. Vivina stopped and smiled.

"Yes. Ginger. Is she around?" Viviana asked. Amy rolled her eyes and shook her head.

"You did not answer my question," Amy snapped. Vivina let out a cackling laugh. "What is so funny, Viviana?" Viviana calmed her laughter.

"I did, Amy, or have you already forgotten? I wanted to meet Gabriel's daughters," Viviana said. Amy shook her head.

"Well," Amy said. "I think our meeting has lasted long enough, so the door is right down the hallway," Amy said as she gestured in that direction. Viviana shook her head.

"Your father invited me, Amy. Why do we not go and see how your father feels about you sending away a newcomer to the family?" Viviana asked with anger in her voice. Amy's eyes went black with rage, and she barred her teeth. Suddenly Gabriel came into the kitchen, causing Viviana to break down, crying.

"Gabriel, your daughter does not like me. She wants me to leave," Viviana said. Gabriel looked horrified at Amy and walked over to Viviana to hold her closely.

"Viviana is staying, Amy. You could use a break from your children and get some proper sleep for once," Gabriel snapped.

Amy looked up at Gabriel with fear and sadness. "Father, what happened?" Amy asked. Viviana smiled at Amy. "She is smiling at me right now, Father." Gabriel looked at Viviana, who turned her expression back to sadness.

"I think it might be best to get some rest, Amy. Please, you need it. You have been working very hard in this family," Gabriel said in his fatherly tone. "Pleas show Viviana where she can tend to your children, Amy, and I shall get us all some refreshments," Gabriel said.

Amy felt disoriented and dizzy from the whole situation and leaned against the wall. "You see, Amy?" Gabriel said. "Feeling tired will do that to a new mother. I guess I can also show Viviana where my beautiful grandchildren are," Gabriel said. Amy shook her head in disbelief as she watched both of them head towards Amy's room. Amy slowly followed them and saw them both enter her bedroom, hearing Viviana making cooing sounds to the children. The children then looked up at her and started to cry. Amy ran into the room and saw Viviana grab a little plush bear from her pocket, which made the children stop instantly.

"How did you do that?" Amy asked astonishingly. Viviana shrugged.

"I guess I am good with children," Viviana said as she grinned at Amy. Ginger suddenly came into the room.

"You must be Ginger," Viviana said as she extended her hand towards Ginger. Ginger looked at Viviana, confused, before she looked over at Amy. "Your father and I have a history together," Viviana said. Ginger scrunched her brow. "Not like anything romantic, but we know each other from a while back. Ginger nodded before shaking hands with Viviana.

Suddenly, Ginger felt this wave of fatigue hit her. "I think I shall take a nap in my room," Ginger said as she walked out of Amy's room. Amy walked after Ginger to find out what just happened. Ginger entered her room and collapsed on the floor.

"Ginger!" Amy screamed. "Ginger!" Nobody came over to help her. Amy put her ear next to Ginger's mouth and could hear her breathe.

The New Guest

Amy walked back to her room and saw Viviana holding Gabrielle in her arms. Gabrielle looked up at Viviana and smiled. Amy felt horrified by the whole situation, especially how lovingly Gabriel looked at Viviana. Amy decided to find out where her mother and Amelia were. Amy decided to walk back to Ginger and still found her on the floor. Amy then walked over to Amelia's quarter and knocked on her door. Amelia opened the door with a confused look.

"Amy, what can I do for you?" Amelia asked. Amy looked behind her to make sure Viviana was not around and made a gesture to enter Amelia's quarter.

"How soundproof is your room, Amelia?" Amy asked as she looked around. "I believe we are in for some dark times, Amelia. Are you familiar with a girl named Viviana?" Amelia gasped. "Okay. That sounds about right. So, she is upstairs right now playing nanny and especially playing my father. I need to get rid of her. She seems to have placed some kind of spell on him, my children, and caused Ginger to faint," Amy said.

Amelia placed her right thumb near her teeth and chewed on the nail nervously. "How did you return from the dead? I thought your father had killed her," Amelia murmured as she walked over to her bookshelf. Amy followed cautiously. "How did she even find out where we live? I believe I did put a spell around our home to keep intruders from knowing the exact location," Amelia said. Amy shrugged.

Amelia looked back at Amy. "What else do you know about her, Amy? Aside from that, your father saw her as a hors d'oeuvres?"

Amelia asked. Amy thought about the time she read her father's journals and occasionally saw her name in some of his writing.

"I recall reading about her in some of my father's journals, Amelia. He wrote about her as if she were such a beautiful and angelic girl. Could he have been jealous of Larry?" Amy asked. Amelia chuckled.

"Your mother was his true heart and blood, Amy. Nobody could ever replace her. Katrina was just a relic for show, but he never gave up on Arabella, nor did he ever let her go to the afterlife. If I know something about that Viviana girl, it is that she was a little sweet treat for your father, but nothing more," Amelia said before she returned her focus back to her books. "Ah, right here. Spells and mind control. I shall see what I can do about our little problem. If your father were to be under her spell, which I would find quite unusual, I would try to help your father regain as much of his conscience as possible. Perhaps you can see what your mother can do as well," Amelia said. Amy nodded.

"Okay," Amy said. "I shall see what my mother and I can do. I should also check up on Ginger and make sure she is awake or at least okay now. Please excuse me." Amy walked back to the main floor and saw how empty it was. She heard faint voices coming from her floor, so she decided to walk back and see what everyone was doing. She noticed Bryan and his brothers were outside of her room, watching Viviana from her room. Amy cleared her voice to get their attention, but their focus remained on Viviana.

"Bryan?" Amy asked. Bryan looked over at Amy and gave her a tiny smile before he returned his gaze back to Viviana. "What are you all doing out here? Larry and Caleb are still out there, you know, and suddenly their girl shows up at our home?" Amy asked.

"Look at how much fun your children are having with Viviana," Bryan said. When Amy entered her room, her children were playing patty cake with Viviana. Amy suddenly felt this nauseous feeling inside her body. Viviana looked up at Amy and smiled.

"Perhaps you should rest, Amy," Viviana said. "I can take your children down to their nursery if you need some time for yourself." Amy shook her head and glared at Viviana.

"I am fine. Perhaps I need something to eat and drink," Amy said as she slowly left the room to see how Ginger was doing. Ginger managed to get on her bed, but she looked quite pale. Amy felt scared when she saw Ginger. Amy then ran over to the cooler, grabbed an unopened bottle of blood, and rushed up to Ginger's room.

"Ginger, please drink this," Amy pleaded. Ginger looked up with glassy eyes. "I had a weird dream, Amy," Ginger said. "I dreamt that we were out in the woods, and Caleb was there to propose to you." Amy quickly undid the screw top and placed the tip of the bottle on Ginger's lips until Ginger gently tilted her head back and let the blood pour down her throat. Ginger started to get color back in her body and managed to hold the bottle in both her hands. She stopped halfway and felt stronger again.

"Ginger," Amy whispered. "We need to get rid of Viviana. I believe she, Larry, and Caleb have something planned. Our father seems to be in some sort of trance whenever he is around her." Ginger nodded.

"Have you spoken to Amelia about spells and enchantments?" Ginger asked. Amy nodded.

"She said we should look into our situation and find out more about Viviana's plans," Amy said. Ginger nodded.

"Good," Ginger said before she handed the bottle back to Amy. Amy finished the bottle and placed it on the floor.

"Perhaps Darcia might also know more about these types of things. I will see what she and Alistair are doing. They might be able to coerce Viviana to leave our home," Amy said before she grabbed the empty bottle and walked out of Ginger's room. Amy walked over to Darcia and Alistair's room and knocked on the door. Alistair answered with a warm smile on his face.

"Amy, what a surprise," Alistair said. "What can we do for you?" Amy looked around and gestured to enter the room. Alistair looked concerned at her, but let Amy enter the room.

"I think we have a major problem right now," Amy said as she approached and walked further into their room. "Are you both familiar with a girl named Viviana?" Alistair and Darcia both exchanged worried expressions. "Okay. That sounds about right," Amy said. "So, she has put some form of spell on my father, and I would like her to leave. How do we go about this problem?" Amy asked. Darcia got out of her side of the bed and walked over to Amy.

"How did she even find us, Amy? I thought Amelia put a spell on this place. Are Larry or Caleb in the area?" Darica asked.

Amy shrugged. "I am not sure, Darica, but I am not sure about anything right now. We need to find a way to get her to leave. I think she has something planned for us, and I am worried." Darcia placed her right hand on Amy's shoulder.

"We will take care of this problem and finally be done with Larry the proper way," Darcia said before she looked over at Alistair, remembering how he never mentioned setting Larry's body on fire that one time.

Alistiar rolled his eyes and sighed. "I love you too, wife," Alistair said. Darcia smiled and looked back at Amy. "Does your mother know about our new guest?" Amy shrugged. "If I know of anything regarding enchantments, it is that they can be quite powerful. If Viviana is some sort of enchantress of some kind, it might weaken our stance. We are shape shifters, but we also have our weaknesses," Darcia said. "See what your mother knows about this situation. Perhaps she can help." Amy nodded and left the room without saying goodbye.

Darcia crossed her arms in anxiety and felt a sense of nausea inside her body. Alistair quickly wrapped his arms around her, holding her close to him. "Are you okay, my love?" Alistair asked. Darcia nodded. "I hope this situation will be temporary. Perhaps we can see who this Viviana girl is?" Alistair asked. Darcia shrugged and nodded.

As they both walked over to where Viviana was, Amy found her mother outside in the courtyard, looking up at the stars. "Mother,"

Amy said with fear in her voice. "We have a problem." Arabella turned around with concern.

"What is the problem, my child?" Arabella asked. Amy walked at a quick pace to Arabella and bent closer to her ear.

"We have a powerful sorceres as a new nanny, but a dangerous one, I think," Amy whispered. Arabella looked at Amy and got to her feet.

"Where is your father, Amy?" Arabella asked quietly. Amy looked up at the window of her bedroom, where the lights were still on. "Does Amelia or anyone else know about her?" Arabella asked. Amy nodded. "Where is your father?"

"He was with her, looking so lovingly at her. I am not sure what happened, but it appears that they both have some history," Amy said. Arabella nodded.

"I have heard about that girl. There is something dark about that one," Arabella said. "We should make sure she does not get near your children, Amy, or she could put a spell on them as well," Arabella said.

Amy nervously started biting her thumb nail. "Where are your children, Amy?" Arabella asked.

"With her," Amy murmuered. Arabella sighed. "She came into the house and mentioned that Father allowed her to be the nanny of the house, even though I already mentioned to him that I have you, Amelia, and Ginger." Arabella nodded.

"Okay. Let me see what your father is doing and see how we can get rid of her," Arabella said before she walked back into the castle. She walked over to Gabriel's office and saw him sitting at his desk with dilated, dreamy eyes. "Gabriel?" Arabella asked. Gabriel looked over at Arabella and smiled.

"It is wonderful to finally have a nanny, is it not, wife?" Gabriel asked. Arabella sighed and closed the door. "Gabriel, what is going on? Why are you acting like this?"

Gabriel smiled and looked over at the door. "Viviana is quite precious. I remember when I saw her back at the tavern. So angelic and pure," Gabriel said. Arabella snapped her fingers at him to get his attention.

"Gabriel, we need to get rid of her. She is causing a lot of problems right now. What do you think? We already have a crowded home anyway."

Gabriel scoffed and shook his head. "Never, Arabella," Gabriel said with a growl. "She is here to stay." Arabella suddenly felt this uneasy fear inside of her. Something she had never felt before. Gabriel barred his teeth at her. Suddenly, there was a knock on the door. Gabriel returned to his usual self. "Enter." The door opened, and Lucien, Vladimir, and Adrian entered the office.

"Gabriel, we were wondering who that new girl is," Lucien said. Gabriel smiled.

"Our new nanny. Viviana. She was once Larry's fiancé, but I think she has fallen for me as well," Gabriel said with a dreamy expression.

Arabella glared at Lucien. "Lucien, there is something going on with Gabriel. He is not his usual self," Arabella said. Lucien nodded.

"Perhaps we should give our Gabriel some alone time and let him gather his thoughts without any interference from us," Lucien said as he guided Arabella out of his office. Arabella walked out of the office with the three guys and waited for the door to click shut. "Arabella," Lucien said as he placed both his hands on Arabella's shoulders. "Everything is going to be okay. We think you deserve a little vacation of some sort, so let the guys take over for now. What do you say? You, Amelia, Darcia, and your children?"

Arabella glared at Lucien and then at the other two men. "I would remove your hands from yours, Lucien," Arabella said sternly. Lucien smiled and removed his hands. "Something is going on, and I will do my best to fix it." Arabella then walked over to where Amy was. She found Amy in her bedroom, biting her beautiful manicured nails with broken, tethered claws. "Amy," Arabella whispered. Amy looked up at Arabella. "Your hands. I think we should get you fed." Arabella grabbed Amy by her arm, pulled her out of her room, and walked over to Ginger, who remained in the same position where Amy left her.

"Perhaps it is time that we girls have a hunt of our own. The blood we have been drinking does not appear to have any effect on decreasing our appetite. What do you say?" Arabella asked as she looked at both Amy and Ginger. They both nodded. "This will be our little secret," Arabella whispered. Before they got a chance to leave Ginger's room, Viviana stood in the doorway.

"Are you girls going out?" Viviana asked. Arabella looked sternly at her. "I would like to join you three for a girls outing if you like."

Amy cleared her throat. "What about my children, Viviana? Should you not read them a nursery rhyme of some sort?" Amy snapped. Viviana entered the room like a slinky cat. "They are all asleep. Babies need many hours of sleep for their development, Amy," Viviana snapped back. "I would like to get to know the Ambrose women a bit better. What do you say?"

Arabella looked over at Amy. "We are huntresses, Viviana. What does that make you?" Arabella asked. Viviana shrugged.

"I do not know what you mean by huntress, but I am quite basic myself, but I can learn to become one," Viviana said. Arabella sighed.

"How do you feel about blood, Viviana?" Amy asked. Viviana's eyes widened. Amy waited for Viviana to respond. "Well?" Viviana shrugged.

"I have seen a lot of blood in my days, so that does not bother me. Look, if you do not want me to join, I can stay, but I was really hoping to meet you three and bond on an emotional level with such strong women," Viviana said.

Amy rolled her eyes and looked over at Ginger, who stared sternly at Viviana. "Well, I guess a hunt for one night with the four of us will not be that bad, so feel free to join us, Viviana," Amy said before she let out an irritated sigh. Viviana smiled.

"Ready when you all are," Viviana said before she left the room and headed down the stairs. Ginger placed her left hand on Amy's shoulder.

"What was that, Amy?" Ginger asked. "Why did you invite her to join us? She gave you the opportunity to have her stay behind, but you are letting her get closer to us. I do not trust her. Mother, please say something," Ginger said.

Arabella sighed. "I want to know more about this Viviana girl and see how big of a threat she is to us," Arabella whispered before she headed towards the front door of the castle. Viviana waited patiently by the door, occasionally checking her nails. Arabella walked down first, then Amy, and finally Ginger followed. Viviana had a smile on her face as she saw the other three approach her.

"What will we be hunting for this evening, girls?" Viviana asked. Arabella smiled and walked past Viviana to open the door. She gestured for Viviana to leave and allowed Amy and Ginger to follow before she closed the door behind her.

"Amy and Ginger have their favorite spots for hunting," Arabella said. "I have had my moments of hunting with my husband, but I have let my children lead the way," Arabella said as she followed her daughters in the direction of the same park where they had an occasional battle with Larry. Viviana stopped at the entrance. Arabella turned around with concern. "Are you okay, Viviana?" Arabella asked.

Viviana did not respond and looked around the park area. "What makes this park so special?" Viviana asked. Amy and Ginger both chuckled. "What?"

"This is one of our hunting grounds, Viviana. You are not scared, are you?" Amy asked teasingly. Vivina glared at Amy and looked behind her.

"I think I might want to return to the castle and make sure your children are not awake," Viviana said. Amy kept her focus on Viviana and wondered if she should follow Viviana to where she was heading.

"Do you need someone to walk you home, Viviana? It might not be safe for a woman to walk by herself in the dark at this time," Amy said. Viviana looked over at Amy and smiled.

"I will be fine," Viviana said as she turned around and headed back in the same direction she came from. Amy, Ginger, and Arabella exchanged glances.

"What should we do?" Amy asked. Ginger looked at Amy with concern. "I want to see where she is going. There is something about her stopping at this park that pricked my ears up."

Arabella looked around and saw how quiet and empty the streets were. "Perhaps we should see what the nanny has planned, my dears," Arabella said as the three of them headed in the direction where they were able to catch Viviana's scent. Suddenly, Amy felt this intense, sharp stabbing pain in her head, which caused her to stop. "Amy, what is going on?" Arabella asked as she wrapped her arms around Amy. Amy started drooling and barring her teeth. She pushed Arabella off of her and fell backward.

Ginger covered her mouth with both her hands. "Mother, what should we do?" Ginger asked. Arabella looked around.

"I need to know where the girl went. Please stay with your sister for a moment," Arabella said before she took off running, shape shifting herself into a wolf, and tracking down Viviana's scent till she reached the castle. She opened the door and saw Gabriel, Adrian, Vladimir, and Lucien sitting with Viviana, looking at her like she was a unique painting.

Viviana stopped talking when she saw Arabella. "The children are fine, Arabella. They are still sleeping so innocently." Arabella looked back and saw Amy and Ginger approaching the castle, where Amy was leaning against Ginger.

"Where are your children, Arabella?" Viviana asked. Arabella returned her focus back to Viviana.

"What did you do to my daughter?" Arabella snapped. Gabriel got to his feet with anger in his eyes.

"What are you talking about, Arabella? Viviana has been with us for some time. And look, here come Amy and Ginger," Gabriel said as Arabella saw how pale and disoriented Amy looked.

"Gabriel, please snap out of it," Arabella said pleadingly. Gabriel held up his right hand to shush Arabella. "Something is going on,

Gabriel. You need to snap out of her spell. Please remember me, your wife," Arabella said. Gabriel shook his head.

"Please take our daughters out for a nice walk, Arabella. Perhaps a little hunt would do you all good," Gabriel said before he sat back down in his chair. Viviana had a faint smile on her face before she placed her hand on top of Gabriel's.

"Your grandchildren are doing well, Arabella. Enjoy a nice treat with your children," Viviana said. Gabriel smiled at Viviana and placed his other hand on top of hers. Arabella felt nauseated about the whole situation and had to find out where Amelia was. Arabella approached Amelia's quarter and waited for her to open up.

"Amelia, this is getting worse. She attacked Amy, I believe," Arabella said. Amelia gestured for Arabella to enter her room.

"We need to find out what Larry is planning before I take any measures. That girl might be puppeteered by him or Caleb, where they are pulling the strings and using the poor girl," Amelia said. "I have been reading up on some of the spells and potions I could use, but we need to make sure this will not cascade or backfire somehow. Do you know of the location of Larry and Caleb?"

Arabella shook her head. "Okay. Perhaps Alistair and Darcia might know where they are. Have you seen them lately?" Arabella thought about it and shook her head.

"How about I help you find them? I want to see who this Viviana girl is in modern times. I have heard about her, but I do not recall ever meeting her in person," Amelia said as she took the lead up to the main floor. When both Amelia and Arabella entered the dining quarter, Viviana was at the table alone, while Gabriel was getting himself a bottle of blood with two glasses.

"Would you care for a treat, Viviana?" Gabriel asked. Viviana smiled and nodded. Amelia sat down, across from Gabriel, but kept her focus on Viviana.

"So," Amelia said. "I must apologize. Forgive me for not introducing myself. I am Amelia, the sister of Gabriel Ambrose," Amelia said as she extended her hand. Viviana looked uncomfortably at Amelia's hand and then grabbed Gabriel's instead.

"It is okay, Viviana. Amelia is a good friend of the family. She is not dangerous," Gabriel said in a soothing tone. Arabella felt her anger rising in her throat. "And my wife, you know, right?" Gabriel said as he gestured toward Arabella. Viviana smiled and nodded. She then took her full glass of blood and took a sip from it. It made her wince.

"Oh dear," Gabriel said. "Are you all right? Is it the blood?" Viviana shrugged. "Perhaps we should open up a new bottle. I believe Hildegard went out for a new trip to a blood bank, as I recall, but is there anything you are able to eat, Viviana?" Viviana smiled and shook her head.

"I am fine, Gabriel. It is just something I need to get used to, I guess. An acquired taste."

Gabriel smiled and looked back at Amelia and Arabella. "Would you care to join us at the table, Arabella?" Gabriel asked. Arabella took a seat next to Amelia and crossed her arms. "Did you need a glass, my love?" Gabriel asked as he looked at Arabella. Here, let me get you a glass." Gabriel got to his feet and walked over to the cabinet for two empty glasses, brought them back to the table, poured a full glass of blood, and handed them to Arabella and Amelia. "What have you ladies been up to lately?" Gabriel asked as he looked over at Amelia and Arabella.

Amelia smiled. "Noting much. I am just reading some of my old books and relaxing as much as possible. Perhaps this might come across as rude, but how did you two meet, and I am not talking about Arabella," Amelia said. Gabriel felt a sense of uneasiness until Viviana squeezed her hand on Gabriel's.

"I remember it like it had happened about a week ago," Viviana said. "I remember seeing Gabriel for the first time, so pure and beautiful with his marble complexion, his black suit, his black hair, and his red black eyes. He had met my fiancé, Lawrence Harrison, and I just remember the moment Gabriel entered the tavern. It was interesting to see how much power he had, but I know how hard it was for him to live the lifestyle he had in our world. Since then, I have wanted to get to know him. My fiancé had been talking about him for so long that I was quite intrigued by who Gabriel Ambrose was. That is how I met him," Viviana said before she loosened her grip on his hand.

Amelia smiled before she took a sip from her glass. "Sounds romantic," Amelia murmured. Viviana looked sternly at Amelia.

"What about you, Amelia?" Viviana said it snidely. "How did you come to be in this family?" Viviana asked. Amelia chuckled and looked over at Arabella, who smiled at Viviana.

"Well, that is quite a long story, but I used to work at this store, making dresses and jewelry with some of my friends, then I blacked out due to some spell of some sort, and I woke up in this castle with Gabriel next to him, cradling me like a baby. He gave me some of his fresh blood, and that is how I came to be who I am. Arabella has a beautiful story about how she met Gabriel, but I think I would like to retire to my bedroom. Thank you for the drink, Gabriel. Arabella, Viviana, I shall see you both around," Amelia said before she got to her feet and headed towards her quarter.

The Trap

When Amelia entered her quarter, she felt a sense of nausea hitting her hard, causing her to throw up her blood. Arabella came running towards Amelia, holding her hair and stroking her back. "What is happening, Amelia? Is this Viviana doing this to you?" Amelia had to catch her breath before she could answer.

"I think so," Viviana said. "I felt a sense of dark power around her as she was holding Gabriel's hand. We need to find out where Larry and Caleb are and see how we can end this situation," Amelia said before she struggled to her feet.

Arabella walked over to Amy's room to find her weak. "Ginger, I need you to keep a close watch on your sister. Perhaps we should hunt for someone and bring her back to our place. Amelia and I are going to try and find Larry and Caleb and see what is going on," Arabella said as she looked down at Amy's weak complexion. "And please keep an eye out for her younglings. I am sure they will also need to feed soon." Arabella leaned down and kissed Amy on top of her head. "Stay strong, my child."

Arabella and Amelia headed for the front door until they heard Gabriel clear his throat. "Ladies, what are you two planning for this evening?" Gabriel asked as he stood about ten feet away from them. Arabella and Amelia exchanged glances. Amelia smiled. "We were just thinking about going out for a nice evening stroll. Just the two of us," Amelia said. Gabriel approached them slowly.

"At this time? It is four o'clock in the morning. I do not want you both out there at this time. Save the evening stroll for tomorrow," Gabriel said with a smile.

Arabella rolled her eyes, causing Gabriel to look over at her with concern. "Is everything okay, wife?" Gabriel asked. Arabella sighed.

"We need to find Larry and Caleb. There is something wrong, Gabriel. We need to fix this problem. We think Viviana has put a spell on you all," Arabella said. Gabriel chuckled.

"What? A spell? My dears," Gabriel said. "She is pure human. She has no spells or powers that could overthrow me, the master and patriarch of shapeshifters." Amelia scrunched her brow and took a step backwards. "Amelia," Gabriel said. "Please do not leave right now. I will talk to Viviana about this. I am sure if there was something dark amongst us, I would know," Gabriel said.

Amelia crossed her arms as she leaned against the front door. "Would you or have you been someone's puppet, Gabriel?" Amelia murmured. Gabriel glared at her and grabbed Amelia by her wrist.

"One more word with that tone, and I will have you in the dungeon, Amelia. Remember how I love you both very much, but I cannot allow such tempers towards me, ladies," Gabriel said before he loosened his grasp on Amelia.

Arabella put her right arm around Amelia, holding her close. "Perhaps a slumber would do us good, Amelia," Arabella said before they both walked away from Gabriel towards Amelia's quarter.

"I shall see you in our quarter, Arabella," Gabriel said before he walked toward the basement. Amelia gave Arabella a worried look. Arabella smiled and gently patted Amelia's shoulders.

"If anything happens, Arabella, promise me that you will run over to me," Amelia said. Arabella nodded and walked over to the basement door, where Gabriel was waiting for her.

"Is everything okay, Arabella?" Gabriel asked. Arabella nodded and gestured for Gabriel to walk down first. Arabella followed, but she sensed some darkness about him. Arabella stopped in her tracks and wanted to turn around until Gabriel grabbed Arabella by her hand. "Arabella, what is going on? Why did you stop walking?" Gabriel asked. Arabella felt fear inside of her, but she did not know how to handle the situation without there being a potential fight between them.

Arabella tried to relax her mind and nodded. "I am fine. I just saw Amy some hours ago, and she looked quite ill, Gabriel. I would like to check up on her, if you would not mind," Arabella said. Gabriel released his hold on Arabella.

"Well, as long as you join me for our slumber, Arabella," Gabriel said before he turned around to go to his bed. Arabella walked back to the main floor and noticed Viviana was at the top of the stairs, which caused Arabella to flinch.

"Apologies, Arabella," Viviana said. "I did not mean to frighten you. What are you doing up here? Gabriel mentioned how you all sleep quite early in the morning."

Arabella gave her a tiny smile before she walked past her. "Are you sleeping elsewhere tonight?" Viviana asked. Arabella turned around and walked towards her. "Viviana, who are you, really?" Arabella asked. Viviana did not respond. "Okay. Have a good morning to you too," Arabella said before she walked over to the staircase. Viviana did not move, which worried Arabella about what she was going to do. Arabella quickly walked over to Amy's room and saw an empty blood bottle next to her bed and Amy and Ginger sleeping together. It relieved Arabella to see how much better Amy looked.

When Arabella walked over to the basement door, Viviana was gone. Arabella decided to walk down to the sleeping quarter and noticed the door to their quarter was open. She remembered Amelia telling her to run if something was off, but she wanted to make sure this tension was all in her head. Arabella walked slowly over to the room and saw Gabriel lying peacefully on his back in the pitch- dark room. Arabella slowly walked over to her side of the bed, where the covers were open for her to enter. Arabella looked at Gabriel again and realized how paranoid she was getting.

Arabella got into bed and turned to face Gabriel. She closed her eyes and let herself drift off into a deep slumber. In her dream, she was back at the farm where she had grown up and remembered how she had met Gabriel there after he slaughtered her family. She looked around and noticed the sun was shining, but she was not burning. She saw all the cows and pigs walking around the area. It seemed like an average day until she heard screaming coming from her home. She ran into the house and saw Viviana standing against the wall with Gabriel across from her. This time, it was Gabriel who seduced her into loving him while Arabella stood behind him.

"Gabriel," Arabella said. "It was me who you had turned. Please, I am your love and your wife." Arabella turned around and looked at her like she was not there. He turned around to face Viviana and took her in his arms, with her whimpering, unable to struggle.

"Gabriel, please look at me," Arabella pleaded. Gabriel turned to face Arabella and saw her this time. "My love, I am your wife." Gabriel smirked and turned his gaze over to Viviana, who smiled back at him, showing Arabella the engagement ring that was originally Arabella's.

"There is only one woman who I can love," Gabriel said as he kept his focus on Viviana. "And it is you."

Arabella woke up screaming, causing Gabriel to wake up. "Arabella!" Gabriel screamed. "What happened?" Arabella got out of bed, turning on her nightstand lamp. Gabriel looked irritated at Arabella. "What happened?" Arabella sighed and relaxed her body.

"I think I had a horrible dream, Gabriel. What time is it?" Arabella asked. Gabriel checked his watch.

"About one in the afternoon. You still have a few more hours of rest. It looks quite bright out there today," Gabriel said.

Arabella sighed before she got back into bed. "What was your dream about, Arabella?" Gabriel asked in a soothing tone. Arabella felt sadness in her throat, unable to talk. Gabriel placed his left hand gently on Arabella's right cheek. "Whatever it was, it was just a dream, Arabella. Nothing more. Try and get some more sleep."

Arabella lowered her body to the matrass, turned off the light, but was not able to sleep. She wanted to do something about Viviana. She knew she had to take care of this problem. Gabriel wrapped his arms around Arabella, holding her close. "Sleep, wife," Gabriel whispered. Arabella closed her eyes and managed to fall asleep again. When Arabella woke up, she felt dizzy and confused, but nightmares could cause a lot of psychological problems. She walked over to the main floor and saw Lucien, Vladimir, and Adrian with Amelia and Ginger in the dining quarter. Arabella checked the time, and it was going on eleven in the evening.

"Good evening, sleeping beauty," Lucien said as he raised his glass toward Arabella. "Care for a drink?" Arabella looked around and felt confused.

"Where is Gabriel?" Arabella asked. Lucien gestured toward Gabriel's office. Arabella walked over to the office and knocked on his door.

"Enter," Gabriel said. Arabella opened the door and saw Gabriel at his desk, with Viviana sitting across from him.

"Oh," Arabella said. "I hope I was not interrupting something," Arabella asked. Gabriel smiled and gestured for the other chair.

"Of course not, Arabella," Gabriel said. "How are you feeling? Were you able to sleep?" Arabella reluctantly sat next to Viviana and felt something dark in the room. "Hildegard came back with another batch of blood, Arabella. You look like you could use some breakfast."

Viviana smiled at Gabriel and looked over at Arabella. "You look rather pale and tired," Viviana said.

Arabella glared at Viviana. "Perhaps I shall," Arabella said before she got to her feet. Gabriel cleared his throat.

"Viviana, would you like a drink?" Gabriel asked. Viviana smiled and shrugged. "I could always consume more sustenance, if you would not mind, Arabella?" Arabella felt anger inside of her.

"If you would not mind, Arabella? Get all three of us a glass from our new source?" Gabriel asked. Arabella nodded and walked over to the dining quarter to find the other members sitting around.

Arabella walked by them and grabbed three empty glasses and a new bottle of blood, placing them on a trey that Hildegard normally used, and brought the trey over to Gabriel's office. Arabella placed the trey on Gabriel's desk, poured three glasses of blood, and sat back down. Gabriel admired the mannerism of Arabella's hospitality. He reached over and touched Arabella's hand. Viviana looked over at the manner in which Gabriel was stroking Arabella's hand, causing Gabriel to feel a sudden, sharp stabbing pain in his head. He clutched his head with both hands. Arabella got up to help Gabriel, but he pushed her away.

"Viviana, stop!" Arabella yelled. Viviana glared at Arabella with fury. "Enough of this nonsense. I need you to leave." Gabriel got to his feet, grabbed Arabella by her wrist, and pushed her out of the office before he locked the door. Viviana relaxed her body. The pain in Gabriel's head subsided.

"I think your wife hates me, Gabriel. I am not sure if I want to stay in this place for long," Viviana said. Gabriel looked up at her with bloodshot eyes.

"You never have to leave us, Viviana. You can stay here as long as you like," Gabriel said weakly.

Viviana got to her feet and wrapped her arms around Gabriel. "I think I shall check up on your grandchildren, Gabriel," Viviana said before she left the office. Viviana undid the lock of the door, opened the door, and saw Arabella standing a few feet away from the doorframe with her arms closed. Arabella kept quiet until Viviana closed the door and waited for Viviana to talk.

"What is with the hostility, Arabella? I mean you or Gabriel, no harm. I have no idea why you are treating me like I am a monster."

Arabella cleared her throat before she spoke. "I know what you are planning. That little trick back there to get my husband to kneel before you with pain and suffering, I know how much you are hurting him. Gabriel is not the best man to have fallen in love with, but he has so much guilt and suffering inside of him as well. To make him suffer after what he has done is wrong, Viviana," Arabella said.

Viviana let out a shrill cackle. "What?" Viviana said. "You think I am causing him pain? Please, Arabella, you are not that dumb to know that I am just here to offer my services as a nanny for Amy's children. Nothing more. Please, would you mind me leaving for those kids?"

Arabella was not able to stop her from going up to Amy's room, but she wanted to do something badly. "You will be gone before you know it, Viviana. Just because you are the puppeteer, dangling

Gabriel like a doll does not give you full power over everyone. Amelia and I have not fallen for your tricks, Viviana. Remember that," Arabella snapped.

Arabella waited for Viviana to be out of sight before she walked back into Gabriel's office, seeing him paler and weaker than before. "Gabriel," Arabella whispered. "Let me help you. Please." Gabriel looked up at her with a dazed expression. "All will be forgiven in the end, so whatever you want to do, I know you will never act like this. Here, have some more blood," Arabella said as she poured him another glass.

Gabriel chuckled before he downed the entire glass in a few seconds. "My eyes are burning, Arabella," Gabriel whispered. "I think I shall rest for a while." Arabella nodded and watched Gabriel struggle to his feet as he left his office. Arabella knew she had to take action. She ran over to Amelia, who was in her quarter, filing her nails. Arabella knocked impatiently on Amelia's door and waited for her to answer.

"Amelia, we must deal with this problem right now," Arabella snapped. "We need to find Larry and Caleb right now." Amelia nodded and got to her feet, and they both headed out until they came across Alistair and Darcia, who came in through the front door of the castle.

"Alistair, Darcia," Arabella said, acknowledging them both. "Would you both be interested in tracking down Larry and Caleb?" Darcia and Alistair exchanged glances.

"They are not at Larry's apartment complex, Arabella. I am not certain where he is now," Alistair said. Arabella and Amelia headed outside anyway to see if they could find Larry and Caleb until they heard Alistair and Darcia chuckling.

"How simpleminded women are in falling for such traps," Larry said as he shifted from Alistair to himself and watched Caleb shifting into Darcia.

Arabella barred her teeth, crouching down. Larry quickly grabbed Amelia from behind, holding his nails to her neck. "If you take one step closer, Arabella, she dies," Larry hissed.

Caleb smirked at Arabella. "What do you want?" Arabella asked, remaining in the same stance. Larry did not move. Arabella returned to her normal self.

"Good," Larry whispered. "I need you both to stop looking for us, or we will go after your grandchildren, Arabella." Arabella scrunched her brow in confusion.

"How did you know?" Arabella asked. Larry and Caleb exchanged glances.

"The real Darcia and Alistair are our captives right now, but they are not anywhere in the most obvious areas. They are being babysat by my sister and friends. Viviana will have Gabriel killed off this time for real, and there is nothing you can do about it," Larry said before he pushed Amelia out of his arms.

Caleb walked over to Larry. "We will take our leave, but you will not see your friends until we know it is safe to release them," Larry said before he turned around. Amelia wrapped her arms around Arabella, hanging onto her for support. "Arabella, what do we do?" Amelia asked in a worried tone. "Please, Arabella, say something." Arabella watched Larry and Caleb leave the premises of their castle. "We need to get the other members involved, but first, we need to get back into the castle and see how Amy and Ginger are doing," Arabella said as she peeled Amelia's hands off her body.

Darcia, where are you? Arabella asked with her thoughts. There was silence. *Darcia, whatever happens, Amelia and I will take care of it all. Hang in there.* Again, there was silence. "Amelia, I need you to tell me more about your spell books and explain to me what each enchantment means. I think we are headed for a spell battle," Arabella said. Amelia nodded as they both headed inside. "First, I must see my daughters," Arabella said. Amelia and Arabella both walked over to Amy's bedroom and saw her asleep with her children on the floor with toys. "It looks good from this angle. What about Ginger?"

Ginger was nowhere to be seen in her room. Arabella walked out of her room and headed for the dining quarter to find her and Gabriel sitting together, drinking blood. "Gabriel?" Arabella asked.

"I thought you needed to rest. Gabriel looked up with clear black eyes. Ginger looked up at Arabella with concern.

"Are you all right, mother?" Ginger asked. Arabella looked at both Ginger and Gabriel, and then at Amelia.

"What is going on, Amelia?" Arabella asked. Ginger smiled at Arabella and looked back at Gabriel. "Come with me, Arabella. I think the situation is more serious than it was before," Amelia said as she yanked Arabella by her arm to her quarter. Arabella and Amelia were in Amelia's quarter, going through different spell books.

"Ginger looked weird, Amelia. Where is Viviana? I must see her," Arabella said. Amelia shushed Arabella. "What? If she harms any of my babies, I will end her, Amelia," Arabella snapped.

Amelia closed the book she was holding. "Viviana is playing a game with you, Arabella; do you not see that? She is bating you in some psychological mind game. Try not to lose yourself in this situation. Ginger might be another one of her puppets, Arabella. We will save them all," Amelia said in a soothing tone. "Right now, we need to play her game. It is a dangerous game, but we will win in the end," Amelia whispered.

Arabella sighed and leaned against Amelia's sofa, closing her eyes. "I hope you are right, dear Amelia," Arabella murmured. "I am so tired of conflicts with Larry, Caleb, and now Viviana. How did Alistair and Darcia allow themselves to get kidnapped like that?" Arabella asked. Amelia did not respond while she was reading some passages on enchantments. *Darcia, please answer me. Are you still alive?* Arabella thought. Again, there was no response. "I am worried, Amelia," Arabella whispered as she was fidgeting with the fabric of Amelia's sofa's pillow she was holding.

Amelia kept going through different pages, but nothing seemed to match the situation they were currently in. "This is frustrating," Amelia snapped before she walked back to her bookcase. "There are ancient spells and stories, but nothing about what Viviana is doing. I am not sure if it would be wise to go into the human world library since most of those books are based on history and nothing about spells or enchantments. Most of those books anyway are just fictional, so that would be more of a waste of time," Amelia said. "Where would I need to look for books about puppeteers?" Amelia asked.

As Amelia and Arabella were trying to figure out this problem, Amy woke up from her nap, feeling tired but also in need of feeding. She got out of bed and struggled to remain on her feet. She leaned against the wall and looked over to see her children crawling around. The three of them looked up at Amy, who was also in need of feeding. "Let mommy get something to eat first before I let you three suck from my life source," Amy said as she walked with her hand against the wall, brushing by her, towards the door. When Amy opened up the door, Viviana was standing in front of her.

"Amy, are you all right? You look rather tired. Did you sleep enough?" Viviana asked with concern in her eyes. Amy gave her a weak smile.

"I am hungry, Viviana; I need to get myself a bottle from the cooler." Viviana smiled.

"I can get you a bottle, if you like. Let you remain close with your babies," Viviana said before she bolted down the stairs. Amy scrunched her brow with confusion before she looked over at her children, who had smiles on their faces.

Amy walked back to her bed and sat on the edge of it, trying to sit up as straight as she could. Viviana came back moments later with the cap off. "Here you go, mommy," Viviana said teasingly. Amy smiled as she extended her hand to take the bottle from her hands. Viviana handed her the bottle and decided to sit in one of the other chairs in her room.

"Any sweet dreams, Amy?" Viviana asked. Amy took a sip from the bottle, which made her wince. "Is everything okay, Amy?"

Amy looked over at Viviana. "What source is this, Viviana? This tastes a bit more bitter than it did before," Amy said as she placed the bottle on her nightstand.

"Oh, I am not sure, Amy," Viviana said. "I got this from the cooler, but perhaps this is a different type of blood? If it tastes bitter, it could have been from an elderly person or from a sick person. I am not sure about such things," Viviana said. Amy looked at her, wondering if Viviana might have spiked the blood somehow.

"Have you seen my father lately, Viviana?" Amy asked. Viviana's eyes widened at that question. "About a few days ago. He is doing well, as is your mother," Viviana said with a smile. Amy nodded.

"What about Alistair and Darica, or even Bryan?" Amy asked. "I have been meaning to talk to Bryan about some things, but lately I just have no energy inside of me," Amy said. Viviana had a sympathetic expression as she looked at Amy.

"No, sadly, but if you tell me, I can find out where they might be and give Bryan the message."

Amy looked over at her with confusion. "Viviana," Amy said. "I was wondering something." Amy wondered if she was going to overstep and cause problems with her question, but she knew that if she could not ask, she might not get a chance in the end. Just then, there was a knock on the door. "Come in," Amy said. Bryan came into the room with his brothers.

"Bryan," Amy said. "What a surprise! I have been meaning to get Viviana to look for you." Bryan smiled at Amy and then at Viviana. Bryan approached Amy and sat next to her, with Viviana on his other side.

"What would you like to talk about, Amy?" Bryan asked as he kept his eyes focused on Viviana. Amy snapped her fingers. Bryan looked at Amy with concern. "Are you all right, Amy?" Bryan asked. Amy looked over at Viviana.

"Could you all give us some privacy for a few minutes?" Amy asked. Viviana nodded and left the room. The other boys followed her instantly. "Bryan," Amy said. "I have not been feeling so optimal, but I was wondering if you could try out the new blood from this bottle?" Amy asked.

Bryan took the bottle from her table and placed it on his lips, but he did not sip. "Hm," Bryan said. "It smells musty. How old is this blood anyway, Amy?" Bryan asked. Amy looked over at him with concern.

"You can smell that it tastes old? Viviana brought that up for me. What could be in that bottle that would ruin such flavors, Bryan?" Amy asked. Bryan smiled and looked over at Amy.

"Do you think Viviana is tampering with our source, Amy? Please, Amy; she is a harmless lamb. I do not think someone like her would do anything like that to us. Larry or Caleb, most likely, but not her. Have you seen the way she engages with your children, Amy? She is like a goddess," Bryan said with a smile on his face.

Amy started to feel sadness building inside of her. "I feel like I am going crazy, Bryan. What should I do?" Amy asked. Bryan placed his right hand on Amy's left shoulder.

"Do not overthink newcomers immediately, Amy. I can understand that new women cause jealousy with other women, but I have no feelings for her whatsoever. My heart belongs to you, if you still want it, of course," Bryan said. Amy smiled and wrapped her arms around him.

"My suggestion to you, Amy, is to get as much rest and relaxation as possible and take care of yourself, okay?" Bryan asked before he released himself from Amy's arms. Amy nodded. "Good. I can see if there is a new bottle for you," Bryan said before he left the room. Moments later, he came back with a new bottle and handed it to Amy. Amy took a sip, which was better than the other bottle. "Look, you are getting some color back in your cheeks, Amy. I am going to see where my parents are," Bryan said before he left the room and closed Amy's bedroom door.

Amy started to feel relieved again. Perhaps she did need to take better care of herself. Perhaps a break from everything and lounging around or having a spa day would help her regain her strength again. Amy got to her feet and picked up Gabrielle to feed her first. Then she picked up Maggie, and then Nathaniel. She then decided to see what everyone else was up to. Amy walked down the staircase and noticed how quiet it was. Perhaps some of them were out hunting or sleeping, but she wanted to see where her parents and sister were. She walked into the dining quarter to find Adrian, Vladimir, and Lucien drinking from a different bottle.

"Good evening, sleeping beauty," Lucien said teasingly. Amy smiled as she approached them. "How have you been? From what I hear around our home, I know how well Viviana is doing. She is such a precious jewel, Amy. You are lucky to have someone to take on some of the responsibilities." Amy frowned at that comment. "Have you seen my father?" Amy asked. Lucien shrugged.

"Perhaps in his study room, sleeping quarter, or perhaps outside?" Lucien said. Amy nodded and headed for Gabriel's study room.

Amy knocked on the door but did not hear a response. Amy knocked on the door again. Again, there was no response. Amy decided to open the door and did not find Gabriel in his office. This was a bit weird, but then again, Lucien did say that he could also be sleeping or outside. Amy decided to head towards the sliding doors towards the patio and saw Gabriel sitting at a table with Viviana next to him. "Father?" Amy asked. Gabriel looked away from Viviana and up at Amy with a smile. Amy looked over at Viviana with concern, but remembered that she could not really overshoot the mark about her strange feelings towards Viviana.

"Amy, my sweet child," Gabriel said. "Please, join us outside for a beautiful evening." Amy looked behind her and saw Arabella and Amelia standing together, talking to each other.

"Um," Amy said before she started to stutter. "Um, nothing," Amy said before she turned around to see what her mother and Amelia were talking about. "Mother, something weird is going on. I can sense it quite well, especially around that Viviana girl," Amy said.

Arabella directed Amy towards the living quarter, with Amelia following them. "We know. Larry and Caleb also have Alistair and Darcia tied up, kidnapped, or something like that. We are not certain about their sons. Do they know anything about their parents?" Arabella asked. Amy looked around.

"I saw Bryan briefly. He looked like he was in love with Viviana. He even called her a goddess," Amy said with sadness in her voice. Arabella placed both her hands on Amy's shoulders.

"This situation will end real soon, Amy," Arabella said in a reassuring tone. "We will find out more about this problem. For now, try and remain low-key till we have gathered the other coven members to our home or at least around a safe area where we can plan our final attack on them."

Amy and Amelia both nodded. "Where is Ginger anyway?" Amy asked. Arabella looked outside.

"I am afraid that she may also be under some sort of spell, or perhaps she is playing Viviana's game. Just then, Ginger came down the staircase and walked over to them with her right index finger against her lips, beckoning them over to her. Amy sighed with relief.

"Thank goodness," Amy said. "Ginger, what is going on? Have you noticed anything odd lately?"

Ginger nodded. "Yes," Ginger whispered. "Father seems to be in some kind of trance whenever she is around him. Remember how she did not want to enter the park where we were going to hunt about a week ago?" Ginger asked. Arabella and Amy both nodded.

Amelia scrunched her brow. "Excuse me? You three were going to hunt without me?" Amelia asked. "Why was I not invited?" Arabella smirked.

"My daughters needed some food inside of them, Amelia. This was just an outing where a mother takes her daughters out for a lovely evening," Arabella said. Amelia rolled her eyes.

"Go on," Amelia said.

"I think we should use our shape-shifting powers to our advantage in finding out more about this trick they are pulling," Ginger said as the other three women nodded in agreement.

The Truth

Gabriel and Viviana returned from being outside and checked the clock in the living quarter. "Good. It is going on five o'clock in the morning. I think I am up for a nice slumber," Gabriel said. He hugged Viviana and wished her a good slumber before he walked over to the basement door. This time, he did not wait for Arabella to join him.

Arabella, Amelia, Ginger, and Amy decided to see where Viviana was headed for her slumber. Viviana remained still as she kept her focus on the four women. "Can I help you?" Viviana asked. The other women kept their focus on Viviana. "The sun will be rising quite fast, you know. Whatever," Viviana said before she headed towards the front door of the castle.

"Do you need a place to sleep, Viviana?" Amy asked. Viviana turned around and shook her head. "We have a castle. I am sure there is a room that Hildegard can prepare, if you like." Viviana gave a tiny smile and shook her head again.

"I am fine. Thank you, Amy," Viviana said before she opened the door and walked outside.

Amy scoffed. "I do not understand her at all. What is she, actually? Is she human? A sorceress? A shape shifter?" Amy asked as she focused her attention on her sister, mother, and aunt. Nobody responded. Amy headed for the staircase. "I think we should rest up before we plan our next attack. I think I will lock my door and windows this time," Amy said, wishing everyone a good night.

After Amy locked her final window, she saw the sun starting to rise. It looked beautiful and magical, but she had to close her curtains before the sunlight might affect her. Amy placed her children in their crib and got into her own bed. In Amy's dream, which seemed like hours had passed after she was asleep, she heard a loud banging on her bedroom door. She woke up in shock, feeling her heart beating fast. "Who is it?" Amy asked.

"It is I, Bryan," Bryan said. Amy looked at the time. It was eleven in the morning.

"Are you sure?" Amy asked. What is my middle name?"

"Rose," Bryan said. "Amy Rose Ambrose, now please let me in," Bryan said. Amy undid the lock and opened the door to find Bryan in a state of panic.

"My parents," Bryan panted. "Are gone. Have you seen them, Amy?" Bryan asked as he paced around Amy's bedroom. The other brothers came into her room. "We are worried, Amy," Bryan said. "I looked everywhere and called out to them, but they are not here. We need to find them," Bryan said. Amy crossed her arms.

"It is still daylight out there, Bryan. I cannot leave until the sun is down. I will help you once it is darker outside, but I cannot leave," Amy said.

Suddenly, Bryan shape shifted into Larry and Raymond to Caleb. "Oh goodness, no," Amy gasped as she started to back away. Caleb got on his knees, holding a ring in his hands. "Amy Marie Ambrose, will you do me the honor of being my bride and let me help you take care of my children?" Amy was unable to breathe, and she woke up in shock. She checked her watch. It was three o'clock in the morning. Amy looked around. It was dark. Her children were still asleep, and she was alone in her room. No Larry or Caleb around. Amy let herself fall against her mattress again and rubbed her eyes. "It was just a dream. Just a dream," Amy repeated to herself.

Amy decided to walk over to Ginger's room. She opened the door gently and saw how peacefully Ginger was sleeping. She closed the door again, and to her surprise, Bryan was standing next to her in the hallway. "Bryan," Amy gasped. "I had a horrible dream." Bryan nodded.

"And I have something to share with you too, Amy. I cannot seem to find out where my parents are. Have you seen them?" Amy suddenly remembered how her nightmare started like this as well.

Amy quickly smacked Bryan across the face, causing him to growl at her and bare his teeth at her. "Sorry," Amy whispered quickly. "I had to know it was you. That is how my nightmare also started, Bryan. You turned into Larry," Amy said as she tried to remain as calm as possible. Bryan relaxed his body and mind before he took a step back.

"I know. My mother, Amelia, sister, and I are going to find out what is going on. We think Larry and Caleb are behind it all," Amy said. Bryan gave Amy a confused expression.

"What do you mean, Amy?" Bryan asked. Amy looked around and noticed how quiet it was, but it was not entirely safe, either.

"I cannot explain that right now, but we will make sure Alistair and Darcia are back home," Amy said reassuringly. Bryan did not move. "Bryan, what do you want?"

Bryan smiled and grabbed Amy's right hand in his. "Bryan, please let go of me," Amy whispered. Bryan smiled as he played with Amy's hands.

"Tell me more about your dream, Amy," Bryan whispered. "You said I was in it?" Amy started to feel uncomfortable. "I shape shifted into Larry, was it?" Amy started to feel scared.

"Bryan," Amy whispered. "Please release my hand. You are scaring me." Bryan looked into Amy's eyes. Suddenly, Amy felt faint and blacked out.

"You are to get married to Caleb and raise your children with him, Amy Marie Ambrose," Bryan whispered before he shape shifted into Larry.

Amy's eyes were pitch black, putting her in a stupefied state. "Yes," Amy whispered. "I shall marry Caleb." Larry smiled at Amy before he released his grasp on her. "Dreams do come true, do they not, Amy?" Larry whispered. Amy nodded mindlessly. "Good. Tell your mother that you have no interest in finding Caleb or me," Larry whispered before he released Amy and snapped his fingers to wake her up from his trance. Amy looked at him mindlessly, watching him leave. Suddenly, Bryan came out of his room, causing Amy to growl at him.

"I know Bryan," Amy whispered. "We think Larry and Caleb are behind this all, including Viviana." Bryan gave Amy a confused expression. "I have no time to explain this situation, but I need to get going; excuse me." Amy walked away from Bryan and headed down the staircase towards her mother, aunt, and sister. Amy checked her watch. It was about one o'clock in the morning. "Okay, we have several hours to find out where Caleb and Larry are holding Alistair and Darcia," Amy whispered.

Arabella, Amelia, Ginger, and Amy all walked out of the front door. They walked over to the park area and looked around for any traces of Larry, Caleb, or any dead people. Ginger raised her nose up to the sky and did some breathing exercises to see if she could inhale any scent of them. Amy looked around, but there was nothing to see.

"Hm," Arabella said. "Where was his home, Amy?" Amy looked around and remembered the exit of the park. They headed in that direction. It was quiet outside, except for a few evening parties that were taking place in people's homes. The loud beats of the music were playing around.

"As I recall, his apartment is around that corner, right there," Amy said as she pointed in the direction of the apartment with some stairs and a handrail. Amy walked up the stairs, but the name had changed to a different name. Was there a name to even begin with? Amy just remembered that when she and her children got kidnapped, she just got shoved into the house, making sure her children were not harmed.

Amy looked back at her mother, aunt, and sister with confusion. "Now I am not so sure anymore. What do we do?" Amy asked. Arabella looked around.

"Well," Arabella said as she was trying to look through the windows, but the curtains blocked her view. "Do you remember what the curtains looked like, Amy?" Amy looked at the curtains.

They looked similar, but she also did not entirely remember the whole scenery either.

"Okay," Arabella said as she was trying to find an answer to the problem. "I think we should wait a few hours, walk around some of the main streets, and see if he might show up. "Perhaps this might work. Amy, see if you can contact Darcia. You were able to communicate with her telepathically, right?" Amy nodded. See if she will respond to you or even Alistair."

Amy closed her eyes. *Darcia, where are you and Alistair?* Amy asked in her mind. *Alistair, where are you two?* Amy kept her focus on them for a few minutes before she opened her eyes. Still nothing. "I am getting worried about them," Amy whispered. Arabella and Amelia exchanged glances. Perhaps I should contact Larry or Caleb," Amy said.

"Absolutely not," Arabella snapped. "You will do no such thing." Amelia shook her head. "What your mother means, Amy, is that it might cause bigger problems if you go looking for trouble." Ginger looked at them both.

"Why? Our father is out of commission, as are his brothers. Then again, Bryan and his brothers are not under Viviana's spell, or are they?"

Amy sighed before she crossed her arms. "How did this all happen in just a few seconds?" Amy asked. Arabella looked over at her.

"What do you mean, Amy?" Amy looked at her with sadness and frustration.

"How do we end up in these turbulent situations, mother?" Amy asked. "Nothing makes sense anymore. I feel like I might be having a panic attack." Arabella wrapped her arms around Amy, holding her close. "I know the feeling, my sweet child. Being brought back from the dead and being a shape shifter was quite the change for me."

Amy nodded. "I think everything will be okay in the end. Do you all agree?" Amy asked. Amelia, Ginger, and Arabella nodded. "An occasional thunderstorm in our lives will not cause too much trouble for us," Amy said. While the four of them waited around to see if Larry or Caleb would show up, Alistair and Darcia were both chained up against each other, back to back, in the basement of the apartment complex, weakened by all of the blood draining.

Larry walked down to the basement. "How are you two holding up?" Larry asked teasingly with a smile on his face. Alistair looked up from his weakened state through his long, dark bangs.

"What are you going to do to us, Larry?" Alistair asked with barely enough energy to talk. Darcia was unable to keep her head up, leaning back against Alistair's shoulders. "How did your friends become so strong, Larry?" Larry crouched down, grinning at him.

"There are many ways of strengthening my friends, Alistair. Perhaps you are losing touch with your strength and got soft for Amy," Larry said with a chuckle.

Darcia managed to open up her eyes. "What are your plans, Larry?" Darcia whispered. Larry moved over to crouch in front of her.

"Have you all killed off one by one? The fact that your sons are not here to save you is something that makes no sense to me. I remember seeing your boys at the park and how they almost had me killed off, but of course my body was not burned, so I could regenerate."

Alistair could not help but smile at the whole situation. "What is so funny, Alistair?" Larry snapped. "You do not seem to mind the whole dying part, do you?" Alistair ignored Larry and looked over at him.

"I am just thinking about how you will end up dying this time, Larry," Alistair whispered. "Perhaps you might scream and cry like Katrina, but then again, you might get rewarded with a quick, painless death. Who knows? Gabriel is quite capable of strategizing," Alistair whispered.

Larry chucked. "Gabriel is under Viviana's spell, my dear Alistair," Larry said. "He might be the first one to go. As a matter of fact, I might want you all to witness the death of your beloved patriarch sometime, real soon," Larry said. "Then your sons can watch you all enter into a deep sleep, and then Amy can watch her beloved Bryan go into a deep sleep. Goodness, how dark I can get," Larry said as he laughed at himself. "Anyway, Bianca is upstairs, with my friends making sure you two will not escape. I think I might want to see what our Amy is doing," Larry said before he got to his feet to head for the stairs of the basement.

"Alistair," Darcia whispered. "Is Gabriel really going to die?" Alistair sighed and shrugged. "We need to find a way to get out of here." Larry overheard the whole conversation and returned.

"All of this talking might not benefit you two. I think I might need to find a way to find a muzzle or a way to quiet you both. Excuse me for a moment," Larry said before he walked up towards the basement door.

"I feel so weak. I keep hearing Amy's voice inside of me, my love," Darcia whispered.

"I know, Darcia," Alistair whispered. "I hear her too. I just do not have much energy to communicate." As they both sat there, trying to keep themselves from losing too much energy, Larry was on the main floor of his apartment complex with Bianca and the rest of his friends, including Caleb.

"Larry," Caleb whispered. "I think we might have some company outside of our place." Larry looked at the front door and saw nobody.

"I do not see anyone, Caleb. Perhaps your eyes are deceiving you. Try and keep your mind as quiet as possible," Larry said. "Bianca, sister dear, we cannot have them killed as of yet. Perhaps give them a little blood pack to distract both Darcia and Alistair?"

Bianca scrunched her brow. "Why, brother dearest? I thought we were supposed to have them killed off. If Viviana has Gabriel under her powers and we have Darcia and Alistair, those are considered the key players in keeping the family in a powerful state, right?" Bianca asked. Larry crossed his arms.

"We cannot do anything drastic right now. We need to distract them and make them think we are the victims of the situation. As a matter of fact, Caleb, would you mind bringing our guests a little treat?"

Caleb looked over at Larry with confusion. "Larry, that might not be wise. I have been around that family for so long. What if they tug on my heart strings with their words?" Caleb asked. Larry smirked. "What?"

"Are you that weak, Caleb?" Larry asked. "All I ask is for you to bring them a blood pack and come back up to our floor. They do not have enough strength to take you down, Caleb. If you do not, I might want to ban you from my group," Larry said sternly. "I need strong stallions to do their job. Are you strong, Caleb?"

Caleb nodded. "Good. Bianca, could you hand Caleb a blood pack?" Bianca nodded and walked over to their kitchen area.

Larry kept his eyes on Caleb, analyzing him until Bianca returned with a blood pack. "Do your job, Caleb," Larry said as he gestured towards the door of the basement. Caleb nodded and walked down to the basement of their apartment complex, feeling a sense of awkwardness at handing two people he once knew some blood. When he saw Alistair and Darcia, their complexions had gone gray, and their eyes had gone darker than before. It was horrifying to see how weak they were.

Alistair looked over with confusion. "Caleb," Alistair whispered. Darcia looked over. "Goodness, what brings you down here?" Darcia asked. Caleb swallowed nervously and placed the blood pack on the floor between them. "Wait!" Alistair said. "Please help us, Caleb," Alsitair said. "If you do, we can save Gabriel, and you can return to our home and be treated like a hero."

Caleb did not move or respond. He just looked at them with pity and sadness. "Caleb!" Larry yelled from the top of the stairs. Caleb walked sheepishly away from them and headed toward the top of the stairs to find Larry with his arms crossed, leaning against the doorframe. "What is taking you so long?" Caleb shrugged and headed upwards till Larry grabbed him by his shoulders, pushing him backwards till his ankles were off the first step.

"If there is any shady business going on behind my back, Caleb, you may join them real soon," Larry snapped before he pulled Caleb inside. "Now, ladies and gentlemen of my family, Caleb and I are going out for a little prowl around the area. Bianca, please make sure our guests do not escape," Larry said before he headed toward the front door, pulling Caleb alongside him.

After Larry pulled the door shut, Amy was able to hear them from about two streets down. "They left their home," Amy whispered. The four of them headed towards Larry and Caleb. They noticed them from a distance and tried to keep a distance between them to avoid drawing any attention to them. Larry and Caleb were heading for the castle. Arabella, Amelia, Ginger, and Amy remained crouched near some shrubs when they noticed Larry and Caleb meeting up with Viviana at the entrance of the park.

"Are you able to hear what they are saying?" Arabella whispered. Amy put her right index finger against her lips.

"How is everything going at the Ambrose castle, Viviana?" Larry asked. Viviana smiled.

"As I had imagined, quite well. Poor old Gabriel has no idea how weak he is getting by the day. Soon he will not be able to function so well, and you both can go in for the full attack," Viviana said teasingly. Both Larry and Caleb smiled with approval.

"What about the children?" Larry asked. Viviana smiled and looked behind. "They will soon forget about their mother, Amy," Viviana said with disgust. "And remember their father, Caleb." Caleb remembered the whole scenario of Amy being lied to and carrying his children rather than Bryan's. He felt a sense of sadness and guilt inside of him. Viviana looked over at Caleb and then at Larry.

"Are you all right, Caleb?" Viviana asked. Caleb quickly nodded. Larry playfully punched Caleb in his left shoulder.

"Of course he is. Both Darcia and Alistair are also in a weakened state. My sister, dear Bianca, is doing a good job as well," Larry said. Viviana smiled.

"Soon, this will all be over. Our revenge will finally come. Anyway, I need to return to the castle before anyone notices my absence, but we will soon speak again," Viviana said before she headed back towards the castle.

At the castle, Gabriel started to see double as he felt like his energy was depleted somehow. Lucien entered his office with fear on his face. "Gabriel," Lucien said with a gasp. "Here, let me get you something to drink." Lucien quickly left the office to fetch a new bottle of blood and walked back to his office. "Here, drink some of this, Gabriel," Lucien whispered. Gabriel waved off the bottle. "Please, you need to feed. You look very weak," Lucien said.

Gabriel leaned against his chair, closing his eyes. "I just need to rest, brother," Gabriel whispered. "I just feel extremely tired." Lucien looked behind him, but nobody was around. "Please leave me alone, Lucien. I will be okay." Lucien started to back away until he heard the front door open and close. He walked over to find Viviana looking at him.

"Oh, it is you," Lucien said. Viviana smiled. Lucien suddenly felt a sense of happiness when he looked into Viviana's eyes. "How was your evening walk?" Viviana smiled. "Quite well, Lucien. How is everything over here?" Lucien chuckled. "I think I will check up on Amy's children. Say, have you seen her as of late?" Lucien shook his head mindlessly. "Okay. It is weird for a mother not to be there for her children, but then again, I am a nanny," Viviana said teasingly, causing Lucien to giggle. "I will see you around."

Lucien smiled and laughed, but suddenly felt this wave of reality after she was gone. Lucien was holding the bottle of blood in his hands and forgot what he was doing. Amy, Arabella, Amelia, and Ginger then entered the castle. Lucien looked over at them. "Viviana is looking for you, Amy," Lucien said. Amy sighed.

"Where is she, Lucien?" Amy asked. Lucien gestured towards the stairs. "Okay, probably playing nanny. Perhaps it might be wise if I go up alone," Amy said before she headed towards the stairs. When she got to her closed bedroom door, she opened it slowly to find Viviana on the floor with her three children, playing with some rattles and balls.

"Amy," Viviana said. "Where have you been? I have been trying to find you." Amy gave her a quick smile before she closed the door. "Is everything all right?" Amy sighed before she got on her knees.

"Where have you been, as well, Viviana? I noticed that you were outside, like near a park area." Amy said. Suddenly, Viviana's eyes went dark. "Right," Amy said. "Your eyes have already betrayed you, Viviana. What are you planning?" Viviana scoffed before she got to her feet.

"I have no idea what you are talking about, Amy, but whatever it is, you will not survive this game," Viviana said in a neutral voice to avoid causing drama in front of Amy's children.

"Will I?" Amy asked sternly. "As far as I am concerned, we already have backup from other members around the world. If you think that you, Larry, and Caleb are going to take us down, you are quite naïve about the whole situation, Viviana. Whatever you are doing to my father needs to stop," Amy snapped.

Viviana chuckled. "Or what? You are going to do something about it?" Amy started to feel her anger rising to her teeth. "If you do anything to me, Amy, your father will not survive that long. If you want to keep him alive and well, you best behave yourself in front of me." Amy sighed. "Good," Viviana said. Amy got to her feet to head over to the dining quarter. Amy opened up the cooler and noticed that the blood had a different color to it. She analyzed the blood and decided to open it up to see why it looked different than before. She sniffed it and noticed the musty smell again. What was Viviana doing to the blood supply? What type of blood did she replace the healthy blood with? Is that what was keeping her in a weakened state?

"Hildegard," Amy said. "Where are you?" Viviana came down the stairs with a smile on her face. "Did I not mention how I fired your beloved human?" Viviana said. Amy sternly looked over at Viviana.

"What did you do to our blood supply, Viviana?" Amy snapped. Viviana smiled.

"What makes you think that I did anything, Amy?" Viviana snapped back. "Perhaps your taste buds are weak." Amy looked around to see if there was a fresher bottle of blood for them. They all looked the same.

"I may have added a personal ingredient to your beloved blood supply, Amy. Perhaps a little juniper might give the flavor a bit more of a bite," Viviana said as she winked.

"Is this what you have been feeding my family, Viviana? Spiked blood?" Amy snapped. "All because you got turned into a shapeshifter like us? You want to take your revenge on us?"

Viviana walked closer towards Amy, but she also kept enough distance to avoid getting hurt. "If I cannot have happiness, then nobody can have it, especially the ones who caused me so much pain and suffering in my past, Amy," Viviana said with sadness in her voice. "I could have had a beautiful future with Larry and built a stable family with some of my own children, but your father was reckless and ruined my future with his impulsive behavior."

Amy sighed. "I did not have the dream past or even future either, Viviana, but I managed to overcome my differences with my father's bad decisions and try to think about the positive sides. You and Larry are both still alive. You can live a beautiful life together, perhaps even still with children. If it was possible for me somehow to have children with Caleb's blood or whatever was injected inside me when I was on that airplane going back to the human world, mostly against my will, of course," Amy said.

Viviana listened to Amy's story, feeling a sense of relief. "You think it is still possible to live like shape shifters?" Viviana asked. Amy shrugged.

"I have no direct answer to that question, Viviana, but I do know that my mother is back in my life, I have a decent relationship with my sister, and I have Bryan in my life. Whether we will ever end up together is something that still needs to be discussed. My father, well," Amy said as she was trying to finish that sentence. Perhaps he is also a victim in his own ways, as well."

Viviana let out a loud, shrieking laugh. "What? A victim? In what way, Amy?" Viviana asked with laughter in her voice. "How is Gabriel Ambrose a victim? As far as I am concerned, he is a monster and will never deserve any form of empathy from his victims. Perhaps you have been around him for so long that you are feeling empathetic for your captor or destroyer, but I do not work like that, Amy," Viviana said sternly. "I think I shall take my leave for today. Your children are probably in need of their mother." Viviana turned around to walk out of the castle.

Amy stood in the dining quarter feeling drained and empty from that exchange with Viviana. She forgot about the tampered blood supply. She checked her watch. It was going onto three o'clock in the morning. She had to figure out where Hildegard was. She decided to walk over to see if her father would know her location. When she knocked on her father's study room, she heard a vague groan and a moan from her father. Amy opened the door and felt horrified at the sight of how weak her father looked.

"Father!" Amy shrieked before she walked to his side quickly. "What happened to you?"

Gabriel sighed before he looked up at her with glassy-red eyes. "Amy," Gabriel whispered. "You are home." Amy tried to see what she should do best for the situation. She walked out of his study room and ran over to Amelia quickly.

"Amelia," Amy panted. "Father is ill. He needs some fresh blood. Viviana tampered with our blood source."

Amelia looked concerned at Amy and got to her feet fast. "Where is Hildegard?" Amelia asked.

"Viviana had fired her somehow. I'm not sure how she managed to persuade Hildegard that our father required no services from her anymore," Amy said. Amelia shook her head in disbelief. "Where is your mother? We need to get to a blood bank quickly before your father can end up in a worse state than before."

Amelia nodded. "Do you know how to drive a car, Amy?" Amelia asked. Amy chuckled at that question. "I never learned how to drive, you know."

Amy smiled and nodded. "Our human parents, Nathan and Emma, taught us around our teenage years, Amelia. Perhaps Ginger might want to join us," Amy said.

Amy and Amelia walked over to Ginger's room, but she was not there. "In here," Ginger said as she called from Amy's room. Arabella and Ginger were with the three children.

"Father is ill," Amy said with concern in her eyes. "Please help." Arabella quickly got to her feet.

"Where is Hildegard?" Arabella asked. Amy looked over at Amelia, who then looked at Arabella and Ginger.

"Fired," Amelia said. "I do not know how Viviana managed to do that, but she also tampered with our blood source as well." Arabella sighed and shook her head.

"She really needs to leave," Arabella said. "Where is that Viviana anyway?" Amy looked around to make sure she did not return.

"She left the castle, but I am not sure if she will be returning anytime soon. Where does Hildegard live, and where did she get our blood supply?" Amy asked.

Arabella thought about those questions. "Not sure, but perhaps we should take your father out for an old-fashioned hunting trip," Arabella said. "I mean, to kidnap humans and bring them here, that would cause bigger problems, unless…" Arabella said, looking over at Ginger. "What did you say was one of your powers as a shape shifter?" Ginger remembered how she was able to get those college students at the airport to give her money for their flight. Does she have similar powers as her father? Playing mind games on humans?

"I could try and use my powers on some people. Could we not see how weak our father is before we decide on our next plan?" Ginger asked. "If he can leave the castle, that should be no problem. What about the children? Would this not give Viviana access to potentially kidnap Amy's younglings?"

Amy nodded. "Well, I guess I could stay behind and let you three help Gabriel, but then again, where are Bryan and his brothers anyway? If Caleb and Larry did mention that Alistair and Darcia are located at their home, should we not have them save their parents?"

Arabella looked over at Amy and could not help but smile. "What?" Amy asked.

"We are just wasting time right now. Yes, I would advise you to tell Bryan and the other ones where their parents are, but then again, they might get overpowered as well. Goodness, when it rains, it pours," Arabella said. "I heard that phrase from some humans a while back."

Amelia smiled. "Okay. Amy, you take care of Bryan, your sister and mother, and I will take care of Gabriel, and you, protect your children," Amelia said before they all went their separate ways. Amy walked over to the room where Bryan was staying and knocked on it. There was no response. She opened it, and to her surprise, the beds were made up, but there was no Bryan or any of his brothers to be seen. "Of course they are not here. What would be the next wonderful surprise?" Amy murmured to herself.

She walked over to Gabriel's study to find her mother, sister, and aunt around him. "How is he doing?" Amy asked.

"Gabriel, are you strong enough to walk for a few minutes?" Arabella asked. Gabriel looked up at her with sadness. "Gabriel, yes or no?" Gabriel nodded as he pushed himself onto his feet. He put his arms around Arabella and Amelia while Ginger walked ahead to open the door.

Amy watched the four of them try to get Gabriel outside of the castle. She decided to go over to her children. Suddenly, the chimes of the castle went off. "Who would be at the door at this time?" Amy got on her knees and snuck around to see if she could see someone from a different angle. Suddenly, she heard a familiar voice. "Amy?" Bryan asked. Silas, Xavier, Raymond, and Joshua were also at the door. Could she trust them, or could they also be Larry and Caleb?

Amy got to her feet and opened the door. "Bryan, is that really you?" Amy asked. Bryan gave her an annoyed look.

"Yes, it is truly me. We found out where our parents are. They look weak from all of the draining. Larry and Caleb managed to build their army. We need Gabriel to summon the other coven members," Bryan said sternly.

Amy beckoned them in. "Father is extremely weak. It appears that Viviana put juniper in our blood supply, which caused my father to get sick, Bryan," Amy said, feeling sadness inside of her.

Are you certain she did that?" Bryan asked. "She looks so innocent." Amy glared at Bryan.

"Never mind, Bryan; if you would prefer to be with her, be my guest. She told me," Amy snapped. Bryan gave Amy an annoyed look.

"Perhaps she is telling the truth, Bryan," Raymond said. "My mind has gone blank, but Amy would not be acting like this." Bryan looked at Raymond.

"I do not trust you either, Raymond. One moment your powers worked, and now they do not." Bryan snapped.

Distraction

Outside the castle, Gabriel leaned against Amelia and Arabella. "Ginger," Arabella whispered. "What should we do?" Ginger looked at her and shrugged.

"It will soon be morning, and there is nobody around. I have no idea where we should even start," Ginger said.

Amelia looked around. "What about a blood bank? Where would we be able to find a blood bank?" Amelia asked. Gabriel moaned.

"Where am I?" Gabriel asked as he leaned his head against Arabella's. "Why am I so cold?"

"We need to get you properly fed, Gabriel. Our blood source got spiked," Arabella whispered. Without realizing it, Viviana was watching them from a distance, trying to find the best way to get Gabriel back under her spell. Gabriel's breathing was slowing down. Arabella saw a fox in the distance.

"Amelia," Arabella whispered. "We might have a little appetizer for Gabriel. Could you fetch us the creature?" Amelia nodded and quickly transformed herself into a wolf. She grabbed the fox with her might and quickly brought the animal over to Gabriel, so he could slurp down the blood.

Gabriel started to feel a bit better after that fresh source, but he knew he needed more. Suddenly, Viviana appeared behind them. "Gabriel," Viviana called out. "What are you all doing here?" Gabriel turned around with fear in his eyes, and suddenly he felt the same sharp pain in his head as he had before. Amelia and Arabella let go of Gabriel, causing him to fall until Ginger caught him before he hit the ground.

Amelia and Arabella got into wolf forms, chasing Viviana, who remained in her human form, and calling out for help. Amelia and Arabella quickly returned to their human form and headed back towards Gabriel and Ginger. Gabriel threw up the blood that he had consumed while Ginger was holding onto him.

"Father," Ginger said. "Here, please take some of mine." Ginger held her arm up to his mouth, but Gabriel pushed it away.

"Gabriel!" Arabella screamed until she was close enough to him. "We need you to feed some more. Take some of our life sources. Please," Arabella pleaded. "You will not survive that long if you keep living so weak." Gabriel groaned as he balanced himself against Ginger.

"I am not sure if I can handle anything anymore, Arabella," Gabriel said with pain in his voice. "I am not certain if I should continue."

Arabella shook her head. "I do not want you talking like that, Gabriel. We will get you fed properly, and you will get stronger before you know it. You need to let Viviana go. She has been the culprit of your problems, Gabriel." Gabriel gave Arabella a tiny smile.

"What makes you think she is behind it all? What about… Larry…" Gabriel said as he felt like he was losing more energy as he talked. "Or…the other guy?" Gabriel whispered.

"Amy heard that Viviana had put juniper in our blood supply. That is what is making you so weak, Gabriel. It is toxic to our kind," Arabella said. "Look, please take some of my life source till you can make it to your next source."

Arabella held her right arm against Gabriel's lips. He placed both his hands around her arm and put his mouth on her arm until he felt another wave of nausea hit him. "I am unable to," Gabriel moaned. Arabella looked over at Amelia.

"What do we do, Amelia?" Amelia looked around and realized that the sun was probably going to rise pretty soon.

"Perhaps we should bring him back to the castle and sleep till the evening time, and then we should go to a blood bank and bring back some fresh blood packs," Amelia said. Arabella and Ginger both nodded before they brought Gabriel back to the castle. As they headed for the castle, Amy started to feel hunger inside of her, but she did not trust their blood source. Bryan and his brothers were fidgeting as well.

"Where is your father anyway?" Bryan asked.

"My mother, aunt, and sister took him out hunting. They should be back soon. It is four o'clock," Amy said. "Did my father ever mention where Hildegard lived?" Bryan looked over at his brothers, and they all shook their heads. The door opened and closed. Amy walked over to see how worse Gabriel looked. "Oh goodness, what happened?" Amy shrieked.

Bryan and his brothers came over to the front door with horror in their eyes. "Gabriel," Bryan whispered. Gabriel looked up at him with glassy eyes. "I cannot believe my eyes. How did this happen? All because of the tampered blood supply?"

"We need to get him into bed. Please excuse us," Arabella said as she and Amelia helped Gabriel down the stairs toward their quarter. Bryan gave Amy a concerned look.

"We need to find Viviana and see what is going on. Brothers, we need to find her," Bryan said before he left the castle again. Bryan headed towards the park where they had their attack with Larry, and to their surprise, he saw Viviana at the entrance, looking in their direction.

"Bryan," Viviana said with relief in her voice. "Amy hates me. I keep trying to tell her that it is all in her mind, but she wants to get rid of me. I am not doing anything to her father."

Viviana was able to fake some tears falling down her eyes and managed to get Bryan to wrap his arms around her. "I just want to be friends with Amy, but it seems like she hates me, Bryan. I do not know where to go. I do not even have a place to sleep. I just sleep on those park benches, which are hard on my back. What do I do?"

Bryan stroked Viviana's back. "You can stay with us. I will talk to Amy about this whole situation. I know you are not doing anything to harm her or her father. You did not put juniper in our blood, did you?" Bryan asked. Viviana looked up with tears in her eyes.

"Never," Viviana said. "Never." Suddenly, Bryan's eyes went black. "I need you boys to do something for me. I need you to distract Amy. Will you do that for me?" Viviana asked as she was hypnotizing Bryan. Then she looked over at Silas, Xavier, Joshua, and Raymond. They all nodded mindlessly. "Good. Now run along back home and try to get Amy to forget about everything."

Bryan's eyes returned to normal. Viviana smiled and waved them off before she walked back to the apartment complex to give Larry and Caleb an update. Amy walked over to where Bryan was.

"Father is finally asleep. We should all be resting for now. It is going on six o'clock in the morning, and I feel exhausted from everything," Amy said as she headed for the staircase.

Bryan, being in a mentally altered state, followed Amy over to her bedroom and stood by the doorway. Amy looked over at him with confusion. "Did you need anything, Bryan?" Amy asked. Bryan just stared at her mindlessly. "Please leave, Bryan. You are scaring me."

Bryan started to back away without any response, walking over to where his brothers were. Amy quickly closed her door and locked it. Her children started to whimper till Amy picked them up one by one, placing them in the crib. The children then tried to crawl out of the crib.

"It is bedtime, my loves," Amy said. "Please go to sleep. You are not hungry or bored."

The children crawled out of the crib and headed for her bedroom door, trying to open it. "Stop it," Amy snapped. "You need to sleep." The children turned around with tiny, sharp teeth, hissing at Amy. "Viviana, what have you done to my children? What is your plan for me?" Amy asked. The children then started to cry. "I need to find that girl, but it is bright out. Goodness, what should I do? Bryan is acting weird. Amy decided to go to Ginger's room to ask her for help. She closed the door behind her to make sure the children would not leave her room. When she entered Ginger's room, she was deep asleep when Amy opened her door. "Dang it," Amy whispered. "Okay. What about Mother and Father?" Amy headed down to the basement area to find her parents asleep in their quarters.

"Mother," Amy whispered as she gently shook her awake. Arabella opened her eyes. "The children are acting weird. I think Viviana has put a spell on everyone. What do I do? I cannot have my children endanger themselves. Please help me." Arabella looked over at Gabriel, sleeping deeply. Then she got to her feet, grabbed her robe and slippers, and they snuck over to Amelia's quarter.

Amelia came to her door, rubbing her eyes. "Ladies," Amelia moaned. "It is too early to be asking me for help."

"My children are acting up, Amelia. How can I quiet them down? I think Viviana put a spell on them. They are trying to find her," Amy whispered. "Do you know of any potions that could calm them down?" Amelia thought about it for a moment and grabbed one of her potions books to put people in a sleeping state. Like a human sedative.

"Here," Amelia said. "We need some lavender and valerian. If I were you, I would mix those two herbs with your milk, Amy, so you could feed them with a bottle. Perhaps that might put the little ones to sleep." Amy looked at her mother. "Do we have any of those?" Amy asked. Arabella smirked and shrugged.

"Hildegard normally did the grocery shopping, but Viviana had fired her. I am not certain. What about you, Amelia? Would you not have some spare herbs around?" Amelia thought about it and shook her head.

"I never keep herbs that long. It dries out, and the effects wear off. Whenever I did spells or potions, I waited to gather the herbs as fresh as possible. For now, perhaps sing a lullaby to them or rock them to sleep. I am afraid I cannot help you during these hours, Amy. I am sorry," Amelia whispered. Amy nodded and walked back to the main floor.

Amy's breathing started to get fast. "Am I having a panic attack?" Arabella quickly walked over to Amy, holding her close to her. "It will all be all right, Amy," Arabella whispered. "These moments will come to an end. I promise you." Amy clung to her mother and rested her head on her mother's chest, hearing her breathing calmly.

Amy started to feel relaxed. "Thank you, mother," Amy whispered. "This is all getting too much for me. I just wish none of this had ever happened. Being born a shape shifter, being lied to, returning with an immaculate conception story, and living this abnormal life. It is getting too much for me, mother. I feel so overwhelmed and scared."

"That is why you have your mother with you to help you through it all. You are not alone, Amy. You will never be alone," Arabella said as she stroked Amy's back until Amy was balanced enough to release her hold. "Where are your children anyway?" Amy looked around to make sure they did not escape outside of the castle.

"I think they are still in my room, mother," Amy said. "Hopefully, asleep. Hopefully, I am just going crazy." Both Amy and Arabella headed for Amy's bedroom. The door was open, and the children were gone. Amy started to panic. "Where are my children?" Amy screamed. Arabella and Amy knocked on Bryan's door until Raymond opened it. Bryan was holding Gabrielle in his arms, with Nathaniel and Maggie next to him. Amy sighed in relief, feeling lightheaded and exhausted.

"Okay. You can keep the children while I slumber. I need to sleep so badly right now. I feel like I am going crazy," Amy said before she left the room. Arabella remained behind the doorframe, looking confused.

"Bryan, are you okay?" Arabella asked. Bryan looked up at Arabella with confusion as well.

"Why would I not be, Arabella?" Bryan asked. Arabella kept her gaze on Bryan, feeling a sense of darkness between them.

"I could take the children from you as well, Bryan, if you need to sleep," Arabella said. Bryan held Gabrielle close to him, cradling her in his arms.

"I do not mind keeping them close to me, either, Arabella. As a matter of fact, I have slept long enough. My brothers and I will care for these children, right brothers?" Bryan asked as he looked over at his brothers standing behind Arabella. Arabella gasped, not realizing how quiet they were.

Arabella then headed for the staircase, but noticed how unusually dark the eyes were of Silas, Xavier, and Joshua. Arabella stood at the top of the stairs and knew something was wrong. Gabriel was out of commission, and both Darcia and Alistair were not around. Perhaps Amelia could help her out. Arabella quickly ran down the stairs and over to Amelia, who undid the lock on her door again and groaned.

"Now what?" Amelia snapped? "I am tired and am in need of rest."

Arabella entered her room, waiting for Amelia to close her door. "Bryan and the other ones are under Viviana's spell. Something is going on, Amelia. What should we do?" Amelia quickly closed her door and locked it before she beckoned Arabella to her living area. Amelia checked her watch. It was eight o'clock in the morning.

"Where is Amy?" Amelia asked. Arabella realized that Amy might not be safe in her room.

"In her bedroom, trying to sleep. I do not want her or Ginger to be alone right now. We need to stay together," Arabella said. Amelia nodded.

Arabella walked over to Amy's room, noticing how peaceful she was. She did not want to wake her up, but she also did not want to leave her either. Arabella walked over to Ginger's room and found her sleeping deeply. Perhaps Arabella was overreacting. Perhaps her lack of sleep and stress were causing her to feel disoriented. Arabella decided to leave everything alone and walked over to her sleeping quarter. She found Gabriel also asleep, breathing softly. Arabella smiled at herself.

"I think we all deserve a little vacation," Arabella whispered before she got under the covers and wrapped her arms around Gabriel. Gabriel moaned gently as he touched Arabella's left hand with his right hand. "Sorry for waking you," Arabella whispered. There was no response, and Arabella closed her eyes. She was dreaming about how she went back to Amy's room. This time, it was not Amy who was in her bed, but Viviana. Arabella screamed for Amy until she saw Caleb and Amy entering her bedroom together.

"Amy," Arabella said. "What is going on? Why is Caleb here? What is going on?" Amy smiled and showed Arabella her right hand with a wedding ring on it. "No," Arabella whispered. "No, Amy, you cannot get married to him. Please, Amy, come back to your senses." Then Larry showed up with Ginger next to him. Arabella felt faint. Before she fell backward, she woke up in shock.

Gabriel was sitting on the edge of his side of the bed, hunched over. "Arabella," Gabriel whispered. Arabella turned to face him. "I need to eat something. Did you actually offer yourself to me last night?" Gabriel asked. Arabella nodded.

"Yes, Gabriel, I did," Arabella said with a tense of excitement in her tone. Was Gabriel returning to his old self again? Arabella did not mind giving up some of her life source for him. She held her left arm near his mouth. This time, he grabbed it and brushed his lips against her flesh. She closed her eyes, remembering the soft sensation of his lips. Then she felt an intense, sharp pain in her arm, causing her to gasp. Gabriel was draining part of her. He was not able to stop himself. "Gabriel, that is enough!" Arabella screamed. "Gabriel!" He released her, leaving a bite mark on her arm. Gabriel licked his lips and felt warmer inside.

"I need more," Gabriel snapped before he got to his feet with his pajamas still on, heading for the main floor. Arabella whimpered at the sight of the bite mark and the weakness she felt. She let herself fall against the mattress while Gabriel was running around, looking for more blood to consume. Arabella had to remind him that the blood supply was tampered with by Juniper. She struggled to get onto her feet, supporting her against the wall with her body.

"Gabriel," Arabella moaned. "I need to tell you something. The blood has been poisoned. Gabriel faintly heard Arabella's voice and returned to her. "What did you say?" Gabriel snapped. "With juniper, was it?" Arabella nodded. "Viviana…did it," Arabella said as she felt herself weakening by the minute. Gabriel felt confused.

"I do not understand, Arabella. What does she have to do with everything?" Gabriel asked. Arabella was not able to answer. Gabriel checked his watch and realized it was going on two o'clock in the afternoon. "Hm. We still have a few more hours before we can go outside," Gabriel said as he headed back for their sleeping quarter.

He put on his black suit and tie with matching shiny black shoes and decided to sit on the sofa where Ginger and Amy had sat the first time he got a chance to talk with them. He felt stressed as he bit the flesh next to his right index finger. He heard Arabella moaning before she fell next to him on the sofa. "Where are the girls? Are they okay, Arabella?" Arabella moaned as she rested her head on Gabriel's shoulders.

Gabriel remembered something important. He could communicate with people with his telepathic power. *Hildegard, where are you? I need you to return to our home as a housekeeper.* Gabriel thought. There was no response. *Hildegard, are you even alive?* Gabriel thought. There was silence. Goodness, perhaps Viviana, Larry, or Caleb killed Hildegard. The poor girl, who had served his family for many years. "How are my brothers? Why have they not brought us new blood if our own source was tampered with? Juniper, was it?" Gabriel asked. Arabella shrugged but remained in the same leaning position.

"Here, Arabella, please have some of my life force," Gabriel whispered as he made an incision with his left thumb on his right wrist, holding it to her mouth. Arabella started sipping from it with her lips till she felt an intense need to feed. Gabriel quickly released himself from her grasp.

"I need more," Arabella moaned. "What do we do, Gabriel?" Gabriel checked his watch. It was now going onto four o'clock in the afternoon.

"Soon, my wife," Gabriel said in his soothing tone. "Everything should be okay." Gabriel decided to head for the main floor. The door opened and closed. "Hildegard?" Gabriel asked. There was no response. Gabriel headed for the door area and saw Viviana standing by the front door with a shock on her face.

"Gabriel?" Viviana asked. Viviana headed for Gabriel until he felt another sharp pain in his head. "You must feed Gabriel," Viviana whispered as she grabbed one of the opened bottles from the cooler, pouring him a glass. He smacked the glass out of her hands. "What are you doing? You should feed Gabriel," Viviana said as she snapped her fingers, causing Gabriel to fall to his knees before her. Suddenly, Arabella came running up to the main floor.

"Gabriel, are you all right? I heard a loud bang," Arabella said. Viviana looked at her with anger in her eyes. "What are you doing here?" Viviana looked down at Gabriel.

"I am here as the nanny of the household. Gabriel had invited me. I came early in case the younglings needed me," Viviana said. Gabriel started to drool on the floor, causing Arabella to walk over to him and pull him to her, cradling her in his arms.

"Stop it!" Arabella snapped. "You are causing him harm, Viviana. You need to leave." Viviana smiled and shook her head.

"Ask him if I should go and let him decide as man of the castle, Arabella," Viviana said provocatively. Arabella did not respond until Viviana was out of sight.

"Gabriel," Arabella whispered, trying to get him back to reality. "Gabriel, you must fight whatever you are dealing with. Come back to me, Gabriel."

Gabriel felt an intense pain flowing through her body, as if he had consumed liquid metal. "Arabella," Gabriel whispered. "Please help me." Arabella held him close to her, stroking his back.

"I will, Gabriel. You need to also remember your daughters, your real family, and me. Please remember," Arabella whispered. Viviana entered Bryan's room, seeing him holding Gabrielle in his arms.

"Good morning, boys," Viviana said teasingly. The boys all smiled at her like she was a goddess. "How are the younglings?" Bryan giggled at her, causing the other boys to join in. "I was thinking about taking the children out for an evening outing," Viviana said.

Arabella checked her watch and then looked outside. The sun was starting to set. She decided to go out and look for a blood bank. Before she did that, she had to help Gabriel into the living quarter.

She grabbed Gabriel by his upper body, pulling him over to the nearest sofa, pushing him onto it, and placing his legs on the sofa. He looked weak, but she could not just sit there. She grabbed her black hooded coat, sunglasses, and gloves, headed outside the castle, and kept to the shadowed areas.

She was not familiar with the area, but she could not give up on her search for a proper meal for Gabriel or herself. She walked over to the main shopping street, where people were at restaurants and bars. As Arabella walked past them, she drew attention to herself by the way she was dressed. She had to walk fast. She started to feel herself getting weaker as she was walking around. She saw the humans enjoying their own meals and drinks, but knew she could not go after them.

Arabella realized that they might know the location of the nearest hospital. Arabella looked around to see if she could see anyone she could ask. Many eyes were on Arabella. She noticed a waiter who was placing new cutlery and plates on an empty table.

"Excuse me, sir," Arabella said as she approached him. The waiter, a young man in his mid-twenties, looked up at her. He had dirty blonde hair and blue eyes, with a slender figure. Arabella admired the boy's beauty. "Um, sorry, do you speak English?" Arabella stuttered as she was licking her lips, feeling how dry her mouth was. The boy nodded. "Where can I find the hospital?" The boy thought about it and explained the directions she had to follow to get to the hospital. Arabella smiled and thanked the boy before she walked in the direction he pointed.

Arabella fell to her knees, causing the boy to run towards her. "Let me call you an ambulance," the boy said with a strong Romanian accent. Arabella smiled and shook her head.

"I am fine, thank you," Arabella said as she struggled with the boys help back to her feet. The boy looked concerned at Arabella. She felt an intense need to feed. She looked behind him and noticed how quiet everyone was. She waddled around the corner, away from the humans, toward the direction of the hospital. The boy followed Arabella.

"Let me take you," the boy said. Arabella smiled.

"You are quite the gentleman," Arabella said. "What is your name?" The boy smiled.

"Florin," the boy said. "And you?" Arabella smiled and ignored the question, but she did not want to come across as a rude person.

"Arabella. I need to get to the hospital. I need to help my family," Arabella said. The boy nodded and wrapped his right arm around Arabella, pulling her along. Arabella could not help but giggle at the way she was being treated. "Florin," Arabella said. "You do not have to hold me. I am okay with just leaning my hand on your shoulder." The boy smiled and released his grasp. Arabella looked at him with admiration for his act of kindness and pure appearance. She looked ahead and saw a tall building with lights inside and outside. It was the hospital. Arabella stopped walking. The boy looked at her with confusion.

"I can take it from here, Florin," Arabella said as she stroked his cheek gently. "Thank you for helping me. Enjoy the rest of your evening." Florin did not move. Somehow, he was intrigued by her beauty and voice. He had never met a woman like Arabella. He watched Arabella enter the main door of the hospital and decided to follow her. He walked into the hospital and noticed she was nowhere to be seen.

Arabella had found the blood supply section of the hospital and engorged herself with about ten packs of blood. She had smudges over her black coat and face. The blood was dripping from her hands. She felt so alive and strong again. Then she grabbed two packs in her hands. How was she going to bring all of the blood back to her family? She needed something like a box or a bag to put as much as she could inside of it. Without realizing the blood on her face, she headed for the hallway and noticed Florin standing about ten feet away from her with horror in his eyes. "Florin, what are you doing here?" Arabella asked. Florin started to run away, screaming.

"Monstru!" Florin screamed as he ran over to the receptionist, pointing in the direction of Arabella. "Monstru, bea sânge!" Florin screamed. The receptionist got to her feet and walked over to the area where Arabella was trying to cover up all evidence of her consuming blood. She walked outside the blood bank and noticed a brunette-haired, short receptionist woman staring at her. Arabella looked at her and then at Florin. "Copilul are o imaginație sălbatică," Arabella said, which meant the child has a wild imagination.

The woman looked over at Florin, shaking her head. "Du-te acasă." Florin left the hospital and headed back home. Arabella headed toward the exit of the hospital, but realized she needed to find some extra blood packs for Gabriel. She waited patiently outside the hospital until the receptionist walked away and headed back into the blood section. This time she found a plastic box that was meant to transport medical supplies around the hospital and started placing some blood packs inside the box. Once she felt that there was enough, she walked outside of the hospital. Florin waited outside from a distance, staring at her with fear.

Arabella felt annoyed at the fact that she had to get rid of him somehow, so she walked towards him. "What are you doing? Should you not be at your job right now?" Arabella asked. Florin kept his focus on her.

"What are you?" Florin asked. Arabella rolled her eyes and shook her head. "Please leave, Florin. I need to help my family," Arabella said as she started to walk away from him. Florin decided to follow her. Arabella decided to let him follow her to the castle and let fate take matters into its own hands.

The Storm

Arabella arrived at the entrance of the castle with Florin next to her. "Enter at your own risk, Florin," Arabella whispered before she turned the knob and walked inside.

Lucien, Vladimir, and Adrian were standing before them. "Boys, this is Florin. A human witnessed something terrible. Perhaps we should introduce him to Gabriel," Arabella said as she walked past them. Florin looked over at the three men in fear. "Do not mind them, Florin. They are harmless, as long as you keep your distance from them."

Florin looked at Arabella. "What are you, exactly?" Florin asked. Arabella smiled as she looked back at him. "You were drinking blood. Are you a vampire?" Arabella could not help but chuckle at that question.

"No, Florin," Arabella said. "I am a woman who needs a lot of iron. Why did you follow me home, Florin? Are you homeless and in need of a roof over your head?" Florin shook his head.

"I wanted to make sure you were going to be okay, until I saw you drink from those packs like an animal," Florin said.

Arabella sighed. "I need to bring this over to my husband for a blood transfusion. I am able to digest the blood, but he requires a different method of getting blood inside of him," Arabella said. She looked at Florin's young features and realized that Gabriel could devour him and regain his strength with the blood packs. Then again, she did not like tricking people and watching death take place in such a manner. "What are you still doing here, Florin? I did mention to you that you should return to your home. Why did you follow me?"

Florin shrugged as he looked at the floor. "You are beautiful," Florin said. "I did not know you lived in such a place and thought we could become friends or something like that," Florin murmured. Arabella smiled.

"We would never work out, dear Florin. I already have a husband and am much older than you are. I am sure there is a girl out there that would match you quite nicely," Arabella said. "I do need you to leave this place, like now." Florin turned around to walk towards the front door and opened it. Then he turned back one last time to look at Arabella, and he walked away.

Arabella knew how wrong it was to have exposed herself like that and not take better measures than to let some kid walk behind her to the hospital. She also knew that she should have sent the child away rather than letting him enter the house. Her lack of blood, the situation going on with Gabriel, and other problems clouded her mind. Arabella placed the crate down on the floor, walked outside of the castle, and saw Florin about fifty feet away from the castle. Should she call him back? She did not want him to expose her secret about a woman who walked among the humans and talked to a male waiter.

Arabella shook her head and walked back into the castle. The three guys looked at Arabella with confusion. "Are you just going to let him walk away after he saw us, Arabella?" Lucien asked. Arabella looked at him and shrugged.

"What would be the worst-case scenario? Nobody would believe him," Arabella said.

Lucien opened the door to the castle. "What if Larry were to go after him and tell him about who we are and let him expose us to a greater group of humans, Arabella? Just like any virus or infection, it starts off small and grows into a bigger problem," Lucien said.

Arabella rolled her eyes. "I have no energy or time. I must have Gabriel fed. He is waiting for me," Arabella said. Suddenly, Gabriel showed up in the area, looking better than before.

"What is all the commotion?" Gabriel asked. Arabella looked at him. "Are we in danger?"

Lucien looked over at Arabella. "I am not sure, Gabriel, but your wife might have exposed our kind to a child," Lucien said. Gabriel looked over at Arabella.

"Why did you do that, Arabella? Where is Hildegard? Why did you go to the hospital by yourself? You could have taken one of us with you. Where is this child?" Gabriel asked. Arabella pointed outside.

"He is a waiter at this restaurant. Forgive me for wanting to bring us a better blood supply, especially after you allowed a sorceress to become a nanny at our home who poisoned our blood supply with juniper," Arabella snapped.

Gabriel shook his head. "We need to take care of our little problem. First," Gabriel said. "I will need two packs of blood to restore my energy levels. Then we will find ourselves a new blood bank area and take care of the other problems after that. Brothers, could you deal with the child?" Gabriel asked. Lucien, Adrian, and Vladimir all nodded before they headed out. Gabriel looked back at Arabella. "Why, Arabella?" Gabriel asked.

Arabella shrugged. "Forgive me for wanting to take care of my husband. How are you even more alive than before? Viviana caused you to throw up my blood, and now you are back on the main floor? I was going to bring this stuff down for you," Arabella snapped.

Gabriel looked over at her. "I had some of our toxic blood and could taste the juniper. It tastes awful and does not make me feel good, but I needed something quickly before I would become immobile," Gabriel said before he leaned down to pick up a blood pack.

"Nothing makes sense to me anymore, Gabriel," Arabella said. "I am feeling overwhelmed, angry, sad, and heading for depression. I do not know how long I can handle living like this, Gabriel. Do you still even love me?" Arabella asked. Gabriel smiled at Arabella. "Of course I do, Arabella. I loved you when you were a human in your farm gown. I loved you before you had Amy and Ginger, and I love you now that you are standing there. My love will never disappear, ever," Gabriel said in a reassuring tone. Arabella walked over to him to wrap her arms around him.

"Will everything be okay?" Arabella asked. Gabriel nodded. "How are you feeling now?" Gabriel smiled.

"Much better. This blood pack tastes better than our own source. Where is Viviana anyway?" Gabriel asked. Arabella shrugged.

"Several hours ago, she caused you harm, and now I am not sure. I wonder if she is with Amy's children. It is going on eight o'clock in the evening," Arabella said.

Gabriel decided to go up to see what Viviana was doing and noticed that she and Amy were in Amy's room with the three children. Viviana looked up at Gabriel with confusion. "Oh," Viviana said. "What a surprise." Gabriel looked at Viviana and smiled at her. "How have you been, Gabriel?"

Gabriel looked over at Amy. "I see that the children have grown accustomed to you, Viviana. Not many humans would be able to handle such children," Gabriel said. Viviana smiled and nodded.

"I just adore them, Gabriel," Viviana said. "Are you okay, Gabriel? You look rather tired. Did you need me to help you with anything?" Gabriel smiled at her while Viviana was trying to put a suppressant spell on him. It did not work this time.

"Dang it, what is going on?" Suddenly, Amelia came into the room, with Arabella following her. Viviana looked at them with fear.

"Did you need anything, Viviana?" Amelia asked. "I was wondering if I could ask you for a little favor?" Viviana felt reluctant.

"I am fine, Amelia. Thank you, though. Perhaps there might be someone else to help you," Viviana said. "What is going on?" Arabella smiled at Viviana.

"Never mind," Viviana said. "Gabriel, did you need anything from me?" Gabriel shrugged. "What is going on? I am only here to assist Amy with her children, and I am getting this weird feeling that you think ill of me. What have I done to make you think that?"

Arabella looked at Amelia. "What have you been doing to us, Viviana?" Arabella asked. "How did you manage to get your hands on juniper and put that in our blood supply? That stuff is toxic to us." Viviana scrunched her brow.

"What? I never did any of that. Perhaps you should ask your housekeeper or even other family members, but I promise you all that I never poisoned your blood supply; it was…" Viviana said as she stopped herself from going on.

"Yes?" Arabella asked. "You were saying?" Viviana looked over at the other ones.

"Bryan, I think." Arabella chuckled. "Yes, I remember him talking about adding a new ingredient to your supply. I think Alistair and Darcia are jealous of you all for living in such beautiful castles while he stayed in motels," Viviana said as she recalled hearing stories from Larry about those names.

Arabella looked over at Amelia and then at Gabriel. Gabriel looked over at Arabella. "Where are they anyway? Bryan, Alistair, or even Darcia?" Gabriel asked. Viviana felt a sense of relief for making up such a story. Amy looked over at Gabriel, and Arabella was shaking her head. After the talk with Viviana, she wanted to find a way to trap her.

"I think I know where they are," Amy said as she got to her feet. "I think Bryan's room is a level above ours. Feel free to follow." Amy walked ahead, over to Bryan and Raymond's room. Bryan answered the door as his usual self with a neutral expression.

"Bryan, could you tell us a bit about Viviana?" Amy asked. Bryan looked over at Viviana and blacked out. Viviana had control over his mind as he spoke. "Viviana is a beautiful and talented young woman," Bryan said. "She would never try to harm us." Viviana smiled at him and went back to being himself. Amy scrunched her brow.

"Bryan, what is going on? Why are you acting like this?" Amy asked. Bryan looked at Amy, expressionless. "We would never poison our blood supply. Suddenly, after this girl arrives, we are having health problems. Why is that Bryan?"

Bryan repeated the same answer he gave before. Gabriel sighed. Viviana looked up at Gabriel. "Gabriel, I would never try to harm you. Please know that," Viviana said. Amelia looked at Viviana.

"Would you like to know why your powers are not working so well on Gabriel this time, Viviana?" Amelia asked. Viviana glared at Amelia.

"Whatever do you mean, Amelia? What makes you think that I am crafting spells around here?"

"In a few words, I will give you a basic answer. I am using a cloaking spell on Gabriel. After Arabella left to fetch him some blood, I decided to give him a bit of my protection while he was in his weakened state and gave him some of my own wrist to drink from to give him extra immunity. Gabriel lied to Arabella about drinking from the poisoned bottle because he knew how sharp your hearing was. Perhaps a trip to the dungeon would help you out more, would it not, Viviana?" Amelia asked.

Viviana looked over at everyone and then at Bryan. "Bryan, please do something," Viviana whispered. Bryan's eyes went dark as he barred his teeth at them. Then he crouched down into pouncing mode and looked for the nearest member to attack. Amy was in front. He licked his lips as his mind went blank and pounced on Amy, biting her hard on her throat, causing her to scream. He did not let go, causing Gabriel, Arabella, and Amelia to try to get him off of her. Ginger came over from her bedroom with horror in her eyes.

"What is going on?" Ginger screamed. "Bryan, what are you doing?" Ginger walked over and tried to get Amy away from Bryan, causing a deep flesh wound on her chest. Gabriel threw Bryan back into the room he was staying in and closed the door, keeping his hand on the doorknob, feeling Raymond banging on the door. Amelia and Arabella both grabbed Viviana. Ginger cradled Amy in her arms, holding her close.

"Where are the blood bottles?" Ginger asked. Arabella looked at Ginger.

"We have three more blood packs available in a crate down the stairs, Ginger. Hurry!" Arabella snapped.

Ginger picked Amy up and carried her down the stairs. She opened up the nozzle of one blood pack, holding it against Amy's lips. Amy started to drink from it while she clutched her chest with her right hand. "Stay with me, Amy," Ginger said. "Do not give into this disastrous moment." Amy took two more sips and stopped. "Keep going, Amy," Ginger said, urging Amy to consume the packs.

Ginger heard screaming from Viviana coming closer to her as she saw Arabella and Amelia pulling the struggling Viviana down the stairs and over toward the basement area where they kept their dungeon. Ginger looked back at Amy, watching her complexion get healthier again. "Come on, Amy," Ginger whispered. "Keep drinking. You will feel better again." Amy tried to continue drinking.

Gabriel did not let go of the doorknob and suddenly saw Silas, Xavier, and Joshua enter the hallway. "Boys," Gabriel snapped. "I need you all to return to your rooms, or there will be severe consequences. The boys, with their blank minds, barred their teeth at Gabriel till Lucien, Vladimir, and Adrian came running over to them, pouncing on them and subduing them. "Put them in the dungeon," Gabriel ordered before he released the doorknob, watching Raymond towards him with Bryan following him. Gabriel dodged their attempted punches and biting, grabbing them both by their necks and pulling them down the stairs with him.

"You all will be forgiven, but I should talk to Alistair and Darcia about improving their parenting tactics with you boys for falling for such illusions," Gabriel snapped. Once they arrived at the dungeons, Amelia and Arabella kept Viviana subdued until the rest had arrived before they released her and ran out of the cells. Gabriel threw the boys on the floor before Lucien closed the gate.

"You cannot leave us here, especially me!" Viviana screamed. "Larry will come over with Caleb and Bianca and his other friends, and they will save me." Arabella and Gabriel both smiled at each other. "You are all going to face such heavy repercussions, perhaps even death, if you do not release me!" Amelia, Lucien, Adrian, and Vladimir headed for the door toward the staircase. Arabella and Gabriel looked back at the boys who were on the floor, looking dark and angry. Viviana suddenly looked at Gabriel.

"Gabriel," Viviana said with sadness in her eyes. "Please do not leave me alone." Arabella looked at Viviana and glared. Gabriel mindlessly headed for the gate until Arabella quickly grabbed him, pushing him away.

"If you keep this up, Viviana, I will have you muzzled like they do with aggressive dogs," Arabella snapped before she grabbed Gabriel by his arm, pulling him towards the door. When Arabella and Gabriel reached the top of the stairs, they both saw how weak Amy looked.

"Father, Amy does not want to drink anymore. What should we do?" Ginger asked. Gabriel picked Amy up, looked down at her, and remembered how he held her in his arms when she was a newborn baby.

"Amy," Gabriel whispered. "Are you okay, my love?" Amy looked up at him with fatigued eyes, nodding softly.

"I will be, Father. I just feel so tired and in need of some rest. Can you take care of my children while I sleep?" Amy asked. Ginger, Amelia, Arabella, and Gabriel all nodded. Gabriel carried Amy up to her room to tuck her in. He decided to sit on the edge of the bed, watching her drift off into slumber. He continued sitting on the edge of the bed. He wanted to be a better father for his children.

"I hope you and your sister will forgive me for all of my horrible acts, my dear child," Gabriel said as he watched Amy sleep softly. "It was inexcusable what I had done. Place you both in the care of humans, lying to you both, creating Caleb," Gabriel said as he felt remorse in his body.

Ginger and Arabella entered the room, watching Gabriel keep watch over his daughter. Arabella came over and sat on the edge of the bed, across from Gabriel. "How is she doing?"

"She is well, I believe," Gabriel said. "I am just very tired. I have been quite tired myself. Say, whatever happened to that child, what was his name, Florin?"

"Lucien just used his powers of persuasion to get the boy to ignore what he had seen. Lucien would never make a scene of death," Arabella said. Gabriel looked over at her and smiled.

"Would you ever have known the moment you started realizing who you were in this world that we would be in this situation?" Gabriel asked. Arabella looked over at him and chuckled.

"Of course, Gabriel," Arabella said teasingly. "I mean, why live boring lives of having a family and a job whereas you can choose to be born into a life of shapeshifters?"

Ginger smiled at both her parents, teasing each other. "What will happen to Viviana or Bryan?" Ginger asked. Gabriel looked over at her.

"We will summon the other coven members and finally put an end to this war. I know there is still some tension regarding the last battle. We also need to find a way to save Darcia and Alistair. Perhaps we can exchange prisoners. If Larry does love Viviana, he would not want to see any harm come to her," Gabriel said. He looked back at Amy.

"I need to see if I can find Hildegard," Gabriel said. He checked his watch. It was going on eleven in the evening. "She might be asleep right now, but we need to get her back. I think I remember where she lives," Gabriel said. "Are you ladies going to be okay while I am gone?"

"I think you might need some backup, Gabriel," Arabella said. "Larry and Caleb would be outside waiting for you." Gabriel thought about it for a moment and shook his head.

"Take Lucien with you, at least," Arabella said. The other two men can stay here with us." Gabriel nodded before he got to his feet. Moments later, Gabriel and Lucien headed outside to find Hildegard. When they got to the house they believed she lived in, Gabriel started to climb up the wall of the house to see if he could see any traces of her. The lights were off, and the curtains were closed. He tried to hold his ear close to the windows to see if he could recognize her breathing.

Hildegard was deep asleep and snuggled under the covers. Gabriel gently opened the windows with his sharp nails and snuck into her bedroom. Lucien shook his head in disbelief, thinking how wrong it looked to watch a man in a black suit enter someone's window at this time of the day. Gabriel hovered over Hildegard and covered her mouth with his hand to avoid her screaming.

"Hush Hildegard," Gabriel whispered. "I need you not to scream right now." Hildegard nodded silently. Gabriel released his hold on her.

"What are you doing at my house?" Hildegard snapped. "Are you even here, or is this a nightmare?"

Gabriel sat on the edge of her bed. "Why did you stop coming to my home, Hildegard?" Gabriel asked. Hildegard gave him a confused and irritated expression.

"You fired me, Gabriel, or at least it went through your new housekeeper; what was her name? Vivienne?" Hildegard asked. Gabriel smiled. Gabriel nodded.

"Viviana, but yes, she was a nanny, but she is no longer of service at my home. She did some terrible things," Gabriel said in a whisper. Hildegard looked at him with curiosity.

"Like what?" Hildegard asked. "I mean, did she expose you all to the humans yet, or did she have herself turned?" Gabriel shook his head.

"No. Viviana used magic on us, especially me, and poisoned our blood supply with juniper. She is quite a tricksy little girl, but she is also quite dangerous. That is why I am here. I need you back as the original housekeeper of the Ambrose family. Are you still up for it, Hildegard?" Gabriel asked.

Hildegard shrugged. "I do not have a job yet, but then again, after living with you all for so long and suddenly entering back into the human world of buying groceries and running my own errands, I suffered from depression after I was let go. Do you still need someone, Gabriel?" Hildegard asked. Gabriel nodded.

"You would always be part of my family no matter what, Hildegard," Gabriel said with a smile. "I did not want to wake you up around this time, but I also needed to take immediate action in case you were gone or even dead."

Hildegard smirked at that comment. "Well, I guess I am still mortal and have aged quite a lot after working with shape shifters, but yes, I get what you mean, Gabriel," Hildegard said. Gabriel nodded.

"You do not have to worry about anyone harming you back at the castle. Viviana is in our dungeon, sadly, alongside Alistair's and Darcia's sons. Amelia and Arabella would welcome you back in their lives again and see you as the young girl they once met," Gabriel said with a smile. "What do you say? Are you up for returning this evening so I can get you resettled, or did you want to be given a few days of packing?"

Hildegard looked around and laughed at the situation. Being in bed with a shapeshifter and wanting her back in his life. Nothing made sense from the moment she got hired as a housekeeper, and it still made no sense to her. Where was she going to get a job, and what kind of credentials and names would she be able to provide for being a housekeeper? Hildegard checked the time.

"I guess I can get myself ready right now and prepare my move back to your castle again, Gabriel," Hildegard said. "I have no other prospects going on for me anyway, and you did eventually come back for me," Hildegard said. "I just need an hour or so to get all of my things. Did you come back in your car by any chance?"

Gabriel shook his head. "No. Lucien is waiting outside right now, making sure Larry or Caleb are not planning on attacking us," Gabriel said. Hildegard nodded.

"Oh right," Hildegard said. "The bad ones." Hildegard got out of bed and allowed Gabriel to open the front door for Lucien to enter while she packed her clothes and other personal items and got dressed in her regular clothes.

Back at the castle, Amy started to feel a bit better, but she still felt sore after being bitten so hard. She sat up against the bedpost, looking ahead at the crib and watching her children. She felt a sense of heartbreak after seeing Bryan attack her, but he was also under Viviana's spell. Amy wondered if Bryan even knew what he was doing and how he managed to get compromised so easily by her. Her feelings for Bryan were shattered after that moment, but she hoped her feelings for him would return.

There was a knock on the door. "Come in," Amy said. The door opened, and Arabella came into her room. "Mother, what can I do for you?" Arabella closed the door and walked over to sit on the edge of Amy's bed.

"You look much better than before, Amy," Arabella said. "How are you feeling?" Amy shrugged.

"I have felt worse, but I do feel better than I did after the bite, mother," Amy said. Arabella nodded. "How is everyone else?"

Arabella shrugged. "I think everyone is shaken, but also relieved that this situation is starting to simmer a bit. Your father is trying to find Hildegard so she can bring us our blood sources again. This time without juniper," Arabella said with a smile. Amy chuckled.

"Goodness, we have survived many storms; have we not, mother?" Amy asked. Arabella smiled and nodded.

"We are strong women. We can handle many things, Amy and Ginger," Arabella said. "I was a ghost for a while, and you girls were in the human world. Yet, we did survive the drama and pain that came with it all. We will survive this as well," Arabella said.

There was another knock on the door. "Yes?" Amy asked. The door opened, and Amelia came into the room. "Amelia, what are you doing here?" Amelia was holding a measuring cup.

"We do not have blood, but I did concoct this serum that should speed up any wounds you still might have, Amy," Amelia said. Amy pulled the collar of her pajama shirt down to show that there was an infected bite mark that had somewhat faded, but it was still visible. "Try some of this," Amelia said as she held the cup up to Amy's lips.

Amy slowly took a sip from it and winced. "What is that?" Amy asked. Amelia smiled.

"Different healing herbs, Amy, like chamomile, lavender, calendula, and jasmine," Amelia said. Amy looked at the wound. It started to heal a bit faster this time. "Good," Amelia said before she placed the cup on Amy's nightstand. "When you need some more, try and finish this cup. It should also help you sleep and heal quicker."

Amy nodded. Arabella got to her feet before she followed Amelia out of the room. Amy closed her eyes and let the relaxed feeling take over her body. Arabella closed the door behind her and walked with Amelia down the staircase.

Back at Hildegard's place, Gabriel and Lucien waited in Hildegard's living room, watching the clock ticking. Hildegard zipped up her two big suitcases. Gabriel and Lucien walked up the stairs to help Hildegard with her baggage. "There," Hildegard said as she grabbed her brown winter coat, fuzzy hat, and gloves. "I am ready." Gabriel and Lucien each grabbed a suitcase, and the three of them headed out of her house and walked towards the castle.

It was going on about two o'clock in the morning. A crescent moon was out, and a few planets were visible in the sky. It was a quiet, but cold, night for humans to be outside at this time. It took them about a half hour to get back to the castle. Lucien opened the door. "Gabriel!" Larry yelled from about fifty feet away from them. "What have you done with Viviana?"

Gabriel turned around and saw Larry, Caleb, Bianca, and about ten members behind him. Gabriel quickly pushed Hildegard inside. Lucien got outside and beckoned for Vladimir and Daniel to join them, who were waiting for them. Larry and his group walked towards them. "Where is she, Gabriel?" Gabriel remained silent till they got close enough.

"Why do you ask, Lawrence Harrison?" Gabriel asked teasingly. "Perhaps she is outside doing girl activities." Larry crouched down and barred his teeth.

"Or perhaps she was a naughty girl and needed a timeout," Gabriel snapped. "I am sure she kept you up to date on what she was doing, right?"

Larry relaxed his body and stood up again. "What do you mean, Gabriel?" Larry asked. "What has she been doing anyway to anger you so much?" Gabriel cleared his throat as he took three steps forward.

"Come on, Larry," Gabriel said. "Your Viviana is a sorceress, is she not?" Larry rolled his eyes.

"If you want to call her that," Larry said. "She put a spell on you, Gabriel Ambrose, leader of all shapeshifters? Goodness, so you do have a weakness about you. Man, I really have lost my respect for you, Gabriel. Well, where is she? Did you kill her for real this time?" Larry asked. Gabriel shrugged.

"Where are Alistair and Darcia, Larry?" Gabriel asked. Larry smirked at that question and looked behind him at his friends.

"Perhaps they needed to be put in a timeout as well," Larry said teasingly, causing his friends and Bianca to laugh. Gabriel felt anger boiling inside of him. "First, answer my question, Gabriel. Is Viviana okay, or did you have her killed for real?" Larry asked.

"She is alive and in our dungeon. I am not sure if I want to release her right now until I know that Alistair and Darcia are safe," Gabriel said. Larry felt anger inside of him.

"What do you propose, Gabriel Ambrose?" Larry snapped. "A prisoner swap?" Gabriel thought about it and needed to see if it was safe enough to agree to that term or if he could think of an alternative way to trick him and have Darcia and Alistair released.

The Plan

Darcia and Alistair remained in their weakened state. "My love," Darcia whispered. "How long do you think we still have before we truly die from starvation?" Alistair felt too weak to answer, but he mustered up enough to respond.

"I am not sure, Darcia," Alistair said. "I feel too weak to even talk. Do we still have that blood pack near us?"

Darcia moved her head slowly and noticed the unopened pack of blood about three steps away from them. "It is, but I do not know how I can reach it, my love," Darcia whispered. Darcia realized how all the humans she and her family had hunted were probably in the same situation of feeling weak and hopeless. She considered switching over from pure human bodies to alternative means of getting the proper nutrients inside of her. She looked at the blood pack with intense hunger.

"My love," Darcia whispered. "Are you able to move your hands in any way?" Alistair shook his shoulders a bit, which hurt from being at the same angle for a while. "Okay. Let me see if I can move over and lean down to grab the pack with my teeth, or did you want to try that?"

"I think that if I lean down, I will just topple over, Darcia. Perhaps you can do it since you are more petite and slender than me," Alistair said. Darcia inhaled and exhaled before moving her weak body a few inches at a time until she was close enough to lean down and find the nozzle of the pack.

The first time she missed, which caused her to lose more energy than she had before. She groaned as she felt intense, sharp pains throughout her body. Alistair felt the need to use the last bit of strength he had to undo the shackles that were attached to his wrists and ankles. Darcia tried it again and missed the nozzle, but she bit down on the plastic side of the pack. She felt the weight of the liquid pulling her down. She let go, but this time the nozzle was angled in a better position, so she could lean down and bite on the nozzle part. She pulled herself up with her last bit of energy and let the pack fall into her lap.

Alistair groaned as she pulled the chains from each side to try to break them. Darcia had a tiny bit of energy left and joined in on pulling her arms from each side to break the chains. They both tugged and groaned at the resistance of the chains until the left side snapped off from the middle part. Darcia and Alistair's left hands were free. Darcia quickly grabbed the blood pack, bit off the cap, and swilled down half the pack. Then she quickly handed Alistair the other half, and they leaned against each other with relief.

"We do make a good team, do we not, my love?" Alistair asked. Darcia smiled at that comment. "I do feel a bit better after that drink, but we both need more to get our strength back again. Wait," Darcia said. "Does it not seem quiet to you?" Alistair listened and was unable to hear anything.

"They might be gone. That means that we can easily escape this place better and quicker," Alistair said. Darcia struggled to move to her right side and started to pull on the chain while Alistair pulled on the other side. About a minute or two later, the chain broke. Alistair and Darcia looked around to see how they could break their ankle chains. There was a broken shard in the corner of the room in the basement.

Darcia was closest to that side of the room and crawled over with bound legs over to the shard and sat down. She tried to break the shackle, but felt too weak to even move. "Alistair," Darcia sighed. "Do you think you can help me?" Alistair crawled over to her with the little energy he had left and started cutting the chain until he felt an intense stabbing pain in his upper back, causing him to stop.

"Ow," Alistair snapped. Darcia grabbed the shard and continued cutting the shackles. Darcia groaned as she noticed little improvement in cutting the shackles.

"It is hopeless, my love," Darcia moaned. "We are never going to leave this place."

Alistair breathed through the pain, took the shard from Darcia's grasp, and continued cutting through the chain. Minutes went by, and he broke through half of it. Then he decided to tug at both ends of the chain until they broke off. The pain that Alistair felt before doubled. "Ow, my body," Alistair cried. "Darcia, you need to leave me," Alistair said. Darcia felt tears building in her eyes and shook her head.

"Never, Alistair. We are going out together. I am never leaving you. We either leave together or we die together, but we are not separating right now," Darcia cried. Alistair lay on his back, massaging his body, while Darcia grabbed the shard and cut as energetically as she could through the chain. She did not care if it would take her an hour. She was not going to abandon her life partner. About twenty minutes went by, and she was able to get through half of the chain. "Alistair," Darcia panted. "Do you think you can pull on one side of the chain while I tug on the other side?"

Alistair sat back up and nodded. The pain of stabbing and the waves from it made it unbearable, but he did not believe in giving up. He pulled on one side, while Darcia pulled on the other side. Seconds later, the chain broke loose. Darcia let out a shrieking howl. "We did it!" Darcia shrieked before she fell against Alistair. They both lied on the wooden floor until they realized that they only had so much time left before Larry and his group would return. They looked over at the broken window. Alistair took off his jean jacket, wrapped it around his right fist, and smashed two of the windows that were already partially shattered. Darcia crawled out first onto the wet leaves. Then she turned around and waited for Alistair to crawl through. He looked at the windows and shook his head.

"I am not sure I can fit through this, my love," Alistair said. "Would it be better for me to use the front door?" Suddenly, Darcia looked over and saw Larry and Caleb heading for the house. Darcia looked at Alistair with tears in her eyes.

"They are coming, my love; what do we do?" Darcia whispered. Alistair looked over at Darcia. "You need to go back to the castle, and you need to let the other ones know about me," Alsitair said. Darcia shook her head.

"No, Alistair," Darcia whispered. "I cannot leave you like this." Alistair urged Darcia to leave. She got to her feet with fear and sadness on her face, snuck around the area where Larry and his friends were, and ran towards the main streets toward the castle.

Larry entered the apartment complex and headed for the basement. "Well, it is your lucky day, Alsitair and Darcia," Larry said with anger in his voice. "You both get to go home where your master is waiting for you." Larry walked down the last few steps and turned the corner with a surprised look.

"Where is the girl?" Larry snapped as he looked at Alistair in anger. "Where is Darcia?" Alistair shrugged. Larry looked at the broken windows and then returned his focus back to Alistair. "Did she escape, Alistair?" Larry asked. Alistair did not respond. He sat there with broken shackles around his ankles and wrists.

Larry walked over to him and grabbed his wrists, looking at the broken chains. "Well, perhaps you did allow little Darcia to escape, Alistair. Do not worry. She will be okay, but your fate has become darker," Larry said before he pushed Alistair's wrists down. "Before we even reunite you both, my sister might want another taste of you, Alistair. Oh, Bianca," Larry said in a singing way. "Would you care for a little taste?"

Bianca came walking down the stairs, looking more beautiful after her taste of other blood packs. "Of course," Bianca said before she got into a pouncing position and jumped at Alistair, causing him to groan. She grabbed the shard that was next to Alistair and cut his throat, causing some blood to spill. Bianca placed her lips on his throat, sucking fast. Alistair's last bit of energy was gone. He collapsed on the floor, but he was not dead. Larry would not want anything to happen to Viviana.

"Good," Larry said. "Have the men drag his body over to the castle, but do not be so easy on it." Bianca nodded as she licked her lips and wiped her mouth with the back of her hand. Larry looked at the deflated Alistair, smirking at him. "I bear you no malice, Alistair, but I know how close you are to Gabriel. This should be his final warning before he does anything unexpectedly," Larry said before he walked back up the stairs.

Alistair was unable to move and felt incredibly weak. How a meek little creature like Bianca could have such an appetite made no sense to him. Three of Larry's male friends came down the stairs. Two of them grabbed Alistair by his arms and the third by his legs as they carried him up the stairs to take him back to the castle.

Darcia felt incredibly weak, but she managed to snatch several small birds and foxes on her way, increasing her strength again. She had to be strong for Alistair. She saw the castle from a distance and jogged in that direction. She managed to get to the front door and rang the bell before falling to her knees. The door opened, and Hildegard stood in the doorway. "Good heavens," Hildegard said. "Darcia? What happened to you? Where is Alistair?"

Darcia panted as she held up her hand. "Kidnapped" was the only thing Darcia was able to say. Arabella, Amelia, and lastly, Gabriel, approached her with horror on their faces.

"Darcia," Gabriel said in shock. "What happened? Where is Alistair?" Darcia reached for Gabriel's hands. He took them and helped her onto her feet. "Kidnapped. Larry," Darcia panted. Gabriel looked behind Darcia out into the open streets with anger.

"Where is he, Darcia?" Gabriel asked as he helped her walk into the living quarter and sat her down on one of the sofas, holding her in his arms.

"Basement," Darcia whispered. "Larry's home." Gabriel looked over at his friends and shook his head with disgust.

"Okay. Hildegard, could you retrieve me a fresh bottle of blood?" Gabriel asked. Hildegard headed for the cooler and grabbed an unopened bottle that she had purchased from a blood bank several hours ago. Gabriel undid the cap and held the tip to Darcia's lips like he was feeding a child.

Darcia swilled down most of the bottle from being starved and leaned into Gabriel's arms. "Where is Larry now, Darcia?" Gabriel asked. Darcia felt stronger than before.

"I saw him return to his house. I had to leave Alistair because he did not fit through the windows. Goodness, I am so worried about him, Gabriel," Darcia said as she felt sadness inside of her. "I do not know what happened to him, but we need to save him."

Gabriel nodded before he gently released Darcia and let her lean against the back of the sofa. He got to his feet and saw his brothers enter the room. "We need to save Alistair," Gabriel said. "He might be in severe danger. Perhaps we should use Viviana as bait to get Larry to come for his lady." Amelia shook her head.

"I do not think that is a good idea, Gabriel. What if they try to trick us?" Amelia asked.

Gabriel looked at her with confusion. "We need to give Larry the impression that we are unaware of Darcia's return and that we do plan to give Viviana back to him," Gabriel said. "We need to trick him first before he gets a chance to trick us." Arabella shrugged. "It is worth a shot, but I do think we should make sure Viviana is not listening, either," Arabella said.

"Or the boys," Amelia said before she looked over at Darcia, who looked confused. "Your boys became enchanted by Viviana's spell. Bryan attacked Amy. Darcia looked at her with concern.

"What?" Darcia asked. "How is that even possible? Bryan loves Amy. How did he become enchanted by that girl?"

Arabella smiled. "As was Gabriel for a while. He became quite ill from our tampered blood supply. Viviana put juniper in our blood supply, causing Gabriel to get sicker by the day. It was horrible to watch him not being able to walk, vomiting up blood," Arabella said. Darcia looked at her with remorse.

"I am sorry to hear that, Arabella. May I see my sons, or would that cause problems?" Darcia asked.

Gabriel looked at her. "Perhaps once this is all over, it might be too soon to bring you in," Gabriel said. "Have no worry; this too shall be over before we all know it."

"Where is Amy anyway?" Darcia asked. Arabella looked at her and then at Gabriel. "She is in bed right now, recovering from the attack," Arabella said. "Amelia gave her some healing herbs for her flesh and blood." Darcia nodded.

Gabriel headed for the door that would lead him to the dungeon. "Wait," Amelia said. "Gabriel, I am not sure you should go down to retrieve Viviana. I think Arabella and I should retrieve the girl. What if she puts another spell on you again, Gabriel? I know the spell I put on you is quite strong, but I do not want to lose you again like we almost did before. Whatever Viviana may be, she is quite strong," Amelia said.

Gabriel gave her a reassuring smile. "I think we will all be okay," Gabriel said before he turned the doorknob and opened the door. Darcia came walking fast over to him.

"I must see my sons, Gabriel. I need to know how they are doing," Darcia said. Gabriel looked over at her and shook his head.

"Not right now, Darcia. Please stay up here while Amelia, Adrian, Vladimir, Lucien, and I go downstairs. Arabella can stay with you, right?" Gabriel asked as he looked over at Arabella.

Arabella nodded. "I think we should, also just in case Larry and his friends were to return with Alistair," Arabella said. Darcia looked at Arabella, feeling scared. Gabriel and Amelia both walked over to the dungeon, seeing the boys fawning over Viviana, and Viviana was in between them.

"Gabriel," Viviana said with happiness in her voice. "You came back for me. Please save me from this horrible place," Viviana said as she tried to use a love spell through her voice. Amelia cleared her throat, moving ahead of Gabriel.

"Do not even think about doing anything, Viviana," Amelia snapped. Viviana glared at Amelia. "Whatever you are trying to do, it shall not work this time. You finally get to return to your own coven, Viviana, if that is even your real name."

Viviana scoffed. "How?" Viviana asked. "I do not see Larry or Caleb anywhere. How do I not know that you are planning like a trick?" Amelia sighed.

"Darcia returned, but Alistair is not here. Would you know what could have happened to him, Viviana?" Viviana smiled and shrugged.

"I was never around that house that often, so I have no idea what you are talking about, Amelia, if that is even your name," Viviana snapped.

Amelia scoffed. "Boys, please undo the locks," Amelia said. The three men undid the locks. Bryan and his brothers looked over at them, growling at them. "Gabriel, what do we do?" Lucien asked. Gabriel nodded for them to open the gate.

"Boys," Gabriel snapped. "How would you all like a tasty little treat?" Gabriel asked. The boys kept their hungry eyes on the three men. "We have fresh blood upstairs if you want." The boys looked at Gabriel, licking their lips.

"Amelia, could you fetch our boys a fresh bottle of blood?" Gabriel asked. Amelia nodded and quickly ran up the stairs. The three men kept their hands on the gate until Amelia returned.

Amelia came down with the bottle. The boys became excited at the sight of the bottle and growled. "We are hungry, Gabriel," Bryan said.

Gabriel nodded. "Of course you are," Gabriel said. "You must promise that we will release you, but you are not allowed to attack us." Bryan looked at Bryan with dead black eyes. "Promise me, Bryan," Gabriel said. Bryan eventually nodded and relaxed his body. His eyes remained pitch black. "Good. Brothers, please open the gates for them to get out." Adrian, Vladimir, and Lucien released their holds on the gate, letting Bryan and his brothers run over to Amelia. She quickly undid the cap. Bryan yanked the bottle out of her hands and started chugging it.

Silas and Xavier tried to grab the bottle, but Bryan refused to let go. "We are hungry too," Raymond said. Joshua looked over at Amelia, licking his lips. "Go up and get yourself as much as you want, boys," Amelia said as she gestured toward the stairs. The other four boys all ran up to the cooler to get themselves their own bottle of blood.

Amelia could not help but chuckle at the sight of them acting so hungry. Darcia saw them with shock in her eyes. "Boys, what happened?" Darcia asked as she ran after them over to the cooler. Raymond was the first to grab a bottle and unscrewed the cap, chugging down the blood. Darcia looked at them with sadness in her heart. "What happened?" Darcia whispered.

Raymond stopped drinking to answer Darcia. "I have no idea, but I am quite hungry, mother," Raymond said before he finished the bottle. Silas, Xavier, and Joshua then drank down their own bottles, feeling sated.

"That feels much better," they all said. Then they looked at Darcia with confusion. "Where have you been?" Joshua asked. Darcia looked at each of her sons with confusion.

"Your father and I got kidnapped. I was able to escape through an open window, but your father's whereabouts are still unknown right now. Gabriel promised he would help us," Darcia said. "What is taking him so long?"

Back in the basement, Amelia wanted to make sure there were no unexpected tricks that Viviana could play on them. "Now, where did we leave off?" Amelia asked. The three men walked over to Viviana and stopped before her. Viviana looked quite sad as she sat there, waiting to be taken away. "Oh, Viviana," Amelia said. "Do not look so somber. You finally get to go home." Viviana did not respond. She let Lucien and Adrian both grab her, letting them escort her to the main floor.

Gabriel was the first to enter the main floor. Arabella sighed with relief as she saw Viviana in Adrian's and Lucien's arms. "Where is Larry? Has he come yet?" Gabriel asked. Arabella looked outside and shook her head.

"I am not sure, Gabriel. I have not noticed anything," Arabella said. Suddenly, Joshua clutched his head. He saw how weak Alistair looked as Larry's friends were dragging him through poison oak plants and muddy waters.

"Father!" Joshua screamed. Everyone looked at Joshua as he was holding onto his head in pain.

Bryan came up the stairs. "What is going on?" Bryan asked before he noticed Joshua. "What happened?" There was no response. The pain in Joshua's head eventually subsided.

Joshua regained his composure, trying to organize his thoughts. "I saw our father being dragged," Joshua said with sadness in his voice. "He looked awful." Bryan growled before he walked toward the front door.

"Bryan," Darcia snapped before she ran over to him. "Stop with what you are thinking. Now is not the time to act irrationally. We need to wait for Larry to return your father. He is stronger than you think. Your father," Darcia said. Bryan felt sadness inside of him.

"Larry needs to die, one way or another," Bryan snapped. "This problem needs to end." Darcia nodded in agreement.

"We are going to do a prisoner swap. Hildegard has purchased new cases of blood for us, so we should be good for about a month, is that right, Gabriel?" Darcia asked as she turned to face him. Gabriel nodded.

"For about a month, as per usual," Gabriel said. Darcia smiled and nodded.

"Gabriel Ambrose!" Larry yelled. Gabriel and the other members heard him scream.

"I guess it is time," Gabriel said as he headed towards the front door of the castle. He opened the door with his brothers holding Viviana, standing behind him.

"Lawrence Harrison, what brings you to my home?" Gabriel said it with a smile until it faded when he saw how horrible Alistair looked in the arms of two men he had never seen before.

"Viviana, are you all right?" Larry asked, dodging Gabriel's question.

"Yes, my love," Viviana said in a hoarse tone. "They kept me in a dungeon and did not feed me." Larry glared at Gabriel before he gestured toward Alistair.

"I believe this creature belongs to you," Larry said as he grabbed Alistair's hair, pulling his head back to expose all the bite marks he had endured. Darcia gasped at how horrible Alistair looked. She tried to walk past Gabriel, but he grabbed her.

"Not yet, Darcia," Gabriel whispered.

Darcia whimpered at the sight of her life partner. "Please, Gabriel, let him come back home to me," Darcia whispered. Gabriel ignored her, keeping his focus on Larry. Gabriel nodded to Adrian and Lucien.

"Bring her with us," Gabriel said as he approached them with Viviana, closer towards Larry's group. "Will you meet us halfway, Larry? Please bring Alistair closer to us."

Larry looked at Viviana and then at Gabriel. "Gents," Larry said. The men released the weakened Alistair into Larry's arms. Larry smiled at Alistair before she pushed him onto the floor. "Take him. Now release Viviana." Lucien and Adrian both released Viviana. She ran into Larry's arms, whimpering and shaking. Lucien and Adrian both picked up Alistair to bring him inside. Darcia walked alongside them in fear, opening the door. She ran over to the cooler and grabbed a fresh bottle of blood. Alistair was unresponsive but breathing softly.

"Alistair," Darcia said. "Please drink." Darcia held the bottle to Alistair's lips, giving him several minutes to swallow the blood. Darcia tipped the bottle gently, so Alistair could lean against the sofa with his head facing upwards.

Larry looked at Viviana, checking her for any wounds. "We will get you fed properly," Larry said before he looked over at Gabriel. "This is not over yet, Gabriel. You got your precious creature back, but so did I." Larry and his group turned around to go back to their home. Gabriel, Vladimir, Amelia, and Arabella watched Larry and his group walk away from them. Arabella sighed with relief before she turned around to head back to the front door.

Lucien and Adrian both came outside, waiting for Gabriel and Vladimir to return. "How is Alistair doing?" Gabriel asked. "Is he recovering?" Both Lucien and Adrian nodded. "Good. For now, we shall have a bit of peace from any conflicts," Gabriel whispered. Everyone entered the castle and locked it up properly.

Back in Amy's room, Amy was dreaming of Caleb and her being in the same woods that she had dreamt of before. Caleb looked at

Amy with love and admiration. She felt scared and uneasy, but she tried to remain as calm as possible. In her bed, she was shaking and turning. Ginger noticed Amy's behavior in bed. She walked over to her and wrapped her arms around her. "Wake up, Amy," Ginger whispered. "Wake up. It is only a dream." Amy woke up gasping.

"Where am I?" Amy panted as she looked around. She saw Ginger and wrapped her arms around her. "Ginger, I had a horrible dream about Caleb again. What is going on?" Amy asked. Ginger stroked Amy's back and held her close to her.

"Nothing, but a dream, Amy," Ginger said in a soothing tone. "You were just having a nightmare, nothing more." Amy pulled back from Ginger's embrace.

"I have had this dream about two times already. What can I do to stop these dreams, Ginger? Please help me," Amy whispered.

Ginger used her persuasive power on Amy. "Listen to me, Amy," Ginger said. "I need you to forget about that dream. It is not real. It was just a dream. Please repeat after me. It was just a dream," Ginger said.

"It is just a dream," Amy repeated mindlessly. Ginger nodded.

"Say it again," Ginger said. Amy repeated the exact sentence. "And one last time, say it again." Amy repeated the same sentence. Ginger snapped her fingers on her right hand to snap Amy out of her power. Amy blinked two times before she looked at Ginger.

"Ginger, what are you doing here?" Amy asked. Ginger smiled and nodded. "You will be okay, Amy. I just know it," Ginger said before she got to her feet. "Hildegard got new blood for us, Amy. When you are ready, feel free to come join us for a drink." Amy felt confused, but also hungry and thirsty. She got out of bed and noticed that she was in her pajamas.

"Let me get dressed. I will be down in a few minutes. Goodness, I must have slept so long. It is going on two o'clock in the morning. I might not be able to sleep tonight," Amy said. Ginger chuckled before she left the room. Amy looked over at her children, who were awake and in need of eating something.

The Dream

Larry opened the door with his weak Viviana hanging on him, guiding her to the living room of their apartment, while Bianca went over to get Viviana a blood pack from their cooler. Larry put Viviana on the couch and held her close to him.

"How are you feeling, my love?" Larry asked. Viviana shrugged.

"Better than I had before, my love," Viviana said. Bianca came back and already undid the cap of the blood pack and held it out for Larry to place it on Viviana's lips.

"Drink," Larry whispered. Viviana started sucking at the pack. She started off with small sips and later grabbed it and swilled down the pack. "Wow, you must really have been starved. Bianca, dear, could you hand me another pack?" Bianca rolled her eyes at Larry and reluctantly got up from the chair she was sitting in to get Viviana another pack.

"For her third pack, you can handle that one yourself, brother dearest," Bianca said. When Bianca had returned, she handed Viviana the unopened pack and sat back down again. Viviana drank down the second pack and sighed.

"Much better," Viviana whispered. Larry smiled at Viviana and released his hold on her.

"I have a question for you, though," Larry said. Viviana looked up at him while she was sipping the last few drops. "How did they find out, you were bewitching them, especially Gabriel?" Larry asked. Viviana swallowed before she spoke.

"Amy found out," Viviana said. "I have no idea, how she managed, but she found out that her father was under my spell, and it all went downhill from there." Larry sighed.

"How did she find out, Viviana? As far as I am concerned, you managed to survive in this world from the moment Gabriel buried you in the woods many years ago, but she managed to find out about your powers; how does that work, Viviana?" Larry asked, feeling his anger rising. "What gave that away?"

Viviana felt guilt and shame washing over her. Larry relaxed his mind, trying to put Viviana at ease. "Look, however it happened, it did, and you are back and well, but I was really hoping that Gabriel could have died this time and perhaps let me drop the guillotine on him," Larry said. Viviana nodded.

"I am sorry, that happened, Larry. I truly am. I mean, how long has it been that I have been at that place? About six months, is it?" Viviana asked. Larry nodded.

"About, but it seems that they are quite strong. I should have actually killed Alistair off, but then again, that would mean they would retaliate and have you killed off," Larry said. "That would hurt me a lot."

Caleb approached Larry. "Larry," Caleb whispered. "I think I know how to take down those creatures, once and for all." Larry looked up at Caleb and smiled.

"Do tell, brother," Larry said. Caleb got down on the floor.

"I keep letting Amy have these nightmares about her and me being husband and wife," Caleb said. "What if I were to play Gabriel and allow him to let me back in his life as his potential son, which was the main reason he created me, and let me seduce Amy?"

Larry chuckled at that idea and shook his head. "What would make you think Gabriel would ever let you return to his home? And what would make you think Bryan would let Amy out of his sight? He is so possessive of her, whether you realize it or not. Amy is like a diamond necklace that is placed under heavy locks in a jewelry store. You would never be able to seduce her," Larry said.

Caleb waited for Larry to finish. "Oh yeah? I have been letting her dream of me, you know, but hang on," Caleb said. "What if I were to seem desperate or needy for her protection? Like, what if I was being chased and harmed by a group of monsters and see if she does not have a sense of protection within her to want to save me?" Caleb asked. Larry rolled his eyes.

"I do not know, Caleb. Those ideas sound dumb and unprepared. You would most likely become a better snack for them than a long-lost family member, Caleb. We can talk about this sometime tomorrow. For now, I feel incredibly tired," Larry said before he got to his feet to go to sleep. "Will you be joining me, Viviana?" Viviana nodded as she headed for Larry's bedroom.

Back at the castle, Alistair felt better, but he was not able to get up without Darcia's support. "I feel incredibly tired, my love," Alistair whispered while he remained on the sofa. "Go on to bed, my love. You need to be able to sleep in a proper bed. I will be okay." Darcia shook her head.

"No, Alistair," Darcia whispered. "I am not leaving your side right now. I will look after you while you sleep. Go on. Close your eyes and let yourself drift off into a deep and relaxing slumber." Alistair smiled before he closed his eyes and fell into a deep sleep. Darcia looked at him and watched him sleep. She felt tired after two hours and fell asleep on the sofa across from Alistair.

When dusk arrived, Darcia opened her eyes and saw that Alistair was still asleep. She checked her watch. It was going on six o'clock in the evening. Arabella and Amelia were awake, getting themselves a glass of blood. Then Gabriel showed up, and eventually the other members slowly woke up. Darcia got hungry and joined the others for a glass of blood.

"Darcia," Arabella said. "Did you get any sleep?" Darcia nodded.

"Yes," Darcia said. "I slept on the opposite sofa to make sure Alistair was okay. I think I might want to bring him an unopened bottle of blood." Darcia grabbed a full glass and downed it in seconds before she grabbed a fresh bottle and walked back to the living quarter.

She had no intention of leaving his side. Moments later, Bryan and his brothers came down for their evening drink. They stopped outside the living quarter when they noticed Darcia sitting by herself. "How is Father doing?" Bryan asked. Darcia looked up at him and smiled.

"I think he is well, son, but he just needs to rest up. He really got drained quite a bit and tortured by Larry's friends," Darcia whispered. "I really hate them for how they treated us. All because of his problem with Gabriel."

Gabriel just then entered the living quarter with his glass. "I heard my name mentioned. Is everything okay?" Gabriel asked.

Darcia looked up at him. "Just fine, Gabriel," Darcia said. "How are you feeling, by the way?" Gabriel looked over at Bryan and smiled. Bryan got to his feet, so Gabriel could sit down. Gabriel turned his focus to Darcia.

"I feel quite well, Darcia. I believe that this problem with Viviana is over, and whatever Larry has planned next, I will not let my guard down this time. How is Alistair doing?" Gabriel asked.

Darcia looked at Alistair. "I hope he will be okay, Gabriel," Darcia whispered. "When I saw him so weak and drained yesterday, it broke my heart. How Larry and his friends managed to kidnap us was quite unexpected, as well. Months ago, Alistair and I thought it would be a good idea to see what Larry was up to while Viviana kept you metaphorically subdued. Then we entered the park where we normally walk, and suddenly there were probably twenty of them out there, and they all piled on top of us, biting us and beating us up. Of course fifteen of them got severely injured, but we were quite weakened by it all, Gabriel."

Gabriel nodded as he waited for Darcia to continue. "Why did you two not try to escape all that time?" Gabriel asked. Darcia looked at him.

"We were quite weak, Gabriel. It was not until two days ago, when Caleb came down to us with a pack of blood from his own source, that I was motivated to not give up on the situation. The fact that Larry and Caleb left to see you gave Alistair and me some extra time to strengthen ourselves back up and try to escape. It was not until I noticed how small the window was that Alistiar would not have been able to crawl through. I refused to leave him, but he urged me to go so I could get some backup. Larry and his friends got to have fun with Alistair with their manner of torturing him until they allowed him to come back home. I wonder if I had stayed, if they would have tortured me as well, or if they would have forced me to watch somehow. I should try to forget about what happened with us and try to look ahead at the positive sides of the fact that we are both back and not dead," Darcia said.

"Keep me posted about any improvements regarding Alistair's improvement. We will make sure there is justice regarding our conflict with Larry. This problem should be coming to an end, Darcia," Gabriel said before he got to his feet and walked back to the dining quarer where he saw his brothers and Amelia sitting together.

"Gabriel," Lucien said. "How is Alistair doing?" Gabriel shrugged.

"He looks quite weak and tired, but Darcia has a fresh bottle of blood for him. That should hopefully help him regain his strength again," Gabriel said before he took a seat next to Amelia. "I want to thank you again, Amelia, for saving me from Viviana. I had no idea Viviana was some sort of sorceress, and when you let me drink from your arm, it brought me back to reality. I sort of felt like I was going in and out of reality when Viviana was here and when she left, but I really felt incredibly scared by how weak I was getting. I never knew we even had juniper," Gabriel said.

Amelia smiled and shrugged. "Sorceress people can find all kinds of herbs and poisons for their victims, Gabriel," Amelia said.

Gabriel nodded. "How did you even find out what she was doing to me, Amelia?" Gabriel asked. Amelia shrugged.

"Intuition, but then again, I did recognize the flavor of juniper while I was studying magic and positions from my past and remembered vaguely that we are quite toxic to vampires. Then I noticed you got incredibly weak and were unable to hold in fox blood that one evening, and the memory of that one paragraph came back to me," Amelia said.

"Well, I am happy to have you in my life, dear Amelia," Gabriel said. "You are quite an important member of our family." Amelia smiled and nodded.

"Oh, stop it, Gabriel," Amelia said teasingly. "You know that Arabella is in the area, right?" The other men chuckled. Gabriel smiled.

"Arabella and I are strong enough to handle an occasional flirting moment with other members," Gabriel said.

"So," Lucien said. "What is the plan for taking down Larry this time, Gabriel?" Gabriel thought about it for a moment, not having an immediate answer prepared for Lucien.

"I think we should just take our time and get Alistair back to his original self again. I know you might think that it should be a good idea to go after Larry right now, but I am not in a rush right now to have to deal with him. I feel content right now with my brothers and Amelia. I do feel sad about Daniel not being here with us any longer. I have not had dreams about him; have any of you?" Gabriel asked.

Each member looked at each other and shook their heads. "Not really," Adrian said. "I do miss him a lot. I just remember how it was the five of us and how we used to go out on our hunting trips and seduce a lot of people. Now it is the four of us, with one member gone forever." Vladimir and Lucien both nodded.

"Yes," Gabriel murmured. "I do miss him a lot. Especially his technical skills on using that computer machine that I have in my office." Everyone smiled at Gabriel.

"Perhaps Amy's son, Nathaniel, might take after him or at least have some type of important skill that would benefit our family."

Amelia chuckled at that comment. "Gabriel, the child is only a few months old. Just enjoy him exploring this world, and let him soon discover his true identity when he is ready. You will be there to witness the development of Amy's and, hopefully, Ginger's children in the future. For now, we still have each other as our main support in this world. I feel quite content with everything right now," Amelia said.

Lucien nodded. "I agree. Right now, everyone is doing quite well. Amy seemed to be doing well, and Alistair will be regaining his strength again. I feel quite satisfied, as well," Lucien said. Gabriel smiled.

"Well, let me check the time. Oh goodness, it is going on six thirty in the morning. Yet, the sun has not risen yet. I think I shall head over to my quarter and see where my wife is," Gabriel said before he placed his empty glass in the sink for Hildegard to clean up.

Gabriel headed down to his sleeping quarter and saw Arabella brushing her hair in front of the boudoir. "Good evening, Arabella," Gabriel said as he took off his blazer and undid his tie. Arabella looked up at him and smiled.

"How are you doing, Gabriel?" Arabella asked. "Do you feel any different after being under Viviana's spell?"

Gabriel shook his head. "I feel much better than I have ever felt. The fresh blood does help," Gabriel said. Arabella nodded. "And you, Arabella, how are you?" Arabella shrugged.

"Quite exhausted from everything," Arabella said before she yawned. "Goodness, I am quite tired from everything." Gabriel smiled and nodded before he got under the covers and waited for Arabella to join him.

Arabella wore her cotton Victorian white nightgown, slid under the covers, and fell asleep instantly. Gabriel then fell asleep. In his dream, he dreamt he was back at the tavern where he had met Larry and saw Viviana as her mortal self again. He looked at them and watched them from a distance. He did crave them, which was weird. He approached the tavern and saw everyone looking at him with anger. He did not recall humans looking at him like they did, but he stopped at the front door.

He put his hand on the doorknob to open the door and stepped inside. This time, Larry's friends were around, with Larry serving everyone a red liquid. Was he serving his guests wine, or was that blood? Larry then looked over at Gabriel and smiled. "Our guest has finally arrived," Larry said excitedly. "Welcome back, Gabriel."

Gabriel looked confused at everyone who had a smile on their faces. Then he turned to leave the tavern, but the door was locked. Caleb showed up in a tuxedo, and behind him was his daughter, Amy, wearing a wedding dress. Gabriel looked at her in shock. He remembered the fake wedding he had until Amy transformed into her shape-shifting self. Larry then placed both his hands on Amy and Caleb's shoulders, like he was uniting them.

"Amy," Gabriel whispered. He was unable to speak. "Amy," Gabriel said again. This time, she looked over at him and smiled.

"Caleb had proposed to me, Father," Amy said. "And I just could not resist this wonderful man. I said yes," Amy said as she showed Gabriel her wedding ring. Gabriel felt scared for the first time in his life. Then Katrina showed up in a pink bride's maid dress with blood in her center, and then Viviana showed up in her white gown with blood in her center, holding a bouquet in her hands.

"Would our best man want to give a toast to the happy couple?" Larry asked. To Gabriel's astonishment, it was Daniel who showed up in a tuxedo with a blood-marked center. "Daniel Ambrose, the uncle of Amy, what would you like to say to the happy couple and your brother?"

Daniel smiled. "Life is very precious. It just takes one painful moment to end such a precious gift," Daniel said. Gabriel could not move. The room started to fade, but it was Gabriel who was close to fainting until he woke up in shock.

Arabella remained asleep. Gabriel checked his watch. It was going on at noon. Gabriel lost his sleep and got out of bed. Arabella moaned as she was trying to reach out to him and felt an empty spot next to her. She opened her eyes and looked up at Gabriel.

"What happened?" Arabella asked. Gabriel turned around to face her. He was afraid and angry.

"I had a nightmare, Arabella," Gabriel said. "I was talking with my brothers and Amelia hours before bedtime, and we were talking about Daniel. It was a horrific dream, Arabella. It felt so real. Remember how I had a fake wedding prepared for Amy and Caleb? Oh, right, forgive me, Arabella. You were still in the form of a ghost."

Arabella rolled her eyes. "Right. The fake wedding was because you wanted Amy to express herself as a shape shifter, right?" Arabella asked. Gabriel waved off that comment and got to his feet.

"I need to speak to Amy about these dreams. I think she might be having them too. I do not want her ever going near Caleb again," Gabriel snapped. Arabella sighed.

"Well," Arabella said. "Whatever you decide, I think I want to get some more sleep before I hear about your plans for Amy or even Caleb." Gabriel did not respond but decided to go up to the main floor for another glass of blood. He entered the dining quarter and saw Hildegard walking around in her usual outfit. She gasped when she saw Gabriel.

"Gabriel," Hildegard whispered. "What are you doing up so early? Should you not be resting?" Gabriel shook his head.

"I had a nightmare, Hildegard," Gabriel whispered. "I need to have a drink." Hildegard grabbed an empty glass and an opened bottle of blood and placed them in front of him. She checked her watch. She had done most of her shopping for her own dinner, so she decided to sit with Gabriel.

"Did you want to talk about it, or would you prefer to sit in silence with your drink?" Hildegard asked. Gabriel smiled.

"I do prefer a bit of company, Hildegard," Gabriel said. "I just feel quite exhausted from even such nightmares. I have been so foolish about everything and disregarded my own children for the sake of my own ideas on how I wanted to see everything," Gabriel said before he chugged down his first glass. Hildegard poured him another and listened to his stories.

"Nightmares are just short-term thoughts, Gabriel. Whatever nightmare you dreamed of will never come to pass. Everything is going to be okay, Gabriel," Hildegard said. Gabriel smiled and placed his hand on hers. Hildegard used to flinch at Gabriel's touch, but this time she felt neutral about his hands. Gabriel slowly released his hold on her.

"How do you handle nightmares, Hildegard?" Gabriel asked. Hildegard chuckled at that comment.

"I just endure the moment, wake up, and usually those dreams disappear throughout my day," Hildegard said. Gabriel could not help but chuckle at Hildegard's response.

"Well, I think I might try to go back to sleep," Gabriel said before he left the glass and bottle for Hildegard to clean up. Gabriel headed down the stairs toward his sleeping quarter. He opened and closed the door to the bedroom gently to avoid waking up Arabella. He gently slid into his side of the bed and closed his eyes. Sleep did not take him for another two hours, until he eventually fell asleep. That evening, he woke up around eleven, a bit later than he normally would have woken up. He felt for Arabella, but her side was empty. He stretched out his body and slowly put on his day clothes.

When he arrived on the main floor, there was a storm going on outside. The rain was pouring down; the lightning and thunder had struck several times. Gabriel looked outside and always found some sort of peace with storms. He admired the trees and plants getting natural water and how rain was like a cleansing of the world. He walked over to the cooler and opened up a new bottle. Hildegard knew she had to retrieve several new bottles, so she took the car that Gabriel had left in their garage to run her errand.

Gabriel sat down in the dining quarter with his empty glass and fresh bottle. He waited for the opportune moment to go to Amy and discuss the dream he had regarding Caleb. He wanted to see if Amy could show up sooner than that, so he had to go looking for her. Lucien, Adrian, and Vladimir came walking into the room. "Good evening, sleeping handsome," Lucien said teasingly. Gabriel looked up at him and nodded at their entrance.

"Good evening to you too, brothers," Gabriel said. "What have you all been doing with your evening so far?" They all shrugged.

"Not much, Gabriel," Lucien said. Every evening is practically the same for us. We sleep, consume some nutritious drinks, and make sure we are not being targeted by potential predators," Lucien said with a chuckle. Gabriel nodded as he looked at his three brothers.

"I had a dream about Daniel while I slept," Gabriel said. The three men sat down in a chair, close to Gabriel. "I had a nightmare that Caleb and Amy were to get married, and guess who the best man was to give a speech. Yes, it was Daniel," Gabriel said. "I woke up in shock around noon and could not get back to sleep for a while, brothers."

The three men looked at Gabriel and then at each other. "How weird," Adrian said. "I mean, you do not think that Larry has such strength to use anyone's sad memories and put them in their dreams." Gabriel shrugged.

"I am not sure. I still have no idea what kind of power he even has. I mean, I am a shape shifter, and I can use my mind to control people's behavior, just like Alistair," Gabriel said. "Speaking of which, how is he? Have any of you seen him lately?" Gabriel asked.

The three men shook their heads. "I think Darcia is overlooking him, and if there was something wrong, I am sure she would notify us," Lucien said. Gabriel nodded.

"Well, I have had my fill for now. I am going to see where my daughter may be. Apparently, she has been having nightmares about Caleb as well. I need to know more about this situation before it gets out of hand. Please excuse me, gents," Gabriel said before he placed the bottle back in the cooler and his empty glass in the sink. He walked over to Amy's room and knocked on it until she responded.

"Yes?" Amy asked. The door opened, and Gabriel entered the room. Amy and Ginger were with the three children. "Father, what a surprise! What can I do for you?" Gabriel got down on the floor next to Amy and saw how precious her children were playing with the toy horses and rattles. He smiled at their beautiful features. "Father, is everything okay?"

Gabriel looked over at Amy and smiled. "Well, yes, but I need to ask you something important. Is this a good time? I do not want the children to sense anything weird about our conversation. If you could step outside with me, that would make it easier for me," Gabriel said. Amy nodded, got to her feet, and headed for the hallway. Ginger looked over at them with interest and decided to join them in the hallway.

"What is it, Father?" Amy asked. Ginger opened and closed Amy's door.

"I had a nightmare about you getting married to Caleb, and I also heard that you had nightmares about him as well," Gabriel said in a hushed tone. Amy looked at him with shock. "By your expression, I know now for sure you have had nightmares. Could you tell me more about your dreams, Amy?"

Amy sighed and thought about how she was going to formulate her answer. "Well," Amy said. "I have had dreams about Caleb proposing to me. Dreams where he and I are outside in some woodsy area with my children, to which he refers, our children," Amy said. Gabriel nodded.

"Okay. Well, whatever happens, do not ever think about going over to Caleb. If you ever see him outside of the castle, do not ever go to him. Is that understood? That goes the same for you too, Ginger," Gabriel said.

Ginger and Amy both nodded. "I will try to find out more about why we are having these dreams. Looking back at the moment we had met for the second time, after eighteen years, I should have never created Caleb, and I should have never forced you to marry him, Amy. I hope this is not like Pandora's box, but whatever happens, it will get resolved real soon. I promise you, Amy, and to you as well, Ginger," Gabriel said with a chuckle.

Ginger sighed and crossed her arms. "I do remember how bad of a plan that was, Father. I remember reading up on Caleb in magazines and thinking how arrogant and weird he looked. It must have been so hard for you to not have been given a son but two daughters," Ginger said teasingly. Gabriel looked at her and placed his right hand on her left shoulder.

"You two are my crown jewels. I never knew I was able to reproduce, either until your mother got pregnant a while back. I never knew any of this was possible," Gabriel said.

Ginger smiled and looked over at Amy, who looked concerned. "Well," Gabriel said. "I will leave you women to tend to the younglings, but please keep me up to date on any dreams that you are having, Amy." Amy nodded and watched her father walk away.

"That was weird," Amy said as she stood in the hallway with Ginger next to her. Ginger looked over at her and shrugged.

"You had dreams about Caleb? For how long?" Ginger asked. Amy shrugged.

"A couple of times, but not that often, just maybe two or three times last week," Amy said.

"Well, you do not have any secret feelings for him, do you?" Ginger asked. Amy shook her head.

"How could you even ask me that, Ginger?" Amy snapped. "Why would I have feelings for someone who lied at me at my high school prom and almost got us placed under arrest at the airport when you and I traveled together? Goodness, Ginger, not nice," Amy said before she opened the door to her bedroom. Ginger stayed outside of her room and decided to get herself something to drink.

Ginger walked down the staircase and saw Arabella walking upstairs. "Mother," Ginger said. Arabella smiled.

"Ginger, is everything okay?" Arabella asked. Ginger smiled and nodded. "Okay." They walked past each other.

"No wait," Ginger said as she headed up a few more steps. "Amy and Father have been having dreams about Caleb and their arranged marriage or something like that. Would you know of anything about that, mother?" Ginger asked.

Arabella thought about it and recalled Gabriel talking to her about her nightmare. "Sort of," Arabella said. "I remember when I was a ghost. I had overheard the whole fake wedding when Gabriel led Amy down the aisle. That was very wrong, dangerous, and plain stupid of your father to have done that to her," Arabella snapped. Ginger nodded. "Other than that, I do not think your father would want them to be together, though having dreams or nightmares about Caleb is probably the result of his bad decisions and planning. Why, what brought that up, Ginger?"

Ginger looked in the direction of where Amy's room was. "Would Amelia be able to know about this?" Ginger asked. Arabella shrugged.

"You could ask her if you want. She is the one who probably has more experience with these matters," Arabella said. Ginger nodded.

"Okay, I think I will find our dear aunt Amelia. See you around, mother," Ginger said before she walked down the staircase.

Arabella headed for Amy's room to see her grandchildren. When Ginger approached Amelia's sleeping quarter door, she knocked and waited for Amelia to open the door. Amelia undid several locks and opened the door with a surprised look.

"Ginger!" Amelia said. "What a surprise! I normally would not have known you to ever visit me." Ginger smiled.

First Round

"Amelia," Ginger said as she sat down on the sofa in Amelia's living quarter. "Are you aware of anything weird going on?" Ginger asked. Amelia could not help but chuckle at that question.

"There is always something weird going around in this family and castle, but go on, is there anything more specifically you wanted to know more about, Ginger?" Amelia asked.

"Both Amy and Father are having dreams about her arranged potential marriage to Caleb," Ginger said. Amelia gave Ginger a concerned look. "I mean, this would all just be purely coincidental, right?" Amelia thought about it and shook her head.

"I will get back to you on that topic, Ginger, because knowing the conflict with Larry and Caleb is still going on and now there are nightmares, I wonder what the next phase will be," Amelia said. "Please let me go through some of my books, and I will let you know if we need to take any precautionary measures," Amelia said. Ginger nodded and left her quarter.

Amelia looked through her bookcase and saw various topics on different spells, potions, and then mind control. Amelia looked through the glossary to see if there was anything on dreams. There was something about how some creatures can use mind control to control their victims, especially when they are in a vulnerable state, like a deep slumber.

Amelia would have never known about that topic until now. She read several pages on the topic of mind control. Ginger walked over to the main floor to see if she could try to find out what was going on. She looked outside at the raining weather and saw some dark silhouette figure in the distance with white gleaming eyes, or was that just the rain cascading off the window? She walked closer to the window, and the same figure just remained in that exact position. Ginger decided to open up the sliding doors to the patio to see if she could get a closer look.

The figure disappeared into the darkness. There was something out there. Ginger quickly ran back inside and closed the door. She then walked away from the window. Caleb remained crouched behind a shrub. He had to try and find a way to persuade Larry that his plan of getting back into the castle would work. He snuck his way around the foliage till he saw the main road that took them to the entrance of the castle. He pressed the doorbell and waited patiently outside the castle. Hildegard opened the door and looked at Caleb. "Caleb," Hildegard said.

"Madame," Caleb said in return. "I was wondering if I could speak with Gabriel."

Gabriel heard Caleb's voice and walked over to him, nudging Hildegard away from him. "What are you doing here?" Gabriel asked. Caleb sighed.

"I would like to earn my way back into your good graces again, Gabriel Ambrose," Caleb murmured. Gabriel just looked at him.

"I am sorry, Caleb, but could you speak up a bit more?" Gabriel snapped. Caleb cleared his throat and swallowed.

"I..." Caleb said that he felt like he was losing a lot of energy. "I would like to return home to you again," Caleb said with a sigh. Gabriel shook his head.

"I do not know why you came here, Caleb, but I need you to leave," Gabriel snapped. He was about to close the door.

"What about the dreams, Gabriel? Does that not have any meaning for you?" Caleb asked. Gabriel grabbed Caleb by his jacket in an aggressive manner, growling at him.

"What do you mean about that, Caleb?" Gabriel asked. "What do you mean about dreams?" Caleb smiled at Gabriel, not wanting to laugh at Gabriel's angry expression. "Speak."

"I know a little someone who may be playing with you, Gabriel. I felt that it was in poor taste to add your deceased brother to your dream, but then again, it always means that your brother is thinking about you," Caleb said with a smile. Gabriel shoved Caleb away, but he had to control himself.

"I am not going to fall for your bait, Caleb," Gabriel snapped before he turned around to go back into the castle. Caleb just stood outside of the castle before he left back home to Larry's apartment. Gabriel sighed before he walked over to the dining quarter to find Ginger looking at him.

"Is everything okay, Father?" Ginger asked. Gabriel walked past her in silence to grab the bottle of blood he had opened before. He placed the sip and drank down the other half.

When he felt satisfied after that drink, he sighed. "Caleb is doing something to us, Ginger," Gabriel whispered. "I am not sure how he is doing this, but he tried to get back into our castle. We need to be on our guard even more than before. I will let everyone know about this problem." Gabriel placed the bottle in the empty crate and walked over to his brothers, who were in the living quarter talking with each other. Amelia came up to the main floor with one of her enchantment books. "Gabriel?" Amelia called out.

"In the living quarter, Amelia," Gabriel called out. Amelia walked over to the living quarter to find Gabriel sitting with his brothers.

"I may have found something out about your dreams, Gabriel," Amelia said. She opened the book to the page where she read about how some creatures are able to control their victims in their dreams.

"How is this even possible, Amelia?" Gabriel asked. "I thought you put a cloaking spell on me against Viviana. Now Caleb has power over my dreams as well."

"Well," Amelia said. "I think there is something else going on, Gabriel," Amelia said. "I need to see what Amy's children are dreaming of, since they are officially from Caleb's blood." Gabriel remembered how he had Amy injected with his serum. He shook his head and sighed.

"What if I were to let myself die off? Do you think that would solve this grand problem we are facing, Amelia?" Gabriel asked.

The other brothers gasped. "Gabriel," Lucien snapped. "You are not going to let yourself get killed off." Gabriel waved off that comment. "Hey," Lucien snapped. "Do not ignore me either. We cannot lose you, Gabriel Ambrose. You are our patriarch. Just because you made some mistakes does not mean you should give up."

"Lucien is right," Adrian said. Vladimir nodded. "This whole situation with Larry and Caleb will end. You are too powerful, Gabriel."

While Gabriel was with his brothers and Amelia, Daria noticed Alistair's complexion was improving. Alistiar was able to sit up, feeling a bit dizzy, but he was aware of his surroundings and recognized Darcia.

"You look much better, Alistair," Darcia said as she watched Alistair sit up against the sofa. "Here, have some more blood. Hildegard came back with another run from the blood bank."

Alistair drank down half the bottle and sighed with his eyes closed. "I think we definitely need a long and relaxing vacation, Darcia," Alistair whispered. Darcia kept looking at Alistair. His complexion was still a bit darker, but as long as he was able to talk, she knew he was going to be okay. Bryan and his brothers came into the living quarter to see Alistair.

"Father," Bryan said. "You are looking better than before. How are you feeling? Alistair opened his eyes and smiled.

"Better than before, son," Alistair whispered. "What have you boys been up to lately?" The boys sat down next to Darcia and Alistair. Darcia shook her head at her boys, regarding the moment they got bewitched by Viviana.

"Your sons have kept themselves busy with evening walks and helping Gabriel out with affairs," Darcia said.

The boys shrugged. "Sounds quite productive," Alistair said. "I will be able to join you all again real soon. I might need another day or two before I feel strong again." Everyone in the room nodded.

"Well," Darcia said. "Go on and attend to your regular activities, boys." Bryan gave her a confused look.

"Can we not stay here with Father a bit longer?" Bryan asked. Darcia nodded. "We have nowhere to be. Amy and Ginger are doing well, and Gabriel seems to be doing well. For now, I think we all deserve a free day of doing nothing."

As Bryan and his brothers stayed with their parents, Gabriel stepped out onto the patio and placed his hands on the bannister, looking over at the courtyard. He felt overwhelmed and angry by everything. He never wanted to be a shapeshifter. He never wanted to crave humans. Arabella came out onto the patio and stood next to Gabriel.

"Gabe, something seems to be troubling you. What is going on in your mind right now? I overheard a bit of drama from your side, but I want you to know that letting yourself get killed off by Larry is not the best strategy," Arabella said. Gabriel looked over at her with confusion. "Do not look at me like that, Gabriel. I heard you from the dining quarter."

Gabriel looked over at the sliding doors, seeing his brothers and Amelia hanging around. "Arabella, I appreciate you coming to me not wanting me to end my life for the good of the future of our family, but what if me finally being gone actually takes care of the problem and conflict with Larry and Caleb?" Gabriel asked. "Look, I am not scared about dying. I am not scared about getting hurt, but the moment those fears come to pass, you or our girls are in danger, Arabella."

Arabella rolled her eyes. "Oh yeah? What about my fears, Gabriel, or have you already disregarded them? We may have had problems, like heavy problems, in the past, but I still care about you for the sake of our daughters. The fact that your relationship with both Amy and Ginger started on the wrong foot does not mean they want you out of their lives, Gabriel Ambrose," Arabella said.

"Are you not tired of all of these conflicts and nightmares, Arabella? If I could give up my life to make sure you all remain safe from harm, I would do it in a split second," Gabriel said. Arabella shook her head.

"You would be a fool to be thinking such thoughts, Gabriel," Arabella snapped. "I think you just want to escape your problems and let yourself get killed off, so the rest of us can deal with Larry and Caleb by ourselves." Gabriel took a step back when his mind went blank. "What was that, Gabriel? Am I making you angry for pointing out an obvious thought?"

Gabriel cleared his throat before he walked back inside. "I do not know what has gotten into you, Arabella," Gabriel said before he opened the sliding doors. The other members dispersed when they saw him in various directions. "Next time, if you are interested in listening to our conversation, feel free to open the sliding doors rather than standing behind them."

Gabriel walked over to his study and closed the door behind him. "I need a break from everything," Gabriel said to himself. He felt a sense of emptiness inside of him, not knowing what he should be doing. He just stood in his office, not wanting to sit or even look at his laptop. He walked over to his window, which was in need of a thorough wash. Perhaps he should ask Hildegard to wash his windows. He wanted the whole Larry conflict to be over. He did not want to kill himself, but he wanted to end the conflict in the quickest way possible. He did not know where to begin. He was not hungry or thirsty. He was not tired, but he needed something. He did remember Amelia talking about how she wanted to analyze Amy's children. He was going to see what Amelia was doing. He walked over to her quarter, but she was not there. Perhaps she was with the children.

Amelia was in Amy's room, engaging with Gabrielle, Maggie, and Nathaniel. She tried talking to them using basic words and showing them pictures of trees, clouds, and houses. The children just pointed at them, trying to imitate her with their own cooing sounds. "So, Amy," Amelia said. "How often have you dreamt of Caleb?"

"Probably about three times, I think. I do not really think it is that big of a deal," Amy said. Amelia looked at her.

"I was wondering if I could borrow your children or at least analyze their sleep patterns?" Amelia asked.

"Well," Amy said reluctantly. "I guess that would be okay, but is there a particular reason for that?" Amelia looked back at her children.

"Perhaps they sense that they are originally from Caleb and are dreaming about them, but your mind is somehow diverting their thoughts over to yours, as protection, I think?" Amelia said.

Amy scrunched her brow. "How do you mean, Amelia? Is it even possible for me to do that mindlessly?" Amy asked. Amelia looked back at Amy.

"In the modern human world, this would seem unusual and fictional, but in our world, Amy, anything is possible. I wonder how they would react if they saw Caleb in person."

Amy quickly grabbed Maggie, holding her in her arms. "Never, Amelia," Amy snapped. "How could you even say that? They are never going near any of those monsters out there. Now I want you to leave and rethink what you are ever going to say to me, Amelia. Now go." Amelia nodded before she left Amy's room.

The children started to whimper until Amy grabbed each one of them a tiny sippy cup of blood and watched them drink it down. "I am sorry, my little loves," Amy said. "You three will never have to suffer like your mother did. I will protect you from all forms of harm in this world. We may not be humans, but we do not deserve to be seen and treated like monsters either."

There was a knock on the door. "Enter," Amy said. The door opened, and Gabriel entered the room. "Father, what brings you to my room?" Gabriel closed the door and approached Amy.

"Amelia told me about her plan, but I think you should reconsider this, Amy. The fact that I had you injected with a bit of Caleb's blood does mean that those children are officially Caleb's. Perhaps those children are dreaming of their father, Amy," Gabriel said.

Amy shook her head. "Absolutely no, Father," Amy snapped. "How can you even say such things? Ginger told me that you sent him away, and now you want him to return to our home? I strongly disagree." Amy got to her feet. "I do not want to hear this talk from you again. That scares me."

Gabriel did not leave Amy's room. "I did not mention anything about you reuniting with Caleb. Amelia never talked about having you give up your children either, Amy. Perhaps we are having these dreams because Caleb is not doing anything to us, but these children feel a connection to him. Let Amelia find out more about these dreams. If there is anything we can do to stop them, I think we should try it out. I would never let Caleb near you or your children, Amy. You have my word," Gabriel said. He opened his arms for Amy to enter his embrace. They hugged for a few minutes until Gabriel released his hold on Amy.

"I am not the best father in the world, but I hope you can see that I am trying my best. I even thought about giving up my life for you and your sister to have a brighter future. Your mother is against it, but if it means that Larry and Caleb will leave you all alone, it is something I have considered," Gabriel said. Amy looked up at him and shook her head.

"Why have you considered that, Father? What would make you think that Larry and Caleb would leave us alone after you are dead? Perhaps they would try to overthrow our family and put us all into servitude or something like that," Amy said.

Gabriel shrugged. "Look, I am just getting you all prepared for the moment that you and your sister take over as queen of our family, or matriarch's, and soon Gabrielle will become the next matriarch, and so forth, Amy. My time as a leader has gone on for a long time," Gabriel said. Amy looked at him angrily, shaking her head. "Amy."

Amy took a step back and turned away from him. "I cannot be thinking of such things, Father," Amy whispered. "I am not there yet. I cannot be queen. I mean, Ginger, perhaps. You cannot leave us right now, Father. I am almost twenty-two years old in human years; I cannot handle becoming queen right now or in a year from now. Please, Father, you need to stay around a bit longer."

Gabriel smiled as he approached Amy, holding her in his arms. "Amy Ambrose, you are more than ready to become queen. The fact that you handled yourself quite well when you were considered human, traveling with a strange family, meeting Katrina and me that one time, remember?" Gabriel asked. Amy nodded. "Being a queen does not mean wearing royal gowns, tiaras, or crowns. It is all about how you help, guide, and support your people. You never gave up on yourself or even your children when you had all the power and right to do what was right for yourself, Amy. Plus, you will have Ginger to support you. You both can make your own mistakes and laugh about them. Plus, Lucien, Adrian, and Vladimir are nowhere near my age to even think about leaving, so you will have your crazy uncles and your aunt Amelia for your support, Amy," Gabriel said.

Amy suddenly felt like she had been stabbed in the heart by Gabriel's words. She felt her eyes water. "Father," Amy said as she released herself from his grasp and turned to face him, drying off her eyes with the back of her hand. "Why do you want to abdicate so badly? I mean, when I met you for the first time, you looked strong and powerful. Now I just see you slowly breaking down. All because of this situation with Larry and Caleb?" Amy asked.

Gabriel shrugged. "Not exactly, but I do feel myself getting more weary and tired every day, whether you realize it or not," Gabriel said. "I think that spell or enchantment that was used on me by Viviana weakened me a lot, Amy. The sad thing is that no matter how much blood I consume, my energy levels are gone at the end of the day. I think there is some leftover magic or something inside of me, Amy," Gabriel said. Amy looked at him with confusion.

"What do you mean, Father?" Amy asked. "What leftover magic? Are you sick?" Gabriel shook his head.

"No, not sick, Amy, but whatever Viviana did to me, it took a lot of energy to get her enchantment out of my body. I mean, I am officially back, but I do not feel like my original self," Gabriel said. "Which is why I need you to be ready to take over the throne if anything were to happen to me."

Amy felt sadness wash over her again. "Why must you throw this at me right now, Father? Why could you not let Lucien, Amelia, or someone else take over? Why me? All because I am your second-born daughter with three children that I never wanted." Amy said. Gabriel did not respond. "I cannot picture myself being queen. I was never popular. I was never a star student. I only had one boyfriend, but now I am wondering if it has always been Caleb."

Gabriel shrugged. "Well, I just wanted to give you a heads up, Amy. In case something were to happen to me, I will see where your sister is. Perhaps she might consider being queen," Gabriel said teasingly. Amy rolled her eyes, wanting to throw her pillow at him. Gabriel smiled and left Amy alone with her children. He walked over to Ginger's room, seeing her in her bed, reading a book about the ancient world. Ginger looked up at him.

"Father," Ginger said. "What a surprise! What can I do for you?" Gabriel held up his left index finger to his mouth and closed the door behind him.

"Nothing in particular, my child, but I had a talk with your sister about me abdicating. How would you feel about becoming queen with your sister, Ginger?" Gabriel asked. Ginger scrunched her brow.

"What are you going on about, Father?" Ginger asked. Gabriel sat on the edge of her bed, telling her the same story he told Amy. Ginger sighed.

"How long do you still have, Father?" Ginger asked. "Why is Uncle Lucien or the other ones not going to follow up on being patriarch, Father?" Gabriel sighed.

"You two are my blood children, and you were originally the next ones to step up to the family throne," Gabriel said. Ginger looked at the door to see if anyone could knock on her bedroom door to distract him. "Ginger, I do not plan to leave you or your sister anytime soon, but I need you both to be ready for when the time does come. At least think about it before you refuse this important step, okay?"

Ginger nodded. "Well," Ginger said. "I know how important it is to keep our legacy going. I mean, we are shape shifters, and for whatever reason, royalty or something along those lines?" Ginger asked. Gabriel waited for Ginger to finish.

"I do not see myself being queen anytime soon, Father. I mean, my mother is a queen. She could continue, even after you are gone," Ginger said. Gabriel shook his head.

"I just need you to consider this important step that you and your sister will soon be taking," Gabriel said before he got to his feet. "I will not bother you both about it anymore, but I just want you two to realize how important our legacy is and how both of you are going to do a wonderful job as matriarchs and queens. I hope you can have your own offspring with whoever you decide, Ginger. The whole Caleb situation was not the smartest decision on my part, but I have changed; ever since you both transitioned into shape shifters after that silly wedding, do you remember?" Gabriel asked.

How could Ginger even forget how traumatizing that was for Amy and how she had no power to stop that incident? "Yes, I remember," Ginger said. "That was one of the dumbest moments of my life. Watching a farce wedding take place, like in medieval times, watching two humans get married to better their station in life," Ginger said sarcastically. Gabriel did not respond.

"Well, I shall see what the rest of our family members are doing, but please keep this thought in mind. Once the time comes, I am sure you will decide wisely," Gabriel said before he left Ginger's bedroom and closed the door behind him.

Ginger sighed and tried to continue reading the book she had placed on her nightstand. She decided to go over to Amy and see how she was doing. She knocked on Amy's door. She heard her sigh before she answered. "Yes?" Amy asked. Ginger opened the door and saw Amy sigh with relief.

"Goodness, it is you," Amy said. "Did Father also talk to you about becoming queen of our family?" Ginger nodded. "Goodness, that man is all over the place. He is inconsistent and obnoxious," Amy said.

Ginger chuckled at Amy's choice of words. "I think this whole conflict regarding Larry is getting to him, especially since he knows that he caused it in the first place. The hunger of a shapeshifter must have been quite strong for him. I mean, do you recall reading about his upbringing in his diaries or only about how he traveled around and created various humans?" Ginger asked.

Amy thought about it and shook her head. "I do not recall any baby stories about him having a mother, father, or even siblings. I know that Mother had several siblings, but him? I wonder if he has more diaries. Then again, if I were in his position, I would not know about writing in journals, due to how humans could see that as a potential threat to their kind," Amy said. Ginger nodded. "Right now, sister dear, I cannot picture myself being in a position to be queen. I cannot ever see myself guiding and ruling over our kind. What about you?"

"Right now, I cannot handle many things at the moment, and being queen, Mother is queen. I have not heard her talk about leaving this world. Everyone seemed to love her, even our family in Rome, Croatia, Greece, and Australia," Amy said as she tried to remember all the countries she had visited. "Whenever they heard the name Arabella, all their eyes would light up." Ginger listened to Amy, smiling at the way she was talking.

"Well, Father is not going away anytime soon. First, we do have to deal with this Larry situation," Ginger said. Amy nodded. "How are your little ones doing?" Amy looked over at her children, who were playing around with their toys. "They are wonderful, Ginger. I mean, this whole idea of having children seemed like a bad idea at first, but seeing those little ones just enjoying their youth does put a smile on my face," Amy said.

Ginger chuckled. Then there was a knock on the door. Amelia came into the room before Amy could respond. "Oh goodness, now what?" Amy asked. Amelia held her hands up like she was surrendering. "Yes?" Amy asked. Amelia approached them.

"I know that your father talked to you about my plans for your children, Amy, but I really think you need to reconsider letting me analyze your children while they sleep. Just to make sure that Caleb is not doing anything to them. Just for one slumber, Amy. Then you can have them back, and I will never bring up my plan ever again," Amelia said.

Ginger looked over at Amy with confusion. "What is she talking about, Amy?" Ginger asked.

Ancestry

Amelia explained to Ginger what could have been the cause for Amy and Gabriel to have such dreams regarding Caleb. Ginger laughed at the whole story and shook her head. "How is this even possible, Amelia?" Ginger asked.

"When we look at our bloodline, many of us do have a sense of intuition about blood versus water. For example, I have no attraction to any of my family members but to people outside of the family. You girls do not feel any romantic feelings towards your father because he is your blood relative. The same goes for Amy's children. They feel a sense of kinship regarding their blood. Does that make sense?" Amelia asked.

Ginger nodded. "Yes, but the problem is, does that mean that sometime or someday, when the children receive a sense of understanding of this world, they will want to see who their father is and perhaps feel a sense of connection with him?" Ginger asked. Amelia shrugged.

"It might be possible, but as far as how your father has handled this situation, it was quite wrong of him to have done that. He should have never forced his will upon any of you or any of us, because he is considered the father and patriarch of our kind," Amelia said.

Ginger nodded. "Well, I feel bad for Amy and her children regarding this situation. I wonder if there is a way to get rid of Caleb or at least persuade him to never return," Ginger said. Amelia thought about what Ginger said.

"We should see how this all transpires. Hopefully, your nieces and nephew will choose wisely. Hopefully they will not take after your father all too much," Amelia said with a chuckle.

Suddenly, Gabriel showed up. "Ahem," Gabriel said. "What are you ladies talking about?" Amelia and Ginger looked at him and smiled. "Whatever the topic was, I would try to avoid using my name due to my sharp hearing," Gabriel said. Both of them nodded. "Good, now what are you all up to?" Ginger looked at Amelia and smiled.

"I was talking with Amelia about the whole dream situation. There might be a problem, Father," Ginger said. Gabriel looked sternly at Ginger. "Well, what if Amelia is right about the whole ancestry and genetic factors in this world?" Ginger asked. Gabriel smirked and crossed his arms. "What if these children are dreaming of their biological father?"

Gabriel rolled his eyes. "There is not much I can do about that, my sweet girl," Gabriel said. "We are just going to have to make up stories for those children to avoid problematic questions." Amelia scrunched her brow, and Gabriel shook her head. "Yes, Amelia?"

Amelia sighed. "Gabriel, here we go again. Creating bigger lies and deceptions. First, Amy and Ginger get lied to, and soon her children get lied to as well. When will it stop?" Amelia asked. Gabriel sternly looked at Amelia. "The truth will come out someday, and you know who will get cast out like a monster? You, Gabriel," Amelia said. "You keep lying to everyone you love, especially over important topics like family and identities," Amelia said with despair in her voice. "It needs to end. No more lies and deception."

Gabriel sighed. "Why must you act so hysterical, Amelia? Why do you even care? When Arabella died, you did not offer to take in my children. I was distraught and half dead inside, but you just held baby Amy in your arms while I held Ginger, handing her over to my brother, Lucien, that evening. Do you remember?" Amelia took a step back and crossed her arms.

"I lied to my children, because," Gabriel said, looking over at Ginger. "I wanted to protect them, especially from me. I never meant to do anyone any harm, but I did that out of love, and I eventually wanted them back. I never gave up on wanting to see my daughters again."

Ginger sighed and looked at Amelia, who looked like she was ashamed and embarrassed. "Well," Ginger said. "The past is the past, but we are now looking at the current situation regarding Amy's children. Caleb was a mistake, but we should not burn that bridge too soon, Father." Amelia nodded. "I mean," Ginger said as she was trying to find the right words to finish her sentence with. "Perhaps we can brainwash Caleb, or at least make use of him somehow?"

Gabriel shook his head. "What is done is done, but we shall wait to see what the future holds. Perhaps Amy's children will take more after her, and we do not ever have to bring up the topic of Caleb. If we do, we will try to see what would be the best way to handle that situation. For now, just go about your day, Ginger. And you, Amelia, I would do more research about the ancestry part. Perhaps there is something that these children sense, so please continue your research and experiments on such," Gabriel said before he turned around and left.

Amelia sighed with relief. "We should be more careful, Ginger," Amelia whispered. Ginger chuckled and shrugged.

"Father can be scary," Ginger whispered. "Then again, he would not be able to do much to us anyway." Amelia chuckled and shook her head.

"Well, I guess I should go back to my own room, Ginger. Enjoy the rest of your evening," Amelia said as she smiled.

"You too, Amelia. Good luck," Ginger said before she headed over to Amy's room.

Amy was playing with her children on the floor. Ginger entered Amy's room before knocking and sat on the ground with Amy, watching the children engage with each other. "How is it going, Amy?" Ginger asked. Amy looked at her and shrugged.

"Better than ever, sister dearest," Amy said. "I do not want to see Caleb again; at least I should be given that luxury in this world." Ginger nodded.

"I agree," Ginger said. "Amelia is doing her research right now about ancestry and blood-related dreams or something like that."

Amy looked up at her with confusion. "Like what?" Amy asked. Ginger shrugged. "My children are not to be experimented on like lab rats. At least make that clear to anyone, or I will be forced to leave. My children are not to be analyzed because of our dreams. If I am protecting them with my thoughts, then I will continue to protect them, but they are not to be touched, especially without my permission.

Ginger nodded. "I agree with you entirely, Amy. You do not have to preach to the choir about your concerns. I know that our father has no interest in such things either, but both he and Amelia just want to see if Caleb or Larry are not trying to pry for any sensitive areas that they can penetrate, or, you know, what? I have no idea what I am talking about," Ginger said quickly.

Amy rolled her eyes at the way Ginger was talking. "Okay," Amy said mindlessly before she focused her attention back on her children. Gabrielle started to whimper. "Oh dear, what is it?" Gabrielle crawled over to Amy. "Perhaps you are hungry. Ginger, could you hand that pink sippy cup over there?" Amy said as she pointed to her night table. Ginger handed Amy the sippy cup. Amy handed it to Gabrielle. Both Amy and Ginger watched her drink down her entire cup with amazement.

"She is a good eater," Ginger murmured. Amy chuckled. "How are the other children?" Amy smiled.

"They all are. I should get some more, unless you want to fill their cups for me, sister dear?" Amy asked. Ginger sighed. "Or ask Hildegard." Ginger shook her head, grabbed the three sippy cups, and filled them with their main blood source.

On Ginger's way down the stairs, she saw Gabriel in the dining quarter with a fresh bottle of blood and his own glass. "Father, would you mind if I filled the sippy cups of Amy's children?" Ginger asked. Gabriel nodded as he placed the bottle closer to Ginger.

"How are those children doing, Ginger? Have you noticed anything unusual or different about them?" Gabriel asked. Ginger shook her head as she poured a blue sippy cup.

"They seem normal to me. They have good appetites, from what Amy has told me," Ginger said. "Other than that, they do not seem to miss Caleb or cry for him." Gabriel nodded.

"Okay. I know that Amelia is doing her own research on genetics and ancestry information," Gabriel said. Ginger nodded before she tightened the last purple-colored sippy cup that was probably Maggie's.

"Gabrielle does look a lot like you, Father," Ginger said. "Have you noticed her eyes and hands?"

Gabriel smiled. "I hope not. They would not want to have much to do with their crazy grandfather, Gabriel Ambrose. I mean, I never even asked Caleb for his last name. Should we find out, or should those children just go by our family name? As the patriarch of the family, our name goes back to my origin, but then again, I have no idea who or where I came from, you know?" Gabriel said. Ginger nodded.

"Well, I best get these cups back to Amy's children. They must be hungry. Gabrielle downed her cup in a moment of seconds, Father. Quite impressive," Ginger said. Gabriel smiled.

"Perhaps she is more like her grandfather," Gabriel said with a chuckle. "Just do not let her leave the house without giving her proper training, including the other two, Maggie and Nathaniel."

Ginger shook her head. "I will see you around, Father," Ginger said as she walked back up to Amy's room. Amy's door was already open, so Ginger placed the three cups down on Amy's night table. Gabrielle was already asleep. Ginger handed Amy a green sippy cup for Nathaniel and grabbed the purple one, so she could feed Maggie.

"They are so cute when they feed, Amy," Ginger said. Amy smiled as she looked at Nathaniel, holding both his hands on his sippy cup.

"They are, Ginger," Amy said. She looked over at Maggie, who also had both her hands on her sippy cup, and smiled at her. "Such precious children. I hope they all become strong and powerful enough to take on any challenges they will be facing. I look forward to hearing such inspiring stories of their successes in their lives, Ginger," Amy said.

Ginger smiled. "You will, Amy. I look forward to guiding them as their crazy aunt Ginger and, of course, giving them treats behind your back," Ginger said teasingly. Amy playfully punched Ginger. "Domestic violence in front of your children. Well done. Do you see children? What does your mother do to her sister?"

Amy chuckled. "I am just showing them how it is done, Ginger. How one should defend themselves," Amy said.

Once the children were done, both Amy and Ginger tucked them next to Gabrielle. "Sleep well, my dears," Amy whispered. Amy and Ginger then walked out of Amy's room and over to the dining quarter. Amy was in need of feeding herself. They both walked over to the dining quarter and saw Darcia and Alistair at the table.

"Ladies," Alistair said. "Good evening." Darcia smiled at both Amy and Ginger. "Good evening to you both," Amy said. "How are you feeling, Alistair? You look better than before."

"I feel much better, Amy," Alistair said. "Darcia and I survived."

"Barely," Darcia said. "We were both quite weak by Larry and his monstrous sister. What was her name? Beverly, Barney?" Darcia said as she was trying to remember her name.

"Bianca?" Amy asked. Darcia snapped her fingers.

"Yes. Bianca," Darcia snapped. "She really did a number on my beloved heart. I had hoped that Alistair could have crawled out of that window sill, but he did come home after getting tortured."

Amy nodded. "Well, would you both care for some company? Ginger and I need to have a drink," Amy said. Both Alistair and Darcia nodded as they gestured for the empty chairs. Both Amy and Ginger grabbed an empty glass from the cupboard and allowed Alistair to pour them a full glass. "So, how are your boys? I remember them being locked up with Viviana after she had hexed them or something along the lines of that?" Amy asked.

Darcia shook her head, giving Amy a stern look. *Amy.* Darcia thought. *We did not want to bring up that memory. Alistair is still recovering.* Amy nodded.

"Perhaps I misunderstood the situation, but how is Bryan?" Amy asked. "I have not seen him for a while."

Alistair gave Amy a confused look. "He has been around," Alistair said. "I am sure he will be around more often." Darcia placed her hands on Alistair's and smiled at him. Alistair smiled back at Darcia. "How are your children, Amy?" Amy smiled at Alistair.

"They are doing good. They have been drinking blood since about two or three weeks ago. They are even getting bigger. Ginger, what do you think?" Amy asked.

"They are amazing. I was wondering if we could ask you something regarding a problem that both Amy and Gabriel have been facing for a while?" Ginger asked. Amy glared at Ginger, shaking her head. "What? Oh, never mind. Amy does not want me to talk about it."

"That is not what I said, Ginger," Amy snapped. "Well, fine. Go ahead and see what kind of insight they can offer." Darcia and Alsitair looked at Ginger and then at Amy.

"Okay. So anyway, Amy and our Father have been dreaming about Caleb. Amelia now mentions that these children could be dreaming of their biological father. Does that make sense?" Ginger asked.

Alistair and Darcia exchanged glances. "Well," Darcia said. "It might be possible for some kind of ancestry or genetics that Amy's children could be dreaming of their biological father. There is, of course, the connection to Caleb's blood." Alistair nodded.

"I am not sure we have ever experienced anything like that before, but what is the upshot?" Alistair asked.

Both Amy and Ginger shook their heads. "No, but Ginger thought it would be a good idea to bring it up right now, but Amelia said she was looking into it," Amy said. Darcia nodded as she was trying to look back at any moments from her past that resembled that situation.

"How often have you both had these dreams? Both Alistair and I were drained a lot when we were held captive at their home, which decreased our hearing," Darcia said.

Alistair downed another glass of blood, and his complexion went back to normal. "Well," Alistair said. "I think I might want to get some fresh air and walk around the courtyard." Darcia smiled before she got to her feet.

"I will join you," Darcia said before she put her long black coat with faux fur cuffs on. Both Alistair and Darcia left the castle through the sliding doors.

"That was insightful," Amy murmured. "As if they would have any idea of our dreams, Ginger."

"Well, Amy, dearest," Ginger said. "It is good to ask such questions, in case Alistair or Darcia might have experienced such situations with their boys. If they had dreams of their boys." Amy rolled her eyes before she placed Alistair, Darcia, and her glasses in the sink.

Amy then checked the time. It was going on four o'clock in the evening. "I think I shall see how my children are doing before I head off to bed," Amy said. Ginger smiled and waved at Amy.

"Sweet dreams, sister," Ginger said. Moments later, Arabella came into the dining quarter and grabbed an empty glass.

"Ginger!" Arabella said. "How have you been?" Ginger gave Arabella a quick smile.

"Just fine, mother. How have you been?" Ginger asked. Arabella sat down across from Ginger before she answered.

"Exhausted and taking each day as it comes, dear child," Arabella said. "Has your father mentioned his potential abdication? I need to keep my eyes out for whatever he has planned. Otherwise, we might need to create some backup plans in case your father decides to leave or do something unexpected," Arabella said.

Ginger scrunched her brow in confusion. "What has Father told you, mother?" Ginger asked. Arabella did not respond, in case it might cause some unnecessary drama in the family. "Mother?" Ginger asked. "Why are you ignoring my question? What has Father told you about abdicating?" Arabella cleared her throat.

"He wanted to deal with Larry by himself and see if that could end him in a quick manner, but to me, that sounds like a bad idea. I mean, your father has many good qualities and is strong in many ways, but his strategic skills are not that strong, Ginger," Arabella said before she downed her glass.

"Father wants to get himself killed? Why would he do that? I mean, why would he even want to leave us in this situation? What if Larry, Caleb, or anyone else tries to do something evil to us, mother? Goodness, where is Father?" Ginger asked.

Arabella got on her feet, holding her hands up. "Please listen. I am just letting you know what he told me. His thoughts and actions do change a lot, Ginger. Do not think that he is out there right now, provoking Larry for a reaction," Arabella said.

Ginger shook her head. "I cannot believe this, mother. Why would Father even want to die? We have been in this castle for over a year now, and now that we are in his life, do we serve no purpose anymore? You are right about him, mother. His strategic skills are bad," Ginger snapped before she left the dining quarter.

"Ginger!" Arabella said. "If I had known this would cause unrest with you, I would have saved it for another time."

Ginger stopped to turn around. "As if that would make it easier. Why would you think that would be a better plan? How could you even say that?" Ginger snapped before she stormed off. Arabella sighed and lost her appetite. Darcia and Alistair came back into the castle.

"Good evening, Arabella," Alistair said. "You are looking beautiful this evening." Darcia hissed at him. "Come now, Darcia," Alistair said. "You know that our love could never break, ever. Arabella looks pretty, does she not?"

Darcia smiled at Arabella and nodded. "You always look beautiful, Arabella," Darcia said. "Well, Alistair and I will be up in our room for the first night. Have a good slumber, Arabella," Darcia said as both she and Alistair walked towards the staircase.

Ginger walked over to Gabriel's study office to find him preparing for his slumber by turning off his laptop and placing his papers neatly in a pile. "Father," Ginger said with desperation in her voice. "How can you think such things about wanting to leave us? I thought you were getting weaker because of Viviana's spell."

Gabriel sighed and gestured for Ginger to sit across from him in the chair.

"Ginger," Gabriel said in a relaxed tone. "I am getting weaker by the day because of what has happened to me. Your mother has taken what I said out of proportion, as per usual, thinking I just want to jump ship when it gets dangerous. The fact is that I will be around for a longer time frame, but for the sake that something does happen to me, in any situation, you and your sister must be prepared to take over."

Ginger rolled her eyes and shook her head. "Unbelievable," Ginger said. "I just cannot picture any of this taking place. Your death, which would lead to Amy and me being queens of our kind? Father, I have only understood who we are for about a year or so, and suddenly you throw this at us? That is so selfish of you. First you make us think we are humans, then Amy, without me, gets to travel around the world with some weird excuse of being chased and hunted by monsters, and then you send us letters about you being our father? How did you manage to do that? Why did you think that was a good strategy?"

Gabriel listened to Ginger's ongoing monolog with his arms crossed on the desk. "Nobody ever gets to choose the life they are given, Ginger," Gabriel said. "I already mentioned many times how wrong I have been, but sadly, just like anything, we are not endless. Alistair almost met his fate had we captured Viviana and bartered her for him. Nobody ever knows what the future holds. I had never known I was going to be a shapeshifter with intense hunger. I never even knew that our kind could procreate. There are many stories about how vampires and werewolves cannot procreate. There are stories about how some humans are unable to do either. Nobody knows per se how it happens. What we do know is our current moment. I am your father. I was the one who made love to your mother on many occasions. I know you are my daughter, including Amy. What I do not know is my own origin. Did I even have a father? Did I even have a mother? Where are they? Are they dead, or did I come from something else?" Gabriel said.

Ginger started to get lost in Gabriel's nonstop talking and leaned against the chair, tapping the armrest. Gabriel stopped talking as he saw Ginger losing interest in his story. "So, to answer your question and conclude my story, I need you both to be prepared for the future. It may seem scary due to the many uncertainties, but you will have many of our kind to support and love you and Amy. You will have Alistair, Darcia, Amelia, and the others to guide you and offer support. Please, for now, try and rest up till the evening, and we can continue our talks if you need, Ginger," Gabriel said.

Ginger nodded before she got to her feet. She felt emotionally drained from everything, wished Gabriel a good night, and walked over to her bedroom. She could not be bothered to wish Amy goodnight, so she put on her pajamas and crawled into bed. In her dream, she heard about her father's passing, and she decided to give herself a traditional coronation by wearing a purple gown and a diamond tiara. Amy was on the sidelines, smiling at her, holding Gabrielle in her arms, while Bryan held Nathaniel and Arabella, Maggie. There was just one throne that Ginger was walking toward. Where was Amy's throne? Why is Amy just standing at the side? Amy did not respond and turned her thoughts off. Gabrielle started getting her sharp teeth. Nathaniel was biting on something soft, and Maggie was still sucking on a pacifier. Something felt off. She wanted to see where Lucien or the other men were. She saw Amelia in the background, but she looked restless and scared. What was going on? Ginger then turned around and saw Gabriel standing in the background, looking healthy. "Father," Ginger said. "I thought you were dead." Gabriel just smiled at Ginger. "What is going on?" Gabriel kept on smiling. She felt scared and wanted to walk towards him, but something caught onto her. Then she decided to head back to the throne and saw Amy sitting there in the exact purple dress, grinning at Ginger. Then there was another throne, and Ginger saw Caleb sitting next to her, holding out his hand for Amy to take.

"Amy," Ginger whispered. "This is not right." Amy then sternly looked over at Ginger. Gabriel approached Ginger and placed his right hand on her shoulders. "Ginger," Gabriel whispered. "This is just a dream; you need to wake up." Ginger then woke up in a gasp. She checked her watch. It was going on three in the afternoon. Ginger sighed with relief but felt uncomfortable and anxious.

"Something needs to happen," Ginger said. "Caleb is now bothering me, but what was Father doing in my dream? Why did he tell me to wake up?" Ginger asked herself. She sat up in bed and pondered her dream, starting where she was queen, and then Amy was queen with Caleb. Nothing made sense.

Ginger got out of bed and decided to put her day clothes on, which were a pair of jeans, black tennis shoes, a pink t-shirt, and a house jacket. She brushed her long brown hair and grabbed her sunglasses before she left her room. She walked down the staircase and saw how bright it was through the curtains. It looked overwhelming to her, but she just wore her sunglasses indoors and headed for the dining quarter. Hildegard was preparing herself some dinner and gasped when she saw Ginger. "Ginger," Hildegard whispered. "What are you doing up so early?"

Ginger shrugged. "I had a bad dream," Ginger said. "How do you handle nightmares, Hildegard?" Hildegard smiled as she poured herself some farfalle pasta and some pesto sauce on a plate and grabbed herself a bottle of sparkling lemon water.

"Care to join me while I eat, Ginger?" Hildegard asked. Ginger smiled and nodded. "Sure, but let me get myself something, as well," Ginger said as she headed for the cooler for an open bottle of blood and grabbed herself an empty glass from the cupboard before she sat down at the table across from Hildegard. "So, nightmares, what was yours about, Ginger?" Hildegard asked. Ginger explained everything, from seeing Amy, then Caleb, and then her father, who was supposed to be dead. Then about the part where Gabriel told her to wake up.

Hildegard listened attentively to Ginger's story. "That sounds quite a heavy dream, Ginger. Goodness, how scary it must have been," Hildegard said. "Well, what I normally do after I have endured a nightmare is to center myself and tell myself that it was all a bad dream, and it was never real. Then I try to distract myself if the dream was quite miserable with fun activities and try to ignore it."

Ginger listened to what Hildegard was saying. After hearing about how Amy and her father both had dreams about Caleb and how Amelia believes that Amy's children are having biological dreams about their father, Hildegard's advice was not going to work for Ginger.

Ginger swilled down her glass and leaned back against the wooden dining room chair. "The problem is that both Father and Amy have had dreams about Caleb being married or proposing to Amy, because Amelia thinks that Amy's children are dreaming of their biological father. These types of nightmares are not dreams to be forgotten, as they are correlated to something big, Hildegard. Have you ever experienced something like that?" Ginger asked. Hildegard shook her head.

"I am human, Ginger, and I have gained and lost in my life in many ways. I gained a life of luxury, but I have lost the experience of being a human and living a normal human life," Hildegard said.

Ginger scrunched her brow. "What do you mean, Hildegard? I thought Father mentioned that you willingly gave up your life to serve or be our human, and in exchange, you would live in a castle and be able to get a stipend for meals," Ginger said. Hildegard nodded.

"Yes, that is all true. There is still that thought that I occasionally think about if I had chosen to live the life of a basic human, living in an apartment, meeting the love of my life, and having children or pets," Hildegard said.

Ginger nodded. "Okay, but what made you decide to take care of our family instead, Hildegard?" Ginger asked. Hildegard shrugged.

"Well, it all started off, to my knowledge of how it happened, that your father was in need of a human housekeeper. I was a woman in my thirties, in need of a job. My college degree in English was not going to get me anywhere at the time and circumstances I was in, so I contacted your father and got to meet him one evening, which at first was odd to me, especially how haunted this place was with dust and cobwebs, where the whole place just looked unkempt. Then I saw your father, with his pale complexion and his long, tousled black hair. He looked quite exhausted from the angle I saw him. My gut told me to run away and never return. Then I saw your mother. How beautiful she looked with her long brown hair and her warm voice. I accepted the deal, and since then, I have not regretted anything. I got to hear about the birth of both you and your sister. I remember how precious you both looked. At the time, I was in my forties, and remembered you. I believe it was the first time I ever got to hold a baby in my arms. Of course, the circumstances were quite bad because of Arabella's death and how she ended up as a ghost. I felt so heartbroken by everything, Ginger. After that incident, I wondered if I would have been in such similar circumstances in human life or the world, or if it would have been better or worse," Hildegard said. "But, enough about my story. Well, I am not sure if I can help you out with this problem. I am certain that if Amelia thinks there is something to be done, it usually gets done."

Round Two

In Larry's apartment complex, Larry was walking back and forth in their living room, pondering his next move. Bianca felt his stress vibes, feeling uneasy. "Brother," Bianca said. "Could you stop pacing like that?" Larry looked sternly at Bianca.

"Sister," Larry snapped. "I am busy trying to figure out our next plan. I regret not having killed Alistair. That could have sent a powerful message over to Gabriel about how we do not negotiate with such monsters." Viviana was filing her nails, trying to block out the sibling bickering. Bianca looked over at Viviana.

"What are your thoughts on our next plan, Viviana?" Bianca asked. Viviana shrugged, keeping her focus on her nails.

"Of course," Bianca snapped. Larry barred his teeth and hissed at Bianca. "What?"

"Do not talk to her like that, Bianca. Viviana is precious to me," Larry snapped. "I am busy figuring out our plan and do not need any interference from anyone right now. Well, maybe from Caleb. Where is he anyway?"

Caleb was in his own bedroom, lying on his bed with his eyes closed, keeping his mind as relaxed as possible. Larry barged into his room, causing Caleb to shriek. "What was that?" Caleb yelled. "You scared me half to death, Larry. I was in my alpha state, trying to get to Amy's children, and you just busted into my room like a bull in a china shop? Goodness."

Larry could not help but laugh at Caleb's response and words. Caleb then started to laugh. "What can I do for you, Larry?" Caleb asked. Larry sat down on the edge of Caleb's bed. "Seriously? We have to discuss it this close? I could also meet you out in the living room if that would work out for you as well."

Larry got to his feet and gestured for Caleb to leave his bedroom. Caleb reluctantly got out of bed and slumped over to the living room to find the other comrades watching television with Viviana next to them and Bianca sitting adjacent to them in her own chair. Caleb sat down in the dining room chair and waited for Larry to join him. "What?" Caleb asked.

"What were you actually doing in your room, Caleb? Are you trying to get in touch with Amy's children, or are you just messing around with Gabriel?" Larry asked. Caleb looked around and leaned in closer to Larry.

"I am trying to get Amy's children to understand how I am their official father and that she has been unfaithful with her lies and deception toward me, Larry," Caleb said in a hushed tone. Larry listened attentively to Caleb. "Once the children get a good understanding of what this world is about, they are going to want to know more about where they came from, right?" Caleb asked. Larry nodded. "So, Gabriel and Amy are obviously going to make up some sappy story about me abandoning them or that I was a threat to them, which is why I was sent away, but as long as I try to get into their minds with my own mind and play around with their innocent minds, I could get them to question both Amy and Gabriel and perhaps let them decide if they want to stay with them or not."

Larry smiled at how Caleb had this wicked side to him. "You almost had me underestimate you, Caleb. I mean, if the children do realize how wrong Gabriel was with his honest ways of wanting to get Amy pregnant, constantly putting his children in danger, or even hosting a fake wedding to get Amy and Ginger to show their shape-shifting sides, that might break the trust and love of Amy with her children, but especially Gabriel and everyone else," Larry said with a chuckle.

Caleb smiled and nodded. "I always want you to underestimate me, Lawrence Harrison. Then, when I do come up with such plans, I enjoy watching your priceless face light up. Right now, I am sure that Gabriel and Amy are getting worried about me being in their dreams, but once the children start to understand what is going on, let the games begin," Caleb said with a chuckle. Larry laughed and looked over at Bianca.

"Sister dear, could you fetch us two packs of blood? I feel like having a toast with one of the greatest masterminds of our world," Larry said. Bianca glared at him and looked over at Viviana.

"I could go for some as well," Viviana said. Bianca mocked Viviana before she got to her feet. Larry sighed and shook his head at Bianca with a disapproving look.

"Perhaps you should get yourself a glass too, sister, dear. It could benefit you," Larry said.

Caleb could not help but chuckle at that comment. Bianca hissed at them both and left for their kitchen. Larry focused his attention back on Caleb. "So Caleb," Larry said. "How long would you give this plan? Right now, I am not really in such a rush to go after Gabriel. Perhaps we can wait about a few years, or so?" Larry asked.

Caleb shrugged. "I want to give my powers and strategy some time, because whenever we go out on a limb with our plans, it always seems to backfire where Gabriel is still alive and well. Our last plan was Viviana, which failed miserably. Going after the most precious and innocent targets is easier than going after the big whale," Caleb said. "I mean, we should also give Gabriel the idea that we have lost interest and have given up, so perhaps that would cause him to let his guard down, and once that happens, we will be right on top of it and go for the full attack. Perhaps we can add some more members to our group. What do you think, Larry?"

Larry looked over at his group members, watching how strong and tough they looked. He shrugged but did not respond. "I am not saying no to that idea, Caleb, but once Gabriel is out of our lives forever, I am afraid we might just end up causing more problems amongst the humans. If we have perhaps another two members, a lot of humans might wonder how everyone is just dying left and right. We shall see what the future looks like," Larry said.

Caleb nodded and saw Bianca return with four packs. She poured them into a glass, handed both Larry and Caleb a glass, and handed Viviana her own glass before she sat back on the couch with the other members, taking little sips from her glass. "I want to propose a toast to my best friend, Caleb. What did you say your last name was? You know what? Never mind. To Caleb for taking up the reins and having his own plan that involves the final attack on our beloved friends, Gabriel Ambrose and Amy," Larry said sarcastically.

The other members ignored Larry and kept their focus on the television. Larry and Caleb tapped their glasses at each other before they took a sip.

Back at the castle, Ginger walked over to Gabriel's study office and saw him focused on his laptop. "Father," Ginger murmured. Gabriel looked up.

"Ginger, what brings you here?" Gabriel asked. Ginger sat down in the same chair in front of him.

"I had that nightmare, Father," Ginger said. "It bothered me. I tried talking to Hildegard about it, but she offered no help. I think Caleb is doing something to us. What should we do?"

Gabriel sighed as he leaned against his office chair and nodded as he remembered that he had promised Ginger that he could be at her disposal. "Ginger," Gabriel said. "Try not to overthink these dreams. Amelia is working on Amy's children from her side. Right now, just try to ignore your dreams until we are certain that Caleb is behind it all. Dreams have no actual impact on the mind. Try to go about your usual day activities, my dear child."

Ginger did not respond or move. "How can you tell me this, Father? I mean, what if Caleb is trying to metaphorically infiltrate our lives with his powers?" Ginger asked. Gabriel sighed. "I did not mean to bother you or interrupt you, but I am really scared right now." Gabriel nodded.

"I understand. For now, we just have to go about our usual activities until Amelia has more information to provide on her part. Please get yourself a drink and try to distract yourself with some fresh air or something fun," Gabriel said with a smile. Ginger sighed before she got to her feet. "Okay, Father," Ginger said before she left his office.

Ginger did not feel reassured or relaxed. She decided to see if Amy was awake yet. She walked over to her bedroom door, which was still closed. "Hm. Perhaps I shall see if there is anyone else around," Ginger said to herself. She walked over to the living quarter and saw Bryan and his brothers hanging around. "Boys," Ginger said as she approached them. They all smiled and waved at Ginger. "What are you all up to?"

Bryan and his bothers exchanged glances. "Not much," Bryan said. "We are just probably waiting to see what old Larry is up to." Ginger smiled as she sat down on one of the empty chairs. "How is Amy doing? Darcia told me that I had attacked her. Is that true? I have no recollection of ever going after Amy or Ginger. You have to believe me." Ginger held up both her hands to quiet Bryan.

"Amy is fine. It is true that you did attack her, but you were under Viviana's spell. All of you were. Amelia told me how you all downed our fresh blood supply in a matter of minutes," Ginger said with a chuckle.

The boys exchanged glances with each other. "Seriously?" Joshua asked. Ginger nodded. "Goodness, how was this possible?" Ginger shrugged.

"Viviana was one of the most powerful sorceresses in our world, I guess," Ginger said nonchalantly. Joshua scrunched his brow before he rolled his eyes. "Yep," Ginger said. "Anyway, we might be facing a big problem in the near future, perhaps in a few days or a week."

The boys all looked at Ginger. "My father and Amy have been having dreams about Caleb. Last night, I had a dream about him as well. It was quite terrifying. My father even told me to wake up," Ginger said. The boys looked confused at Ginger. "I am glad you are all looking at me like that, because I have no idea why I am dreaming of that creature."

Bryan got to his feet. "Where is Amy anyway? I feel like I want to explain myself to her. I do regret my actions, whether I was under someone's spell to ruin my relationship with her," Bryan said. Ginger shrugged.

"I would wait for her to wake up. Amy is still asleep, and perhaps the last thing that would reconcile you both would be to ruin her sleep," Ginger said with a chuckle. The other boys chuckled along. Bryan looked up at the floor where Amy was sleeping.

"I just do not understand how Viviana could have been behind it all, Ginger," Bryan said. "She seemed so kind and helpful, like a loving aunt to those children." Ginger shrugged.

"Amy told me that you called her a goddess," Ginger said. "My my, Bryan, I thought Amy was your goddess." Bryan glared at Ginger. "What? You did refer to that witch creature, that she was a goddess, in front of Amy, whom you claim to love? Whatever Bryan. Good luck trying to get Amy back in your life."

Ginger got to her feet and walked over to the dining quarter, where she saw Lucien, Vladimir, and Adrian sipping from their glasses. The three men glanced over at Ginger with confusion. "Is everything okay, Ginger?" Lucien asked. Ginger looked over at them.

"Just fine, Uncle Lucien," Ginger said sarcastically. She grabbed an empty glass and headed for the cooler until Lucien picked up the bottle on the table.

"Care for a drink?"

Ginger rolled her eyes before she walked over to them, allowing Lucien to pour her a cup of blood. "Does that feel better?" Lucien asked teasingly. Ginger ignored that comment and sat down across from the men. "What is going on? You can trust your uncles, you know." Ginger looked over at Lucien, scrunching her brow.

"Since when do you guys want to talk to us girls?" Ginger asked. Lucien did not respond but smiled calmly at Ginger. "That Bryan can be quite foolish, you know?" Lucien and the other men smiled at that comment. "Bryan wants to apologize for being under Viviana's spell for attacking Amy, and plus, to rub salt over her actual wounds, she even referred to Viviana as a goddess in front of her," Ginger said.

Lucien and the other men got to their feet quickly. "No, wait a moment, you guys. Do not worry about that right now. I have already put him in his place. If something needs to happen, let Father take care of it," Ginger said. The three men reluctantly took their seats again. "Good. Do not worry about that Bryan kid. He is just foolish.

Lucien downed his glass and sighed. "So, what are your plans for the rest of the evening?" Ginger asked, trying to take their minds off of family drama. "Father advised me to go out for an evening walk. Would you guys want to join me for a stroll? The three men exchanged glances and shook their heads.

"No, thank you, Ginger. We will just hang around till we are needed for the evening," Lucien said. The other men nodded.

Up in Amy's room, she slowly woke up from her slumber. She checked her watch. It was going on one o'clock in the morning. She overslept this one time, but then again, she had nowhere to be either. This time, she had no nightmares or dreams at all. Amy got out of bed and grabbed her robe and slippers before she headed out. She walked down the stairs slowly and entered the dining quarter with tousled hair. The three men smirked at Amy, causing Ginger to glare at them.

"What is so funny?" Ginger asked. The three men glanced over at Amy and then back at Ginger.

"The true picture of a mother who needs plenty of sleep," Lucien said. Ginger rolled her eyes.

"Uhuh," Ginger said sarcastically. "Well, perhaps you all have had enough for the evening?" Lucien smiled before he got to his feet and placed his glass in the sink.

"Perhaps you want to spend some time with your sister?" Lucien asked in the same tone. Ginger gave him a sarcastic smile and waited for them to leave. Amy walked over with an empty glass and finished the bottle of blood.

"Good evening to you, Amy," Ginger said. "How are you feeling? You sounded like you slept like the dead." Amy smiled before she let out a big yawn and leaned against the chair with her eyes closed.

"Those children love to keep their mother up a lot, you know," Amy said. "The beauty of having children." Ginger smiled at Amy's comment. "What have you been up to this evening?"

Ginger shrugged. "Can I tell you something scary?" Ginger asked. Amy smirked.

"I have not had my first sip for the day and already get asked to hear about something scary. Okay, go for it," Amy said with a chuckle. Ginger leaned in closer to Amy.

"I had a bad dream about Caleb. Then I heard Father's voice inside of me telling me to wake up. It made no sense. Have you had any dreams about Caleb?" Ginger asked.

Amy gave Ginger a confused look. "No, but why is he now bothering you?" Amy asked. Ginger shrugged.

"Amelia is still working on the dream analysis from her side, so hopefully we will hear more about our dreams from her within a short time frame," Ginger said. Amy nodded.

"Well," Amy said. "Sorry about your nightmare. Sleep deprivation or any sleep problems can result in a bad day for many."

Ginger smiled at Amy, watching her sleepily drink from her glass. "If you are interested in going outside for an evening walk within the courtyard, that might be fun. Let our mother be with her grandchildren while you and I have some sibling bonding time," Ginger said. Amy smiled and nodded.

"I would like that. Just get out of this castle for once and enjoy a bit of fresh air," Amy said.

Back at Larry's apartment complex, Caleb remained in a relaxed alpha state as he gained access to Amy's children through their slumbering. Gabrielle sensed Caleb and had a dream of being in his arms, watching her mother Amy look horrified at the situation. Gabrielle felt a sense of happiness in being in Caleb's arms, but she also sensed fear and sadness from her mother. Gabrielle reached for Amy and whimpered for her love until Amy shape shifted into Viviana, and she grabbed Gabrielle. Gabrielle knew something was wrong and wanted to cry. Viviana hummed a hypnotic lullaby and put Gabrielle into a relaxed state, which she did the first day she was a nanny. Then Gabrielle saw her other siblings whimpering for their mother. Gabrielle woke up crying until Arabella came into the room and picked her up.

"Hush now, my child," Arabella said in a soothing tone. "Your grandmother is here." Gabrielle felt safe, being in a familiar pair of arms. "Goodness, I wonder if you also had a bad dream about Caleb," Arabella whispered. Gabrielle just made cooing sounds. Then Hildegard came into the room with some baby products, soaps and creams.

"Do you need any help with the children, Arabella?" Hildegard asked. Arabella nodded. "Is little Miss Gabrielle being fussy right now?"

Arabella shook her head. "I think she may have had a nightmare, hopefully not of Caleb," Arabella said. Hildegard gave Gabrielle a sympathetic smile and grabbed Maggie. "Wow, your children are growing up so fast. Soon, I will not be able to bathe you all anymore." Hildegard smiled at how Arabella engaged with her grandchildren.

"How does it feel to be holding a baby, Arabella?" Hildegard asked. Arabella gave Hildegard a confused look. "Oh, no, Arabella, I meant no harm with my question," Hildegard said. "No, what I meant to ask was, did you miss out on holding Amy and Ginger when they were babies?"

Arabella rolled her eyes. "Why yes, Hildegard," Arabella snapped. "I would have loved to have had the opportunity to hold Amy and Ginger when they were babies and not allow those two humans to hold them and raise them with family pictures." Hildegard nodded.

"Forgive me, Arabella," Hildegard said. "That was stupid of me to ask. You just look so perfect with a baby in your arms." Arabella shrugged and nodded.

"No worries about that, Hildegard. I sort of understood what you meant. It is sort of bittersweet knowing that Amy is the mother but that Caleb is the father," Arabella said with sadness in her voice. "Gabriel can be quite foolish when it comes to plans, Hildegard. Especially how he ruined my family with his impulsive acts. I can see how Larry has this intense hatred for Hildegard. I am not saying that I respect or admire Larry, but when people act so hastily, it can break a lot of situations or even families."

Hildegard nodded. "I agree, but I have also respected Gabriel for all the things he has done. He may not be the most popular family member in our world, but he is also not the most hated either," Hildegard said.

Arabella smiled at Gabrielle with her beautiful strawberry blonde curls and blue eyes, sucking her thumb. "Hildegard, dear," Arabella said. "Do we have any bite rings for the little ones? I think they might be teething real soon, and I do not want them to start biting Amy or anyone else." Hildegard nodded and walked off.

"I think I may have purchased some. I got many types of baby supplies, from blankets to bottles to pajamas, and ah, here we go. A bite ring," Hildegard said as she walked back to the room, handing the ring to Arabella.

Arabella dangled the bite ring above Gabrielle till Gabrielle reached for it with both her hands and placed the ring inside of her mouth, sucking on it. Arabella smiled down at her granddaughter. Nathaniel then started to whimper. Hildegard picked him up and carried him over to the nursery to bathe him. "Such precious angels they are," Arabella said as she focused her attention on Gabrielle. Maggie sat close to Arabella's feet and reached for her.

Arabella leaned down and picked Maggie up, holding each baby in her arms. "Maggie, you look so much like Gabriel, with your eyes and facial structure. You will never be like him. I guarantee this to you," Arabella whispered. Just then, the door opened. Amy entered the room and smiled at her mother.

"How are the children?" Amy asked as she looked at both her daughters. Arabella smiled at Amy.

"Such wonderful creatures. We are about to bathe them all and then feed them. What have you been doing with your evening, Amy?"

Amy shrugged. "Ginger and I are about to go outside for a stroll. Father recommended that to Ginger. Apparently, she has been dreaming about Caleb as well. Goodness, that man is driving us all crazy," Amy said. Arabella scrunched her brow.

"Gabrielle woke up crying as well, but perhaps she was just in need of some love from her grandmother," Arabella said. Amy focused her attention on Gabrielle and remembered what Amelia was talking about how her children may be dreaming about Caleb. Amy quickly shook her head to distract herself from it all.

"Are you all right, Amy?" Arabella asked. Amy gave Arabella a quick smile before she turned around. "Amy?"

Amy turned around and smiled. "Just fine, mother," Amy murmured. "I just needed to check up on the little ones, but it looks like they are in good hands. Literally," Amy said with a chuckle. Arabella smiled before she left for the nursery. Hildegard had drawn a bath for the children and helped Arabella get them washed and dried.

As Amy headed down the staircase, Amelia waited at the bottom for her. "Amy," Amelia said. "I think I may know what is going on." Amy stopped and waited for Amelia to continue. "I think your children are dreaming of Caleb, since he is their biological father. I know it may seem scary, but we might need to invite him over, of course, without Larry, Viviana, or whomever may be out there." Amy did not respond. "I can see how that is distressing you, so I shall give you some time to think about it, Amy," Amelia said. Amy quickly shook her head again.

"No, I just need to talk to my father about this. Does Gabriel know?" Amy asked. Amelia shook her head.

"No, because I wanted to let you, as their mother, know first, so you can decide what would be best for you and the children," Amelia said.

Amy sighed. She started to feel overwhelmed. "Amelia," Amy said as she started breathing fast. "I...I cannot handle this right now," Amy said as she panted. "I...I...I...need to speak to my father about this. I do not know if I can decide on such heavy topics, Amelia," Amy whispered. Amelia quickly grabbed Amy and guided her towards the living quarter. Ginger waited by the sliding doors and saw Amy.

"Amy," Ginger gasped. "What is going on? Are you okay?" Amy nodded. "What is this?" Amelia held her hand up.

"Give Amy some space, Ginger," Amelia said. "She just felt a bit overwhelmed. I think I might know what is going on with those dreams you all are having." Ginger sat down next to Amy and put her right arm around her shoulder.

"Ginger!" Amy panted. "What should I do? Amelia suggested that Caleb should come over and let us take care of this problem. Caleb is probably the one who is sending out such memories and turning them into dreams."

Ginger gave Amelia a confused look. "How is that even possible, Amelia? Why is he doing this?" Ginger snapped. Amelia shrugged.

"Well, I think either they wish to see their father or he might be doing something on his part. I think the children wish to see who their actual father is. Amy will talk to her father about my suggestion of inviting Caleb over," Amelia said. Ginger released her hold on Amy and crossed her arms. "That sounds like a bad idea, Amelia," Ginger said.

"That is why we should see what Gabriel has to say. Perhaps he might disagree with it as well, but it should be mentioned," Amelia said. Ginger shook her head. "I just wanted Amy to know what I had found out. Forgive me for this news."

Amy nodded and sighed. "Okay, I think the panic attack is over. Ginger, are you still up for going outside?" Amy asked. Ginger nodded and got to her feet, holding out her right hand for Amy to take. Both Amy and Ginger walked outside the castle, walked down the stairs, and walked alongside the courtyard.

"Amy," Ginger said. "I find it a bad idea to invite Caleb over to our home. I am sure we might face another attack or battle of some kind." Amy nodded mindlessly as she looked ahead. "Amy," Ginger said as she snapped her fingers.

"What? I was just deep in thought. Look, what if Caleb is doing something on his part?" Amy asked. "What are we doing to stop him from infiltrating our dreams, especially the dreams of my children?"

Ginger sighed. "What if he has a secret and unknown plan where he ends up kidnapping your children or causing great harm to our father, Amy? What if Viviana is a shape shifter?" Amy moaned as she stopped walking. "What? These are important questions to respond to, Amy," Ginger said sternly. "I care about you and your kids; is that so weird of me, Amy?"

Amy smiled and nodded. "Not weird at all, Ginger," Amy whispered. "I just hate the fact of these dreams. What if he does something and the children decide they want to be with him, Ginger? What if he is brainwashing or poisoning their minds?" Amy asked. Ginger rolled her eyes. "Seriously, Gin," Amy said. "What if this is just a plan of his, so my children want to find him and be with him and hate me for whatever reason Caleb will tell them?"

"I just think inviting him over is the worst idea ever, Amy, but if you and Amelia think that it is a good idea, be my guest. If anything does happen to your kids, Amy, I am afraid I will have to say that I told you so," Ginger said sarcastically. Amy sighed and stopped walking.

"I think I am done for the evening. I want to see what our father is doing. Excuse me," Amy said before she headed back for the sliding doors. Ginger watched Amy return with frustration.

The Decision

Once Amy arrived back at the castle, she headed for Gabriel's study office and saw him on his laptop. He looked up before she even knocked. "Enter," Gabriel said. Amy opened the door. "Amy, what a delight to see you." Amy quickly closed the door.

"Has Amelia told you about what she has found out, Father?" Amy asked. Gabriel shook his head.

"No, Amy. Do tell. What has she found out about these dreams regarding Caleb?" Gabriel asked.

"Well, apparently my children are dreaming of their biological father. Amelia thinks it might be a good idea to invite Caleb over and see what is going on. I found it a bad idea and wanted to see what you had to say, Father," Amy said. Gabriel nodded.

"As do I, but I do wonder what Caleb has planned for us. Perhaps he is the one who is trying to reach out to your children, Amy, or at least using some type of strategy to bait you or me, Amy. Then again, it might also result in some major problems as well," Gabriel said. Amy nodded.

"Okay, so what is the plan, Father? If Amelia thinks it is a good idea, should I tell her that we should wait a bit longer?" Amy asked.

Gabriel shrugged. "What exactly did Amelia actually say to you, Amy? Why would she find it a good idea to invite Caleb over?" Gabriel asked. Amy took a few steps closer to Gabriel.

"She wants to see how the children react. If it turns out that Caleb is trying to get in contact with them, we would take action, but if it turns out that the children feel some sort of connection through their blood with Caleb, we might need to do something else. I mean, as long as Caleb shows up alone without anyone else, that might be something we should consider," Gabriel said. Amy looked at him like he was crazy. "Do not fear anything right now, Amy. These are just vague, first-phase plans. If you truly feel uncomfortable about it all, we do not have to do anything."

Amy nodded. "Well, I think we need to think about our plans before we take any action," Amy said. "I mean, Ginger is entirely against it. Then again, I am not in the mood to have such nightmares about getting married or engaged to Caleb, like that fake wedding I had to endure. Do you even know how traumatizing that was to me, Father?" Gabriel sternly looked at Amy. "What?"

"I have already apologized and suffer with guilt from my actions, but yet here you are, a princess of the castle, alive and well," Gabriel snapped. "I know what I did was wrong, but I am not going to suffer the rest of my life because of my supposed actions that I believed were good at the time."

Amy shook her head. "Whatever," Amy murmured. Gabriel sighed. "I will see what Amelia has to say, Father. I will keep you posted on any plans and see what would be the best course of action to take." Gabriel nodded and gave Amy a tiny smile before she left his office. Gabriel leaned in his chair, his hands covering his eyes, massaging them, and then his temple.

"Our family is not an easy one to deal with," Gabriel told himself. He decided to get himself a glass of blood. He walked over to the dining quarter and opened up the cooler. "Hm. Hildegard may need to go out for another blood run." Gabriel saw two full bottles and grabbed one of them. He undid the cap and grabbed an empty glass from the cupboard.

Hildegard came into the dining quarter and looked at the crate of empty bottles. "Master Gabriel," Hildegard said. "I shall get you all some more blood bottles this evening," Hildegard said. Gabriel nodded.

"You smell interesting, Hildegard," Gabriel said as he inhaled the air that lingered behind.

"Perhaps it is the baby powder and bath products, Gabriel," Hildegard said. "Those children are growing quite fast." Gabriel smiled.

"I do worry about the fate of those little ones," Gabriel said. Hildegard looked confused at Gabriel. "Amelia wonders if the children are trying to communicate with their biological father. I mean, what was I thinking, Hildegard? Thinking that Amy and Caleb would end up together? Why?" Gabriel asked. Hildegard sat down next to Gabriel and grabbed both of his hands. Gabriel smiled. "Gabriel," Hildegard said. "From all the years of being a housekeeper in your home, I have seen the way you think and live, and from what I have seen up until now, you need to take a break from it all and go on a little vacation."

Gabriel pulled his hands out of her grasp and smiled. "What makes you think that?" Gabriel asked. Hildegard sensed Gabriel's irritation and got up fast. "Have no fear of me, Hildegard. I am just curious enough to wonder why you feel that I need a break from it all." Hildegard took a step back and sighed.

"You look tired, Gabriel. I would recharge my battery if I were in your situation, because of all the conflicts. I mean, I have been hearing about you wanting to abdicate from your metaphorical throne. Perhaps let Amy and Ginger be part-time rulers and give them some experience of what they would be as queens of this castle, Gabriel," Hildegard said.

Gabriel nodded. "I do agree with that in many ways, Hildegard. I do feel quite tired and exhausted, and as a matter of fact, I have proposed the queen position to both my daughters, but they seem very reluctant to take over as queen, Hildegard," Gabriel said. Hildegard nodded.

"Of course they would, Gabriel," Hildegard said. "You are the patriarch. They feel that they cannot match up to your standards. Many of the covens in your world have feared, hated, and respected you, Gabriel. Many might see Amy and Ginger as potential pushovers and weak-minded girls."

Gabriel scoffed at Hildegard. "Weak-minded girls? Amy and Ginger? Oh, please, Hildegard. Amy and Ginger are strong and capable of handling anything they are faced with. The fact that both Amy and Ginger's bond grew stronger when they faced me. The fact that Amy traveled around the world with Alistair and Darcia's family," Gabriel said as he kept bringing up all the moments his daughters have been strong and capable. Hildegard held up her hands in surrender mode.

"Forgive me, Gabriel," Hildegard said. "I just gave you my perception of the situation."

Gabriel sighed and relaxed his shoulders. "I know Hildegard," Gabriel said. "I know that you do have good intuition about the situation. I just wish I could just sleep for a while and not let anything bad happen while I was indisposed." Hildegard nodded.

"Well, you can always take a nap and let your mind wander for about a few hours. But I should get going before people wonder why this elderly-looking woman is constantly buying blood for her family," Hildegard said with a chuckle.

Gabriel smiled and gestured for Hildegard to leave. He got to his feet and headed for his slumber chamber. Alistair and Darcia then entered the dining quarter with Bryan and their children. Alistair opened the cooler and sighed.

"What do you say about going on a family hunt?" Alistair asked. Darcia smiled and looked at their sons. They all smiled and nodded. The seven of them left the castle and headed outside toward the main streets near the castle. It was about two o'clock in the morning, which meant that most humans were asleep in their beds. They walked around the area until they found something like a party or club, but it seemed almost impossible.

Alistair and Darcia held hands as they walked together. "Hm. There do not seem to be a lot of humans outside right now, my love," Darcia said. Alistair nodded. "Should we try a hospital, or would that draw too much attention?" Alistair shrugged. "I mean, what kind of human would be outside at this time? Unless people are either drunk or are night owls."

"Well, we can check out a few more parks and see if there are a couple or some teenagers out there," Alistair said. Darcia shrugged and nodded.

"Okay," Darcia said. As they walked further around the city area, there were some humans working nightshift in some areas, like gas stations, convenience stores, and hospitals. That would draw too much attention. "Blood bank it is," Darcia said. The seven of them headed toward the entrance of the hospital and saw two security guards.

"Bună seara," said a male security guard with a strong build and short hair, wearing a bulletproof vest, hat, and boots. He had his gun on his right side. He had his arms crossed but had a stern look on his face.

"English?" Alistair asked. The other security guard, a blonde, strong-built man with the same uniform, stepped up.

"Good evening. Do you need help?" asked the male security guard, who spoke English with a heavy accent. Alistair looked over at Darcia, who pretended to be dizzy with her pale complexion, and held her close to him.

"Yes, officer," Alsitair said as he was using his persuasion powers on both men. "My wife is not feeling well and may need something like a blood transfusion. The officers both nodded and gestured toward the night nurse. The nurse was a petite white girl with short brown hair that she clipped in the back with a hairclip. She was wearing white scrubs behind her computer.

The security guards approached the nurse and spoke to her in the Romanian language, explaining how Darcia needed some help. The nurse quickly got up and approached Darcia.

"Eşti bolnavă, doamnă?" the nurse asked.

"English?" Alistair asked. The woman nodded and repeated the question in English. Darcia nodded.

"I need some iron. We women often need a lot of iron to keep ourselves healthy," Darcia said in a sickly tone. The nurse let Darcia lean on her as she led her into an observation room and let Darcia lay on the bed.

"I will get a doctor in here," the nurse said before she left the room. The five boys moaned with irration.

"This is a bad idea, Father," Bryan said. "Why are we pretending that Darcia is ill? Why not use your powers to tell them that we are just looking around or something along the lines?" The other boys nodded.

"Look, Arabella told us what had happened to her when she went to get blood for herself and Gabriel, and how she almost got caught," Alistair said. "We are just taking some stricter measures to avoid getting caught by humans, boys," Alistair said. "This way, Darcia can continue needing iron every so often, so we do not have to depend on Gabriel or Hildegard for providing us with fresh blood."

The nurse came back with a male doctor. A young white man with dark brown hair and dark brown eyes, wearing a white doctor's coat, held a clipboard in his hands. "Good evening, Darcia, was it?" the doctor asked. Darcia nodded. "The nurse told me that you are in need of iron. How low is your iron level?" the doctor asked. Darcia shrugged.

"Since we do not have you on file with your medical records, I am not sure that would be the best solution for you. Many pharmacies have iron tablets that you can take, but you do look awfully pale," the doctor said.

Alistair nodded. He used his powers on the doctor and nurse. "You will give us each a pack of blood, so in total, you will retrieve seven packs of blood for us, doctor and nurse," Alistair said. The doctor and nurse blankly nodded as they headed out toward the blood sector of the hospital.

"Now we are talking," Bryan said. Darcia smiled. "That is how we do it in our family."

Alistair felt a bit tired and sat down in the circular stool that doctors normally sit in. "My love, are you okay?" Darcia asked. Alistair nodded.

"Using my powers twice in one session does take a lot of energy out of me. I know I am hungry as well, so that does not help."

Darcia nodded. Five minutes later, the doctor came in with the seven packs of blood. Then they walked out of the room. All seven of them sipped the pack of blood till it was gone. Everyone sighed with relief and pleasure.

"That feels much better," Darcia whispered before she started on the second half. Alistair nodded, feeling a bit more energetic than before. The five boys did not say anything as they were too focused on their beverage. Once the packs were empty, they just threw them away in the trashcan in the room and left the room. The security guards greeted them as Alistair and his family left the hospital. Alistair checked his watch. It was going on three thirty. "I think we should head back to the castle," Alsitair said. Everyone else nodded in agreement.

As they were heading for the castle, Alistair heard a rustling sound behind some bushes. This time, Alistair and Darcia had their sons with them for backup and protection. Caleb came out with his hands up. "Caleb?" Darcia asked. Alistair sighed with relief. "Where is Larry?"

Caleb shook his head. "Larry and I had a fight just now, and he sent me out. I was just slumbering in some of those shrubs back there and realized that I needed a better place to sleep. Are you all headed back to the motel or castle?" Caleb asked. Alistair ignored him, and he gestured for his family to ignore him. "Please, Alistair," Caleb begged. "It was never my intent to see you both suffer like that. Larry can be a monster in many ways, including now."

Darcia stopped in her tracks. "What happened, Caleb?" Darcia asked. Alistair cleared his throat to get Darcia's attention and shook his head.

"It does not matter, Caleb," Alistair said. "Darcia, let us go back to our home." Darcia looked over at Alistair and then at Caleb.

"Why are you out here by yourself, Caleb? Is this a trick, or is there really a conflict between you and Larry?" Darcia asked. Alistair chuckled out of frustration.

"Why do you suddenly care, Darcia?" Alistair asked. "Why should we even listen to this little turncoat?"

Caleb sighed and started to walk away. "You see? There is nothing to worry about. Let Caleb figure out his own problems while we all get ready for our slumber," Alistair said. Darcia nodded. Caleb kept a distance between him and Alistair's family before he snuck around behind them, keeping his focus on where they were headed. Caleb then saw that they were headed for the castle.

"Okay," Caleb said to himself. "This might get a bit trickier, but perhaps it is not impossible. Caleb snuck around outside of the castle and saw all the curtains being closed by an elderly-looking woman. "Hildegard," Caleb whispered.

Hildegard then looked out in his direction with concern before she continued closing all the curtains. "Hildegard," Caleb whispered again. This time, she stopped closing the curtains and walked over to one of the windows to open it. She poked her head out and looked around. "Hildegard," Caleb whispered.

"Who is out there, and what do you want?" Hildegard snapped. "It is I, Caleb," Caleb said in a singsong voice. Hildegard shook her head and quickly closed the door and then the curtain.

"Darn it," Caleb whispered. "Okay, well, we have all the time in the world now." Caleb headed back toward Larry's home.

Larry was sitting in the living room with his friends, Viviana and Bianca. "Caleb," Larry said. "Where have you been?" Caleb took off his black jacket and shoes before he entered the living room and sat down in the chair next to the couch.

"I have been observing Alistair and Darcia and tried to get Hildegard's attention, which only worked for a few seconds before she closed the window and curtains on me," Caleb said.

Larry could not help but laugh at Caleb's plan. The other ones joined in and laughed. "What is so funny, Larry?" Caleb asked. Larry stopped laughing and tried to hold in his laughter, which did not work for a few minutes.

"The way you described her closing the window and curtain on you, like you were a suitor, Caleb," Larry said with a chuckle. Caleb rolled his eyes and shook his head.

"Okay, but that is what I have been doing with my evening. What about you, Larry? Sitting here watching evening television or drama videos of human problems?" Caleb asked. Larry shrugged as he sat between his sister and fiancé.

"So far, there is not much we should be doing. Are you still trying to communicate with your biological children, Caleb?" Larry asked.

Caleb nodded. "I am, Larry, but I should not do it too often, because otherwise Gabriel could sense that I am intentionally doing something mischievous and could cause him to get his other friends from around the world involved. I am just subtly strategizing," Caleb said. Larry nodded.

"Okay, good job, Caleb," Larry said. "Just try not to woo Hildegard too often, or there might be a wedding to be planned."

Viviana and Bianca both laughed at that comment. Caleb waved them all off before he headed for his bedroom. Larry smiled before he checked his watch. He saw the sun slowly rising through the curtains. "I think we should all get ready for the evening," Larry said. Everyone nodded in agreement, and then headed for their own sleeping spot.

Back at the castle, Arabella helped Amy put her children in their crib and sighed with exhaustion. "I think I might want to take tomorrow off, if you would not mind, Amy?" Arabella asked. Amy smiled and nodded.

"Of course, mother," Amy said. "Everyone deserves a break." Arabella kissed Amy on top of her head before she left the room. Amy looked at her children and saw how big they were getting.

"Soon, I might need to get you three of your own beds," Amy said. There was a knock on the door. "Yes?" Amy said she was wondering if it was her father. Bryan opened the door.

"Amy," Bryan said as he held up his hand to her. "I just need to tell you this. I have no idea I was the one who attacked you, but I am so sorry for what happened."

Amy smiled and nodded. "Look, I know you were under Viviana's spell and enchantment. It was not fun, and it hurt a lot, so

I know how your victims feel about your attacks, but I forgive you," Amy said. Bryan still felt guilt and shame inside of him.

"How could you even forgive me, Amy? I would understand if you would never want to see me again," Bryan said. Amy shrugged.

"Look, I am an easily forgivable person, especially towards my father, who caused me to suffer a major identity crisis. Bryan, I have known you for several years, and I know how loving and caring you are toward me. Whatever happened back then is something I know you would never do out of your own volition. Are we okay?" Amy asked.

Bryan nodded and looked over at the bed. "So, I shall leave you to get ready to sleep," Bryan said before he headed for the door.

"Wait, Bryan," Amy said. "Would you like to stay with me for the evening?" Bryan scrunched his brow and looked outside to make sure his parents or Gabriel were not out there.

"Well," Bryan said with hesitation in his voice. "If that is what you want, of course." Amy smiled and nodded.

"Like old times?" Amy asked. Bryan felt more relaxed and nodded.

"Like old times, huh?" Bryan asked teasingly. Amy smiled, opened up her side of the bed, and waited for Bryan to enter from the other side.

Arabella walked down the stairs toward her sleeping quarter and noticed Gabriel sitting on his private sofa with a glass of blood in his hands. "My love, are you okay?" Arabella asked. Gabriel looked up at Arabella and smiled.

"Quite well, my love," Gabriel said before he returned his focus back to his glass. Arabella sat down next to him. "What is going on?"

"I am feeling quite tired and exhausted from everything. I want Amy and Ginger to take over my position. The blood is not giving me the proper energy that I once had, Arabella," Gabriel said. Arabella wrapped her left arm around Gabriel, holding him close to her. "Arabella, I am not dying anytime soon, but could you perhaps talk to our daughters and see if you can persuade them?"

Arabella shrugged. "I know they are prepared to become queen of the shape shifters, Gabriel. I do not want to push them either," Arabella said. Gabriel nodded. Arabella smiled, got to her feet, and walked over to their bedroom. Gabriel remained in the same position for a while. Arabella did not fall asleep immediately. "Gabe, are you still coming to bed?"

Gabriel finished his drink, got to his feet, and joined Arabella for a slumber. Gabriel felt incredibly tired and fell asleep in his suit. Arabella ignored Gabriel, put her nightgown on, and got under the covers. She could not sleep. She sat up in bed and looked down at Gabriel with concern. In Gabriel's dream, he was back at the tavern. Gabriel entered the tavern, but it looked empty and practically torn up. He looked around and saw broken windows and shards on the floor; the floorboards were half-broken in some areas of the tavern.

Gabriel was looking around and suddenly heard infants crying behind a closed door. Gabriel looked around to make sure nobody was behind him. The crying started to get louder. Gabriel put his hand on the doorknob, opened the door, and saw Amy's three children, but they were about five years old, crying on the floor, covering their eyes with their hands. Gabriel heard the door of the tavern open and close.

Caleb stood about ten feet away with a hungry look on his face. "Caleb," Gabriel gasped. Caleb smirked at Gabriel, grazing his sharp nails along the nearest wooden table. "What are you doing?" Caleb shrugged as he kept his focus on Gabriel. "Why are Amy's children in the closet?"

Caleb headed for the bar, grabbed an unlabeled bottle from the bar, popped the cork, placed the bottle in his mouth, and swilled down a dark red liquid. Gabriel opened the door again, but this time the children were gone. Gabriel looked back at Caleb and saw him wipe his mouth with the back of his right hand. "Caleb!" Gabriel screamed. Caleb cleared his throat and sighed. "Where are the children?"

Caleb looked out of the broken window and nodded. Then Larry showed up with Bianca and Viviana, and slowly the other members also entered the tavern. Larry and Caleb fist bumped each other and focused on Gabriel. Viviana used her subjugation on Gabriel, causing him to clutch his head and fall to his knees. Viviana kept her powers focused. Gabriel gritted his teeth because of the pain. Then Larry got on his knees in front of Gabriel, barred his teeth at Gabriel, and was about to bite Gabriel till Gabriel woke up in shock.

Arabella woke up from the tossing and turning. "Gabe!" Arabella screamed. "Gabe, it was just a nightmare." Gabriel sighed and sat up against the bedpost.

"Was it about Caleb again, Gabriel?" Arabella asked. Gabriel nodded and tried to relax his body. "We need to take care of this problem, Gabriel." Gabriel nodded and wrapped his arms around Arabella, holding her in his arms.

"Everything is going to be okay, Gabriel," Arabella said in a soothing tone. "Caleb and Larry will be taken care of real soon." Gabriel felt tired and released his hold on Arabella, snuggled under the covers, and let Arabella wrap her arms around. He fell asleep seconds later. The night fell upon them, and Arabella held Gabriel till he woke up.

Gabriel woke up and looked better than he did before. Once Gabriel and Arabella were dressed for the evening, Gabriel decided to summon all of the covens at the invitation of Caleb. Gabriel did not feel so energetic like he did years before he met Viviana, so he decided to gather up all the coven members and invite them to Romania. He opened up a video chat for everyone to access from their own homes.

Dante and Francesca were both sipping from two blood packs. Alarick and Vanessa sat patiently but looked quite tired in front of the camera. Kristjan, Helen, and Logan showed up with Mackenzie, shaking his head. Mackenzie still looked upset over the loss of Audrey. "My fellow coven members and friends, I am not sure if you are all up to date on what has taken place at our home, but it has been quite disastrous," Gabriel said as he sat in front of his laptop.

The other coven members kept their focus on Gabriel. "To make a long story short, I got enchanted by this young girl, who is officially Larry's fiancé or wife, not even sure about that anymore, and she drained me of my energy where blood has no effect on my improvement anymore. Caleb is threatening Amy's children through their dreams, which causes Amy, me, and I believe Ginger to also have nightmares about Caleb. I am inviting you all to help me take care of Larry, Caleb, Bianca, Viviana, and a few others that I have not really seen as of late," Gabriel said.

Logan shook his head and placed his left arm around Mackenzie. "I think we will pass, Gabriel. I am sorry for all of the things that have taken place in your life, but the loss of my wife is still hard to bear. No other woman can match up to Audrey," Logan said.

Gabriel nodded. "Nobody can replace Daniel either, Logan. I had a nightmare about him a while back, and that haunted me until today, especially since I had another nightmare about Caleb and Larry last night. Arabella can vouch for me," Gabriel said. Logan shrugged.

"But still," Logan said. "I can understand your loss, but you still have two or three more brothers, as I recall, but when your life partner, with whom you have a child wife, is gone? That is something that can never be replaced. I am not saying that losing Daniel should be easy, but I am not sure if I can put myself out there for the sake of Mackenzie or even lose her. Then I would most likely follow them, wherever they may be, Gabriel," Logan said.

Gabriel sighed and looked at the other members. "Dante, Alarick, Francesca, Helen, Vanessa, Kristjan? Gabriel asked. "Look, what happened the other day with that big fight with Larry, I blame myself entirely. I have mentioned to my wife that I would love nothing more than to grant them peace if I am gone, but somehow, Arabella thinks that Larry would continue going after her, Amelia, or my other brothers, or even my own children," Gabriel said.

Dante shrugged and nodded. "I would be more than happy to back you up, Gabriel," Dante said. Francesca nodded along. Then Alarick and Vanessa both nodded, and lastly, Kristjan and Helen also nodded.

"So," Dante said. "When is the big day? Are we to be expected anytime in the next twelve hours?" Gabriel shrugged.

"Well, I was hoping to propose this idea to Caleb once we are done with our talk and see if he is willing to stop by alone," Gabriel said.

Helen raised her hand. "How would you know Larry or that Phoebe is not going to be there?" Helen asked. Gabriel scrunched his brow.

"Who is Phoebe? Do you mean Bianca?" Helen quickly nodded and chuckled. "Well," Gabriel said as he was trying to hold in his laughter. "We would try to find a way to avoid that. I will keep you all posted on all of my plans regarding this invite with Caleb, and I will send you all a personal electronic invite."

All the members except for Logan and Mackenzie nodded. "Okay. Well, enjoy the rest of your evening," Gabriel said before he signed off from the video chat.

The Invite

Gabriel walked over to the dining quarter and saw his three brothers and Arabella sitting at the table with a bottle of blood and four glasses. Gabriel sat down in one of the empty chairs and saw Adrian grab him an empty glass. Lucien poured Gabriel a glass of blood and pushed the glass toward him. "So brother," Lucien said. "What is going on?"

Gabriel took a sip of the blood and sighed. "Most of the coven members, except for Logan and Mackenzie, will arrive whenever the invite has been accepted by Caleb," Gabriel said. The other men and Arabella gave Gabriel a confused look.

"What do you mean, Gabriel?" Arabella asked. "Why would you invite Caleb and the other coven members?"

Gabriel sat up and clasped his hands together. "Remember how I told you, Arabella, that I was feeling weaker? Well, I think the time has come to finish our little problem with Caleb and Larry by bringing in our own backup," Gabriel said. "Look, do not take this personal at all. You all are very strong and capable of handling Larry and Caleb, but I do not want to repeat any mistakes like last time, my friends and love."

The three men exchanged glances, and Arabella rolled her eyes. "Well," Lucien said. "Inviting Caleb over is quite a big step to take, Gabriel. I mean, what if Larry, Viviana, or that Bianca girl are in the back somewhere with their own backup plan? What if Viviana enchants you again, Gabriel? What are the other coven members going to do? Once you get metaphorically possessed or blacked out, you could end up harming one or some of us," Lucien said.

Gabriel smiled and shook his head out of frustration. "What do you mean by that, brother?" Gabriel said as he gritted his teeth. "I would never harm anyone or let myself get possessed," Gabriel hissed. The brothers all exchanged glances again.

"You have done that, Gabriel, or perhaps not in that exact way with an attack, but you did not want to get rid of Viviana; do you not remember that?" Lucien asked.

Gabriel shook his head. "No, but then again, the last thing I remembered was that Amelia had fed me from her wrist and put another spell on me, like a cloaking spell, and I felt like myself again. Whatever happened before that is all just a blur for me," Gabriel said. Arabella moved over two chairs so she could sit closer to Gabriel and grab his hand.

"Whatever happened, we have a new plan, so Gabriel will gather the other coven members, and we shall invite Caleb and make sure he has no backup plan for us," Arabella said. Gabriel smiled at Arabella. "So, that would mean there would be about twenty-one of us against Larry's group." Gabriel nodded. "I am not sure if I want Amy and Ginger to take part. They can stay with the younglings and Hildegard."

"I agree," Gabriel said. "Amy and Ginger should probably relocate or leave for a while while we have our final battle with those monsters." Lucien rolled his eyes.

"Uhuh, and leave them alone with a human and three children? Gabe, what if Larry's friends overthrow your kids? Look, the last time we had our fight, Amy was pregnant and stayed in her room," Lucien said.

Gabriel remembered that moment and felt a sense of guilt for not being there for Amy. Arabella managed to help her, but he wanted to see the entrance of his grandchildren into the world. "I remember that fight. The fight, which ended my relationship with Logan, as well," Gabriel said. Nobody said anything. "Amy and Ginger are strong enough to handle Larry's friends. Plus, if Larry or Caleb do not know where my children are, that could increase their chances of survival in this world. I will see how my children feel about taking a little vacation away from everything," Gabriel said before he got to his feet.

Arabella got to her feet as well. "Absolutely not, Gabriel. Amy and Ginger will remain here until the battle is over," Arabella snapped. "I will not leave my daughters out there while we are here together. We would do better if we were all together."

Gabriel sighed and shook his head. "I cannot always be there for them, and neither can you, Amelia, or the other ones, Arabella. Getting Amy and Ginger as far away as possible from all forms of harm would increase their chances of survival, including Amy's children. Let me just throw this idea out at the girls and see how they react. If they disagree, they can do whatever they want. I cannot allow Caleb or Viviana to do anything to my children or grandchildren. I would not be able to bear that, Arabella," Gabriel said.

Arabella sighed and shook her head. "I disagree with separating our family," Arabella said. "Go ahead and see how Ginger and Amy react to your proposal." Gabriel walked off. Arabella sat down again.

"Lucien, please talk some sense into Gabriel. If Amy and Ginger are separated, that could increase the chances of putting them in great peril," Arabella said. Lucien nodded.

"I agree. I do not think Amy and Ginger would want to leave this place, Arabella," Lucien said. Arabella shook her head, got to her feet, walked over to Amy's bedroom, and saw Gabriel, Amy, and Ginger in her room.

"Father," Amy said. "I cannot see myself running away with three children, Ginger and Hildegard." Ginger nodded. Gabriel sighed and turned around when he heard Arabella enter.

"Mother, are you aware of what our father is talking about?" Amy asked. Arabella nodded.

"Look!" Gabriel said. "I want to make sure that you all are safe and away from Larry, Caleb, or even Viviana. If you all are away, I do not think they would go after you three at first, because I am the main target, and if I know that you are near me, they might attack you both and perhaps kidnap your children, Amy."

Amy sighed and shook her head. "I do not feel comfortable about this, Father," Amy said. Gabriel started to feel tense. "Why are you acting so weird?" Gabriel crossed his arms.

"Caleb is to be invited, and I am inviting other covens, but if Bianca and Vivaiana are outside somewhere, coaxing or seducing your children, Amy, you could easily get attacked by Larry or even get kidnapped like last time. Do you remember, Amy? Your children got kidnapped, and then you got kidnapped. That was so scary, Amy," Gabriel said.

Amy remembered being kidnapped by Larry and seeing his parents for the first time in many years. "Look, where would we have to go?" Amy asked. Gabriel snapped his fingers.

"Australia," Gabriel said. "You all can stay with Logan and Mackenzie." Arabella remembered that Logan and Mackenzie were staying behind and nodded.

"That might be something, Amy," Arabella said. "I mean, Logan and Mackenzie are our shape-shifting members. They might dislike Gabriel, but they would love to see you again and even see Ginger again after hearing about her."

Amy sighed with despair. "Seriously? For how long?" Amy asked. Arabella looked over at Gabriel.

"About a month, give or take," Gabriel said. Ginger started to feel nervous, especially about how she remembered traveling from Oregon to Romania with Amy and how scary it was for both of them.

"Can I just think about this plan, Father?" Amy asked. Gabriel nodded.

"Of course, my dears," Gabriel said before he left Amy's room. Arabella stayed behind.

Arabella shook her head. "You know what? I do not feel comfortable having you all go by yourselves to Australia, not because it is not safe for shape shifters, but because Logan and your father are not entirely best friends. If you all want to stay here, I am sure you all can handle Larry and Caleb," Arabella said. Both Amy and Ginger nodded.

"As much as we do need a vacation, Gin," Amy said. "I do not feel comfortable traveling with my children." Ginger nodded.

"I agree. I wonder why our father is being persistent in wanting us to leave. I mean, first he wants us to become queen, and now he wants us to leave because of this upcoming meeting with Caleb? We could just stay in one of our rooms and keep each other safe," Ginger said.

Amy nodded and sighed with relief. "I agree. We should just stay and let our mother let us stay," Amy said before she let herself fall on her bed. Ginger sat on the edge of the bed, going through the whole process in her mind.

"Well, now that we are safe enough, I think I shall go to my own room," Ginger said.

Amy gave Ginger a tiny wave and watched her leave her room. There was a knock on Amy's door. "Yes?" Amy asked, confused. The door opened up, and Bryan came in.

"Amy, I keep hearing about how Caleb is coming over. Why?" Bryan asked with frustration in his voice. "What if Larry or the other ones are around, Amy? I do not feel comfortable about this," Bryan said.

Amy nodded. "I do too, Bryan, but my father managed to get the other coven members involved, so that would be our backup," Amy said.

Bryan rolled his eyes. "Well, perhaps that is better than I had thought, but I really do not want to see him again. Everything those monsters represent is just something I would never have known existed in our world, Amy," Bryan said. Amy nodded. "I agree," Amy said. "I mean, there are mean girls that I have dealt with during my high school years, but knowing that there are worse predators in this world is just too much."

Bryan nodded. "I agree. I mean, humans can be cruel towards each other, but knowing that there are monsters like ours, it can become quite unbearable," Bryan said. Amy nodded.

"So, Bryan," Amy said. "Are you going to join in on the strategizing and planning with your parents?" Bryan shrugged.

"Probably not, because Alistair and Darcia will probably take part once the other coven members arrive," Bryan said.

Amy nodded. "My father almost had Ginger and me sent back to Australia to stay with our supposed uncle Logan and our cousin Mackenzie while Caleb was here. It is like he has no faith or trust that we can protect ourselves against Caleb," Amy said. Bryan scrunched his brow.

"Why?" Bryan asked. Amy shrugged. "Does your father not know that splitting up can increase problems and attacks? How old is he again? Over a thousand, and he has no common sense," Bryan said.

Amy chuckled at watching Bryan. "What?" Bryan asked. "Look, I care about your wellbeing, Amy, and to watch your father make more unethical strategies and plans angers me." Amy smiled and nodded.

"I am not laughing, because I find it funny, but I appreciate you being there for me, Bryan," Amy said. "You have more common sense than my own blood-related father."

Bryan smiled before he wrapped his arms around Amy. "I do care about you, Amy Rose Ambrose," Bryan said. "When I saw you back in Oregon, my heart broke, but I could not show much compassion toward you. We had to be strong and protective of you, and you have no idea how much my heart broke to see you suffer, crying, and being lied to. I sometimes feel like I was an accomplice in lying and deceiving."

Amy started to feel Bryan's compassion and hugged him tighter. "I do not blame you for anything, Bryan," Amy said as she felt sadness in her throat. "I just wish we could have met a different way, but this ended up being the silver lining." Bryan released his hold on Amy and sat next to her. "I mean, I was lied to for eighteen years. Unexpectedly, after walking those two dogs from Emma and Nathan, you all showed up. Ginger was still at college, and I was overwhelmed and angry. I mean, you all seemed friendly, which is what our health class teacher told us to watch out for," Amy said.

Bryan nodded. "I know how bad that sounds," Bryan said with a chuckle. Amy could not help but laugh at the situation. Bryan did feel bad about hearing Amy's perspective like that.

"If you are laughing out of nerves, I do not blame you, Amy, but nobody should ever have to go through what you and Ginger went through. No matter how common it may be in certain areas, it is still not right what Gabriel has done to you both. He had Amelia, who could watch over you with Hildegard, and he had his four brothers at the time to emotionally support him, but instead he has you sent off. No, Amy, what he did was not right," Bryan said. "Here he goes again with more dumb plans. I am glad you both are putting your foot down. Whatever Gabriel has planned for you two is just absurd and disorganized," Bryan said.

Amy nodded, realizing all the pain she had to repress during the last year or so. Bran sensed Amy's sadness and quickly grabbed her in his arms again. "I am sorry for bringing up those horrible memories, Amy," Bryan said. "I did not mean to cause you any harm." Amy shook her head and sighed.

"No, Bryan," Amy said. "I know what you were saying and explaining to me, and deep down inside, I do feel like I never got a chance to fully process all of what has taken place. Everything just happened in just a matter of seconds for me, including getting a fake wedding thrown at me, and now there is this meeting with Caleb," Amy said. "I do not know what to feel or think anymore, Bryan."

Bryan stroked Amy's back, seeing if she wanted to shed some tears, but Amy just gently nudged Bryan off of her. "Thank you for trying to help me, Bryan, but I just need some space right now, if you would not mind?" Bryan nodded.

"I understand, but if you do need to see me, you know where to find me," Bryan said before he left Amy's room.

Amy nodded and suddenly felt the urge to want to cry, but it took her a while. Back on the main floor, Arabella approached Gabriel sternly. "Gabe, I do not think it is a good idea to send our daughters and grandchildren off to Logan's right now," Arabella said. Gabriel sighed as he quickly turned around to face Arabella.

"Now what?" Gabriel asked. "I am just planning for the safety of our family, Arabella, and now you want them to get closer to danger?" Arabella rolled her eyes and shook her head out of anger.

"Why do you go through such extremes, Gabriel?" Arabella asked. Gabriel stood in front of Arabella. "Yes?" Gabriel turned around to head for the cooler and grabbed a fresh, unopened bottle of blood and an empty glass for himself.

"I would love some too, you know," Arabella said. Gabriel shrugged as he undid the cap of the unmarked bottle. "So this is how you want to play it? I mean, what makes you think Amy and Ginger would approve of going back to Australia? Gabriel, have you not ever heard that splitting up the family is far more dangerous than remaining in a close bond? What if Larry has connections around Australia or at the airport?"

Gabriel shrugged as he poured a full glass of blood. "Everything that I have done for you and the girls is for the sake of protecting you all and keeping you all safe from harm. I already apologized for my actions many times, Arabella, but yet I constantly feel like I am being scrutinized and harassed, even though you all are safe and alive," Gabriel said.

Arabella rolled her eyes as she grabbed herself an empty glass. Gabriel then poured her glass full and placed the bottle in between them. "Whatever Viviana had done to me, Arabella, that came across so unexpectedly. I do not wish for my daughters or even you to suffer like I have suffered Arabella," Gabriel said. "I do feel weaker than I have before, which is why I contacted our friends from around the world to come over as backup support."

Arabella did not respond immediately. "I do not wish for anything bad to happen to anyone either, Gabriel, but sending them off again is not something I approve of, and I know that both Amy and Ginger are not that interested in leaving either," Arabella said. "At least understand their concerns, dear Gabriel." Gabriel did not respond and poured himself another glass. Lucien, Adrian, and Vladimir all entered the dining quarter. Amelia joined them moments later.

"So," Amelia said. "Are we actually inviting Caleb over?" Gabriel nodded.

"Yes, but I may need someone to give him his invitation, as I have no other way of communicating with him. He has to know that there will be no other members, except that might be hard, and that he has to come alone," Gabriel said. Arabella could not help but chuckle at the situation.

"You really think Caleb will come here on his own accord and not know that there are other enemy members around, Gabriel?" Arabella asked.

Gabriel gave Arabella a quick glance before he continued. "I mean, I could also go outside and meet him and keep him there while you all stay close behind the door, in case there is something sinister that Caleb has planned," Gabriel said. Nobody responded. "If Caleb knows that he is not in for a trap, he might be okay with coming over." Everyone exchanged glances at each other.

"Gabriel," Lucien said. "I think it would be better to invite him inside the house and interrogate him rather than baiting him and potentially ruining our own plans."

The other members nodded. "Look, Caleb will most likely not show up alone, but we cannot send you outside by yourself either. Perhaps Arabella can join, or even better, Amelia," Lucien said. Amelia quickly shook her head. "No, listen to me for a moment. If there is a woman present, that could ease the situation a bit more than if it is just Gabriel."

Amelia started to feel nervous about the plan. "I mean, I was happy that I was able to protect Gabriel from Viviana, but whatever," Amelia said. "If that would help with getting him here and seeing if he is not somehow going after Amy's children, or her? I would be happy to take one for the team and join Gabriel outside of the castle."

Gabriel chuckled at Lucien's suggestion, but then again, he had no actual plan either. "Okay. How do we invite Caleb over to our home?" Gabriel asked. Suddenly Hildegard came into the dining quarter.

"I almost got enchanted by Caleb a few nights ago," Hildegard said.

"Were you ever going to mention that little piece of information to us, Hildegard?" Gabriel snapped.

"I thought I was going crazy, due to the last few nights of getting readjusted to my position as housekeeper," Hildegard said. "What if I was used as bait while Amelia and Gabriel waited, like behind some shrubs? I am certain Caleb would come for me, and then you two jump out to catch him?"

Everyone in the room started to laugh. "What is so funny?" Hildegard asked. "Can you picture that, everyone? Amelia and I are hiding while Caleb is talking to Hildegard," said Gabriel with a chuckle. Hildegard sighed and started to walk away.

"Well, hang on there for a moment," Lucien said. "Perhaps sending out a human could bring him over quicker? I mean, Hildegard goes over to put in the envelope with her name on it. Since Caleb did try to communicate with her, Hildegard could be used as human bait. Sorry to refer to you as that, Hildegard, and once he comes over, out comes the king of the castle, ready to bring him into our dungeon. That way, Amy and Ginger are safe from harm, and you have the other coven members backing Gabriel up and acting as a means of extra support. I actually like that plan. What do you think, Gabriel?"

Gabriel could not help but chuckle, but knowing that Caleb did try to get in touch with Hildegard, that was a risk he was willing to take. "Okay, so I shall compose a handwritten letter, and Hildegard delivers it over to them during daytime hours, so nobody is around to bother her. Okay, we have ourselves a good plan," said Gabriel before he left for his office to write out a letter for Caleb. Gabriel grabbed a blank page from a pile of printing paper, grabbed this gold fountain pen with black ink in it, and composed his letter.

Dear Caleb,

I am cordially inviting you to my home once you feel comfortable enough by yourself. I would like to discuss a few things regarding potential dreams that my daughters and I have been having. I can understand that this is something you might shy away from, but if we can perhaps negotiate or strike up some type of deal, I would be interested in seeing what you are hoping to gain from it all. My housekeeper, Hildegard, would be more than happy to meet you out front if you find my presence too much to handle. I hope we can come to some type of agreement if you are interested in it. Once you have your answer, please feel free to drop in at any time that suits you.

Cordially,
Gabriel Ambrose

Hildegard grabbed the letter with Caleb's name on it, headed over around ten o'clock in the morning to the apartment complex where Larry and Caleb were staying, slid the envelope inside the mailslot, and walked away. Without realizing this, Caleb was watching her with the curtains closed, grabbed the envelope, opened it, and laughed when he saw Gabriel's name on it.

"Okay, this is going to be easier than I had expected," Caleb said as he walked back to his bedroom and sat on the edge of his bed. Caleb finally got his chance of getting back into Gabriel's castle, so he could get closer to Amy's children, who were also his children, and take further steps. Caleb managed to fall asleep and wake up the next evening. He walked into the living room, seeing Bianca and Larry sitting at the table with their own glass of blood. Caleb held his letter in his hands and handed it to Larry.

Larry looked at Gabriel's name and laughed. "Wow, I was not expecting the king of the castle to propose that you come over to their home, Caleb. Whatever you did, I am proud of you," Larry said. Caleb smiled and nodded. Larry handed the letter to Bianca. She could not help but smile.

"I am impressed by this, you guys," Bianca said. Viviana just entered the dining room, yawning and stretching out her body.

"What is with all of the commotion?" Viviana asked. Bianca handed Viviana the letter. "Oh goodness, Gabriel has finally lost it. Perhaps my enchantment spells have a side effect or an aftereffect," Viviana said.

Larry let out a sinister cackle and sighed with happiness. "Gabriel is losing his touch. I am sure that you are not going by yourself, Caleb. This is what I think is important. You go and meet that Hildegard," Larry said as he looked through the letter. "The girls and I will be in the background to make sure you do not enter the castle and get locked up in their dungeon."

Caleb thought about it and remembered that dungeon. "Oh, right, I completely forgot about that part of their castle. I mean, why would I go by myself? Oh, please, how weak is Gabriel?" Caleb asked. Larry smirked at him and shrugged.

"Whatever it is, Caleb, we now have a chance of getting closer to him," Larry said. "Okay. This is what you will do. Do you have your phone with you, Caleb?"

Caleb nodded. "Good. Perhaps we might be in the park area or somewhere a bit further away from the castle while you go over to the castle and look up that housekeeper of his, and you let us know what is going on. If anything happens, just give us a quick call, and we will be right within a few seconds next to you for support," Larry said.

Caleb nodded. "Okay," Caleb said. "We will keep in touch. I hope they are not planning to trap me, you know. That dungeon was not fun or clean at all. I will do my best to see what Gabriel has planned. Perhaps we might come to a good agreement of some kind."

Larry smiled and nodded. "Yes, you will, Caleb. I know that Amy will be quite protective of her children, so try to avoid that topic, but you can always bring up the fact on earning sympathy points from that housekeeper that you do feel some kind of connection to Amy's children and that you had wished you could have been a father in your life. Something like that and maybe Hildegard might allow you to get closer to Amy's children, and even kidnapping one child would make Gabriel rethink what he has done to us all," Larry said.

Caleb smiled and nodded at the other two women as well. "Well, it is going on ten o'clock in the evening. What should I wear?" Caleb asked.

Third Round

Hildegard was getting the castle prepared for Gabriel's guests. "So, how many of our guests will be arriving, Gabriel?" Hildegard asked. Gabriel counted all the names with his fingers.

"About fifteen or so," Gabriel said. "That does mean that Alistair's boys have to give up two of their rooms to accommodate the other guests. I am sure they will be okay with it."

Hildegard nodded. "I will make sure all of the rooms will be ready for our guests," Hildegard said. The castle chimes went off several times. Gabriel had greeted Dante and Francesca, then Kristjan and Helen showed up, and lastly, Alarick and Vanessa showed up. It was going on about midnight, and Hildegard decided to gussy herself up with one of Arabella's evening gowns. Then she did her hair and makeup, and she looked like a different person. Hildegard was even given a fake purse with a cell phone. Gabriel looked over at Hildegard and nodded.

Gabriel decided to invite his guests to the dining quarter and grabbed several unopened bottles. Hildegard breathed in and out, trying to keep herself as composed as possible. Arabella and Amelia remained behind the front door to keep their eyes on Hildegard. Hildegard started to feel nervous about being outside past midnight. She got used to doing blood bank runs, but being used as bait to lure a shape shifter into the castle was something she overestimated. She stood about forty feet away from the castle and started biting her nails on her right hand.

Back at the castle, Arabella and Amelia started to feel impatient as they checked the clock in the living quarter. Arabella decided to go over to Gabriel. "Gabe!" Arabella said. "Have you heard anything from Caleb yet?" Gabriel grabbed his cellular device and checked his messages, but there was nothing new to see. Arabella nodded and walked back to the front door to see Amelia shrugging.

Outside, Hildegard was looking around and feeling tired from the waiting. Suddenly, Hildegard heard distant footsteps coming towards her, and it was Caleb wearing a grey suit with a black tie, holding a bouquet of flowers. Hildegard gave a confused look and turned to face the closed front door of the castle and look back at Caleb.

"Good evening," Caleb said as he extended his hand to Hildegard. "You must be Hildegard, the housekeeper of Gabriel Ambrose." Hildegard started to feel awkward but had to look neutral. Hildegard shook hands with Caleb.

"Yes," Hildegard said with a stutter. "Pleasure to meet you." Caleb smiled and nodded. "So, what brings you to the castle, Caleb?"

"Gabriel sent me this invite," Caleb said as he grabbed the note from inside his blazer. "I never like to show up empty-handed. Hildegard nodded.

"Ah, right, well, I wanted to…" Hildegard said, clearing her throat. "Um… I wanted to get to know you. I heard you the other evening, and I feel like I could have shown a bit more respect."

Caleb chuckled and took a step back. "Respect? Oh heavens, Hildegard, you do not ever have to apologize to me," Caleb said. "So, is the man of the hour inside?"

Hildegard started to feel uncomfortable and was told to keep him outside, so he could be lured in. Hildegard started to sweat a bit as she was licking her lips. She started to back away and quickly adjust herself. "Gabriel is still getting the setting prepared for you, Caleb, but perhaps we can just wait outside?" Hildegard asked.

Caleb started to sense something was off. "Gabriel never mentioned this part, Hildegard," Caleb snapped. "I think I may want to leave." Just then, the front door opened, and Gabriel came out with a jovial charade.

"Caleb," Gabriel said with a high-pitched tone. "Forgive me for having you wait. Thank you, Hildegard, for keeping our guest entertained. Please enter." Caleb looked behind him, which caught Gabriel's gaze. Gabriel looked behind him and nodded.

Larry is in the area. Keep your mind and intuition sharp, Gabriel thought. The other members dispersed into the dining quarter and walked up the staircase. Caleb sighed and headed for the front door, wondering if he had noticed other people.

"Oh," Caleb said as he started to back up. "If you have other people here, we can reschedule for another evening."

Gabriel shrugged and kept his focus on Caleb. "Are you sure, Caleb? I mean, I have an entire meal planned for just the two of us. If you did notice someone, Arabella and Amelia were around," Gabriel said. Hildegard smiled uncomfortably at the whole situation and headed inside the castle. Caleb looked back at him again.

"Do you have someone around, Caleb?" Gabriel asked. Caleb did not respond, looked back at Gabriel, and shook his head.

"Not at all, Gabriel," Caleb said. Then Caleb decided to head toward the front door and handed Gabriel the flowers before he stepped over the threshold.

The dining quarter looked made up with a red tablecloth, two plates, and glasses, and Hildegard finally put on some classical music in the background. "Oh," Caleb said. "It looks a bit romantic." Gabriel shrugged as he walked over to his chair and waited for Caleb to sit down. Hildegard walked over to the kitchen area and grabbed an opened bottle of blood and poured Caleb a full glass in a wine glass, and then Gabriel. Then she bowed and left the room. Gabriel held up his glass to Caleb and waited for Caleb to raise his glass.

"To us guys," Gabriel said. Caleb smiled and raised his glass. "Caleb, the reason I wanted to invite you over here is because I wanted to see how you were doing." Caleb looked around uneasy, as before he even took a sip from his glass. He put it down and looked over at Gabriel in confusion.

"Why, Gabriel?" Caleb asked. "Out of the ten years I got to be your son, I got thrown out because Arabella does not like me, and you allowed that to happen, and now you want to know how I am doing?"

Gabriel was about to respond until Caleb held up his hand. "I am not done here, Gabriel," Caleb snapped. "You broke my heart and you broke my life because of your own unethical reasons, Gabe." Caleb finished talking, which gave Gabriel a chance to talk.

"Caleb," Gabriel said with a sigh. "I have no words to describe what I have done. I was grieving about everything, and when I saw you, how similar we looked, even though you obviously were no biological son of mine, I really thought I gave you a better deal in life."

Caleb scoffed before he got to his feet out of anger. "Where are you going?" Gabriel asked. "Why can we just not talk out our grievances, Caleb? I mean, obviously you are hurting a lot, and I feel like we can resolve our grievances right now with some good blood."

Caleb shook his head. "I just feel like I am wasting my time with you, Gabriel," Caleb snapped. "I just feel like you would not care about my feelings or reasons at all and just overrule me with your own reasons to persuade me to agree with you." Gabriel shook his head and shrugged.

"Caleb," Gabriel said before he got to his feet. "I just want to explain myself, and I would never persuade you to agree with me."

Caleb felt sadness building inside of her and turned his back to Gabriel so he could control himself. Gabriel walked toward Caleb until Caleb turned around with tears in his eyes.

"Caleb," Gabriel said with empathy in his tone. "Please come back to the table and let me explain myself. If you do not want to listen to me, feel free to leave and go back to Larry." Gabriel headed back to the table and waited for Caleb to sit down. To his surprise, Caleb sat back down again.

"Caleb," Gabriel said. "I want to apologize for what I had done, but then again, I saw how well you were developing and growing in our home. I really felt a bond, like you were my actual son. I loved you, Caleb. I really felt that I did the right thing, but then I realized that I needed my daughters back. I never wanted you to leave, Caleb. Then I realized that Arabella would take my daughters away from me because of how I had treated them, including her, which was not entirely positive from my side. I did change, Caleb."

Caleb sighed out of anger and shook his head. "How did you change, Gabriel?" Caleb asked. Gabriel swallowed and nodded.

"I realized that once I put my daughters up for adoption, I completely messed up. Of course, I was so upset and heartbroken by Arabella's death that I could not think straight. I know I could have listened to my brothers and Amelia a bit better, but I really could not handle this additional stress. My daughters resented me for a long time, Caleb, and especially with Amy's pregnancy situation," Gabriel said.

"About that," Caleb snapped. "What was going on with you about that weird wedding, getting Amy pregnant with my life source, and then sending me away? Goodness, Gabriel, I am not sure how long I can stay here listening to your sappy responses." Caleb got to his feet again and headed toward the door. Gabriel started to get angry, got to his feet, and ran to the door before Caleb could reach it.

"Let me ask you something, Caleb," Gabriel snapped. "Are you the one who is causing my daughters and me to have dreams about you? For revenge?" Caleb chuckled and shrugged. "Well?"

"What if I am Gabriel? What are you going to do about it? Kill me? Your beloved son?" Caleb said it sarcastically. "Oh, please, you would not do any of that to me." Gabriel started to feel anger inside of him, barring his teeth. Caleb started to back up toward the table and grabbed his cellular device from his jeans pocket.

"What are you doing, Caleb?" Gabriel snapped. "Calling for backup?" Caleb started to run toward the sliding doors, but they were locked. Caleb then pressed Larry's name, and seconds later, the doorbell chimes went off.

"Caleb," Gabriel snapped. "Hildegard, do not answer that door. We are not expecting anyone right now." Hildegard nodded and headed back to the living quarter, where Arabella and Amelia were.

The doorbell chimes were ringing uncontrollably. Gabriel covered his ears with both his hands while Caleb was trying to escape the castle.

The other coven members came down the stairs in their evening clothes, looking hungry and pale. "You are a deceiving liar, Gabriel Ambrose!" Caleb yelled. "You have backup, whereas you denied me any form of backup?" Gabriel barred his teeth and ran toward the front door, where he saw Bianca and Viviana standing at the entrance. Gabriel suddenly felt an intense, sharp pain shooting around his head when he saw them, which gave Caleb the chance of escaping.

Once the three of them were gone, Gabriel lied on the floor, curled up in a ball, looking defeated. The other members surrounded Gabriel with pity and sadness, except for Dante and Kristjan. "What happened?" Dante asked as he crouched down to put his left hand on Gabriel. Gabriel looked up at Dante with bloodshot eyes and blood on his lips from biting down on them from the pain. The pain slowly subsided, and Gabriel was able to get back on his feet with the help of Helen and Francesca.

Arabella and Amelia joined them as they were all huddled together with concern on their faces. "This was a bad idea, Gabriel," Arabella said as she walked toward him, wrapping her arms around him. "I did not think it was well planned to have the rest of our members on the second floor while you were in the same room with Caleb. The kid obviously has some heavy grievances toward you, Gabriel, and sometimes it is not possible to ever persuade someone to follow your mindset, especially with his broken heart from you," Arabella said.

Gabriel gently pushed Arabella away and walked away from the crowd so he could finish the bottle of blood, which was still on the table, and throw Caleb's glass away. The other members slowly headed for the dining quarter, took seats where they could, and waited for Gabriel to say something. "What happened back there, anyway, Gabriel?" Arabella asked.

Gabriel remained silent for a while and shook his head. "I do not think I handled him all too well, but he is not an easy creature to deal with," Gabriel said. "I believe in being honest about my feelings, but if he keeps disregarding me, shutting me off, and walking away from our talks, I cannot always be an understanding and sympathetic person. I can only handle someone's rude behavior and anger up to a certain extent until I cannot handle it anymore."

Everyone else exchanged glances with each other. Gabriel drank down the entire bottle and turned around to face the other covens. "I tried my best, so I will leave it at that. If there is a battle in the near future, we will all be more prepared than last time," Gabriel said.

Dante was not certain if what he was going to propose was going to come across as being rude, but he decided to give it a shot. "So, Gabriel," Dante said. "Have you ever considered letting one of us males, for example, take over as head-of-shape-shifters?" Gabriel scrunched his brow at Dante.

"What? Why would you ask me such a question? If I were to leave my position as head of shape shifters, I already proposed this to my daughters, Dante," Gabriel said.

Francesca put her hand on Dante's shoulder and looked up at Gabriel. Arabella looked over at Francesca and then at Dante. "Never mind, Gabriel. I felt bad when I saw you on the floor, and I apologize for my question. I did not mean to cause you any suspicion about me, Gabriel. In case you may need a strong male figure, I am willing to help you out," Dante said.

Gabriel shrugged and ignored Dante. Lucien, Vladimir, and Adrian then came down the stairs and headed for the dining quarter. "Where have you been?" Gabriel asked. Lucien growled at Gabriel.

"We were keeping your daughters and grandchildren safe, Gabriel," Lucien snapped. "The fact that Arabella and Amelia were down here gave Caleb a sense of safety, because if we were around, Gabriel, that would cause Caleb to distrust the situation even more."

Gabriel nodded. "Fair enough, but I wonder if you heard the lovely commotion that took place?" Gabriel asked. Lucien and the other men nodded.

"No, inviting Caleb over was the worst plan ever. I did not think it would go like this, but okay. Let the battle commence."

Everyone exchanged glances. "Is there any other in-between step we could take, Gabriel?" Lucien asked as he looked at the other members. Nobody had an immediate answer. Amy then came out of the room and walked down the stairs. "What if I talk to Caleb?" Amy asked. Gabriel quickly got to his feet.

"Absolutely not!" Gabriel yelled. "You or Ginger are never to be around those guys."

Arabella looked over at Amy with confusion. "Why would you say something like that, Amy?" Arabella asked. Amy approached the dining quarter and stood next to Arabella.

"I can be used as bait to lower his guard and give Caleb a chance to trust me," Amy said. Arabella looked over at Gabriel to see what he was thinking.

"No, Amy," Gabriel said. "I do not want you to be used, because that could also be the end of you. Look, we can just give this some time to diffuse and think about a new plan."

Ginger then came down the stairs and walked toward the dining quarter. "What is going on?" Ginger asked. Gabriel rolled his eyes and sighed. "Mother?" Arabella smiled and looked over at Gabriel.

"We are now in a new planning phase," Arabella said. "What are you doing down here? Where are the children?" Suddenly there was a broken window again, and the infants started to cry in Amy's room. This time, half of the coven ran outside, and the other half ran to Amy's room.

There was nobody outside, and the infants remained in the crib. There was a brick with a note on it.

Dear Ambrose family,

Next time, do not lie or deceive your guests anymore with false lies. We did not kidnap your children, but your grandchildren will be coerced into hating you for your lies, Gabriel. We will talk soon.

There was no name, but it was obvious who had sent the letter. Gabriel held the moist and muddy brick in his right hand, looked outside, and saw nothing but darkness. Darcia and Alistair entered Amy's room. "Where have you two been?" Gabriel asked.

Darcia looked outside. "We scoped the areas, Gabriel," Alistair said. "We saw Larry from a distance and saw Viviana and Bianca closing in on the castle." Gabriel shook his head.

"After they had you both kidnapped? Alistair, brother, dear," Gabriel said. "Why must you and Darcia act like this?"

Dacia cleared her throat and looked over at Alistair. "Gabriel," Darcia said. "We are not children, nor are we weak. The fact that we got kidnapped was because we scoped Larry's house a while back to see what was going on, and his strong friends managed to overpower us. Now that we are strong and healthy again, we do not shy away from seeing them again. Please do not talk to us like we are juveniles," Darcia snapped.

Alistair chuckled at Darcia's response and stopped when Gabriel glared at him. "You want to know why I act like this?" Gabriel asked. "I do not enjoy getting angry at anyone, but I act like this because I am worried about everything. Is that not a good reason for me to act like this?" Gabriel said as he was raising his voice.

Darcia shook her head and left the room, and Alistair followed. "I do not like being spoken to by him, Alsitair," Darcia said once they reached the top of the stairs. Gabriel quickly ran over to both Darcia and Alistair.

"Forgive me for my actions, Darcia, Alistair," Gabriel said. "I was really hoping that Caleb would understand rather than act so extreme. I do not consider myself a monster, as I still have no idea where I came from, how Arabella got pregnant, or anything else. I wanted a son, found Caleb, and gave him a beautiful life. He even looked like he was enjoying it."

Alistair and Darcia gave Gabriel a blank stare. "We want to help you, Gabriel, but for the love of our relationship, especially since we have been wonderful family members to Amy on her journey, we would love to have more respect and admiration and less criticism and frustration towards us. Besides, I thought you wanted to be alone with Caleb," Darcia said.

Gabriel nodded. "That is all true, but I am also me, someone who has feelings and someone who can only handle criticism up to a certain extent, as well. I did try my best," Gabriel said.

Alistair nodded, but Darcia still felt a bit reluctant to accept Gabriel's response, especially since they did put their lives and relationship with Gabriel at risk, especially during their trial. Darcia rolled her eyes and sighed. "Okay, Gabriel. You are a man of feelings and can only handle criticism up to a certain extent," Darcia said sarcastically. Gabriel smiled.

Darcia then walked down the stairs, headed for the dining quarter, and saw that the time was going on to two o'clock in the morning. Alistair joined Darcia and wrapped his arms around her. "Everything is going to be okay, Darcia," Alistair whispered. Darcia sighed and turned around to hug Alistair.

"I feel so drained from everything, Alistair," Darcia whispered. Alistair held Darcia in his arms.

"I know, Daria, as do I," Alistair whispered. They stood in each other's arms till they heard the other members entering the dining quarter.

Gabriel remained up with Amy to make sure he was not going to do anything behind his back. "Amy, you must promise me and really take my request seriously to not go over to Caleb, even if you think this might help," Gabriel pleaded. Amy nodded. "I want you to say it, Amy. Nodding has no value in this important agreement. If you ever go near Caleb or Larry, there would be a high-risk chance that you will die within minutes because of how they would want to see me suffer or that they would be worried that I sent you out to spy on them."

"I promise, Father, that I shall not go over to Caleb," Amy said as she kept her eyes focused on his. "Especially since the children do need their mother." Gabriel nodded and smiled.

"A good reason, Amy. Think about the fate of your children if something were to happen to you. Of course I would not send them off to the human world, but it might not even work to bring you back, like what happened with Daniel.

Amy nodded, remembering how out of it she was when she stood in the back of the courtyard during the funeral. "Okay, Father," Amy said. "I will not do anything to increase dangerous situations." Gabriel smiled before he gently kissed Amy on top of her head and left the room. Arabella and Ginger then followed Gabriel down to the dining quarter with the other oven members.

Amy sighed and looked over at her children, who were wobbling as they walked, which made Amy smile. She admired their beauty and wondered what kind of powers they may have. Amy shrugged and decided to open up her curtains to see what the sky looked like. Then she noticed a figure standing at a distance and wondered why nobody was outside chasing it away. Amy decided to walk down the stairs and walked over to the sliding doors, and the figure disappeared. Amy felt like she was losing it.

Everyone was drinking from fresh new bottles and ignoring Amy's presence. Amy then walked back to her room to make sure she was not going crazy. This time, the figure appeared there again. Amy decided to get Bryan in her room to see

if he could see a figure. Amy walked over to Bryan and Raymond's room. Joshua opened the door. "Amy," Joshua said. "What a surprise."

Bryan looked over with confusion. "Amy," Bryan said. "Is everything okay?" Amy shook her head and beckoned for him to join her in his room. The other boys giggled and clapped at both Amy and Bryan.

"Nice," Joshua whispered. Bryan growled at his brothers.

"Head out of the gutter," Amy snapped. "Bryan, could you please come over? As a matter of fact, you all should come to."

"Goodness no, Amy. I cannot join you two," Silas snapped. The other boys continued to chuckle. Amy sighed and shook her head.

"There is something out there, and I want someone else to see if that individual is still there or not," Amy snapped before she left the doorway and walked back to her room. Moments later, Bryan entered the room, followed by his other brothers. Amy looked outside, and the figure was not there anymore. Amy sighed as if she had lost her mind.

"Amy, are you okay?" Bryan asked as he placed his left hand on Amy's right shoulder. Amy looked over at him and then outside again. "A lack of sleep and stress could cause one to see things that are not there, you know." Amy rolled her eyes and kept looking ahead.

"There was something out there, Bryan," Amy said. "I went downstairs, and the figure did not appear to be there, but after I called you in, the figure probably took off."

Bryan and his brothers exchanged glances. "Well, this was pointless," Silas said before he, Joshua, and Xavier headed back to their single room since they had to forfeit their room to Dante and Francesca. Joshua stood next to Bryan and suddenly got a vision. Caleb was trying to communicate with Amy, but every time he got closer, she left the room or area.

Bryan looked over at Joshua, scrunching his brow. "Joshua, are you okay?" Bryan asked. Amy looked over.

"Joshua?" Amy asked. "You saw something, did you not?" Joshua returned to normal. Joshua sighed and nodded.

"Caleb is trying to contact you, Amy," Joshua whispered. Bryan looked over at him and then outside again.

"Okay. What do we do?" Bryan asked. "I want to tear that creature to shreds," Bryan snapped before he headed out of Amy's room and walked down the stairs. Joshua looked over at Amy and shrugged.

"Be careful, Amy," Joshua said before he left the room and walked over to the other boys, explaining the situation. Silas, Raymond, and Xavier left the room to head down the stairs.

Once Bryan arrived at the dining quarter, Alistair and Darcia both looked up. "Caleb is outside, trying to communicate with Amy. We need to keep Amy confined in this castle," Bryan said. Gabriel got up and looked outside the sliding doors, but he did not see anything out of the ordinary and chuckled.

"Boys," Gabriel said. "Next time, do not try to prank your father figure. I enjoy humor, but I am feeling quite tense."

"Joshua saw something, Gabriel," Bryan snapped. Gabriel locked eyes with Bryan and looked over at the other boys.

"What did you see, Joshua?" Gabriel asked. Joshua approached Gabriel and nodded.

"It is true, Gabriel," Joshua said. "Caleb kept trying to get Amy alone, but she came down here before, and it seemed like he would then disappear. Gabriel sighed and smiled.

"Well," Gabriel said. "Hildegard, perhaps we should send him another letter and see if we can meet at the park again, this time for the final battle." The other coven members looked concerned and shook their heads.

"Gabriel," Dante said. "What makes you think we will succeed this time? Last time, you almost got drained by Larry and some of his friends, till Arabella and Amelia saved you."

Gabriel sighed and grabbed his glass to put it in the sink. "Okay. Well, I may need some time to create a plan," Gabriel said before he headed for his study office. Gabriel opened and closed the door behind him, saw his office chair, and shook his head. "This is all getting too much," Gabriel whispered to himself. "I think I may want to speak to Caleb myself again. My powers may not work, but a form of psychology might work."

There was a knock on the door. Gabriel opened the door and saw Arabella standing in front of him. "Gabe, there have been various topics going on regarding our plan, but I would like to know what you are planning as well," Arabella said. "Arabella," Gabriel said. "I am feeling pressured about this plan, but my death would help out," Gabriel said. Arabella sighed and shook her head.

"Stop that," Arabella snapped. "Dante is hungry to become head of all shape shifters, even though he knows Amy and Ginger are to be queens."

Gabriel sighed and crossed his arms. "I cannot picture any other plan, Arabella," Gabriel said. "What other plan could we use to get rid of Caleb harassing our daughter and me?" Arabella shrugged.

"Have patience while the other coven members are planning while we are here. I just cannot be around them for that long anyway," Arabella said with a chuckle. Gabriel smiled and chuckled.

"Take all the time you need, Arabella," Gabriel said. "Having guests can be exhausting."

Back in the dining quarter, Alistair and Darcia were joining the other coven members in discussing their plans. Alarick and Kristjan were talking about how they should leave the problem up to Gabriel while they left. Dante thought about seeing what Gabriel was planning. Gabriel and Arabella returned about an hour later, catching the attention of the other coven members.

"Gabriel," Dante said. "Where have you been?" Gabriel ignored him and sat back down in the dining quarter. "Helen, Francesca, and Vanessa have already decided to slumber, leaving us men awake to wait for you." Arabella sat back down next to Gabriel, and Darcia was on her left side.

"So," Gabriel said. "What have you all been discussing?" Alistair cleared his throat.

"We were thinking about giving this situation a bit of a break and seeing if anything else transpires with Caleb. We should make sure Amy is never alone, so perhaps Bryan and Amy could be together during their slumbering hours and Ginger and Amy during the evening hours," Alistair said.

Communication

Amy remained in her room the entire time. Suddenly, she heard a knock on her bedroom door. Gabriel, Alistair, Darcia, Dante, Alarick, Kristjan, and Arabella entered her room. Amy felt scared and intimidated by them. "What is going on?" Amy asked. "The coven members and I have discussed that you need a lot of protection right now, Amy," Gabriel said.

Amy sighed as she leaned against the bedpost. "Now what? Am I to be sent to Australia and sent back to Croatia and Greece?" Amy asked. Gabriel chuckled and shook his head.

"No, but you will be confined within the castle for a while, and you get to have Bryan with you during your slumbering times and Ginger and the rest of us during your awakening hours," Gabriel said.

Amy moaned as she got under the covers and put them over her head. "This is a nightmare," Amy murmured. Gabriel nodded at the other members.

"Well, it is about four o'clock in the morning now. Go and enjoy a nice slumber," Gabriel said. The other members nodded and left to join their wives. Arabella remained in the same room with Gabriel.

"I found that this was a better plan, Amy," Arabella said. "I would not want you to go back to Australia and be away from the rest of us. This way, it will be less painful for everyone."

Amy pushed the covers backward and sat up in bed again. "Why am I the one who is constantly suffering and not Ginger?" Amy asked. Both Gabriel and Arabella smiled at each other. "Glad you both find this amusing, but I hate this. I hated being forced to carry children against my will by someone I did not even love. Now, the father of these little creatures wants to do something with me. Just wonderful."

Gabriel sat on the edge of Amy's bed. "Look, you are quite strong and capable of handling everything, Amy Rose Ambrose," Gabriel said as he moved part of Amy's hair behind her ear. "Nothing is forever. This conflict will be over real soon, Amy. I promise that once everything is back to normal without any conflict, you can decide on whatever you want for your future. If you do not even want to be queen of shape shifters, I cannot force you or Ginger, but only persuade with good intentions."

Amy nodded. "Oh, look, your curtains are still open. Here, allow me to close them for you." Gabriel headed for the door and looked down to see two dark silhouette figures heading for the front door of the castle. "Arabella, make sure Hildegard does not open the front door." Arabella walked over to the window and quickly ran down the stairs. Nobody rang the bell. A thick envelope fell onto the floor in front of the door. Gabriel walked down the stairs and stopped right next to Arabella on the last step.

"Gabriel," Arabella whispered. "What is going on?" Gabriel did not move. He looked around to see if anyone else was around, but nobody was. Gabriel slowly snuck over to the front door and looked through the stained glass to see nobody outside. He grabbed the envelope and walked back to the stairs to open it with Arabella. Caleb had written a handwritten note addressed to Amy.

Dear Amy,

I have been trying to contact you for the last several hours. I need to speak to you in person. I know your father would not approve of it, but perhaps you could come over to our place and take the children with you so I can see my own younglings in person. I will make sure the other members will not be around, as I know that they would pose a threat.

If your father does want to come over, he can, but there is one condition. I do not want him to mention anything about my grievances because I feel like he does not respect my perception of what has happened to me. When you are ready, please write back to me with a proposal time and day so I can have a nice evening planned for us.

Cordially,
Caleb

Gabriel scoffed at that letter. "As if," said Gabriel. Arabella sighed with relief. "No, Amy is not ever going to go over to Caleb or Larry's home. He made it clear that he had no intention of making peace with me. No, this is not going to take place, ever."

After Gabriel and Arabella both headed for the basement area, Amy stood at the top of the stairs, overhearing her parents' conversation. "How can they still treat me like I am a child?" Amy asked. Amy looked around to see if anyone else was around. Ginger's bedroom door was closed. Amy did not feel tired anymore; she was just angry. What does Caleb even want from her? Why is Caleb trying to get in touch with his supposed children? He left the family to join Larry's group. I mean, he could have talked to me about his grievances and let me deal as the intermediary party. No, she needed to know what was going on."

Amy checked the time. It was going on a quarter past four. The sun had not risen yet, but she needed to find out more. Amy, without realizing what her conscience was telling her to do, grabbed her cloaked coat and walked outside the castle. Bryan left his room to enter Amy's room. He was surprised to find it open, and he walked down the staircase and inhaled her scent, which led him toward the front door.

"Oh heavens no," Bryan whispered before he left the front door of the castle to chase after Amy. Amy remained in her human form, entered the park, and saw Caleb sitting on one of the benches, looking at the fountain.

"Morning, Amy," Caleb said. "I am glad you read my note, but I did not expect you to come to me so soon." Amy shook her head out of disbelief.

"I did not," Amy said. "I overheard my father talking about your letter. I felt so angry about what was going on that I was foolish enough to be out here before dawn. What are you even doing out here anyway?"

"Enjoying the last bit of the darkness, Amy. Look, I was hoping to talk to you alone," Caleb said. Suddenly, Bryan showed up.

"Amy!" Bryan screamed. "You need to come back to the castle right now." Amy looked over at Bryan and then at Caleb.

"The sun will rise soon, Amy. Please," Bryan said as he held out his hand for Amy to take.

Amy turned back to Caleb. "I am not sure if I trust you enough to not harm me, Caleb," Amy said. Bryan took Amy's hand and pulled her toward the entrance of the gate. Amy shoved Bryan off angrily.

"Amy, please," Bryan begged. "I am supposed to be looking after you." Amy turned around to face Caleb again.

"What if I do accept this invitation of yours, Caleb?" Amy asked. "Do you promise to make sure your friends are not around?"

Caleb nodded. "I can draw for you, if you like," said Caleb. Amy quickly shook her head and headed toward the entrance of the park.

"We will talk soon, Caleb," Amy said as she and Bryan ran back to the entrance of the castle. When Bryan had opened the door, Gabriel stood at the entrance with Arabella next to him, glaring at both of them.

"What did I just say to you, Amy?" Gabriel snapped. Amy was about to respond. "No buts, Amy. You promised me that you would not go out to see that creature and look at you. Dressed in that?"

Amy felt overwhelmed, feeling tears building inside of her from sadness, frustration, and anger. "Amy, Bryan, go upstairs right now," Gabriel snapped. Amy nodded and walked ahead. Gabriel looked over at Bryan.

"Next time, do not take so long to get yourself ready to slumber, Bryan," Gabriel snapped. "Make sure that Amy does not leave her room." Bryan nodded quickly and headed for the staircase.

Arabella shook her head with disbelief. "I do not understand them, my love," Arabella said. "Why would Amy endanger herself and go over to Caleb?" Gabriel rolled his eyes before he headed back toward the basement door and walked down the stairs. Arabella followed and looked back to make sure Amy did not go outside again. It was five o'clock in the morning when they managed to get under the covers and fall asleep.

The next evening, Gabriel and Arabella both headed for the main floor and walked over to Amy. It was eight o'clock in the evening. Amy's bedroom was still closed, so they headed toward the dining quarter, seeing Vladimir, Adrian, and Lucien standing near the cooler. "Good evening, Gabriel," Lucien said as he headed for the table while Vladimir and Adrian walked to the cupboard for three empty glasses. Then they noticed Arabella and grabbed an empty glass.

"Arabella," Lucien said, acknowledging her presence. Arabella nodded and sat down next to Gabriel at the table. Lucien poured everyone a full glass of blood and sat down again.

"So," Gabriel said. "We have a big problem." The other members at the table looked at Gabriel. "Caleb is trying to communicate with Amy. She even went over to him, broke my promise of not seeing him, and decided to meet him at that same park." The other brothers exchanged confused glances at each other. "Right. So, we need to keep Amy more confined in this castle and never allow her near Caleb. If Caleb wants to come over, he best behave himself and only deal with me."

The other brothers and Arabella nodded. "Agreed," Lucien said. "Operation, protect Amy. This time from our own home." Arabella smiled and looked over at Gabriel, who was not amused.

"I am serious," Gabriel snapped. "Caleb was created by me, so he has some of my blood and charm in his system. If he is charming and seductive enough, Amy might fall for it, and then Larry has leverage again."

The other brothers nodded. "Okay," Vladimir said. "We will keep our eyes on Amy and make sure she does not leave. I thought you wanted Ginger to keep her eyes on Amy during her awakening hour."

"True," Gabriel said. "I need a bit more backup. I will be with our guests, with Arabella, I hope," Gabriel said with a smile. Arabella smiled and nodded.

"Okay, good," Gabriel said. "So, where was I? Oh yes, Ginger. She will be part of keeping Amy safe from Caleb."

Moments later, Dante and Francesca came down the staircase, then Kristjan and Helen, and lastly, Alarick and Vanessca showed up. The three men and Arabella walked away, so Gabriel could tend to his guests. Amelia then came up from her slumber. When Lucien, Vladimir, and Adrian walked up to Amy's bedroom, Ginger opened her door and stepped out. She gasped when she saw the three men. "What are you all doing out here?" Ginger asked.

The three men smiled and nodded. "Your father wants us to make sure Amy does not leave the castle," Lucien said. Ginger scrunched her brow and looked at Amy's closed door.

"What makes you think she is still sleeping?" Ginger asked. "I shall see if she is asleep, but next time, I would like to be notified about this earlier and not have you three standing outside of our bedrooms like that. Goodness."

Ginger knocked on Amy's door and heard a faint "Yes?" Ginger then opened the door and poked her head around the door to find Amy still under the covers. "It is going on ten o'clock in the evening, Amy. Would you like to get up?" Amy smiled with her eyes closed and wrapped the covers more around her.

"Soon," Amy said. "What have you been up to?"

Ginger entered her room and closed the door behind her. "Um, not much. I just got up myself. Gabriel's three brothers are out here, watching over you. Are you aware of that, Amy?" Amy scrunched her brow and sat up quickly in bed.

"Seriously? What is this about? I need to speak to Father about this," Amy said before she grabbed her robe and slippers. Amy hurried down the stairs, and the three men started to follow her.

"What is this?" Amy snapped. "Back off." Amy walked over to her father quickly. "Father, what is going on? Why are you having your brothers follow me?"

Gabriel held up his hand to Alarick, who was in the midst of his plan for Larry. "One moment, Larry, my daughter needs me for a moment. Yes, Amy? Right. We need you to be confined. After you broke my trust by going to meet Caleb, even though I told you not to, you did it anyway, especially before the sun rose. Why?" Gabriel asked.

Amy saw the other covens looking at her with concern. "I would like to discuss this with you in private," Amy said before she left the dining quarter. The other three men remained inside the dining quarter. Gabriel excused himself and walked over to his office. Amy stood outside his door and walked inside. Gabriel sat in his chair, across from Amy.

"What you did yesterday was very dangerous, Amy," Gabriel said in a calm tone. "Why did you decide to meet up with Caleb around four o'clock in the morning?"

Amy sighed. "I am sorry for doing that, Father," Amy said in a monotone voice. "I was hoping to see what Caleb really wanted. I heard the message he had sent me and how he wanted to meet with me. Why would you not share that with me?" Amy asked. "I am not a child. Of course I would be your child forever, but had you shown me his message that you did not want me to find Caleb, that would have helped."

Gabriel kept his focus on Amy and waited for her to finish. "Okay. I understand, but you need to understand this, Amy," Gabriel said. "I cannot guess or wonder if you would still try to meet with him, Amy. I need you to understand that Caleb's trying to lure you over to meet with him is a tactic that not everyone will understand. If you were not my daughter and not educated enough, you would have been kidnapped by Caleb and brought over to Larry. Do you understand how dangerous that is?"

"I understand that, Father," Amy said. "I will not go near him again. I know how stupid I was being." Gabriel nodded. "Okay. I did not mean to worry you, so I will remain in the castle."

"I will make sure of that as well, Amy," Gabriel said. "Let my brothers keep their eyes on you, so I can keep my guests tended to, with your mother and Hildegard." Amy nodded. "Okay. I am glad we had this conversation. Now, go ahead and get yourself dressed," Gabriel said.

Amy got to her feet and walked back to her room. Lucien, Adrian, and Vladimir followed Amy over to her room, and Ginger walked inside Amy's room. Amy put her clothes on, brushed her hair, and walked over to the dining room. All the other coven members, including Arabella, were gone. Amelia remained behind to finish her final glass.

"Good evening, Amy," Amelia said. "How have you been lately?" Amy gestured toward the three men. Amelia nodded and felt sorry for Amy. Amy grabbed herself an empty glass and sat down across from Amelia.

"I hate this, Amelia," Amy said. Amelia nodded and poured Amy a full glass of blood.

"Well, once this problem with Larry and Caleb is over, you will have more freedom to do whatever you want to do. Whether you decide to stay here, go back to the United States, or wherever you decide to go, I do not want you to go back to Australia again, Amy. Not that there is something wrong with that country, but what if Caleb or Larry were to travel over there as well?" Amelia asked.

Amy nodded. She was sipping from her glass and listening to Amelia. "Why is it always me, Amelia? Why not Ginger? She could also be in danger, so Gabriel could also pursue her if she got captured," Amy said. Amelia nodded.

"You do make a good point. Ginger may not be the main target, but she could also be used as well. I will let Gabriel know about that as well. She is also his daughter. Please excuse me," Amelia said before she left the dining quarter.

Darcia and Alistair came into the dining quarter and saw Amy looking sullen. "How are you feeling, Amy?" Darcia asked before she sat down next to Amy. Alistair grabbed himself two empty glasses and sat down next to Darcia, pouring two full glasses.

"Well, at least we do not have to put our lives on the line," Darcia said before she winked at Lucien and his two brothers. The other men did not respond. "Sorry, but no, this is quite serious. Are you still allowed to go outside in the courtyard?"

Amy shrugged before she looked at Lucien. "Am I?" Amy asked. Lucien nodded.

"As long as it is within the castle property, you can still walk outside, but do not leave the front door," Lucien said. Darcia smiled.

"Okay. At least you can still get some fresh air. This conflict will soon, hopefully, be resolved. Alistair and I will go out on a nice vacation somewhere in Italy, Greece, or Spain," Darcia said. Of course, we keep to the evening hours. I hope you will have your freedom back again, Amy. As much as I saw you suffer during our trip together, I did enjoy our time together. Remember how I took you out to that mall?"

Amy smiled and chuckled at that memory. "Yep. I remember how scared and angry I felt about meeting the big-grand Gabriel Ambrose for the first time," Amy said. Everyone at the table smiled. "I remember how we had to wear suits to meet him. How bourgeois, of course, but perhaps those are silver lining memories." Darcia smiled as she placed her hand on Amy's and sighed.

"Gabriel is quite something, Amy. He has his wonderful moments of being loving and supportive, and then his crazy moments of being chaotic.

Lucien cleared his throat, staring down at Darcia. "Um, yes," Darcia said. "I will not say much about him. He does love you and Ginger, Amy. Do not ever forget that." Then Darcia smiled and winked at Lucien. Lucien looked away. Darcia and Alistair sat with Amy for a few minutes, drinking the blood. Then Darcia and Alistair walked away. Ginger came into the dining quarter.

"What did you do?" Ginger snapped as she looked down at Amy sternly. "Why do I need to be babysat as well, Amy?"

Amy shrugged and smiled. "You are also Gabriel's baby, too, Ginger, so you may also need some extra looking out for," Amy said before she chuckled. Ginger growled at Amy before she walked over to Gabriel's office.

"Father, why must I be confined? Larry obviously wants you, and he is using Caleb to get at Amy. How am I included in this mess?" Ginger asked. Gabriel sighed before he looked over at Ginger.

"Amelia mentioned how you are also just as important to me as Amy is. Amy may have a weaker stance regarding her children, but what about you, Ginger?" Gabriel asked.

"What about me?" Ginger asked. "I am of no importance to Larry, Caleb, or Viviana. Why am I included in being looked after?" Gabriel waited for Ginger to finish her ranting.

"What if they decide to use you as leverage, Ginger? You are strong and capable of fighting off any potential predators in our world, but I do not want to increase any chances of you being put into such circumstances." Ginger sighed, rolling her eyes at her father. "We need to make sure they do not hold any type of power or leverage over us, so we have a good chance of taking down their group, Ginger. Hopefully, within a month, it will all be over."

"A month?" Ginger snapped. "Having Lucien, Vladimir, or even Adrian follow me around the castle? Please Father." Gabriel started to feel frustration building inside of him from Ginger.

"Enough. My word is final, Ginger. Go about your own schedule, but do not think about leaving this castle," Gabriel snapped. Ginger felt sadness inside of her. Gabriel never spoke to her like that. Attack, yes, but snapping at her was something she never thought would happen.

"Yes, Father," Ginger said before she turned around and left his office, leaving the door open. Gabriel sighed, got out of his chair, and closed his door. The other coven members were in their own bedrooms, talking with each other and sharing stories of their backgrounds. Bryan was in his own room with Raymond and Joshua until Joshua got another vision.

Bryan and Raymond exchanged glances. "Josh," Bryan whispered. "What is happening?" Joshua had a vision of Caleb, who was shifting himself into Amy's friend Jenna and making up some story about how she met her parents, Emma and Nathan, and wanted to know where Amy was. Joshua returned to his normal self. "We need to warn Gabriel about this, and Amy," Joshua said before he left the room.

Silas and Xavier heard the three boys leaving and decided to follow them downstairs. When Joshua reached Gabriel's office door, he knocked gently on the door and waited for Gabriel to respond. "Enter," Gabriel said as he was focused on a book in his hands. He looked up in confusion at the five boys. "Yes?"

Bryan nudged Joshua to talk. Joshua cleared his throat, swallowed nervously, and licked his lips before he felt comfortable enough to speak. Gabriel put the book on his desk and leaned back. "Um," Joshua said, trying to find his voice because Gabriel's looking at him made him feel nervous. "We, or I, um, wanted to let you know that Caleb is planning something new."

Joshua sighed with relief. Gabriel cocked his head, keeping his eyes on Joshua. "Yes, Joshua. Go on," Gabriel said with tension in his voice. "What does Caleb have planned?" Joshua sighed as he was fidgeting with his hands. "What are you doing? Please do not think that you should be afraid of me, Joshua. Look, I never did anything bad to you boys, so why must you see me as someone who is out to get you? What does Caleb have planned from your vision, Joshua? Please tell me."

Joshua sighed. "He will try to pose as one of Amy's old high school friends and ring the doorbell here to ask for Amy. We need to keep our eyes out for anyone who looks like someone that Amy knows," Joshua said. Gabriel nodded. "The boy is getting clever," Gabriel said. "Caleb, I mean. Okay, we need to take some stronger measures and keep Amy away from any potential visitors who might be looking for her. Thank you, boys, especially you, Joshua, for your amazing hard work."

The boys left Gabriel's office. Joshua closed his eyes and sighed with relief. "No matter how often I need to talk to Gabriel, I have a hard time talking to him, brothers," Joshua said as he felt a bit lightheaded from his talk. The five boys headed for the cooler, drinking down an entire bottle of blood. Amy was outside on the patio with Gabriel's three brothers, including Ginger. The five boys decided to join Amy and Ginger.

"Good evening, girls," Bryan said as he stepped outside onto the patio. The three men looked over at the boys. "We are not Larry or Caleb, so have no worries. So, it looks like you both are confined inside the house. We have something we need to share with you, Amy. Caleb might try to shape shift himself as your old friend Jenna, if you remember what she looks like."

Amy started to feel scared. "Jenna? Seriously? Now he is going to go after people that I once knew from my past? Sheesh. That boy needs to be dealt with as soon as possible. How do you even know that, Bryan?" Amy asked. Bryan looked over at Joshua. Then Amy looked over at Joshua. "One of your visions? Goodness, but thank you, Bryan, and, of course, Joshua. Man, this situation is making it almost unbearable, boys. What can I do to keep my sanity in tact?"

Ginger shook her head out of disbelief. "I think there is not much we can do about anything, sister dearest," Ginger said. "Nothing can make our situation better." Amy started to feel sad inside. She looked back at when she was a little girl, wearing princess dresses and shoes, playing with her dolls and stuffed animals, and meeting Jenna for the first time, and then she got to be with Martha for a while. She wanted to have a normal life in college, meet the guy of her dreams (unless it was Bryan, who is the man of her dreams), get married, have a job, and have a beautiful future. No shapeshifters, drinking potions, traveling around the world, feeling scared and angry. Amy shook her head and tried to forget about her past.

"Okay, well, thank you for letting me know, boys. I will make sure that if I see a Jenna figure around that, I will ignore it and walk away," Amy said.

Fourth Round

Caleb remained in his bedroom at Larry's home, trying to figure out his next plan. He kind of regretted how he got mad at Gabriel. He could have also played him and seen how far he could get. Anyway, he needed a new plan. He walked over to the living room to find Larry and Bianca sitting with their other friends.

"I think I may have another plan in mind, friends," Caleb said. Larry looked up with interest. "What if we get some of Amy's old acquaintances involved as bait?"

Larry smiled and chuckled. "What happened with your date with Gabriel, Caleb?" Larry asked. Caleb shrugged.

"He was starting to get to me, Larry. I could not handle his lies and deception any longer. I was worried that he would lure me into his seduction or use his persuasion powers on me, Larry. I had to leave," Caleb said before he sat down in one of the chairs across from Larry.

"That is disappointing to hear, Caleb," Larry said in a calm voice. "I needed you to play the game so you could get closer to Amy and her children." Caleb remembered the moment in the park and his letters to Amy.

"I forgot to mention this part as well," Caleb said. Larry kept his focus on Caleb, blocking out the sounds of the television. "I did lure Amy out into the same park where we often spar or fight with Gabriel's friends. Remember?" Larry nodded. "Okay. I lured Amy out, and I managed to get her outside. I told her to keep in touch with me. Obviously, Gabriel was already one step ahead of me in keeping Amy detained. That is why you, even Bianca, or I can shapeshift into Jenna to lure Amy out. If Gabriel will not allow that, we can always try to track down some of Amy's friends."

Larry smiled at Caleb and then laughed. "I love your evil side, Caleb. Do whatever you feel is appropriate for this situation," Larry said as he leaned back against the couch. "Good work." Caleb smiled and walked over to the kitchen to get himself a drink. He started to remember Gabriel looking at him and started to feel a bit remorseful about the whole situation.

Viviana looked in the direction of the kitchen and walked over to Caleb. Caleb leaned against the kitchen counter, holding his glass in his left hand. Viviana entered the kitchen and crossed her arms, analyzing Caleb's demeanor. "Are you okay?" Viviana asked, causing Caleb to gasp. "Jumpy?" Caleb smiled and shook his right finger at Viviana.

"I am just deep in thought, Viviana, nothing much," Caleb said. "I am just trying to figure out my plan."

Viviana kept her eyes focused on Caleb. "Uhuh, so how are you feeling about it?" Viviana asked. Caleb shrugged.

"Just fine. I mean, I wonder when Larry is going to also start planning. It does get exhausting," Caleb said. Viviana did not respond.

"Any remorse, Caleb? Did Gabriel do anything to you to cause you to feel upset or unwell?" Viviana asked.

Caleb started to feel uncomfortable being interrogated by Vivivana. He walked past her until Viviana grabbed him by his left arm, causing his glass to shake. "If you still have any feelings for Gabriel, I completely understand," Viviana whispered. Caleb smiled and nodded until Vivivana released her hold on him. Caleb walked back to the couch and sat next to Larry to distract himself. Viviana joined them, smiling over at Caleb.

"What have you two been talking about?" Larry asked. Caleb shook his head as he focused on the television, not knowing what he was looking at.

"Nothing, Larry. I am not sure what Viviana is doing, but I am here sipping my drink," Caleb said. Larry rolled his eyes before he focused back on the television screen.

Back at the castle, Gabriel walked over to Joshua, Silas, and Xavier's bedroom. Joshua answered the knock and gasped. "Gabriel," Joshua whispered. Gabriel smiled.

"Evening, boys," Gabriel said. "Joshua, could I have a word with you again?" Joshua looked over at his brothers, who smiled and nodded at Joshua. "If you want to invite me in so you do not have to be alone with me, that would work."

Joshua stepped aside to allow Gabriel to enter the bedroom. Bryan and Raymond headed into the room. Gabriel turned around.

"Yes?" Gabriel asked. Bryan and Raymond smiled, gesturing at the bedroom. "I need to speak with Joshua, but feel free to join in." Bryan and Raymond both entered the room and closed the door behind them.

"So," Gabriel said as he faced Joshua. Joshua sat down nervously, biting the side of his right thumb nail, looking up at Gabriel with confusion.

"Joshua, when you saw a vision of the fake Jenna showing up at the front door, when is he planning to do this?" Gabriel asked. Joshua took his thumb out of his mouth, sighing. "Well?" Joshua made clicking sounds with his tongue, rubbing his hands together.

"I am not sure, Gabriel. These visions that I have do not come with a timeframe. It just happens. Plus, not every vision does come true," Joshua said.

"Okay. Could you give me an example of when your visions have not come true? I need to make sure that Amy does not know about our potential guest," Gabriel said.

Bryan cleared his throat and raised his right hand. "We may have already told Amy about Caleb being Jenna," Bryan said. "I am sure nothing bad will happen." Gabriel looked up, feeling more at ease.

"Okay. Well, we should keep our eyes and ears focused on potential intruders. Larry will probably be changing his tactic constantly to make sure we do not let our guard down," Gabriel said. "I will take my leave, but keep Amy distracted and away from the front door for a while."

The boys nodded simultaneously. Gabriel smiled and turned around to leave the bedroom. Gabriel headed for the dining quarter to find his brothers and Amelia drinking blood from their own glasses. "Evening Gabriel," Lucien said, raising his glass to Gabriel's entrance. Gabriel grabbed his own glass and sat down across from Amelia.

"We need to make sure Amy does not go near the front door, in case Caleb has something planned for her," Gabriel said. The other members nodded.

"How does Amy feel about this situation, Gabriel?" Amelia asked.

"Well," Gabriel said. "Amy is not happy about having my brothers babysit her. Speaking of which, make sure when Amy is awake that you three watch her closely." The three men nodded. "And Amelia, perhaps give Amy some girl time and help her get through these moments. What is Arabella up to lately?"

Amelia shrugged. Arabella entered the main floor from the basement in an evening gown, with her hair behind her shoulders. "Evening friends, Gabriel," Arabella said. Gabriel got to her feet to get Arabella a glass and placed it at the head of the table. Arabella sat down next to Gabriel, at the head, waiting for the bottle to be passed to her. Gabriel poured Arabella a full glass of blood and placed the bottle next to her glass.

"What are you all talking about?" Arabella asked. Amelia looked over at Arabella. "We should make the girls, both Amy and Ginger, feel more comfortable about this situation, my love," Gabriel said. Arabella took a sip and placed the glass down.

"How do you mean?" Arabella asked. "I mean, she can still go out onto the courtyard, and she normally does her own thing in her own room and around the place anyway."

Gabriel sighed as he leaned against his chair. "What I mean is to keep her relaxed and calm and avoid any anger or frustration. She has Bryan, who is most likely to be her actual true love, so that should also keep her distracted and occupied. I mean, what do Amy or Ginger normally do anyway?" Gabriel asked.

"Coming from someone who has not known anything about their children," Arabella said teasingly. Gabriel growled. Arabella got to her feet to walk away.

"Arabella, please do not go. Forgive me for growling, but that topic is still quite sensitive," Gabriel said. Arabella nodded.

"I understand. It was not appropriate to mention that, but why would you not know what they normally do, Gabriel? Have you not talked with them about their interests and hobbies?" Arabella asked.

Gabriel shrugged. "We sort of talked, but I am not entirely sure about their hobbies or interests. I mean, Amy loves Bryan and Ginger; I am not entirely sure who she loves," Gabriel said. Arabella sighed. Gabriel looked over.

"Now what? Arabella, I do not go into their love and intimate lives. I feel that is more your topic, Arabella. If Caleb were my son, I would want to hear about his romantic interests, but my daughters? I feel that no boy is actually good enough for them, my love. Sons are important, but daughters hold a special spot in my heart that no other boy or man should even be on my mind," Gabriel said.

Arabella smiled. "That was beautiful, Gabriel," Arabella said. Amelia smiled. "I wish my parents had spoken to me like that," Amelia said. "I wished I was important and not just seen as a relic or just a member." Gabriel shook his head.

"Just because you all are members does not mean that each of you is less important to me as your headmaster, leader, or father figure," Gabriel said. Suddenly, they heard a bedroom door open on the second floor and then close. "Brothers, could you check in on the girls?" Gabriel asked. The three men nodded and went up the stairs. "Okay, I think the other ones will show up. Please excuse me, ladies."

Arabella and Amelia then got to their feet to see how much blood was still needed for their guests. "Hildegard," Arabella said. Hildegard came into the dining quarter with her coat on.

"Yes, madam," Hildegard said. "What can I do for you?"

"Could you do another blood run? They are quite thirsty," Arabella said. Hildegard nodded.

"Okay. Well, I will do the blood run, but then I might need to stop at my old house for some time," Hildegard said. Arabella nodded.

"Okay. You will return to our home, right?" Arabella asked. Hildegard nodded.

"Of course, I forgot something and need to get it," Hildegard said before she grabbed the crate with the empty bottles to put it in the car that Gabriel had purchased for her. Arabella watched Hildegard leave for the garage, wondering what Hildegard needed to do.

"Amelia," Arabella said. "Did Hildegard seem okay with you, or does she seem somehow secretive?" Amelia looked over at Arabella.

"Not sure, but she did seem kind of jittery, Arabella," Amelia said. "Well, see how she seems when she returns to our home." Arabella nodded.

"I guess," Arabella said. "So, anyway, what have you been up to lately?" Amelia shrugged.

"A little of this and a little of that. I mostly waste my hours reading books for Gabriel," Amelia said.

Arabella nodded. "I hope he is not overworking you, Amelia. We should enjoy ourselves a nice evening sometime, just us girls," Arabella said. "Perhaps there would be like a twenty-four-hour open spa or something like that." Amelia smiled.

"A spa is something I have never been to, but I am not sure if we actually need that type of relaxation, but it could never hurt, I guess," Amelia said. "Well, I guess I should hit the books again and read up more about potential hazards and benefits that our kind may need," Amelia said before she left the dining quarter. Alarick, Vanessa, Dante, Helen, Francesca, and Kristjan then entered the dining quarter.

"Evening Arabella," they all chimed. Arabella nodded. "How are we doing with the blood supply?"

"Our housekeeper is doing a blood run, but she will stop at her house, but we should have plenty by tomorrow evening," Arabella said.

"Okay," Francesca said. "Is there enough for the rest of us?" Arabella nodded.

"Of course, feel free to take as much as you need, my friends," Arabella said. Francesca, Alarick, Vanessa, and Kristjan grabbed some glasses and placed them on the dining table, while Dante and Helen grabbed two bottles to serve to each other. Gabriel entered the dining quarter and acknowledged his guests.

"The girls are entertaining themselves as per usual," Gabriel said. My brothers are watching over them, so we should be good for now." Arabella smiled and nodded.

"Good to hear, Gabriel," Arabella said. "I think I might want to see what they are up to. Excuse me." Arabella walked up the stairs toward the second floor to find Alistair and Darcia heading down the staircase. They waited for Arabella to walk upstairs.

"Good evening, Arabella," Darcia said.

"Good evening to you both," Arabella said as a response. "How have you two been holding up?" Alistair and Darcia both shrugged.

"We just take each day as it comes, Arabella," Alistair said. "I mean, we are just waiting around to see what Caleb has planned for us.

Arabella nodded. "Other than that, we just hang around and occasionally go outside, but we actually stopped our need to hunt humans," Darcia said. "Remember that time, my love, when Bryan saw a girl that looked like Gabrielle and he sort of felt protective of her?" Alistair smiled and nodded.

"I remember that," Alistair said. "Bryan was telling me how he wanted to become the father figure of those children. That was interesting to notice."

Arabella smiled. "Bryan does seem to love those kids, at least whenever I see them together," Arabella said. Darcia nodded.

"I believe so," Darcia said. "Well, my love, shall we get ourselves something to eat or drink?" Alistair smiled and nodded.

"See you around, Arabella," Alistair said with a small wave. Arabella watched the two walk down the stairs and then decided to walk over to Amy's bedroom. She knocked on the door and waited for Amy to answer.

"Yes?" Amy asked. Arabella opened the door and found Amy feeding her children with a bottle.

"Oh, I see you are busy. Sorry, my sweet," Arabella said. Amy smiled and shook her head.

"Oh, come on, mother. If you want, Nathaniel is quite hungry. Gabrielle already had her fill. She is a good eater. Maggie, on the other hand, is a bit fussy, so if you could give my son his bottle, that would help me," Amy said. Arabella smiled and nodded. She grabbed a full bottle of blood and sat down next to Nathaniel. He crawled into her lap, holding his hands out to the bottle.

Arabella adjusted Nathaniel on her lap and placed the bottle in Nathaniel's mouth. He clasped both his hands on each side of the bottle and drank. Arabella watched Nathaniel drink, which awoke some sad feelings inside of her. "This is what it feels like to watch a child drink? I wish I got to experience that with you and Ginger, my sweet child," Arabella said as she kept her eyes focused on Nathaniel.

Nathaniel drank down the bottle in just a few minutes and closed his eyes. "Where is Hildegard, anyway?" Amy asked. "She normally helps me with my children, like giving them a bath, putting on a new diaper, stuff like that." Arabella looked up at Amy.

"I have gotten some training and experience from Hildegard while you and Ginger were out together. Do you remember?" Amy thought about it and nodded.

"Right. Of course. Plus, you are the grandmother of my children, so you should be able to help me out," Amy said. Arabella smiled and nodded. Arabella helped Amy in the nursery, bathing Nathaniel in the sink and waiting for Amy to turn up with Gabrielle and Maggie in her arms.

Suddenly, the garage door opened and closed. "Hildegard," Darcia said. "Good to see you here again. Did you need help with anything?

"That is all right, Darcia. I just bring in two crates from the trunk of the car and bring them in at my own pace. I hope the blood is to your liking," Hildegard said.

"Oh yes, Hildegard. The vintage is quite nice this time. Is there anything different from the donors?" Darcia asked. Hildegard appeared to have bruises on her wrists, and her lower lip looked a bit swollen. "Are you all right?"

"Hm? Oh yes, dear Darcia. I am just fine," Hildegard said. The other members, including Alistair, looked over at the housekeeper, analyzing her. "I just mildly injured myself. Nothing much." Then Hildegard walked back to the garage to grab the second crate and bring it into the castle. She placed some of the new bottles in the cooler.

Darcia looked back at Alistair with concern. *Do you think Caleb is behind any of the injuries, my love?* Darcia thought. Alistair looked at Darcia and then at Hildegard, watching how frail she looked. Where did Hildegard have to go?

She does look different. Perhaps Gabriel should look her over for any potential bite marks or scratches. Alistair thought. Both of them kept their focus on each other until Gabriel entered the dining quarter.

Darcia looked over at Gabriel with concern. "Is everything okay in here? It almost sounds too quiet," Gabriel said. Alistair made a gesture towards Hildegard and pointed at her wrists. Gabriel approached Hildegard as she was putting the other bottles in the cooler. Gabriel stood ten feet away from Hildegard and cleared his throat.

Hildegard turned around and gasped. "Master Gabriel," Hildegard whispered. Gabriel smiled and looked Hildegard up and down. Gabriel crossed his arms. "The new load of blood is ready for you." Gabriel nodded and looked over at Hildegard's wrists.

"May I?" Gabriel asked as he reached for Hildegard's hands. She quickly pulled them back to her body and crossed her arms. "Hildegard, may I?" Hildegard started to shake because of her nerves, shaking her head.

"Are you okay, Hildegard?" Gabriel asked, adding some of his persuasion powers to his voice. Hildegard's eyes went black.

"Larry," Hildegard whispered. "He fed from me." Gabriel turned with anger at his group. "Caleb lured me to his home while I was at my home, and they fed."

"What were you doing at your home, Hildegard?" Gabriel snapped. "We had all of your items and personal belongings brought here."

"I forgot…" Hildegard whispered. "A locket that I wanted to give to Amy for her birthday. It was meant for me, but I never had children, so I wanted to secretly give it to Amy so she could put her children's pictures in it." Gabriel released his hold on Hildegard's mind and took a step back.

"Did you need some blood, Hildegard?" Gabriel asked. "This is none of our blood, so it is purely human donor blood."

Hildegard shook her head. "I just need to consume some food with iron in it. Nothing more, master Gabriel," Hildegard said. Gabriel nodded.

"Well, I am sorry that happened to you, Hildegard. Perhaps avoid your house, and perhaps even allow one of my family members to tend to your evening errand of blood banks," Gabriel said.

Hildegard shook her head again. "That is okay, Gabriel. I promise not to let it happen again," Hildegard said.

"It is not about a promise, Hildegard. It is about how weak-minded humans are to our powers. This is not an attack on you for being weak, but I think I know why Larry chose you. You were used as bait before to lure Caleb over, so now they think you are up for grabs. We need to be extra careful now. I wonder if the other coven members would like to invite their humans over," Gabriel said.

The other coven members shook their heads. "Absolutely not," Dante snapped.

"Yes, I agree with Dante," Alarick said. Kristjan nodded along with them. "We are not going to offer our humans up for you, Gabriel. You have this beautiful Hildegard, and we have ours. Do not think about persuading or coercing us into surrendering our humans to you.

Dante sighed, shaking his head. "I am starting to feel unsettled being in this castle. Francesca, if you would like to leave, I will support you," Dante said. Francesca shrugged.

"I think we should see what this Larry creature still has planned, for the sake of knowing that Larry is a potential threat to us all, my love," Francesca said. Dante sighed. Helen and Vanessa both nodded.

"I mean, what should we do right now, Gabriel?" Kristjan asked. "Should we not at least go for a full attack? I mean, we can keep playing games with persuasion or other powers, but I think we are up for the final time of ending Larry and Caleb." Dante smiled at Kristjan.

"I do agree with Kristjan on his plan. We have been sitting here doing nothing while Larry and Caleb are causing drama and harm to our team, Gabriel. We could swill up your blood source till all the blood banks are empty, or we could finally see how far we can get this time. What do you think, Gabriel? Leave your daughters and your grandchildren alone here," Dante said.

Arabella overheard the conversation that was taking place as she held Maggie in her arms while she entered the hallway. Amy saw her mother. Ginger then came over from her room. "What is going on?" Ginger asked. Arabella turned around and shook her head.

"They are planning their final attack, my dears," Arabella whispered. "I cannot believe how they feel that it is the best option. Here, Ginger, please take Maggie and put her in the crib. I need to see what your father is planning."

Arabella entered the dining quarter, causing every member to turn to face her. "My love," Gabriel said. "Is everything okay?" Arabella shook her head.

"I can ask you the same thing, Gabriel," Arabella said. "What is this about you planning the final attack? Why now, Gabriel?" Gabriel looked over at Hildegard.

"Larry attacked our housekeeper, Arabella," Gabriel said. "I am starting to get tired of it."

Arabella looked over at Hildegard. "Is that true, Hildegard? How did you get attacked?" Arabella asked.

"Not now, Arabella," Gabriel snapped. "She went over to her house to get Amy a locket for her children and got lured over by Caleb." Arabella shook her head with disbelief.

"Why did you have to get that right now, Hildegard? I mean, you were sort of used as bait to lure Caleb over, and you decided it was the right moment to do that? Hildegard, why?" Arabella asked. "You could have died."

"Arabella, enough. I already spoke to her about it. She understood and promised to never go outside without an escort again," Gabriel said. Arabella felt anger building inside of her.

"Now you all want to fight? Are you all certain you will win this time? Burn them all and rip their bodies apart. Are you?" Arabella sternly asked. "If anything were to happen to any of you, especially you, Gabriel, you are like the king on a chess board. If you were to die, it would be game over."

"No, Arabella," Gabriel said. "Amy and Ginger would take over. You can remain queen for as long as you want, but if anything were to happen to me, life will continue on." Gabriel said. Arabella waved off Gabriel and headed back for the staircase. Darcia and Alistair felt Arabella's frustration.

"Perhaps we should rethink this plan, Gabriel," Darcia said. Gabriel started to chuckle. "I mean, we need to make sure we are fully prepared for the final battle, and not because Hildegard got injured, no offense."

Hildegard walked over to the kitchen area to prepare herself a steak with some spinach grilled in garlic butter. The other members walked over to the living quarter. Amelia came up to the main floor and walked over to the dining quarter. "Goodness, something stinks in here," Amelia said. "Oh, sorry, Hildegard. Nothing about you. I am just not used to smelling human food right now. But hey, what is with your wrists, Hildegard? Are you okay?"

Hildegard nodded. "Fine, Amelia," Hildegard murmured, returning her focus back to the pan and watching the steak cook nicely. Amelia walked over to Hildegard, trying not to let the nausea get to her.

"If you need some iron or a blood transfusion, you know where to find me. That looks like it was quite painful. Did Gabriel allow you to do that?" Amelia asked. Hildegard quickly shook her head.

"Of course not. It was…" Hildegard said. Amelia kept her focus on Hildegard. "It was…Larry."

"Oh goodness, Hildegard. Here, let me help you. I can help you regain your strength fast," Amelia said as she put her hands on Hildegard's arm to pull her in the direction of Amelia's sleeping quarter.

"No, thank you, Amelia. Please let go of me," Hildegard snapped. Amelia felt surprised by Hildegard's response. "Sorry, but with this steak and spinach, I should regain my iron levels again, Amelia."

Amelia nodded. "Okay, but if that is not enough, please do not hesitate to knock on my door, even if I am asleep. You are an important member of our family, Hildegard. Even if you are human," Amelia said. Hildegard smiled, nodded, and walked back to the pan, which started to crisp up her steak quicker. Amelia left the dining quarter and saw the other members in the living quarter.

"Good evening, friends," Amelia said. The other members smiled and greeted Amelia. "So, what is this about wanting to fight Caleb and Larry for the final time? Why do you all think it is a good time to go on the full attack?"

Gabriel sighed. "Did Arabella have you come to complain about it as well, Amelia? Look, right now we are just discussing. We have not taken any steps toward going over to Larry's home. After Hildegard got attacked, we are starting to feel the need to take strong measures, Amelia. If you do not want to take part, which I will completely understand, you and Arabella can stay with my daughters and grandchildren. Nothing bad is going to happen right now, okay?" Gabriel said.

Amelia sighed before she turned around to get herself a glass of blood. Hildegard cleaned up the pan and sat at the table, eating her dinner. Amelia grabbed herself a full glass of blood and sat across from Hildegard, raising her glass to Hildegard. Hildegard chuckled and raised her wine glass to Amelia. "To the end of everything, I guess," Hildegard said. Amelia smiled.

"I guess so, Hildegard. Gabriel is off to running around and creating unrealistic plans, and then running back home in pieces," Amelia said. "Goodness, I should not be talking about Gabriel like this. I hope he knows what he is doing. The last time, we lost two of our members to several of Larry's. So, Hildegard, I have been meaning to ask you. What made you want to stay at this place anyway?" Hildegard swallowed the last steak piece.

"I had two choices: either end up in potential poverty or live a life of luxury. Of course, the second option came with a big price. The price of living amongst shapeshifters and sneaking around blood banks. How about you, Amelia? How did you become a shapeshifter, or are you more of a sorceress?" Hildegard asked. Amelia nodded. "Well, I used to live around the world doing tricks for a living. Then I came across Gabriel at one of those bars around Romania. I was doing a little trick, and he was quite intrigued by my skills. He was quite handsome. I think he may have seduced me, but he told me that he could add me to his family. I just remembered the first night I was invited into his home. Arabella was beautiful. Her youth, her strong eyes, and her lips. They were both beautiful to look at. I think they felt the same about me as well," Amelia said.

Hildegard listened to Amelia's story. "Sounds beautiful," Hildegard said. "Did you have love in your life with children?" Amelia smiled and shrugged. "No, not really. There were many suitors that I came across, but I enjoyed the life of a bachelorette. I mean, Gabriel was quite handsome, but Arabella does deserve him. They make a beautiful couple," Amelia said.

Hildegard felt a sense of jealousy coming from Amelia and wondered if Amelia wanted to have Gabriel to herself, but she did not dare ask such questions to a shape shifter.

First Step

Back at Larry's apartment complex, Larry was flossing his teeth. "What was that with that housekeeper?" Caleb asked. "Me, luring that housekeeper over to our place? Larry, we may have signed our death warrant. "Look, we need to focus on the main plan, which excludes other members, such as humans. I think they might come for us, but if you think we are prepared for a final battle, Larry, you are out of your mind."

Larry ignored Caleb. "Right. Just ignore your conscience. If something were to happen tonight, Larry, I might not want to be part of your battle. I do not feel ready to fight," Caleb said. Larry felt anger boiling inside of him, grabbed Caleb by his shoulders, and shoved him against the wall.

"Now you listen, Caleb," Larry snapped. "I did what I felt was right. I need Gabriel to understand that we are not weak, but that we are in the midst of preparing for the final battle ourselves. Were you able to get that girl to show up to our home, Caleb?"

Caleb nodded. "I used Amy's voice," Caleb said, mimicking Amy's voice. Larry smiled.

"You almost sounded like her for a moment, Caleb. I never knew you had that power. What other powers do you have?" Larry asked. Caleb shape shifted into Gabriel.

"I am Gabriel; I am mister tough guy," Caleb said jokingly. Caleb returned to his original self. "Gabriel taught me how to shape shift. Remember how you thought he was me? I have some of Gabriel's blood life inside of me, so I should be able to do whatever Gabriel can do."

The doorbell rang. Jenna was at the front door with her backpack and suitcase, but felt confused when she saw the two men smiling at her. "Um," Jenna said. "Is Amy around?" Both Caleb and Larry smiled as they gestured for her to enter. "Amy?" There was silence. Jenna then turned around in fear. Viviana and Bianca showed up behind her with their arms closed. "Dang it, I should have known I was going to be had," Jenna said.

"Had?" Larry asked.

"What?" Jenna asked. "It means that I got hoodwinked, tricked, and fooled. Look, if you want money, I can ask my parents to wire it over." Larry smiled, shaking his head.

"No money is needed, Jenna, was it?" Larry asked. "No, we know where Amy lives. We need you to understand the whole situation before you see her." Jenna scrunched her brow.

"Um. What are you even talking about? Look, where is Amy?" Jenna asked. Larry put on his charm as he approached Jenna. Using his persuasion powers, he grabbed Jenna by her shoulders. Jenna's eyes went dark.

"Amy is with her father in a castle. She is a shape shifter, and she would love to invite you over to her home," Larry said. "Before I do, would you be interested in trying something new?" Jenna nodded mindlessly. "Bianca, Viviana, please bring our special guest a little drink." Bianca headed for the kitchen, grabbed a blood pack, and handed it to Larry. "Now okay. Tilt your head backwards and let the liquid go down your throat." Larry poured some of the blood from the pack, which caused Jenna to wince. "It is an acquired taste, dear Jenna," Larry said. Larry snapped his fingers until Jenna woke up.

Back at the castle, Gabriel was in his office with Lucien, Vladimir, and Adrian, writing out a plan. "Has Joshua noticed anything new, brothers?" Gabriel asked. The other men shrugged. "I mean, Caleb shape shifting into Amy's friend? That could become a potential danger to both my daughters."

The other men nodded. "I agree," Lucien said. "I am glad that we have someone like Joshua who could foresee such incidences, because Amy would definitely fall for Larry and Caleb's trap." The other men nodded.

"We need to keep Joshua close to us, brothers," Gabriel said. "He did mention that his visions either change or are not always accurate, so we need to see if there are any changes to Caleb's plan," Gabriel said. The men nodded. "So, perhaps we should go over to Joshua. For some reason, he seems uncomfortable whenever I approach him. The other boys, like Bryan, seem to have no problem communicating with me," Gabriel said. "Why is that?"

The other men smiled at Gabriel. "Probably, because you are the patriarch and headmaster of us all. That could be a bit intimidating for someone like Joshua," Lucien said. Gabriel waved him off, shaking his head.

"Whatever," Gabriel murmured. "So, perhaps one of you three or one of you could engage more with Joshua?"

The other men exchanged glances. "What about Alistair being the go-between, Gabriel?" Adrian asked. Gabriel sighed. "I mean, you are quite close with Alistair, and he respects you." Gabriel shrugged and nodded.

"If that is the best plan you can think of, okay, we can use Alistair. We do need to keep in frequent contact with him regarding Joshua's visions," Gabriel said. "Okay. That is one step in our plan. Perhaps we should take a break for now."

The other men smiled and nodded. "I could not agree more with you, brother," Vladimir said before the four of them headed for the dining quarter. The other coven members were in their rooms, talking with each other and catching up on as much rest and relaxation as possible, so they would be physically prepared for their upcoming battle.

Suddenly, the doorbell chimed from the castle. Gabriel and the other men smiled as they exchanged glances. "I wonder who that could be," Gabriel said teasingly. The other men chuckled. The four of them walked over to the front door, but Hildegard beat them to it. Jenna stood at the entrance.

"Good evening. I am Jenna, Amy's best friend," Jenna said. Amy, with her sharp hearing, heard a familiar voice and came running down in her speed until Gabriel grabbed her, holding her back.

"Father, what are you doing?" Amy snapped. Jenna smiled and waved at Amy.

"Amy, it is so good to see you again," Jenna said. "I was wondering if I could come in?" Amy struggled against her father's strong arms.

"Of course you can," Amy snapped. "Father, please let me go."

"Brothers, close the door now," Gabriel snapped. Lucien closed and locked the front door.

"What was that?" Amy snapped as she was released from Gabriel's arms. "Jenna, you are welcome to stay here. Father, please open the door.

Bryan overheard the commotion and remembered telling Amy about how Caleb was shapeshifting into her best friend. He remained in his room with Raymond and Joshua. Joshua started to fidget. "Joshua, what is going on?" Bryan asked. Raymond looked over with confusion. "Are you all right?"

"Caleb is back at the house, Bryan," Joshua whispered. "The real Jenna is outside of the castle. Caleb is trying to get Jenna to see the true identity of Amy, so that would hurt their friendship."

Bryan looked at the bedroom door, opened it, and left to run downstairs. "Wait!" Bryan screamed. "That is not Caleb at the door. It is Jenna." Gabriel scrunched his brow in confusion and looked at the closed door.

"Are you sure about that, Bryan?" Gabriel asked. "Why did Joshua not come to us about his new vision?"

"I am not sure, but we need to invite that girl inside before she goes back to them. She might have been used as a pawn to lure Amy out. Caleb is back at the house," Bryan said. Gabriel quickly undid the lock and opened the door, but Jenna was nowhere to be seen.

"This is your fault, Father," Amy snapped. "Now Jenna is probably going to be a hors d'oeuvre for Larry or Caleb. I need to find her."

"No," Gabriel snapped. "Let Lucian, Adrian, and Vladimir find her, Amy. You cannot ever leave this place." Amy felt tears building in her eyes.

"Everything is your fault, Father. Everything!" Amy screamed. "From the moment I was born to being lied to! How could you?" Amy started to punch Gabriel until Bryan grabbed Amy from behind, pulling her backwards and holding her in his arms. "Now my best friend is going to die. All because of you."

Amy released herself from Bryan's hold on her, ran up to her room, and slammed the door. The men sighed and left the castle, leaving Gabriel and Bryan alone. "I should talk to her," Gabriel said. Bryan held up his right hand.

"No, let me," Bryan said. "She has a lot of grievances and anger toward you, Gabriel. I can at least try to simmer her fire." Suddenly, Arabella and Amelia came over to the front door area.

"What happened?" Arabella asked. "Why was Amy screaming at you, Gabriel?" Gabriel waved her off so he could finish his blood drink in the dining quarter.

"Gabriel," Arabella said. "Please do not ignore me. Why was Amy screaming at you?" Gabriel took two gulps of blood before he felt like himself again.

"There was a bit of a mishap, Arabella," Gabriel murmured. "Amy's friend showed up at the door. I thought it was Caleb who had shifted into her friend and closed the door on her. Joshua had a vision of Caleb shape shifting into Jenna or something like that."

Arabella sighed, shaking her head. "How do these things keep happening, Gabriel? Was it Caleb?" Arabella asked. Gabriel shook his head.

"It was the actual human girl, Arabella," Gabriel said. Amelia crossed her arms and looked over at Arabella.

"Well," Amelia said. "I am not sure what I should do right now. I think I will retire to my sleeping quarter and see what I can do for the upcoming battle. Please excuse me."

Arabella returned her focus to Gabriel. "What will happen to that girl?" Arabella asked.

"I sent my brothers to go looking for her. Amy is upstairs in her bedroom, upset at me, my love," Gabriel said. "I try my best, you know. I do not intentionally create problems for the fun of it."

Arabella sighed. "I know, Gabriel," Arabella said. "There does come a time to use common sense. I am sure you did not intentionally hurt Amy just now, but Amy does have a lot of trust issues, even if you cannot see that right now. She has a lot of anger towards you and perhaps even me. Darcia and Alistair were more like parents and supporters for both our daughters. They are not the best, but they are also better than other supporters."

Gabriel listened to Arabella. "I did not mean for anything to happen, Arabella," Gabriel whispered. "None of this was meant to be. I was never meant to be a shapeshifter, unless there is some parallel universe that says otherwise. I was not meant for any of this, unless I reincarnated as this, due to my past life." Arabella smirked at Gabriel's choice of words. "What? I never meant for anything to happen. Plus, I have apologized and lived with guilt and remorse, and there is not much I can do about this situation. Please, Arabella, try to get Amy and Ginger to be easier on me. There is not much I can do to compensate them. They got educated for the most part, got to live in a secure home, and now they are the princesses of this castle. What more can I do to make them feel happier than before?"

Arabella shrugged. "I am sure you did your best, Gabriel," Arabella said. "I can talk to Amy for you. That is something I am willing to do." Gabriel nodded and smiled.

"I appreciate that, Arabella," Gabriel said before he walked over to her to hug her. Arabella placed her fingertips on Gabriel's shoulders, not feeling entirely comfortable with his hugs. Gabriel released his hold on her and walked back to his chair. Arabella walked over to the staircase to head up to Amy's bedroom.

Back at Larry's apartment complex, Jenna returned to his home. "Well, how did it go?" Larry asked. Jenna shrugged.

"Not sure. I believe it was her father, the one who looks quite handsome, who held Amy in his arms, and this other rugged-looking man with greasy long brown hair closed the door on me and locked me outside. "Amy did seem happy to see me, which was nice. That man who held Amy seemed quite overprotective of her, holding her close in his arms. Is that her father? I mean, I do not really see much resemblance, but if so, she is lucky to have some of his genetics. How old is he anyway?" Jenna asked.

Larry rolled his eyes. "Yes. Quite handsome," Larry snapped bitterly. "I am not sure of his age, but perhaps you should go with Caleb sometime. Gabriel and Caleb have history."

"Gabriel? Is that the man's name?" Jenna asked. Larry jokingly tapped his forehead with his right hand.

"Oh dear. I should probably give you more details on those people, if that is what you would want to call them," Larry said.

"What do you mean, if you want to call them that? What are they? Vampires or werewolves?" Jenna asked. Larry did not respond. Jenna chuckled. "Right. Amy was born into a family of supernatural creatures. Perhaps that is why she combusted into flames at school. The sun or moon must have damaged her sensitive skin." Jenna laughed at her own ridiculous phrase. "Whatever they are, they seemed somewhat impolite about meeting new people."

Larry nodded. "They are, dear Jenna," Larry said. "Gabriel is not a friendly man." Jenna shrugged.

"Perhaps Amy takes more after her mother," Jenna said. "Whatever it is, would it be wise for me to invite her over to your place, Larry?"

Caleb looked over at Larry, shaking his head. "Well, sweet Jenna, Amy might not be allowed to leave her home to come here. Her father will not allow that. Perhaps you should try it again, but perhaps also leave out the part about being here with us at the moment," Larry said.

"Why?" Jenna asked. "Does this Gabriel have something against you?" Larry nodded.

"I am afraid so, sweet Jenna. You should not worry about such thoughts. If you want, you can ask Amy to join you out for a little evening walk, or perhaps even allow her to invite you in," said Larry. Jenna shrugged.

"I guess I could do something like that, Larry, was it?" Jenna asked. Larry smiled and nodded. "Amy and I are close enough to be sisters, so I guess I could try to allow her to let me inside her home. I mean, was that a castle, Larry?"

Larry chuckled and nodded. "Yes, it is, sweet Jenna," Larry said. "Amy lives in a castle. Perhaps your theory about mystical creatures may make more sense." Jenna shook her head with disbelief.

"I do not believe in such stories, Larry. Amy looked fine to me. She looks beautiful, but I have not noticed anything different about her," Jenna said. Larry shrugged. Suddenly, there was a chime from their doorbell. Larry and Caleb exchanged glances.

"Who could that be?" Larry asked. "Caleb, could you see who would be ringing our door at this hour?"

Caleb reluctantly walked over to the door and peaked into the little hole, seeing Lucien and two other men next to him staring at the door. "Larry, Caleb," Lucien said as he was pounding the door. "Let the girl go." Caleb walked back to Larry.

"Larry? We might have potential dangerous visitors at our door. What should we do?" Caleb asked. Larry quickly got to his feet, assembling the other members on their feet.

"Whatever Gabriel has planned this time, boys and girls, we will not allow him to harm us," Larry whispered. The banging got louder and louder.

"Larry!" Lucien screamed. "Open the door and release the girl!" Larry exhaled slowly, heading for the door. Caleb stepped aside, giving Larry some space. Larry placed his hand on the doorknob, turned it, and slowly opened the door. Lucien pushed himself through it, causing the other members to hiss and growl.

Jenna gasped and backed up toward the nearest wall in fear. "Oh goodness, what are you guys?" Jenna whispered. "Monsters. Larry was right." Larry turned around with sharp teeth and black eyes, growling in Jenna's direction. Adrian and Vladimir quickly ran into the apartment, seeing about forty members in one direction and Caleb and Larry behind them. Jenna was panting and whimpering in a corner. Lucien saw Jenna and headed towards her until Viviana and Bianca stood in front of Jenna.

"What were your plans with the girl?" Lucien asked. "Gabriel got a mixed vision story from Joshua, seeing Caleb shape shift into that girl. Now, it appears that you brought an innocent human into our world, Larry. That was not only dangerous to us but also to you, Larry. Exposing ourselves to the human world."

Jenna placed both her hands over her mouth to block out her moans and squeaks. Lucien looked over at the girl with sympathy in his eyes. "What do we do about this?"

"I know," Larry said. "How about you take the girl and allow her to see her best friend?" Vladimir and Adrian looked over at Larry, growling at him. "Or, you can end her right here." Lucien sighed, shaking his head.

"Jenna," Lucien said as he crouched down. Both Viviana and Bianca remained in front of Jenna, glaring at Lucien. "Do not be frightened, child. If you want to see Amy, feel free to come with me and my brothers."

Jenna was hyperventilating throughout the whole situation. "Who are you?" Jenna asked shakily. "What are you?" Lucien sighed and rose back up.

"Larry, this will all be included in your future funeral speech," Lucien said. "Doing such a dangerous act toward our kind. I am deeply disappointed and ashamed of our kind. You are more dangerous than Gabriel."

Jenna's hyperventilating caused her to faint on the floor. "Okay, here is the plan," Lucien said. "If you let us take the girl, we can tell her that it was all just a bad dream." Larry scoffed and laughed, causing the other members to join him. "Poor ignorant Lucien," Larry said. "What makes you think we will allow you to take her? What makes you think you will even leave our home alive?"

Lucien nodded at his brothers. The three of them took off their coats, threw them on the floor, and took off their watches, placing them gently near their coats. "Well, I guess we have no other choice than to defend ourselves," Lucien said. The forty members stood near them, getting into fighting positions. Lucien nodded at his brothers again, and the group charged and jumped on the three men. Larry and Caleb stood in the back, near the front door. Lucien was able to take down five of the group members, while Adrian was able to take down two, and Vladimir was able to take down three of them.

Suddenly, there was more growling and hissing around the entrance of the apartment complex. Darcia and Alistair showed up with Dante, Alarick, and Kristjan. Darcia decided to leave Larry up to the men so he could go attack a few of his group members. The fighting was turning into a heavy load for Larry's group. Dante and Alarick grabbed Larry, throwing him across the room. Caleb bolted out of the apartment complex and saw Gabriel approaching the group with Arabella and Amelia.

Caleb quickly got to his knees with his hands clasped together. "Please, Gabriel," Caleb begged. "It was never my fault." Gabriel growled at Caleb, grabbed him, and threw him across the street toward the other building. Amelia and Arabella then ran into the room until Arabella noticed a girl on the floor in the corner. Larry quickly grabbed Jenna and held her in his arms.

"Nobody move, or the girl gets it," Larry snapped. Everyone stopped with their fighting, holding each other in a headlock or biting position.

Suddenly, Amy and Ginger came running toward the apartment until they saw Gabriel approaching Caleb on the ground. "Father!" Amy screamed. Gabriel turned around, and suddenly Caleb jumped on Gabriel, causing him to fall. Ginger quickly ran over to Caleb, yanked him off, and pinned him to the ground. Gabriel looked over at the apartment, noticing how quiet it was.

Suddenly, there were sirens and lights turning on. "Oh dear," Gabriel whispered. "The humans have called about our fight. We must leave immediately. Arabella, Amelia, brothers," Gabriel whispered. Nobody came out. Gabriel quickly ran inside to find Larry holding Jenna cradled against his chest. Gabriel was in shock over everything.

"Well, well, well, the man of the hour decided to show up," Larry said teasingly. Gabriel looked over at his brothers.

"What happened?" Gabriel asked. Then he checked his watch. It was going on four thirty in the morning. "We need to go. Everyone, disperse the situation." Amy quickly ran into the apartment with Ginger next to her and gasped.

"No," Amy whispered. "You heartless monster." Gabriel quickly grabbed Amy, holding her to him. "No."

"Amy, we need to go. We will get your friend back," Gabriel said as he started to back away. "Everyone, we should head back to the castle. The sun will rise real soon." Amy started to struggle against her father's embrace. Ginger started to cry at the whole situation, seeing Amy in distress and the whole fighting just taking place. "Come." Dante released his hold on two of Larry's friends, Alarick backed away, and Kristjan quickly punched one of Larry's friends till Larry growled at him.

"We shall speak again soon, boys and girls," Larry said. "Now off to bed." Gabriel left the apartment with Amy in his arms. Ginger, Arabella, and Amelia then followed, and the rest left the apartment complex. There were police cars out in the front, holding their guns at the group.

Gabriel used his persuasion powers on the police enforcement about how it was all just a bad dream and how nobody called them and told them to leave. Seconds later, the police took off. Gabriel felt exhausted from everything and tripped over his feet. He released Amy from his grasp and got back to his feet to continue walking back to the castle.

The Change

When Amy made it back to her bedroom, she broke down crying. She sat on the edge of her bed, covering her face with both her hands, crying long tears. Ginger came into the room and sat down next to her, holding her in her arms. Arabella then came up and stroked Amy's back.

"I am so sorry about everything, my girls," Arabella whispered. "I never wanted any of this to happen to you both."

Amy exhaled. "I hate him," Amy whispered. "For everything that he stands for, I have not had one moment in my life of feeling happy when I was around him." Arabella ignored Amy's anger but nodded anyway. "Everything. From lying to me to deceiving us? Why are you not angry at this, mother?"

Arabella smiled. "I have been angry at Gabriel for many years, my child, but I want to focus my attention and devote my energy to my girls," Arabella said.

Ginger listened to both her mother and sister. "I agree with Amy," Ginger said. "Father has done nothing but create problems. Now that Jenna is in danger, this is a new kind of low, mother." Arabella looked over at Ginger. "What?"

"Jenna will be okay. Larry would not cause any harm to that girl. Larry is smart enough to not jeopardize his future as well. Right now, just relax as much as you can, my girls. I am going to see what the other members are up to," Arabella said before she left Amy's bedroom.

Amy saw that it was going on around five o'clock in the morning. She felt so hopeless to know that her best friend was in the clutches of Larry, the monster. She wished she could just go outside and bring Jenna back to her castle. This was perhaps the worst moment of her life. Losing perhaps the last person that grounded her in her life. She could not handle the fact that she was so close but yet so far away from her. Amy was quite exhausted from everything, but she was not able to sleep so well that morning. She tossed and turned many times and only got about four hours of sleep.

When it was five o'clock in the evening, the sun was starting to set. Amy got out of bed and remembered she had not even put her pajamas on. She put her shoes on and headed down to the dining quarter. Amy was quite thirsty. Instead of grabbing herself a glass, she opened up an already-opened bottle of blood and swilled it down. Amy heard footsteps walking toward the dining quarter. "Amy," Gabriel said in a hushed tone. "I need to speak with you."

Amy felt sadness building in her throat. "Yes, Father," Amy said. "What would you like to speak to me about?" Gabriel grabbed himself an empty glass, placed it on the table, and grabbed a new bottle of blood. Amy stood by the cabinet and did not sit at the table. Gabriel sat down, poured himself a full glass, and looked up at Amy.

"I will sacrifice myself for your friend, Jenna," Gabriel said. Amy felt tears falling down her cheeks. "Please listen to me, Amy. If anything were to happen, I would take full blame and make sure you were all taken care of. I will go over to Larry's home alone without my friends and bargain myself up for Jenna. I know he wants me dead, and perhaps that would give Jenna a chance of returning home safely."

"Why?" Amy whispered. "Why must it always end so badly in this family?" Gabriel swilled down a glass of blood, got to his feet, and headed for the door. Amy ran after him. "Stop! Father, you cannot leave us right now. I am sure Jenna will be okay. I cannot lose you right now. Please."

Gabriel turned around and ignored Amy's pleas. He opened the castle door and saw how shadier it was getting. Arabella came over to the front door.

"What are you screaming at, Amy?" Arabella asked. Amy broke down as she was pointing at Gabriel, leaving them at a distance.

"No," Arabella said. "What is he doing now?" Amy was unable to speak as she felt like she was choking on her tears.

Arabella ran over to Lucien's sleeping quarter, banging loudly. "Lucien!" Arabella screamed. Lucien opened the door with fear in his eyes.

"What?" Lucien snapped. "What could be so important to be waking me up so early, Arabella?"

"Gabriel is going to sacrifice himself for that human girl," Arabella said. Lucien sighed, shaking his head.

"What is wrong with him?" Lucien asked. "Hang on and let me get my affairs in order. Could you wake up Adrian and Vladimir?" Arabella nodded and knocked on Adrian's door first, told him what Gabriel was planning, and then knocked on Vladimir's door. The three men got themselves dressed and ready to track Gabriel down.

Once Gabriel arrived at the apartment complex, he smelled the human quite clearly. He looked over to see if he could find a doorbell of some kind and pressed it. The doorbell chimed, but nobody answered the door. Gabriel pressed the bell again, and this time, Caleb showed up at the door with shock in his eyes. "Gabriel," Caleb gasped. Gabriel nodded. "What are you doing here? I am not in the mood to fight again. My body still hurts from yesterday."

Gabriel sighed. Caleb noticed Gabriel's sense of defeat and stepped outside to close the apartment door. "What is going on, Gabriel?" Gabriel sighed, shaking his head.

"I am here to bargain with you both. Take me and end me, and let the human girl go back home," Gabriel said. Caleb had a look of horror and shock in his eyes.

"Are you serious?" Caleb asked. Gabriel nodded.

"My daughters both hate me for everything that I have done to them, and now with this girl here, how is she? Is she even alive?" Gabriel asked.

Caleb nodded. "Yes, she is, but you? Wow. I never knew this moment would come to pass, Gabriel. I always thought you would dodge all potential deaths and end up winning in the end," Caleb said. Gabriel had tears building in his eyes. "How sad you look, Gabriel. Just standing here wanting to die," Caleb chuckled. "Well, will you and Larry let the girl go?" Gabriel asked. Caleb sighed and shrugged.

"Perhaps you might want to come inside. Please be careful of the broken glass and broken chair pieces, Gabriel," Caleb said as he gestured for Gabriel to enter the apartment complex.

Slowly, the other members started to wake up and enter the living room. Then Larry showed up in his drawstring pajamas and bathrobe. "My goodness, tell me this is not a dream, Caleb," Larry said. Caleb shook his head.

"He is here to bargain his life for the human girl," Caleb said. Larry chuckled as he looked back at Gabriel.

"Are you serious? The moment where the big old Gabriel Ambrose, head of all shape shifters, will cease to exist?" Larry asked. Gabriel shrugged.

"Huh," Larry said. "Well, the girl is on the couch right now. I am not sure if she is awake, but she probably feels quite exhausted. I need to get myself a little morning beverage. Please, Gabriel, join me at the table."

Gabriel walked over to the table, sat down, and waited for Larry to return. Caleb sat down at a seat adjacent to where Gabriel was sitting, looking at him with pity. Larry came back with his blood pack and a glass from his kitchen cupboard, sat down, and poured himself a drink. Larry started to laugh as he poured himself a drink. "Why would you want to give up your life to a simple human girl, Gabriel?" Larry asked.

"She is Amy's best friend, and if anything were to happen to me, Amy would probably suffer greatly, Larry," Gabriel said. Larry smiled at Gabriel. "How did you manage to find her anyway?" Larry licked some of the blood off his fingers.

"That was not an easy task, but I do remember Amy's high school, where I often picked her up, and I managed to find something like a directory or some archive of students that went there, used Amy's voice, of course, and managed to find that girl," Larry said.

Gabriel nodded. "Clever," Gabriel said. Larry chuckled after he took his first sip. "May I see the girl?" Larry looked over and snapped his fingers for one of his friends to bring Jenna over to the table. Jenna, with her sleepy eyes and drowsy expression, walked over to the table. "Goodness, have you fed off her, Larry?" Larry shook his head.

"Of course not, Gabriel. She was just used to baiting you both. Due to the fact that Caleb tried to lure you both here with his dreams of your grandchildren, which failed, I had to take stronger measures. Or at least, Caleb did most of the work, right, Caleb?"

Caleb nodded. "Well," Gabriel said. "I am not sure if I actually believe you, Lawrence Harrison. She looks quite ill to me. Jenna, dear, may I analyze you for a moment?" Jenna walked over to Gabriel, allowing Gabriel to check her neck, wrists, ankles, and thighs, and then looked deep in her eyes. Gabriel used his persuasion power on Jenna. "Are you hurt?" Gabriel asked. Jenna nodded and moaned. "Larry, what is going on? She obviously looks more ill than yesterday. What did you do?"

"Jenna, could you tell Mr. Gabriel why you do not feel so well?" Larry asked. Jenna moaned and opened her mouth. "Okay, I will tell him. I fed her some of our blood supply, or mostly, my own blood supply," Larry said.

"You heartless monster," Gabriel snapped as he grabbed Jenna. "If you do not release her back home, we might need to have another fight." Caleb then locked the front door when he noticed Lucien and his two other brothers, along with two women, were headed for their apartment.

"Are you willing to risk exposure again, Gabriel?" Larry asked. "Or should we just end you right now?"

Gabriel placed Jenna on the chair where he was sitting, took off his blazer, and rolled up his sleeves. "I guess there is no other option than to end you, Lawrence Harrison," Gabriel said. The other members, some of whom looked bruised with scratch and bite marks around, were on one side of the apartment. Viviana and Bianca then showed up, yawning and stretching till they saw Gabriel.

Larry jumped on top of Gabriel, causing Gabriel to push him off, then Caleb pounced on Gabriel while he was still on the floor, and soon Viviana and Bianca tried to hold him down. Gabriel, with his strength and skills, managed to push everyone off of him. Before Gabriel got a chance to get back up, Larry pounced on him again and bit him hard on his throat, causing Gabriel to scream in pain.

The doorbell was chiming louder and louder until Lucien managed to break down the door and go after Caleb. Bianca stayed in the background this time, looking around at various objects to use. Arabella then came in, grabbed Larry, and held him in a headlock to give Gabriel some time to get back to his feet. Then two other members of Larry's group attacked Gabriel from behind, and Gabriel threw both of them across the room.

Vladimir and Adrian then took off their blazers and ran toward the other group members, while Amelia was trying to get Jenna out of the house. Once Amelia got Jenna outside, she ran back in for support. Gabriel then went after several other members, until some of them curled up in fear.

"Please," some of the members begged. "We never meant to harm any of you." Gabriel looked back at Adrian and Lucien, holding Larry, while Vladimir had his eyes focused on Caleb.

There was a loud coughing sound and a throw-up sound coming from outside. Amelia walked outside to see if that was Jenna. Jenna started to writhe in pain and spasm. "What is going on?" Gabriel asked. Amelia stepped inside.

"Whatever Larry did to her, she is to become one of us soon. If she does not get the proper transitioning process, she will die. Gabriel, you need to give her some of your life source."

Gabriel felt an intense, sharp pain in his body, but not from any of Larry's friends. "Gabriel, you must do it," Amelia snapped with sadness in her voice. "Do it." Gabriel headed for the open door, hearing Jenna gasping and choking. Gabriel knew it was probably going to end his relationship with Amy. His plan of bargaining for Jenna failed. He looked down at Jenna with guilt and shame, grabbed a glass shard from the floor, slid his left wrist, and let the blood drip into Jenna's mouth. Gabriel felt sadness inside of me.

"Brothers, Amelia, and Arabella, take Larry back to the castle with us. This problem needs to come to an end. I do hope it is tonight," Gabriel said as he picked up the rigor mortis Jenna in his arms, carrying her back to the castle. Caleb, Viviana, and Bianca followed them to the castle from a distance, watching them.

"What do we do, Caleb?" Bianca asked. "They cannot kill my brother. He is the victim in all of this."

"I know Bianca," Caleb said. "We need to see what they are going to do with Larry. Please follow me over to this area where we can see their dungeon through stained glass. Larry's other group members stayed behind in fear and anxiety. Caleb led the two women over to the shrubs, where they could see the dungeon with their sharp vision.

Gabriel carried Jenna over to his sleeping quarter in the basement, placed her on the bed, and left back to the main floor to see what his brothers, Amelia and Arabella, had planned. He felt so sick and nauseous from everything. Amy came over to where they were and gasped at the sight of Larry. "What is he doing here?" Amy snapped.

Gabriel was on the main floor and walked over to the front door area. "Please follow me to the dungeon area, brothers, and ladies," Gabriel said.

"Father, please tell me what is going on," Amy asked as her lip was quivering. Gabriel looked over at Amy with tears in his eyes.

"Soon, my sweet and beautiful child," Gabriel said as he led the group over to the dungeon. Amy followed them and saw Larry being pushed behind bars while Lucien locked up the prison cell.

"Father!" Amy begged. "Please tell me. What is going on?" Gabriel gestured for everyone to walk ahead while he and Amy brought up the rear. "Please."

"Amy," Gabriel said as he swallowed. "Jenna is being transitioned right now." Amy gasped and shoved her father out of grief. "Listen to me, Amy. Jenna will survive, but not like a human. I tried to bargain my life for hers, but Larry had already given her some of his blood. This is not like those movies, Amy, where vampires or werewolves bit each other. Our kind is our reality. I had a feeling Larry was not going to be easy on us, but it happened."

Amy got to her knees, sobbing loudly and covering her eyes. Whenever Gabriel would try to console her, she would take a step away from him. "I hate you," Amy snapped. "I really hate you." Gabriel felt sadness inside of him, but this time he refused to leave Amy. "Why are you not going over to get yourself a drink, Father?" Amy snapped. "What are you doing staying here with a broken toy?"

Gabriel did not respond. He kept his gaze focused on Amy and wrapped his arms around her while she was trying to push him away, squirming in his strong embrace, screaming, whimpering, and trying to get away from him. Moments later, she lost all of her strength and energy and fell into his arms. Gabriel carried Amy in his arms over to her bedroom, tucked her in, and closed the curtains to let her rest. When Gabriel left the bedroom, Arabella waited for him outside in the hallway. "My love," Gabriel whispered. Arabella was unable to speak. "Are you okay?" Arabella shook her head. "No, Gabriel," Arabella whispered. "I will never be okay. How is that girl?"

Gabriel forgot about how he left her alone in their bedroom. "She is hopefully still asleep in our bed, Arabella," Gabriel said. Arabella nodded. "I will check up on her." As Gabriel headed down the stairs, he saw Alistair and Darcia heading down the stairs as well. When Gabriel looked up at them, they knew something bad had happened, but nobody said anything.

Gabriel then walked down toward his sleeping quarter, opened the door to their bedroom, and saw a motionless figure in their bed. Gabriel walked over to Jenna and heard her soft breathing. That gave Gabriel a reassuring feeling, knowing that he did the right thing at the right time. Gabriel headed back to the main floor and saw the other members slowly approaching the dining quarter. They all looked shocked at Gabriel.

"What happened?" Alarick asked. Kristjan and Dante then looked over at Gabriel. Gabriel shook his head.

"Larry may have transitioned Amy's best friend. He lured her over here, pretending to be Amy, and gave her some of his life source," Gabriel said. The women gasped as they almost dropped their glasses. The men sighed with disbelief.

"I know," Gabriel said. "I feel this intense burning and stabbing pain inside of me. Amy will never forgive me, which I have respected. I just cannot handle anything anymore, my friends."

The members did not react. Alistair and Darcia heard the sons waking up. "Well," Gabriel said. "Whatever you all decide on, you can leave whenever you want. We have Larry in our dungeon right now. Caleb and the other ones stayed behind."

"Really?" Darcia asked. "So, Larry is here. Does that mean we can end him forever, Gabriel?"

Gabriel shrugged. "I might want someone else to do the honors. Perhaps Amy and that girl," Gabriel said. "Let them get their anger and frustration out on him for what he has done." The other members looked confused.

"Well," Dante said. "Francesca, whenever you are ready to go back home, I will support you. The other members also nodded.

"I am ready to leave Romania. Perhaps forever," Francesca said. "I did not bring much with me this time, so once you are ready, we can head back home."

Gabriel felt a sense of loneliness and loss inside of him, watching his friends leave him. Gabriel grabbed himself a glass, but he did not feel any hunger inside of him. Ginger came down the staircase over to the dining quarter.

"What is going on?" Ginger asked. "Why is everyone leaving right now?" Gabriel held his hand up to Ginger to quiet her down.

"My child," Gabriel said. "Have yourself a glass. We have some sad news to share with you."

Ginger sat across from Gabriel without her drink. "What happened?" Ginger asked. Gabriel looked around to find everyone focused on them.

"Amy's friend is in the transitioning phase right now," Gabriel said. Ginger gasped. "No," Ginger said. "That cannot be."

"Yes, Ginger," Gabriel said. "It can, and it happened. Jenna is down in our sleeping quarter, resting up. Amy is in her room, resting from exhaustion. I am sorry about everything, my child."

Ginger felt tears inside of her. "This does not make any sense. I am so heartbroken and disgusted to hear this. What is the plan now?" Ginger asked.

"Larry is in the basement right now. I think I might want Amy to be the one to drop the blade or swing the axe. At least let them get this justice," Gabriel said. Ginger sighed with disbelief.

"I feel so dizzy right now, Father," Ginger said. Gabriel nodded and gestured for one of his family members to get Ginger a glass.

Vladimir grabbed an empty glass from the cupboard and placed it in front of Ginger. Gabriel then poured a full glass of blood for her and placed it in front of her again. "Go on, Ginger," Gabriel said. "Drink." Ginger mindlessly grabbed the drink and took a few sips.

"Amy is going to be heartbroken, Father," Ginger said. Gabriel nodded, knowing how horrible it was going to be to tell Amy.

"I know, my child," Gabriel said. "I will wait for Amy to wake up to tell her how it all happened. I never meant for any of this to happen to you or your sister, Ginger." Ginger shrugged. "I never meant for any of you to have been placed in this life as shape shifters and suffer greatly from everything that has happened." Ginger remained silent. "Now we have ourselves a little changeling. Jenna is going to need plenty of support and training. Goodness, that was something I never knew Larry was capable of doing."

"What do you expect, Father?" Ginger snapped. "Of course someone like Larry is going to use such tactics against us. I mean, you are old, but not dumb. You must have had years of experience with such incidences, Father." Gabriel shrugged.

"This is going to be something we need to work on, but it will be okay," Gabriel said. Ginger shook her head, placed her empty glass on the table, and walked over to the staircase. It was going on one o'clock in the morning. Gabriel felt exhausted from the whole evening. He decided to go downstairs to his sleeping quarter to see how Jenna was doing.

Once Gabriel entered the bedroom, Jenna quickly sat up and gasped. "Who are you? Where am I?" Jenna whispered, placing her hand against her throat. "Why does my throat hurt?" Gabriel held up his hands to calm Jenna down.

"Okay. Jenna, is it?" Gabriel asked. Jenna nodded quickly and got out of bed fast. "Easy. You might need some time to get used to your new body and life, Jenna." Jenna gave Gabriel a confused look. "Do you remember anything, Jenna?"

Jenna shook her head. "I had this horrible dream about going on a plane, meeting someone named Larry, and getting fed blood. I felt tired and disoriented," Jenna said before she collapsed. Gabriel caught her before her body hit the floor and tucked her back into the bed. Gabriel sighed. Arabella came into the dining quarter, looking at Jenna.

"Poor thing," Arabella said. "This is going to be quite a disastrous moment with you, Amy, and Jenna."

Gabriel nodded. "I know, Arabella," Gabriel snapped. "I know, I know, I know." Arabella rolled her eyes, shaking her head. "What?"

"Nothing. This new situation is going to change everything, Gabriel. Jenna's parents are probably wondering if she is even having a good time with Amy, doing girl activities like shopping, watching movies, and stuff like that," Arabella said.

Gabriel looked over at her with confusion. "Uhuh. Well, they can still do that with this new lifestyle of theirs," Gabriel said. Arabella scoffed and headed for the staircase. "Wait." Arabella turned around. "What can I do to ease the pain and suffering, Arabella? What could you advise me to do?"

Arabella sighed. "Well, I could play a role with my motherly ways of helping Jenna cope with the new situation and to help Amy adjust to this new change," Arabella said. "Perhaps you can play the father role and stay in your office room while I take care of the girls." Gabriel nodded.

"Okay, I can work with that, Arabella. If you need me for anything, please do not hesitate to involve me in your plans," Gabriel said. Arabella smiled.

"What would you do without me, Gabriel Ambrose?" Arabella asked. Gabriel smiled and hugged Arabella tightly.

"I think about how blessed I am to have you back in my life, my dear Arabella," Gabriel said. "The thought of losing you was the worst moment of my life. I could not function at all." Arabella smiled as Gabriel released his hold on her. Arabella then placed both her hands on each side of Gabriel's shoulders.

"There is a price for everything, Gabriel," Arabella said. "The price of keeping me alive in a ghost was hopefully worth it in the end, but you did cause disruption with your relationship with both Amy and Ginger, especially with this new situation," Arabella said.

Gabriel sighed. "I know. I sometimes feel that I should not be around because I seem to make situations and matters worse," Gabriel said. "What do you think?" Arabella shrugged.

"I agree with some of the things you have said just now, my dear Gabriel, but ending your life when it gets harder and tougher to handle is never the answer. So, try to learn from your mistakes and improve them when you get the chance and opportunity. The fact that you helped Ginger transition must have been a good bonding moment. The fact that Amy felt depressed about leaving Alistair and Darcia is a negative point. I will deal with Amy and see how well that goes once she wakes up. Perhaps Amy and Jenna might become best friends in the future. Perhaps one of Darcia and Alistair's sons might fancy Jenna. Who knows?" Arabella asked. "I mean, I am certain her parents will send out law enforcement to look for her in Romania, but as long as she has her new lifestyle, we can send them a letter that she decided to attend a university here, or something like that."

Gabriel smiled and nodded. "Sounds like a plan," Gabriel said. "I will go back to the main floor and see what needs to be done. If Amy is around, I will try to ease the situation, try to talk to her about what happened, and see if her mother is willing to step in." Later that night, the other coven members returned to their own homes.

Fifth Round

Back at the apartment complex, most of Larry's friends were angry. "Why did you go after that human girl, Viviana?" Larry snapped. "Look at what happened. Gabriel shows up, wants to bargain, and the girl is back in a safe environment." Caleb sighed.

"You do realize she is not officially a shape shifter yet, right, Viviana?" Caleb asked. Viviana shook his head. "Seriously? The process of becoming one of us involves biting each other. You just fed her some of your blood, which had a negative effect on her health, causing that witch girl to have Gabriel give some of his life force to her. Are you certain she is a shape shifter?"

Viviana shrugged. "I never knew shape shifters even existed until I became one, Caleb," Viviana said. "I never knew shape shifters were to be bitten. It does explain a lot as to how I became one, but Jenna? That, to me, is still new and confusing. What are your experiences, Caleb?"

Caleb shrugged. "I just remember seeing Gabriel, feeling this weird but also comfortable feeling about what happened next, and waking up in this castle feeling disoriented and thirsty," Caleb said. Viviana nodded.

"Were you bitten?" Viviana asked. Caleb did not respond. "I mean, I did not recall seeing any bite marks on you. Is Gabriel's blood that powerful?"

Caleb shrugged. "I do not know how to answer that, but perhaps since he is the father of our kind," Caleb said. Larry smirked and then chuckled at that comment.

"Father of our kind. Awe, Caleb," Viviana said teasingly. "Do you have daddy issues?" Caleb waved off that comment. "Would you like Father Gabriel to read you a nighttime story and tell you of his past as a shape shifter?"

"Enough," Caleb snapped. "He is not my father, but he is the main creator, from what I have seen and experienced." Viviana leaned back against the sofa, basking in her own humor. "Well, I think I might head off to bed and try to forget about everything that has happened in this place."

Viviana waved Caleb off and saw the other members heading over to their bedrooms of bunk beds and cots. Viviana and Bianca shared a room together next to Larry's empty bedroom. Bianca closed all the curtains and made sure no light would enter any of the rooms. Then she went over to her bedroom and laid down. She felt tired, but not tired enough to sleep. She felt anger inside of her. Anger towards Gabriel for abandoning her in the woods. Anger towards Gabriel for ruining her chance of ever having a happy life. She wanted to tear into Gabriel and make him suffer like he had suffered before.

The time was going on seven o'clock in the morning. The birds were out chirping, which started to drive Viviana insane. She grabbed two cotton balls and shoved them into her ears, as if that were going to take care of the sound problem. Viviana drifted in and out of reality, wondering if she was even asleep. Hours went by, and the time made it up to about four o'clock in the morning. Viviana felt a bit drowsy, but she also wanted to get out of bed. The sun was still shining through the curtains, but it did not bother her. Viviana decided to get dressed and prepare herself for the evening. Once it was about five o'clock, she stepped outside of her room, headed for the kitchen, grabbed herself a pack of blood, and sat down in the living room where the other members normally sat.

Caleb entered the living room, fully dressed. He grabbed himself a pack of blood. "We might need to get more, Viviana," Caleb said. "Where did Larry get our blood stash from?"

"Blood banks and hospitals," Viviana said. "Perhaps you and I can head over to this one twenty-four hour hospital and see if there are any leftover donated blood packs."

Caleb nodded. "Okay. It sounds like a good evening plan. When did you want to do that?" Caleb asked. Viviana checked her watch.

"About seven o'clock in the evening? I mean, humans are probably going out to eat, so we should avoid heavily crowded areas," Viviana said. Caleb nodded as he grabbed the final blood pack and poured it into a glass. He sat down next to Viviana on the couch.

"Tell me, Viviana," Caleb said. "What was your human life like? Did you have a family, a job, children?" Viviana smiled.

"I had Larry as my fiancé. I worked at this tavern where I got snatched from, but I must say that I did enjoy my life as a bartender. My mother fell ill, so my father had to take care of her. My siblings helped with the care of the house, cooking, and shopping at markets. I was becoming the woman of the house to earn the money. That was not until I met Larry. How beautiful he looked! I knew we were meant to be together. He had a father who looked tough, and his mother was beautiful. How I loved the life I was in, Caleb. I really loved it," Viviana said.

Caleb nodded as he continued to listen to Viviana's story. "What about you, Caleb? What was your human life like?" Caleb shrugged.

"I was a modern-day university student in the United States. I enjoyed traveling around the world. I loved meeting people all around the world through networking. I just remember meeting Gabriel for the first time. Mind you, I never had a loving and supportive family when I grew up. Gabriel might have sensed that about me and seduced me, which sounds weirdly phrased, to join him. I just remember how caring he sounded. Like the father I have always wanted. He sounded so happy to have a son in his life. I remember him using that phrase, son," Caleb said.

Viviana nodded. "Sounds about right," Viviana said. "Gabriel is quite a seductive creature. I mean, I remember how fatherly he was to me as well." Caleb nodded.

"But it still does not mean that he did well with us, Viviana," Caleb said. "Gabriel is a powerful shapeshifter and a monster. He should not be given any quarter because of how sad and depressed he may seem. Surely, him going after you and Larry was not a mistake. Surely, he would have known better than to act upon his impulsive feelings."

Viviana nodded. "I agree with you, Caleb," Larry said. "Just because someone is goodhearted and loving on the surface does not mean they are good on the inside." Caleb nodded. Once it was about seven o'clock in the evening, Caleb and Viviana headed out toward the hospital, where Larry often grabbed the blood packs. Upon their arrival at the hospital, there was heavy security of several humans in uniform.

"Bună seara," said one male officer in uniform. Caleb and Larry exchanged glances. "English?" Larry asked. The officer thought about it.

"Do you need help?" Another officer asked a woman with blonde hair and brown eyes in the same uniform.

"We need to get inside for medicine," Viviana said. The female security guard analyzed both Caleb and Viviana.

"Appointment?" The woman asked. Viviana and Caleb both exchanged glances again.

"Um, yes," Viviana said. The female officer entered the hospital and asked this male assistant about appointments. The officer returned.

"Names?" The female officer asked. Caleb and Viviana sighed as they took a step forward. The woman grabbed hold of her gun, which was still in her holster. "Names?" The officer repeated.

Viviana started to feel uncomfortable and started to walk away. Caleb looked at the officer. "Our names are not on there, but we are in need of urgent care," Caleb said. Viviana stopped walking to see what Caleb was planning. "My sister needs blood," Caleb said. The officer gave Caleb a confused look. The first officer leaned over to the woman to say something to the female officer, and they both nodded.

"What kind of problem does your sister have with blood?" The female officer asked.

"With all due respect, madam," Caleb said sternly. "I only discuss health problems with a doctor. If you are not a doctor, I will not answer any more medical questions." The officers sighed and stepped aside for Caleb to enter. Viviana quickly followed and sighed with relief when they reached the assistant.

"Bună seara," the medical assistant said.

"English?" Viviana asked this time. The assistant looked over at both Viviana and Caleb, feeling a sense of danger.

"One moment," the assistant said before he pressed a button on the phone keypad. Two night doctors showed up in white coats, approaching Caleb and Viviana. The assistant explained that Caleb and Viviana were foreigners, and from what he had overheard, they needed blood. The doctors then beckoned for Caleb and Viviana to enter two different examination rooms.

"Viviana, what should we do?" Caleb asked. Viviana sighed and started to panic inside. "Okay, gentlemen," Viviana said. The men turned around. Viviana pulled them both into one room, letting Caleb enter and closing the door.

Caleb, do you know how to persuade these men?" Viviana asked. Caleb looked over and felt a sense of fear inside of him. Was Caleb able to use the persuasion powers Gabriel had? What if it was not going to work? What if it was going to end badly? Caleb sighed and focused on what persuasion was about. He looked at both men and then closed his eyes. Then he opened his eyes again.

"We need blood," Caleb said in a deep voice. "My sister needs blood for her medical needs."

The doctors kept their focus on Caleb. Caleb was not sure if he was persuading them. Caleb repeated the same sentence again. The doctors kept their focus on Caleb.

Then Viviana got to her feet, headed out of the room, and walked over to the blood section of the hospital. Caleb quickly followed behind Viviana. The two doctors remained in a stupor while Viviana and Caleb grabbed the last ten packs of blood from the section and put as much as they could in their jacket pockets. As they were about to leave the hospital, the security guards called out to them.

Viviana sighed and turned around, holding three blood packs in her arms. The security woman analyzed him and leaned toward a male colleague. "Caleb, when I say run, we need to run," Viviana whispered. Caleb kept his focus on the male colleague, who had his eyes focused on him. "Okay. Now," Viviana whispered, and both Caleb and Viviana bolted in their shapeshifting speed back to the apartment complex. The security guards called for backup and ordered a search party for two men carrying blood packs.

Once Viviana and Caleb arrived back at the apartment complex, it was going on ten in the evening. Viviana let out an excited shrill once they entered through the front door. Caleb was still panting. "Well done, Viviana. Now we have a search party for us. What is wrong with you?" Caleb asked. Viviana gave Caleb a pat on his shoulder.

"This will soon fade, Caleb," Viviana said. "Give the humans a few days, and soon they will forget about anyone carrying blood packs."

Caleb sighed, shaking his head. "Okay, but what if they do not, Viviana? How are we going to get more blood supplies for the upcoming weeks?" Caleb asked.

"We can send out the girls the next time," Viviana said. "Girls with their womanly problems? Hm? I am sure nobody would be able to refuse a woman needing some iron," Larry said. "Anyway, we are good for now. We just have to keep it low-key for a while."

Bianca came into the room. "What is going on?" Bianca asked. "Why are there sirens blaring around the area?" Larry opened the curtain next to the front door, seeing police cars riding around. Where is Larry?" Both Viviana and Caleb exchanged glances.

"We had to fill up on our supply, Bianca, but we will try to help Larry escape," Caleb said. Viviana walked over to the kitchen to place the blood packs from her coat pocket and the ones in her arms in the cooler. Then she walked back to the living room to find Larry's coven lounging around.

Bianca felt worried about Larry's fate and was unable to distract herself. Viviana came back and felt Bianca's senses. "It will be okay, Bianca. Larry is quite strong and capable of handling any situation that comes his way. I would not worry too much about what Gabriel might do to him," Viviana said. Bianca did not respond.

At the castle, Larry was in the dungeon, sitting on a cold concrete bench, staring at the grey concrete blood-stained floor from the dead rats. Larry realized that justice was not going to be on his side. He was the victim of Gabriel's actions, and yet he gets labeled as being a troublemaker. He felt tiny and alone. Just because Gabriel managed to get his children back home to him does not mean he is innocent in his actions. Gabriel, the head father of everyone, with his strong powers, is the real perpetrator and monster that needs to be ended. How was Larry going to manage his strategic plan this time? Was Jenna a shape-shifter, or did her body have a reaction to shape-shifting blood?

Suddenly, a door toward the basement opened. Footsteps came down the stairs. Gabriel, with his black suit and tie and his silky, clean black hair down his shoulders, approached Larry. Larry looked up at him with confusion. "Can I help you?" Larry asked. Gabriel stood five feet from the bars with his arms crossed.

"How does it feel to be you, Larry?" Gabriel asked. Larry sighed and did not respond. "I mean, going after a human child?"

Larry then looked up at Gabriel. "Like you, Gabriel? Viviana and I were both children, as well," Larry said. "Have you forgotten that part from your past?" Gabriel did not respond. "I mean, how does it feel to be you, Gabriel? The biggest hypocrite?"

Gabriel waited for Larry to finish his ranting. "Well, there is a difference between you and me, Larry," Gabriel said. "I still have no idea where I came from. At least you know." Larry let out a shrill laugh.

"That is hysterical, Gabriel," Larry said as he laughed sarcastically at Gabriel. Gabriel did his best to remain quiet.

"You managed quite nicely, as did Viviana," Gabriel said. "That young child who is still sleeping might not survive that well in our world, Larry." Larry shrugged.

"Who does, Gabriel? You obviously never cared about keeping your daughters safe. I remember the first time I met Amy," Larry said. "I could have killed her on the spot when I had invited her out to lunch or breakfast. I did not, Gabriel. That is something you would do with your carelessness and ruthlessness."

Gabriel exhaled as he felt anger building inside of him. "Just because we are two different people does not mean I will not give you any quarter, Larry. I am glad you would never be that ruthless to my daughters, but this girl that you lured and harmed will cause humans to go looking for her, and if that girl mentions how she got kidnapped by shape shifters, our kind will slowly go extinct, including you, Larry. I have no idea why you even felt that this was the best move to make," Gabriel said.

Larry did not respond. "I will see how Jenna is doing, but if she is a shape shifter, Lawrence Harrison, you will not survive the evening in our home," Gabriel snapped before he left.

"Wait!" Larry screamed. "I am sorry for what I did to that girl, Gabriel. If I die, Caleb and the other ones will avenge me." Gabriel shrugged.

"How is that going to save the situation, Larry? The fact that humans are now going to be looking for a human girl that went off to Romania. How are you planning to fix this, Larry?" Gabriel asked.

"What if I let Viviana use her powers against law enforcement or even Caleb?" Larry asked. Gabriel did not move or respond. "Viviana is a powerful sorceress. She managed to get you good, right?" Gabriel barred his teeth and growled at Gabriel. "Okay, I get it."

"I will discuss your plan with my family, but you are not ever leaving this cell," Gabriel snapped before he left the dungeon area and headed back up to the main floor.

Amelia came over to Gabriel. "Is it true, Gabriel? Are we supposed to relocate?" Amelia asked. Gabriel held up his hands.

"We are not going to go there right now, Amelia. Larry just made a giant mistake, but we will find a way to handle this situation. I must drink," Gabriel said before he headed toward the dining quarter. Adrian, Vladimir, and Lucien were at the table, drinking from a fresh bottle. Gabriel grabbed himself a glass, poured it full, and drank it down in less than a few seconds.

Lucien looked over at Gabriel with confusion. "What is Amelia talking about, Gabriel? Are we to relocate soon?" Gabriel sighed as he looked at his empty glass.

"Ever since Larry kidnapped that human girl and potentially changed her, we might have to. The fact that humans will have a search party for that girl has compromised our kind," Gabriel said.

"Let me have him," Lucien snapped as he got to his feet. "Please Gabriel." Gabriel shook his head. "Not right now, brother. We need to inform the other coven members and have them live low-key for a while. No more hunting and only sending out their humans to blood banks, but not too often," Gabriel said. Gabriel walked over to his office, opened up his laptop, and called all the members who had recently arrived back at their homes.

"We have a problem," Gabriel said. The other members looked at Gabriel. "Larry may have exposed our kind to the human world. Larry kidnapped a human girl and may have changed her into a shapeshifter." The other members gasped and growled. "I know how this sounds, but we need to be careful about allowing our humans to go on blood runs. If law enforcement goes around our home, we can easily get into so much trouble, no matter how often we use our powers against them."

Nobody said anything till Dante cleared his throat. "How did this happen, Gabriel?" Dante asked. "How did Larry manage to kidnap a human girl and bring her over to Romania?"

"Well, he did not kidnap her, but he lured her over to his home with a fake promise that Amy wanted to invite her over to spend some vacation time together at least that was what I had understood from the situation," Gabriel said.

The other members looked confused, scared, and disgusted at the whole situation. "Well," Alarick said. "We will make sure our housekeeper is informed of this situation. Kristjan also nodded. "As will we." Dante then nodded as well.

"My my, Gabriel," Dante said. "How does this situation make you feel?" Gabriel smiled and shrugged.

"Just like any other day at the Ambrose household," Gabriel said with a chuckle. The other members joined in. "I am sure this will all blow over soon. We will be able to dodge the human law and live our lives as we used to."

The other members nodded. "Okay," they all said simultaneously. "We will keep our eyes open to any potential danger. Gabriel nodded.

"Stay safe, my friends," Gabriel said before he walked off and walked over to the dining quarter. Arabella, Amy, and Ginger showed up together.

"Amy," Gabriel said. Amy glared at Gabriel and turned her back to him before she got herself a glass. Arabella shrugged.

Give her some space, Gabriel. She is quite upset at the whole situation, Arabella thought. Gabriel nodded and sat down next to Lucien.

"Okay," Gabriel said. "I have to inform you all of what Larry has done, which may have compromised our lifestyle. The other members, except for Amy, looked over at Gabriel. "Since Larry had that girl brought over here," Gabriel said.

"Girl? What girl?" Amy snapped. "Oh, you mean by best friend, Jenna?" Gabriel nodded.

"I understand that you are upset with me, Amy, but I must tell you all something important. Since Larry brought Jenna into our lives, her parents could send out a search party for their daughter. If there is any kind of mischievous or unordinary activity, like Hildegard purchasing or bringing us back blood, she might be placed under arrest, and she could expose us," Gabriel said.

The other members sighed with disbelief. "How do you know this, Gabriel?" Arabella asked.

"It is obvious, Arabella," Gabriel said. "Bringing a human into our lives, especially having a girl lured, could result in many problems." The other members nodded. Amy felt tears building in her eyes. Gabriel noticed and walked over to a different cabinet to get her some tissues, dropping them on the table.

Amy grabbed them, threw them at the sliding doors, and walked away. "This family is toxic," Amy whispered. "Where is Jenna?"

"In our bedroom, Amy," Gabriel said. "If you want, you can go and see her and see how she feels." Amy ignored Gabriel and walked over to the basement sleeping quarter until she reached the bedroom door. Amy gently opened it up and saw Jenna staring at the ceiling, awake, but she looked different.

"Jenna," Amy whispered. Jenna looked over at Amy. She was Jenna, but her eyes had something darker in them.

"How are you feeling?" Amy asked as she approached the bed and sat on the edge. Jenna just looked dazed and confused at Amy.

"What happened?" Jenna asked. "I got you on the phone, went over to the address that you told me to go to, and you were not there." Amy realized that Larry or Caleb might have used a voice changer on her over the phone.

"Yeah," Amy said. "Before I can answer that, do you feel like nothing has happened or do you feel different?" Jenna thought about it.

"I can see the tiny bits of blood on the ceiling, Amy. Your housekeeper or maid does not do a good job with the cleaning," Jenna said. Amy could not help but giggle at Jenna's response. "What?"

"Like, are you hungry or thirsty for something?" Amy asked. Jenna licked her lips and noticed how dry they felt.

"Sort of. I mean, do you have water for me?" Jenna asked. Amy nodded. Amy was not certain if she should already give her some blood. "I think I may want to get out of bed." Amy held her hands up and quickly faced them upward.

"Okay, did you need any help or support?" Amy asked. Jenna sat up, sort of hunched over.

"I think I got it," Jenna said as she wobbled over to the door. Amy quickly grabbed her and led her over to the staircase.

Amy helped Jenna up the stairs and had Jenna hold onto the handrail while she opened the door. Amy nudged Jenna onto the main floor and let Jenna hang onto her as they both walked over to the dining quarter. Gabriel, Lucien, Adrian, Vladimir, Arabella, Amelia, and Ginger looked over at Jenna with shock.

"Goodness," Ginger said. "She needs something to eat and drink." Gabriel quickly grabbed a fresh bottle of blood. Amy waved him off angrily and led her to the faucet, grabbed Jenna and the glass from the cupboard, and filled the glass with water.

Jenna swilled down the water and leaned against Amy. The other members just watched Jenna. "More?" Amy asked. Jenna nodded. "Here, drink as much as you want." Gabriel felt confused.

"Jenna," Gabriel said as he approached her. Amy blocked Gabriel from walking nearer. "Amy, please, this is important. Jenna, how are you feeling?" Jenna turned around.

"You look quite ill. Did something happen to you at that apartment?" Gabriel asked. Jenna placed the glass on the counter and supported herself by leaning against the counter.

"I do not remember," Jenna said. "I just remember entering the apartment, and Amy was not there. I felt angry and confused, but after that, my mind went blank." Gabriel nodded.

"How do you feel physically?" Gabriel asked. Jenna shrugged.

"I have had better days," Jenna said with a chuckle. "I do feel quite tired, and for some reason this water is not helping." Gabriel nodded and looked over at Amy.

Father, no, Amy thought. *You cannot have her consume any blood right now. Please.* Gabriel sighed and looked over at Jenna. "This will come across as a weird and unusual question, Jenna, but how are your iron levels?" Gabriel asked. Jenna shrugged.

"Not sure, why?" Jenna asked. Gabriel took a step back and crossed his arms. "Would you like to try something different?" Gabriel asked. Jenna looked over at Amy, who had fear in her eyes.

Jenna then looked back at Gabriel. "What kind of a drink?"

New Times

Gabriel walked over to the cooler and grabbed a bottle of blood. Suddenly, Amy grabbed him by his left arm, holding him back. "No, Father, please," Amy begged. Jenna started to feel uncertain about what was going to happen.

Amy begged Gabriel not to go any further with his plan to feed Jenna some blood. "Amy, I need to see how her body will react to the blood. Please step aside." Gabriel grabbed an empty glass from the cupboard, but only poured about three teaspoons of blood into it and placed it in front of Jenna.

"Whenever you are ready," Gabriel said, gesturing for Jenna to take a sip. Jenna looked over at Amy, who had sadness in her eyes.

"I might not want to, sir," Jenna said. Gabriel looked over at Amy. "I mean, I have never tried blood before, if that is what is in that glass."

"You obviously drank from Larry's body, have you not?" Gabriel asked. Jenna thought about it.

"I thought that was a nightmare, but yes, I believe I did drink or got pushed into it," Jenna said.

Gabriel nodded. "I want to see if your thirst will be quenched with this since none of us drink soda beverages," Gabriel said. Jenna looked back at Amy, who kept her eyes focused on her. Jenna swallowed, grabbed the glass, inhaled, exhaled, closed her eyes, poured the liquid down her throat, and swallowed.

After Jenna placed the glass on the table while her eyes remained closed, she licked her lips and suddenly felt that her thirst had disappeared.

"I guess my thirst is gone?" Jenna said it with uncertainty in her voice. "I mean, it tastes a bit tangy and unusual, but I feel okay." Gabriel sighed with relief, but he knew how upset and angry Amy felt.

"Did you want more?" Gabriel asked. Jenna held out her glass to Gabriel. Amy walked away with defeat, feeling angry about the whole situation. Nothing made sense. She felt uneasy and angry at the whole situation. Amy then thought that it was technically Larry's fault for bringing her here. Amy marched down to the dungeon area and saw Larry look up at her with a smile.

"Good evening, madam Ambrose," Larry said teasingly. "What brings you down to these chambers?" Amy growled and hissed at him with all the pent-up anger she had. "Oh dear, are you well, Amy?"

"How dare you, you heartless monster?" Amy snapped. "Bringing an innocent young woman over to our home as bait. How dare you?"

Larry cocked his head as he smiled. "Like your father, Amy?" Larry asked. "How dare he go after me and my Viviana?"

"That is different, Larry, and you know it. My father was ruthless, but that does not mean that other shape shifters have to imitate his nature," Amy snapped.

"Oh really? You are just a child to me, Amy Ambrose," Larry snapped back. "As far as I am concerned, I have more years of experience and knowledge than you. Just because you are the child of those hideous creatures upstairs does not mean that you have the same amount of skill, power, or knowledge as us, who were created way before your time, my dear."

Amy growled. "I already knew something was wrong with you from the moment that we first met," Amy growled. "Sending me handwritten notes and wanting to meet me out in the middle of nowhere? That sounds like your typical move."

Larry chuckled. "Is that what you came here to tell me, princess?" Larry asked.

Amy growled and hissed even louder until the door to the basement opened up and footsteps came running down. "Amy," Gabriel gasped. "Go upstairs right now."

Amy looked over at him with concern and felt sadness inside of her.

"It is both your fault and what happened to Jenna upstairs," Amy said as she felt tears falling down her cheeks. "Both of you."

Gabriel grabbed Amy and guided her toward the staircase. "You are to never come down here without anyone else's supervision, Amy. Please go upstairs," Gabriel said. Amy reluctantly walked up the stairs, opened the door, and slammed it behind her, causing Larry to chuckle.

"You are never to speak to any of my family members again, Larry," Gabriel snapped before he left for the staircase.

"She came down here on her own accord, Gabriel. I did not have anything to do with her being here," Larry said. Gabriel waved Larry off, walked up the stairs, opened the door to the basement, and closed it gently behind him. Amy and Jenna were still in the dining quarter. Moments later, Lucien, Adrian, and Vladimir came over to the area for their evening feed. They saw Jenna and looked over at Gabriel with confusion.

"Why is the human here, Gabriel?" Lucien whispered. Gabriel shook his head.

"She is no longer human, brothers. Larry fed her, so I had to counteract his blood with mine," Gabriel whispered back. The other two brothers looked surprised at Gabriel.

"How is that possible? Normally we often exchange or drain victims, but how did this happen?"

Gabriel shrugged. "I cannot answer that right now, brothers. Try to make Jenna feel at home without any judgment," Gabriel said before he headed for his office. Lucien grabbed three glasses, while Vladimir grabbed a new, fresh bottle of blood from the cooler. Adrian sat down across from where Jenna and Amy were sitting. Amy quickly put her right arm around Jenna, holding her close.

"So, you must be the new girl. I am Lucien, one of Gabriel's brothers. This is Adrian," Lucien said, pointing to Adrian sitting next to him. "That guy coming over to us is Vladimir." Jenna smiled and nodded at each of them.

"Gabriel told me that you had changed or something like that," Lucien said. Jenna shrugged.

"If you want to know more, please do some research," Amy snapped. "I will not allow you three to intimidate my friend." Lucien rolled his eyes and leaned back.

"We are not intimidating your friend, Amy," Lucien said in a calm tone. "We are just curious as to how one becomes a shape shifter. As far as we are concerned, we went through a different transition than receiving blood from another source."

"Ask Amelia," Amy snapped. Lucien looked over at Amy with frustration.

"I understand that you feel protective, Amy, but that is no way to be talking to an elderly member. Gabriel will always be your father, but we also deserve respect as well."

Amy scoffed, got to her feet, and held her left hand up for Jenna to take, so she could bring Jenna over to a different area of the castle. Jenna got to her feet and walked over to her bedroom. When Amy and Jenna got to the staircase, Darcia and Alistair were at the top, on their way downstairs. "Amy," Darcia said with glee in her voice. "Who is your friend?"

Amy shook her head. "Has my father mentioned anything to you both?" Amy asked. Darcia and Alistair both shook their heads.

"Jenna may have transitioned, my fellow friends," Amy said. "By the way, Jenna, meet my aunt Darcia and my uncle Alistair. I believe you may have seen them or perhaps met them briefly when they were at school a few times," said Amy.

Jenna thought about it for a moment and suddenly remembered how Amy had to leave school for a while.

"Sort of," Jenna said. "Before I continue, I remember how you had to leave school for a while. Did they have anything to do with your absence?" Amy nodded.

"Hm. So, what does that make everyone in this family anyway? Are you vampires or werewolves?" Jenna asked. Darcia and Alistair both chuckled.

"Well, Amy, perhaps you can answer that question," Darcia said. "I should get myself something to drink and eat. Pleasure meeting you, Jenna."

Both Alistair and Darcia left for the dining quarter. Amy led Jenna up to her bedroom. At the closed door, Ginger came out of her room and gasped.

"Amy, what is going on?" Ginger asked. Amy held up her hand and beckoned for Ginger to enter her bedroom. Once Jenna and Ginger were inside the room, Amy closed the door.

Jenna looked over at the crib with the three children inside of it. "Amy?" Jenna asked. "Are they yours?" Amy felt a sense of shame inside of her.

"Yes. They are also Caleb's children," Amy said. Jenna was in shock and was unable to respond. "I know how that sounds, Jenna. You are taking it much better than I did when I heard the news."

Jenna walked over to the edge of Amy's bed to steady herself from the news.

"Anyway, Ginger, Larry may have transitioned my human friend, Jenna," Amy said. "Ginger, meet Jenna. Jenna, meet Ginger."

Ginger looked over at Jenna with confusion. "How do you mean transitioned, Amy?" Ginger asked. Amy smiled and chuckled at the way Ginger asked that question, but mostly because she was angry at the whole situation. "What?"

"Father gave Jenna some of our blood supply, and that seemed to have quenched her thirst, as Father had phrased it," Amy said.

"Oh goodness, no," Ginger whispered. "Where is Larry anyway? Back at home, popping a bottle of champagne?"

Amy shook her head. "No, he is in our dungeon," Amy said. Ginger scrunched her brow.

"Where are the other ones? Bianca, Viviana, or Caleb?" Ginger asked. Amy shrugged.

"Not sure, Ginger. Nothing makes sense, and I feel this intense fatigue washing over me. I cannot focus right now on anything," Amy said.

Ginger saw Amy slowly entering an emotional breakdown. "Well, does Jenna have a place to sleep?" Ginger asked. Amy looked at her bed.

"My bed is big enough," Amy said.

"I know, but we do live in a castle. Perhaps place her on one of the other floors, also to keep her away from the boys," Ginger said.

Amy looked up at Jenna. "Would you like to explore the castle a bit, Jenna?" Amy asked. Jenna shrugged.

"Well, I guess. I do have an important question to ask you, Amy," Jenna said. "What do I tell my parents?"

Amy looked over at Ginger. "Um, I am not sure. Look, I need a moment. Please excuse me," Amy said before heading for the sliding doors toward the courtyard.

"Amy," Gabriel said. "How is everything going with that girl?" Amy turned around and headed outside toward the courtyard. Jenna watched Amy screaming and running around outside, causing her to feel scared and anxious.

"Ginger!" Jenna said. "What are we, exactly?" Ginger looked over at Jenna.

"A shape shifter," Ginger said. "We are all shape shifters. Amy and I are both shape shifters."

Jenna looked at Ginger with fear. "Amy has always been a..." Jenna said it with a stutter. Ginger nodded.

"Yes. So was I. Have you met the other members?" Ginger asked. Jenna looked at the door.

"Some, I believe. Your aunt and uncle," Jenna said. Ginger nodded and sighed.

"I am sorry this happened to you, Jenna," Ginger said. "You were not meant to become a shapeshifter. I am sorry that Larry and Caleb lured you in with Amy's voice to bring you here for vacation. Instead, you become one of us."

"This does not make any sense, Ginger," Jenna said. "I cannot be… It makes no sense." Jenna's breathing was getting faster.

"Relax, Jenna," Ginger said. "Please." Jenna fainted, but Ginger caught her before she hit the floor. "Oh dear." Ginger held Jenna, balancing her against her body, opened up Amy's side of the bed, and placed Jenna under the covers. Ginger then walked outside of Amy's room and saw Bryan and his four brothers leaving their room.

"Ginger," Bryan said. "Is everything okay?" Ginger mindlessly nodded and headed for the staircase. "Who is that girl?"

Ginger turned around and quickly walked back toward the closed door. "She is to be left alone for now, boys," Ginger whispered. "Please come downstairs with me." Bryan and the four other boys walked over to the staircase to head downstairs. When they arrived in the dining quarter, Bryan made a gesture towards the staircase.

"Bryan," Alistair said. "We might be facing a great problem regarding our dear friend, Larry."

Bryan chuckled as he sat down. "Now what?" Bryan asked. Alistair sternly looked deep into Bryan's eyes.

"This is no laughing matter. Larry may have caused a great exposure of our kind," Alistair snapped.

Bryan looked at Alistair. "We have been hunting humans at bonfires for many years, Father," Bryan said. "What has little Larry done this time to cause exposure? How about Hildegard making a lot of blood donation runs to feed us?" Alistair waited for Bryan to stop talking.

"He has turned Amy's friend, who is probably upstairs wandering around, into a shapeshifter."

Bryan sternly analyzed Alistair's facial expression. "Seriously? Is that who the girl is in Amy's bed?" Bryan asked. Alistair nodded. "What should we do? Is that girl informed of our kind? How did this happen?"

Gabriel cleared his throat. "Bryan, please take it easy for a moment. I know this sudden situation is a big change to process, but we are all worried and scared, as well," Gabriel said.

"Where is Larry anyway?" Bryan asked.

"In our dungeon, but nobody is to go to him right now, Bryan. I had to make that clearer to Amy before she left down the stairs," Gabriel said. Bryan sighed.

"This is a problem," Bryan said. "What is the plan?" Gabriel looked at each member of the room.

"We have to remain low-key for a while, Bryan. Perhaps we should contact Jenna's parents and either persuade or manipulate their minds, or perhaps Jenna can return home. I do not know what I am saying," Gabriel said before he got to his feet.

Alistair and Darcia looked up at him with concern. "This is a big problem, my friends. Something must be done, or we will have to constantly be traveling, which could be quite exhausting and dangerous," Gabriel said. "Please excuse me."

Gabriel walked away. Amy came back into the dining quarter through the sliding doors. "Amy," Bryan said. "What have you been up to?"

Amy walked past him with tears in her eyes. "Please leave me alone. Everyone!" Amy begged.

Alistair looked at Bryan. *Give her some space, son. Amy will come around before you know it.* Bryan nodded. Bryan got himself an empty glass and poured a full glass of blood, taking sips from it.

"This is crazy," Bryan said. Darcia and Alistair looked over at him. "How we all ended up in a situation like this. Now we have to be extra careful? Did we not have problems with some law enforcement officials or something like that?"

Alistair and Darcia nodded. "Yes, we have," Alistair said. "At the hospital, when we were feeding from their blood donations." Bryan nodded.

"Right, I remember. I remember how you used your powers on that doctor to bring us some packs while we just drank those packs down," Bryan said with a chuckle. Alistair and Darica both shook their heads.

"We may have been the cause of it all," Alistair said. "We were apparently not that cautious enough." Darcia placed her right hand on top of Alistair's, linking her fingers through his.

Arabella came into the dining quarter. "How is the girl?" Arabella asked. Alistair and Darcia both shrugged.

"Asleep," Bryan said. "What else would someone be doing in bed at this time of the evening?"

Arabella nodded. "Is it true that we have to be more low-key about our lifestyle? I think I may have caused some suspicion around the area when I had to feed Gabriel after he was weakened by Viviana a while back," Arabella said.

Alistair and Darcia exchanged glances. "At the hospital?" Darcia asked. Arabella nodded. "How?"

"I felt incredibly hungry and tired, so I walked alongside that one street with all the restaurants. I asked this busboy where the hospital was. He escorted me over to the hospital, and without me even realizing him standing there, he may have noticed me drinking a lot of blood, causing people to think vampires were among them," Arabella said.

"What happened then?" Alistair asked. Arabella thought about that question for a moment.

"I think Gabriel's brothers took care of him, but they never reported back about how he acted after they used their powers on him. Hopefully he may not have caused too much drama on his part," Arabella said.

"What could have caused law enforcement officials to stand guard outside of that hospital, anyway?" Darcia asked.

Arabella thought about it some more. "I wonder if we, taking a lot of blood packs, drew their suspicion towards us," Arabella said. "Where does Hildegard get our blood supplies from?" Darcia shrugged. "I think I shall ask her to be certain that we are not taking too much blood from just one source. Please excuse me." Arabella walked over to the bedroom, which was reserved for her alone on the third floor, and opened the door gently to find her deep asleep.

Hildegard took off her eye mask. "Yes?" Hildegard asked.

"Apologies, Hildegard," Arabella whispered. "I did not realize you were asleep. We will talk tomorrow, or I will leave you a note in the dining quarter before we slumber ourselves. Sorry." Arabella closed the door gently and stood outside of her bedroom for a minute or so. Arabella then walked over to Amelia's slumbering quarter, knocked on her door, and waited for the door to open.

Amelia opened the door. "Arabella," Amelia said. "What a surprise." Arabella nodded. "What can I do for you?"

"I feel quite anxious about this whole situation to which we may be exposed. What are your thoughts, and what do you have planned for this situation?" Arabella asked.

Amelia shrugged. "I normally leave such questions up to Gabriel. If he wants me for something, he knows where to find me, but other than that, I try to stay as low-key as possible," Amelia said. Arabella gave Amelia a disapproving look. "What?" "Do you think everything is going to be okay, Amelia, or is this going to be the final days of our kind?" Arabella asked.

Again, Amelia shrugged. "I would not overthink or worry about this problem right now, Arabella. Try to take your mind off of this problem by focusing on your grandchildren," Amelia said. Arabella nodded.

"Perhaps that is the only thing I could do for the time being, I guess," Arabella said before she left Amelia's quarter and headed back up to the main floor.

Gabriel returned to the dining quarter. "Arabella," Gabriel said, beckoning her to him. "I think I may have a plan. Larry did propose to use Viviana against the law enforcement officials with her magic. What do you think of that?"

Arabella gave Gabriel a confused expression. "Do you really believe him?" Gabriel shrugged.

"I think we could use him as a tool for once, my love," Gabriel said. "If he misbehaves, it will not end well for him."

Arabella looked at Alistair and Darcia. "What do they think?" Arabella asked. Gabriel looked over at Darcia and Alistair.

"Not yet, but I feel that we should use Larry and make sure that we have leverage on her, and if something happens, he will cease to exist, once and for all. This time we will have a celebratory bonfire," Gabriel said.

Arabella sighed. "I do not feel comfortable about that, my love," Arabella said. "If you truly think it will work, go ahead and give it a shot. If something were to happen again, Gabriel, I am not sure if I can handle another blood bath."

Gabriel nodded. "I agree." Gabriel then walked over to Alistair and Darcia to explain the plan. Darcia and Alistair both cocked their heads to the side.

"Are you certain this will work, Gabriel?" Alistair asked. "Then again, there are seven of us, excluding your daughters, and one of him, or even two of them, including Viviana."

Gabriel nodded. Darcia rolled her eyes. "It seems like we are constantly strategizing battles and fights in this family, and never anything fun and relaxing," Darcia said. Gabriel shrugged.

"I understand that, Darcia," Gabriel said. "Then again, would you prefer to live a boring life of doing the same activities of running errands, attending your sons' school activities, and things like that?" Darcia shrugged.

"Sometimes that fantasy would make life more meaningful than constantly being on guard against the human world," Darcia said.

Alistair wrapped his left arm around Darcia. "It is funny how the human world has fake mystical creatures and even humans that pretend to be us," Darcia said with a chuckle.

Alistair smiled. "They have that holiday in October where humans dress up in various costumes and even have balls and galas based on the immortal lifestyle. The grass is always greener on the other side. Just wait for those humans to see what it is like to avoid the sun, only drink blood, and not be able to keep your friends because of death or boredom," Darcia said.

Gabriel nodded. "I sometimes wonder what it would have been like to have been a human. The food looks quite awful to look at, especially when Hildegard prepares her meals, but I always wondered what it would have been like to walk in the sun, go out to the coastal areas, and admire the beauty of such oceans and landscapes," Gabriel said.

Alistair smiled and nodded. "As do I, Gabriel," Alistair said. "When we were traveling amongst the humans in those airplanes, hearing various languages and conversations, and watching people with different expressions, from happiness, anger, or even sadness. There was that one moment where Bryan and Raymond caused a scene in one of those airports, causing us to bolt over to the nearest woodsy area. Do you remember, Darcia?"

Darcia nodded. "I would never be able to forget that moment, Alistair," Darcia said. "I remember how we were called monsters, or something like that." Gabriel gave a concerned look.

"Oh right. Then I came in for the rescue of my daughter Amy that one time," Gabriel said. "Goodness, how you all could have caused a giant problem for us all."

Darcia nodded. "I believe the humans that saw us only saw two teenagers fighting and nothing more," Darcia said. "At least that is what I hoped." Gabriel nodded.

"I just remember how heartbroken I felt about seeing Amy, who did not recognize me immediately. She looked so beautiful, my friends," Gabriel said. "She looked so much like her mother."

Darcia and Alistiar both nodded and smiled. "She does, Gabriel," Darcia said. "Ginger looks a lot like you."

Gabriel smiled. "Poor thing," Gabriel said teasingly, causing Alistair and Darcia to chuckle. "Ginger is quite strong and capable of handling herself. I mean, I did not want to make our reunion all too complicated, but yet I remember how hard it was for me to see Amy in that black suit that one time. She looked so strong and determined to not let anything happen to her. My actions were not that good, even though they looked quite different in my mind."

Alistair nodded. "That is normally the case, Gabriel. We all have a certain idea in our minds and think it will work, but then when the time comes, it flops," Alistair said. Darcia nodded. "I am sure you did have good intentions, Gabriel. I know how hard it was for you. First with Arabella, then with two children who later became shape shifters. That is quite hard."

Darcia smiled and nodded. "Well, I may need a break from this topic for a bit. My love, care to go outside for a bit and walk around the courtyard?" Darcia asked. Alistair smiled and nodded.

"I think we should commence with the plan tomorrow evening, Gabriel," Alistair said. "For now, try and enjoy the rest of your evening."

Gabriel smiled and nodded. "Okay. Enjoy the outdoors, my friends," Gabriel said, and he walked over to the living quarter to find his three brothers hanging around.

Sixth Round

The next evening, back at the apartment complex, Bianca sat pensively on the sofa next to Larry's friends, biting her nails nervously. "Whatever you both did, you may have ruined our kind forever," Bianca snapped.

Viviana looked over at Bianca. "I think our future is going to come to an end real soon, Bianca," Viviana said. "Shape shifters and humans do not mix."

Bianca growled at both Viviana and Larry. "Bianca, please give us a break for now. Those sirens will dim real soon. Try to watch a bit of what is on the television screen," Larry said.

Bianca rolled her eyes and watched whatever was on the screen, but that did not take her mind off of her stress and anxiety. The doorbell chimed, causing Bianca to flinch. Everyone exchanged worried glances. The doorbell chimed again, and then again. Caleb sighed and walked over to the front door. He opened the door to find two male officers.

"Good evening, officers," Caleb said. "What can we do for you?" The officers showed their badges.

"May we come in?" The shorter male police officer, with brown hair, brown eyes, and a strong build, asked. Caleb nodded and gestured for both officers to enter. "The people in this area have complained about an occasional fight around this house," said the taller, blonde man with a strong build. Caleb looked over at the other group members, who looked scared.

"Not that we know of, Caleb said. "I mean, what kind of fighting, officers?"

The shorter guy looked around and noticed some bloodstains on the table. "Is that wine you all are drinking?" The short officer asked. Caleb nodded.

"Yes. We drink a lot of wine in this family and friend circle," Caleb said before clearing his throat. The taller officer looked around and saw broken glass and shredded pieces of curtain.

"We also got a call from an American law enforcement agency about how there is a missing girl, Jenna," said the short officer.

"We have no one by the name of Jenna in this family, nor have we ever heard of such a girl. She got kidnapped, or what?" Caleb asked.

"Her parents made a call in to see if Jenna had arrived safely in Romania, but they have not heard anything from her yet. They wondered if she was kidnapped," said the short officer.

Caleb shook his head. "Do you have a picture of her, in case she might be around the area?" Caleb asked. The shorter officer grabbed a photograph of Jenna's high school picture and handed it to Caleb. "Oh, what a pretty girl! I will keep my eyes open to anything that appears to be Jenna," Caleb said with a smile.

"What happened there?" Asked the taller officer. "How did your window and curtain break?" Caleb looked nervously at Viviana.

"Oh dear. That is what happened to my candles. They must have caught fire and caused the windows to break. I knew I smelled something smoky. That is what the other people must have thought when they heard glass breaking," Viviana said.

Caleb laughed nervously. "Oh dear, that is why we never light candles near the window," Caleb said. The shorter police officer scanned the area and noticed clawed-out paint on the windowsill. Bianca showed up in her negligee nightgown and fur-cuffed robe.

"Evening officers," Bianca said seductively. The men turned around and smiled at Bianca. "What seems to be the problem?"

The tall officer smiled at Bianca and nodded. "We heard some complaints from some of your neighbors, but your friend or sister appeared to have burned some candles. We will make note of that." Bianca strutted seductively, like a prowling cat, towards the officers.

The shorter officer smiled nervously at Bianca until she was about a foot away from them.

"I will make sure our family keeps it quiet from now on," Bianca whispered. Both men were sweating and nodded before they headed for the front door.

Bianca waved to them and made sure they were out of sight. "Goodness," Bianca said. "I still have the moves."

Caleb and Vivana both burst out laughing, causing the other members to join in. "That was quite something, Bianca," Viviana said. "I almost thought I had to use my powers on them, but you are someone who can probably get by with anything. Nice," Vivaina said.

Caleb smiled, admiring how seductive Bianca looked. "I was also quite impressed with how you were able to pull off going from a pile of anxiety to a seductive cat, Bianca. Larry would have been proud," Caleb said. Bianca smiled and nodded. "Speaking of Larry, we need to find a way to release him from Gabriel's grasp. How should we take care of this problem?"

Bianca and Viviana both exchanged glances. "Um," Viviana said. "We can perhaps try to bargain with Gabriel. Too bad he managed to let the human girl escape. I wonder how she is doing. Would she still be alive?"

Bianca shrugged. "That is a good question. If we all knew how ruthless Gabriel is, I am sure he would have easily turned her or at least enjoyed her as an evening snack," Bianca said.

Caleb was in the process of strategizing. Suddenly, the house phone rang. Bianca sighed. "I will not be able to seduce anyone over the phone this time," Bianca said. Caleb approached the phone, grabbed the horn, and held it to his ear. Caleb did not respond. It was quiet on the other end.

"Caleb?" Larry said.

"Larry?" Caleb said. "Where are you? Were you able to escape that castle?"

"No," Larry said. "We have a big problem. I may have caused a lot of exposure for our family. It was not wise of me to bring over that human girl."

"Yes, I know that, Larry," Caleb said. "We just had two human police officers show up at our home, asking about her and telling us that our neighbors find us too loud."

"Oh dear," Larry said. "The reason why I am calling is because I am standing with Gabriel, his three brothers, and the happy couple regarding how we may need Viviana to use her powers on those law enforcement officials to distract them and divert their attention towards their search for our kind."

Viviana looked over at Caleb with confusion at Bianca. "Who is that on the phone?" Vviana asked. Bianca shrugged.

"I do not know," Bianca said. "It looks quite serious." Viviana nodded as she focused her gaze on Caleb. Caleb turned to face Viviana and beckoned for her to come over. "Yes?" Viviana asked.

"Hang on for just a moment, Larry," Caleb said. "So, Larry is on the phone, realized he made a big mistake by bringing over that human girl, and wants you to use your magical powers on something like creating a video regarding the search for mystical creatures. Would you be up for that?"

Viviana shrugged. "Whatever will help to decrease our chances of more exposure, but I can do something like that, sure," Viviana said. Caleb nodded.

"Great. So, Viviana is up for helping us, Larry. What should we do and where should we do it, and how do we get you back home to us?" Caleb asked. Larry looked over at Gabriel.

Gabriel shook his head. "I think that is enough for now, Larry," Gabriel said before he hung up the phone.

"Larry?" Caleb asked. "Are you still there, hello?" Caleb looked at the phone with concern, and then at Viviana. "What should we do?"

Viviana shrugged. "I think we should wait for further instructions, or at least, that is what I would do," Viviana said. Bianca sat next to one of the female friends of Larry's, a young, petite girl with a black bobbed hairstyle and black eyes, wearing a t-shirt and jeans.

"Well, let me know if you hear anything else from Larry. I feel that I have done my part quite well for now," Bianca said. Caleb looked back at Viviana.

"Perhaps we should wait and see what the plan is." Viviana nodded.

Back at the castle, Gabriel crossed his arms, examining Larry's demeanor. "So, we need to figure out how we can get the humans to forget about the fighting and the blood banks," Gabriel said. "Please go back inside the cell, Larry. Once we get more information, we will keep you posted on our plans." Larry shrugged and walked back reluctantly to the bench he sat on. Lucien turned the lock on the cell, and the rest of the members walked back up to the main floor.

Amy, Jenna, and Ginger were at the dining quarter. Both Amy and Ginger had two full glasses of blood, but Jenna's glass was still empty. Gabriel approached the dining quarter. "Evening ladies," Gabriel said.

"Evening Father," Ginger said. Amy ignored Gabriel and looked back at her glass.

"Evening, sir," Jenna said.

"Jenna, dear, you do not have to respect my father just because he is the man of the castle," Amy said.

Gabriel looked over at the three girls, shaking his head. "You do not have to respect him for what he has done to you, Jenna," Amy said.

"Your father never brought me here, Amy. I mean, I do not see your father as the wrongdoer in this situation. It was that other man or boy that looked like an overactive surfer with his morose friend at that apartment building," Jenna said.

Gabriel smiled at Jenna's comment about how she saw Larry and Caleb. Amy noticed Gabriel smiling and growled at him. "I did come across some interesting books from your library about shapeshifters, immortal creatures, vampires, werewolves, and other topics. Are you all aware of the term daywalkers?" Jenna asked.

Gabriel looked over at Jenna. "Perhaps there are or have been creatures called daywalkers that go out into the daylight, even though they are one of us," Gabriel said. Amy looked back at Gabriel.

"Do you mind, Father?" Amy asked. "Why must you always intervene in my life?" Gabriel smiled and looked back at Jenna.

"The girl is interested," Gabriel said. "Are you informing your friend of the different types of species, Amy?"

Amy waved off that question and tried to focus her attention back on Jenna.

"What other species are there, Gabriel?" Jenna asked.

"Seriously Jenna? Please stop engaging with him. Look at you! Are you not at all upset about what has happened to you?" Amy asked with a raised voice. "Why are you not upset or angry?"

Jenna gave Amy a stern look. "Of course I am, Amy. I just process such things my own way. How am I supposed to explain this to my family? What if I cannot have children like you, Amy?" Jenna snapped. Amy was astounded by Jenna's reaction. "If your father wants to help me, I want to get as much information and resources as I can, rather than trying to guess things. Am I actually a shape shifter? Just because I was able to drink some blood does not mean I can turn into a different person or creature, right? I do not recall even being bitten," Jenna said.

Amy looked back at her father. "What does this mean, Father?" Amy asked. "What should we do?"

Gabriel sat down at the head of the table, with Jenna on his left side and Amy on his right. "There is one thing we can try, but it can also be quite dangerous," Gabriel said. "We could have Jenna go out into the daylight and see what happens." Amy scoffed.

"Absolutely not," Amy snapped. "No, I will not allow that to happen." Gabriel did not respond to Amy.

"Amy," Gabriel said. "You and your sister were able to withstand the sun. Perhaps Jenna has not fully transformed yet. Perhaps she just has a new diet."

Amy felt overwhelmed. "What if she were to perish, Father?" Amy murmured. Gabriel placed his right hand on Amy's hand.

"Just for a few seconds. I mean, we can also wait a few weeks, but how long were you expected to stay here for vacation, dear Jenna?" Gabriel asked.

"About three weeks," Jenna said. "Then I am to go over to my mother's family for a while after that, and then I will start my second year of college."

Gabriel nodded. "Okay. Well, you have been here for about four days now. We can give you perhaps three more days and see from there if there are any changes about you, Jenna," Gabriel said.

Jenna nodded. "Sounds scary, but I would like to know what is going on with me as well," Jenna said.

Amelia and Arabella entered the dining quarter. "Have you met Amy's children yet?" Arabella asked. Jenna nodded.

"They look cute," Jenna said. "Who is actually the father? Was it that one guy, Brandon, Byron?"

Amy chuckled. "Bryan? Sadly, no," Amy said. "The father is not in our family per se, but you have already met him. Caleb."

Jenna gasped. "Him? How did you ever fall in love with that guy, Amy? Bryan is ten times cuter than him."

Amy did not respond and looked at Gabriel. *Should I tell her, Father? About what happened to me?* Amy thought.

That might not be a good idea right now, Amy. Perhaps this topic will be brought up in the near future, Gabriel thought. Amy nodded.

"Well," Jenna said. "I think I may want to slumber for a bit. I do feel a bit tired."

Amy got to her feet.

"Has our housekeeper provided a bed for you, Jenna?" Amy asked. Jenna shook her head.

"I have slept in your parents' bed and then yours, so I am not sure where to sleep," Jenna said.

"Father, where is Hildegard?" Amy asked. Gabriel looked around.

"Not sure. She may be asleep, but perhaps you two can share your bedroom for now, Amy," Gabriel said. "I will make sure Hildegard has a room for Jenna."

Amy nodded. Amy led Jenna to her bedroom.

"It is going on five o'clock in the morning," Gabriel said as he noticed Alistiar and Darcia entering the sliding doors.

Lucien and his two brothers walked over to their slumbering quarter. Gabriel then heard Hildegard open her door around six o'clock. Arabella looked over at Gabriel. "Are you coming to slumber, Gabriel?" Arabella asked. Gabriel nodded.

"I just need to speak to Hildegard about preparing accommodations for Amy's friend," Gabriel said.

Arabella smiled and nodded. "Okay," Arabella said before she headed for the basement stairs.

Hildegard gasped when she saw Gabriel. "Master Gabriel," Hildegard whispered. Gabriel held up his hands to Hildegard.

"Good morning, dear Hildegard," Gabriel said. "I may need you to prepare a bedroom for Jenna as soon as possible."

Hildegard nodded. "Okay. I shall make up a bedroom on the third floor. Is there any particular color I should use for her?" Hildegard asked.

"Well, you could see if they have blue, purple, red, pink, or even black sheets. I mean, she is not meant to move into our home, Hildegard. Hopefully, she is not a shapeshifter like us. If she is even a daywalker, that would make our situation easier to manage," Gabriel said.

Back at Larry's home, Caleb and Viviana looked at the sunrise, while Bianca and the other members prepared themselves for their slumber. "Well," Caleb said. "We should probably get some sleep, so we have our strength and energy to save Larry and perhaps take care of our human problem as well."

"Are you talking about that human girl?" Viviana asked. Caleb shook his head.

"What do you mean? I mean, divert the attention of the humans from looking for anything suspicious in our area, Viviana," Caleb said. "No, I will not eradicate that Jenna girl. I am not that cruel."

Viviana remained confused. "So, we are not to get rid of that girl, but only distract the law enforcement humans?" Viviana asked. Caleb nodded.

"Exactly. I will prepare our home for our slumber," Caleb said as he headed back into the apartment complex. "Are you coming?"

Viviana nodded. "Yes," Viviana asked as she walked into the apartment complex, while Caleb waited for her so he could lock up and close all the curtains in the main area before he headed for his bedroom.

Caleb went to lie down on his bed and closed his eyes. In his dream, he was back at the castle. He went to the dining quarter to get himself a drink and noticed Gabriel sitting at the table. "Evening, son," Gabriel said as he kept his focus on the blood in his glass. "We have fresh blood in the cooler for you."

Caleb walked over to the cooler, but then turned around to find Gabriel's gaze on him with a smile.

Caleb placed his left hand on the cooler handle while he locked eyes with Gabriel. Caleb then opened the lid and forced himself to look inside the cooler. He gasped and took a step back. "Is something wrong, Caleb?" Gabriel asked.

Caleb noticed how fast he was breathing. "You monster," Caleb whispered. "How did you manage to kill Larry?"

Gabriel walked gracefully, like a cat, over to Caleb. Caleb was unable to move. Gabriel placed his hands on Caleb's shoulders, then grabbed Caleb's chin with his right hand to force Caleb to look at him.

"You are next, dear Caleb," Gabriel whispered before Lucien, Adrian, and Vladimir appeared from behind Gabriel with their teeth barred. Amelia and Araeballa then appeared behind them, followed by Alistair and Darcia. They all hovered around Caleb. Caleb tried to escape Gabriel's strong embrace and shook himself awake in a state of panic in his bedroom.

"Goodness," Caleb panted. "Is Gabriel now doing this to me?" Caleb checked his watch and saw that it was going on eleven o'clock in the morning. Caleb fell back onto the bed. "Gabriel, what are you doing to me?" There was a knock on Caleb's bedroom door. Caleb walked over to the closed door, opened it, and saw Bianca standing in front of him. "Bianca, what are you doing here?"

"Did you by any chance have a dream about Gabriel?" Bianca asked. Caleb nodded.

"Me too. What was yours about, Caleb?" Bianca asked. Caleb beckoned for Bianca to enter his bedroom.

"I saw Larry dead in the cooler, and Gabriel's group was about to attack me," Caleb said.

Bianca nodded. "My dream was about how Gabriel had proposed to me, and if I did not, Larry would be ripped apart. I woke up in shock and was unable to fall asleep again," Bianca said. Caleb nodded.

"If you want to sleep here, you are more than welcome to," Caleb said. Bianca shrugged.

"I am fine, Caleb, but thank you for the offer," Bianca said. "I just wanted to make sure I was not going crazy."

Caleb nodded. "You are not crazy. I think Gabriel may be taking revenge on me for going after Amy's younglings," Caleb said. Bianca nodded.

"I understand, but I will try to get back to sleep, Caleb. Sweet dreams," Bianca said teasingly, causing Caleb to giggle.

"You too," Caleb said before he closed his bedroom door and crawled back into his bed.

Back at the castle, Larry started to feel achy and weak due to the malnutrition he suffered from in the dungeon. Larry heard the squeaks of rats in a different cell and made clicking sounds with his tongue to beckon the rat. The rat looked up at him and approached him. Larry felt this intense need to feed. The rat was then about ten feet away from him. When Larry lunged at it, it ran away.

"Darn it," Larry whispered. "I need to feed. This is torture."

Larry checked his watch. It was going on noon. When was he to be released from this castle, so he could have Viviana distract the humans? Larry started to feel sadness inside of him. He looked back at when he worked at that tavern and how he met Viviana. How disapprovingly her father looked at him whenever he looked at his daughter. How clean and pure she looked in this floral white dress! How she made his heart race and his mind race by thinking of her. The moment she accepted his proposal, it was perhaps the best day of his entire life.

Larry laid down on the concrete slab that was supposed to be a bed and closed his eyes, due to how extremely exhausted he had felt from everything. Larry wondered what would have become of his fate had he never engaged with Amy? Would he even be in this situation? Would he have found Viviana in a different way? Why did Viviana never try to look for him? Perhaps she was scared about being a shapeshifter. Perhaps she did not care about him after all.

Larry shook his head fast. No. Viviana does love him and cares about him. She was probably just scared and was hiding a lot, eating rodents and birds. That makes more sense than to think she preferred someone else's company to his. Larry was unable to sleep due to how much pain he felt and how angry and sad he felt. Larry decided that his fate was to be accepted as being stuck in a cage forever.

How was Larry even going to get Viviana to enter the castle? What if Gabriel refused because of how she had treated him and the other members? What if Caleb and Viviana were meant to be together? Would he be able to forgive Caleb for abandoning him? Larry then started picturing Caleb and Viviana getting married and how they would share a life together while he remained in the cold. He pictured Viviana and Caleb traveling together, forgetting him, and not even showing up to offer their respects upon his departure from his grave. Larry then knew he had to do something. Would he be able to break the lock on the cell? If so, he would have to get past that housekeeper. He would not be able to end her so quickly because that would probably seal his fate. Larry knew he had to be more strategic this time and avoid causing unnecessary problems. He had to play the game of strategy, and this time he would have to make sure he would win and not end up in the dungeons again.

The Tests

As dusk approached the castle, Gabriel woke up feeling better than he had been in the last several years. Arabella noticed Gabriel waking up and also decided to get ready for a new evening. "Good evening, my dear," Gabriel said. "I have not slept this well in many years."

Arabella smiled. "Good to hear, Gabriel," Arabella said. "Any sweet dreams?" Gabriel shrugged.

"It was quiet slumber for once. No interruptions. No nightmares, just a quiet and relaxed slumber," Gabriel said. Arabella nodded and smiled as she placed her nightgown on the chair and grabbed a green velvet gown from her closet. Gabriel watched Arabella with admiration in his eyes.

"Green was always your color, Arabella," Gabriel said. "It suits you and your complexion."

Arabella smiled. "Fall colors work best with me, Gabriel. I am not much of a pastel girl," Arabella said.

"I remember you wearing a green gown the first time we officially met," Gabriel said. "You were quite beautiful with your curly brown hair and your eyes. I remember how blessed and lucky I was to have met such an attractive young girl."

Arabella then sat at the boudoir, putting a bit of makeup on, such as mascara and a light pink lipstick. Gabriel watched her and smiled at her as she brushed her hair. "What are your plans this evening, Arabella?" Gabriel asked.

Arabella shrugged. "Amy's children have grown, Gabriel. Have you seen them lately? In just a few days, they are now walking. The process of their development amazes me. I do feel a sense of sadness whenever I think back on when I transformed into a ghost and how I was not able to take care of my own children," Arabella said.

Gabriel felt a sudden sense of sadness inside of him when he thought back to the moment he saw Arabella screaming in pain as she was pushing out both Amy and Ginger. How angry and overwhelmed he felt! Gabriel put on his evening suit and walked up to the main floor. Arabella watched him leave with confusion. "Is everything okay, Gabriel?" Arabella asked.

Gabriel did not respond. He headed for the dining quarter, grabbed himself a fresh, unopened bottle of blood, and started drinking from it to distract himself from his memories. Amelia came up to the main floor and grabbed an empty glass. Gabriel turned around to face her. "I hope I am not interrupting you, Gabriel," Amelia said.

Gabriel shook his head. "No, Amelia," Gabriel said. "I suddenly got quite thirsty." Amelia placed her glass on the table and waited for Gabriel to pour her a glass.

"So," Amelia said. "I have been thinking about this. If Amy's friend is one of us, we should at least try to find out more about her skills and powers. I mean, does she burn in the sun?"

Gabriel shrugged. "I wanted to propose that idea to Jenna, but Amy is against it. I can understand it, for the sake that it could burn her or lead to her grave," Gabriel said. Amelia nodded.

For some reason, Gabriel, we need to know more about this situation because we need to make sure we keep our kind a secret. Has anything else happened?" Amelia asked.

"Anything else happened? What do you mean by that, Amelia?" Gabriel asked. Amelia sighed. "Have you noticed other humans in the area looking for that Jenna girl?"

Gabriel shrugged again. "I do not know, Amelia, but if they are looking for her, we will keep her confined in this castle for as long as it takes," Gabriel said. Amelia nodded.

"Okay. I will see what Amy is up to and how Jenna is doing. Please excuse me, Gabriel," Amelia said before she left for the staircase. Gabriel remained in the dining quarter, watching his three brothers, Darcia and Alistair, enter the dining quarter.

Amelia walked toward Am's closed door, knocked, and waited for Amy to respond. "Yes," Amy said. Amelia turned the notch on Amy's bedroom door and entered. Amy looked up with a surprised expression.

"Amelia," Amy said. "What brings you to my room at this time?" Amelia closed the door behind her.

"I was wondering if I could borrow Jenna for a while and see what her situation and condition are regarding her potential change," Amelia said.

Amy's expression turned to a frown. "What is this with you and my father wanting to see Jenna's condition? She obviously is a shape shifter, so why must you bother her about that?" Amy asked.

"Amy," Amelia said. "I am not trying to do anything wrong or bad regarding this situation, but perhaps Jenna might be a daywalker or perhaps not even a shape shifter at all. If Viviana, your father, or even Ginger could use their persuasion powers on humans, and Jenna seems to be okay, we may have dodged an important bullet in our lives."

Amy sighed. "Seriously? I cannot handle anything regarding stress anymore, Amelia. I get lied to and deceived, and now Jenna might be or might not be a shape shifter? You cannot see how ill everything has made me, but due to our lifestyle, I will remain healthy forever," Amy said.

Amelia nodded. "I understand, but if we have a chance to save our kind Amy, that would save us a lot of problems, and one day or a few days out of our lives will result in the lifelong happiness of having everything return to normal. What do you say?"

Amy rolled her eyes and sighed. She looked over at her children and realized that it would also save their futures. Amy nodded. "Okay. Go ahead and experiment on Jenna," Amy said. Amelia nodded and leaned in to hug her.

"You may have saved us all, Amy," Amelia said. "I will go and find our new guest. Enjoy the rest of your evening."

Amelia headed for the next staircase toward the third floor and came across a new section, which she had never even known existed. There were paintings of Gabriel from different angles. There was also a female painting, which Amelia believed was Arabella. Amelia walked down a hallway and saw the name Hildegard on one of the doors. She then looked at the other doors, which had no name on them. Amelia used her sense of smell and hearing to guide her to Jenna's room.

A few doors down, Amelia stood in front of a closed door, which she believed was Jenna's bedroom. Amelia knocked on the door and waited. There was no response. Amelia knocked again. Again, there was no response. Amelia gently opened the door and pushed it forward by a few inches. "Jenna?" Amelia asked. "Are you in this room?"

Jenna was in bed, but she looked depressed as she just stared at the wall. "Jenna, is everything okay?" Amelia asked. Jenna looked over at Amelia. Her complexion and eyes had changed. "Wow, you look different."

"Am I?" Jenna asked. "Am I different? It seems like everything is going downhill for me. What did you say your name was?"

"Amelia," Amelia said. "Perhaps we did not get off on the right foot with proper introductions, but I am the family's sorceres."

Jenna rolled her eyes. "Wow, a sorceress in the family. What does that make the rest of us?"

"That is what I wanted to find out," Amelia said. "I wanted to run a few experiments on you to see if you are one of us or if you are different." Jenna clicked her tongue. "I know how this sounds, but do you remember the man who lured you over to his apartment that one evening, pretending to be Amy?"

"Caleb?" Jenna asked. "I feel sorry for Amy's kids. How did Amy even find that man attractive?"

Amelia chuckled. "That is kind of a long story, but I just have a few questions for you. How are your hearing, vision, and hunger levels?"

Jenna thought about that question for a moment. "Well, I am not entirely sure how different my hearing and vision have been since

I even came here, Amelia. My hunger, well, I do crave hamburgers and steaks, so perhaps I do need iron. What more can I say?" Jenna asked.

Amelia nodded. "Well, I was hoping you could come over to my slumbering quarter and let me test you on some things, and lastly, see if you are able to go out into the sun without dying or getting burned," Amelia said.

Jenna shook her head. "I feel like I got hoodwinked by Caleb or that other weird guy into thinking a vacation for three weeks in Romania was going to be fun, since I had never been to any country in Europe before," Jenna said.

Amelia shrugged. "Neither have I when I was about your age, but I enjoyed traveling and exploring new areas till I met Gabriel. He was quite handsome, loving, and kind till you got close to him, and goodness, he is something different than what he appears to be on the outside," Amelia said.

Jenna listened attentively to Amelia. "How did you feel about being here for the first time, Amelia?" Jenna asked. "Were you coerced, lured, or pushed into being a shapeshifter?"

Amelia thought about Jenna's question. "Well, I do not really remember how it all happened. From what I do remember, we met at this museum of some kind. This museum showed various ancient paintings of how humans used to live and what combat was about. I was focused on this one painting. What was it called again? I would have to ask Gabriel about it, but I was focused on the detail of how the painter managed to capture it quite nicely. He came up next to me, and he explained something to me. His voice was so deep and velvety. I felt breathless at the way he was explaining something to me. I remember how hot it seemed to be in that museum. Nobody looked at us, since they were too focused on the other paintings. I grabbed my fan and waved it gently till he mentioned he had a castle nearby and how he loved inviting beautiful people to his home to talk about the romantic topics of art and music," Amelia said.

Jenna noticed Amelia's expression of laughter and started to chuckle at the way Amelia explained her encounter with

Gabriel. "Forgive me for asking this, but did you have any strong romantic feelings toward Gabriel?" Jenna asked. Amelia nodded mindlessly.

"All the men and women who had their encounter with Gabriel were quite something. Powerful and passionate," Amelia whispered. Jenna smiled.

"I can see that," Jenna said. "When I first saw him, I felt scared and uneasy, but for some reason, he managed to put me at ease about this situation."

Amelia nodded. "It could have been his pursuasion powers as well, Jenna," Amelia said. "Gabriel is not that evil of a man. He can be ruthless and reckless, but he has decent toward good intentions, except for what happened to both Larry and Viviana."

"Who are Larry and Viviana?" Jenna asked. Amelia looked confused at Jenna. "Larry and Viviana are friends of Caleb, the man who you believed was the father of Amy's children," Amelia said.

"What happened to Larry and Viviana?" Jenna asked. Amelia shrugged.

"Perhaps I am not the one who should explain that story to you, Jenna, dear. What I should do is see how your condition affects your potential new life. Are you ready for a few tests?" Amelia asked.

Jenna nodded. "As much as I can be, Amelia," Jenna said. "It will not hurt, will it? Those tests?"

Amelia shook her head. "No, dear Jenna. Perhaps the sun might, but I shall do that as a last restort, so we can be certain about your situation, okay?"

Jenna nodded. Amelia led Jenna over to her slumbering quarter, which took them about twenty minutes to get to. Amelia opened the door with her special key and gestured for Jenna to enter. Jenna looked around at how clean and white Amelia's quarter looked.

"I like to keep my workspace clean from everything," Amelia said. Amelia walked over to the living area and sat on the sofa, beckoning Jenna to sit next to her. "Okay, I have some books on shapeshifters, vampires, werewolves, and mystical creatures. I want you to look outside of this window and see if you can spot that tree, and describe every detail of what you can see of that tree. Everything," Amelia said.

Jenna looked outside her window, spotted the tree, and squinted her eyes to try to get as much detail as possible. Jenna shook her head. "It looks just like an ordinary tree to me. A brownish bark with green leaves," Jenna said. Amelia looked at Jenna, analyzing her closely.

"Anything else?" Amelia asked. "Are you able to see the tiny drops of dew from the leaves? Are you able to see tiny sprouts of new leaves?"

Jenna analyzed it and shook her head. "No," Jenna said. "I cannot see that far ahead." Amelia nodded.

"That is fine, Jenna. Okay, let me try another thing. I am going to brush this light feather against the wall. If you have sharp hearing, it will sound like a broom sweeping the floor," Amelia said. Jenna nodded. Amelia brushed a white feather that she had in one of her drawers and brushed it along her wall, keeping her eyes focused on Jenna.

Jenna closed her eyes and drowned out any other noise in the area. "Well?" Amelia asked. Jenna shook her head. "Okay. Well, let me try out another thing. You said you were craving hamburgers or steak; I have a flask with some fox blood in it. If I hold it out to you, would you crave it?" Jenna shrugged. Amelia held it out for Jenna to take. Jenna took the flask and looked at the red liquid inside. Jenna's mouth felt dry, and she was in need of something to drink. Jenna quickly took a sip from the flask and exhaled. Then Jenna took another sip and another until it was empty. "Interesting. Okay. Well, your hearing and eyesight are not that sharp like Gabriel's, but let us see how you do with speed and strength."

Amelia brought Jenna down to the dining quarter and saw Darcia sitting at the table with her glass of blood. Darcia looked up at Amelia with concern. "Is everything okay?" Darcia asked. Amelia nodded.

"I am just running a few experiments on the girl, but I was wondering if I could borrow you for two tests?" Amelia asked. Darcia looked over at Alistair and smiled.

"What kind of tests, Amelia?"

"Strength and speed. Jenna does not have sharp hearing or vision, but she did drink down the fox blood sample I had," Amelia said.

"You want me to race and fight, Jenna?" Darcia asked. "What if something goes wrong? Can you not fight her, Amelia?" Amelia sighed.

"I just need to see for myself how much Jenna has developed after the incident with Larry. Please do this for the sake of our kind, Darcia," Amelia said.

Alistair placed his right hand on Darcia's, patting it gently. "I am sure everything will be fine, Darcia," Alistiar said. "As a matter of fact, would I be able to watch them?"

Amelia nodded. "Of course. I want to see how Jenna is doing and see if she has any strengths or powers," Amelia said.

Alistair and Darcia both nodded. "Well, let me first finish my glass, and I will meet you both outside once I am done," Darcia said.

Amelia smiled and nodded before she led Jenna out through the sliding doors. Jenna looked outside and saw how beautiful the sky looked. Amelia looked around, made sure there were no potential threats in the area, and led Jenna down the marble staircase toward the open courtyard. Jenna followed and looked at the different statues and shrub designs. "Wow, this is where Amy lives?" Jenna asked.

Amelia turned around and nodded. "Well, I should not be talking about another person's experiences, but both Ginger and Amy managed to live normal human lifestyles until they were expected to return at the age of eighteen. Perhaps you will not experience the transition for now until you get that real, deep carnal hunger for a human or even an animal. Hopefully, you will be able to return to your parents' home or your college dorm and live the rest of your life as if nothing bad had happened to you. And here are Darcia and Alistair," Amelia said.

Darcia and Alistair both approached the courtyard area. Darcia took off her black leather jacket, handing it to Alistair. "So, what kind of race do I need to take part in?" Darcia asked.

"Running," Amelia said. "I need both you and Jenna to run toward the end of that one tree that I pointed to Jenna earlier and return. If Jenna wins this race or if the race is tied, we will know. If Jenna loses and collapses from being winded halfway there and back, we can check that part off the testing part. Okay ladies, get on your marks, get set, and run."

Darcia took the lead in the speed race and heard Jenna's panting from thirty feet behind her. Once Darcia reached the tree, she looked to see where Jenna was. "Are you tired, Jenna?" Darcia asked. Jenna held up her hand as she bent down, placing her hands on her knees. "Did you want me to carry you back?" Jenna shook her head.

"I just need a moment," Jenna said. "So, if I am not a fast one, does this mean I cannot be a shape shifter?"

Darcia shrugged. "We should go back to Amelia and see what she has to say," Darcia said. "Are you able to run, or would you prefer to walk?"

"I can run a little bit," Jenna said. "You can go on ahead." Darcia looked around and saw how dark and eerie it looked.

"We can also walk together, Jenna," Darcia said. "Here, take my hand." Jenna accepted Darcia's hand, and they walked back together.

Amelia observed Jenna, seeing how pale and tired she looked. "Did you want to continue the experiments tomorrow, Jenna?" Amelia asked. Jenna nodded.

"I think I have done my quota of experiments for now, Amelia. I just need to rest up." Amelia nodded.

"Okay, well, happy slumber," Amelia said before she walked back toward the sliding doors. Darcia and Alistiar walked Jenna back up to the sliding doors.

"That was quite brave of you, Jenna," Darcia said as she gestured for Jenna to enter through the sliding doors. Alistair closed the door behind them. Gabriel approached Amelia.

"How did the testing go?" Gabriel asked.

"Well, she does not have speed, strong eyes, or hearing, but she did drink the fox blood. What could that mean, Gabriel?"

Gabriel thought about it for a moment. "She has not been bitten yet. Do you have books on shape shifters becoming one of us from just blood drinking?" Gabriel asked. Amelia thought about it.

"Well, I would have to double check on some of the topics, because if it is possible that she is undergoing something you went through as well, Gabriel, it could possibly be the same as what you underwent. Let me not draw such conclusions right now, Gabriel. Please excuse me," Amelia said before she walked back to her sleeping quarter.

Gabriel looked over at Jenna. "So, Jenna, how are you feeling?" Gabriel asked. Jenna shrugged.

"I feel kind of tired and swimmy, but other than that, no different than before," Jenna said.

"Perhaps I might want to try something out with you tomorrow evening, if you are up for it? Amy and the other ones can take part in it as well if they want. Would you be up for a different flavor?" Gabriel asked.

Jenna started to feel nervous. "Well, I am not sure if I want to do that, sir," Jenna said. "Can I just return home?"

Gabriel thought about it and shook his head. "I am not sure I can allow that right now, Jenna. You are not a prisoner, but we need to make sure you are not one of us, with the lack of experience and control that could result in a lot of problems for our kind. See what Amy has to say about it. She could perhaps guide you and help you out," Gabriel said.

Jenna did not know what to say or think. She felt kind of nauseous and tired from everything, but she did crave more blood. What was going on? Jenna walked over toward the staircase and saw everyone heading off toward their quarter. Jenna then decided to go over to her quarter instead and wondered if she should talk to Amy. Jenna felt sort of uneasy about being in this place. She looked outside and saw how the sun was going to rise pretty soon. Jenna decided to walk onto the balcony outside of her room and felt the soft wind on her face. She felt scared and alone. She wanted to be back at home rather than stuck in a castle. Was she even allowed to contact her parents? She did not want to engage anymore with the other shapeshifters, wondering if they were all just pranking her or distracting her. How did shape shifters even exist in this world? Jenna just felt more confused as she looked outside.

The sun started to break through. Jenna looked at how beautiful the sun was as it was rising slowly above the trees. She admired such beauty and remembered something her father once told her. Enjoy the tiny bits of beauty in life. Material possessions are fun for a while, but the bits of nature, sunrises and sunsets have more value in making people happy. She watched the sun rise slowly and saw the sun slowly touching the ground in the courtyard. Jenna started to feel her heart racing a bit, and she felt a sense of panic hitting her. Jenna quickly walked back into the bedroom and closed the curtains. What was going on? Are shape-shifters real? Is she to be a shape shifter as well? Will she be able to return home to her parents, or is she stuck in this castle? Jenna felt her breathing getting faster the more she was thinking. Jenna did not feel tired or worn out, but like she wanted to escape.

Jenna opened her door and saw a door open, and an older woman in regular clothes left the bedroom and closed it behind her. Jenna tried to get the woman's attention, but she was unable to speak or make any sound. Hildegard walked down the staircase. Jenna followed her and cleared her throat till Hildegard looked up at Jenna with shock.

"My dear," Hildegard said. "Are you lost? Are you one of Gabriel's pets?" Jenna scrunched her brow.

"What? What does that mean?" Jenna asked in the form of a whisper. Hildegard looked around, but nobody else was around.

"Are you lost, my child?" Hildegard asked. Jenna nodded and shrugged after that.

"I am not sure, but how do I get out of this place?" Jenna asked.

Hilegard beckoned for Jenna to follow. "You sound disoriented. Here, let me guide you toward the front door. Perhaps you are not meant to be a snack, I am guessing," Hildegard said.

"A snack? Do these people eat other humans?" Jenna asked. Hildegard looked confused at Jenna.

"Um, I am not sure what I should be thinking right now, but you seem quite young to be in this place. What is your name, dear?" Hildegard asked.

"Jenna. Amy and I used to go to school together till she had to leave for some family reunion or something like that," Jenna said. Hildegard nodded.

"Oh right. I get it," Hildegard said. "I remember you. You are the potential new creation of Gabriel's. Goodness, how I have been forgetting a lot of things lately. So, what did you actually need, dear Jenna?"

"I need to get out of here," Jenna said. "I feel like I am going crazy and feel incredibly scared right now."

Hildegard placed both her hands on Jenna's shoulders. "It is all right, Jenna," Hildegard said. "You are safe right now. Try to breathe," Hildegard said. Jenna inhaled and exhaled. "Okay. "I am not sure if I can allow you to leave right now, Jenna. Gabriel has offered you lodgings, and unless he is fine with you just leaving right now, I am not up to date on his decisions. Just wait for him to arise. I am sure he can let you go home. Try to get some sleep, Jenna," Hildegard said.

Jenna felt a sense of hopelessness, but she thought about waiting for the housekeeper to be out of sight before she bolted out of the castle. Jenna nodded and headed back toward the staircase. Hildegard then walked toward the dining quarter to fix herself some breakfast. Jenna placed her hand on the doorknob, and it was locked. "Darn it," Jenna whispered. "Well, I can try to head toward the basement area." Jenna did not remember which area went where, so she tried a different basement area, not knowing she was heading toward the dungeon.

The Game

Larry heard footsteps approaching his area and suddenly noticed the girl he had lured over to his apartment complex. Larry's mind and eyes had awoken. "Psst," Larry said. "Over here." Jenna approached the cell with Larry inside of it. "Jenna?" Jenna nodded.

"You are?" Jenna asked. Larry chuckled.

"Of course you might not remember me, but I am Larry, from the apartment complex. I had you come over to me, thinking Amy was in the area," Larry said.

Jenna scrunched her brow. "Oh dear, you are that guy?" Jenna asked as she backed away from him.

"Please wait. I am sorry for what I have done to you, Jenna. That was not right of me. I need your help," Larry said.

"What kind of help?" Jenna asked.

Larry looked around at the cell. "I am stuck in this cell against my will, under Gabriel's orders. I need you to help me return home to my friends. They are worried about me," Larry said.

Jenna analyzed Larry's demeanor. "How did you end up in this place anyway?" Jenna asked.

"Well," Larry said as he was making clicking sounds with his tongue. "It is kind of a long story, but they think I am the cause of exposing our kind, which is not true, by the way." Jenna looked around, feeling uncomfortable and confused. "I can see that the circumstance of you seeing me like this is unusual, but I am also in desperate need to eat and drink. I feel quite exhausted from the lack of nutrition I had to suffer with for the last week or so."

Jenna suddenly felt a sense of pity for Larry. "I am not sure if I can get you out, but I could ask Gabriel once he wakes up," Jenna said. Larry looked deeply at Jenna.

"That might be too late for me, Jenna," Larry said. "If you could come over to the lock, perhaps you can help me break it, so I can return home to my warm bed."

Jenna approached the cell and looked at the lock.

"It looks quite sturdy. I am not sure I have the strength to open this for you, Larry, but I will see if Gabriel could help out," Jenna said.

Larry shook his head. "That might be too late. I need something to drink right now, Jenna. What can you give me or find for me that would keep me from passing right now?" Larry asked.

Jenna thought about it for a moment. "I think I may know where Gabriel keeps some blood. Would that work?"

Larry smiled and nodded. "Absolutely," Larry said. "I knew you were a smart girl when I saw you for the first time, Jenna." Jenna smiled nervously. "Come now. I am sure all your teachers, professors, and parents are incredibly proud of you."

Jenna giggled nervously. "I hope so," Jenna said. "Let me see what I can find for you, Larry. I shall return momentarily." Jenna left back toward the main floor and did not notice any traces of the housekeeper. She walked over to the dining quarter and opened up the refrigerator and other cabinets until she came across a metal box in a corner. Jenna used her strength to open the box and found over a dozen dark red, unlabeled bottles. She grabbed one and dropped the lid, causing a loud bang. Jenna looked around to make sure nobody would wake up from it, and she walked back toward the dungeon area.

Larry got to his feet and approached the metal bars when he saw Jenna walking towards him. "Goodness, Jenna, you are an angel," Larry said. When Jenna handed him the bottle through the bars, Larry looked down at Jenna's wrist and arm and felt this intense hunger inside of him. He reached for the bottle, grabbed Jenna's wrist, and without too much thought, he yanked her arm into the cell, causing Jenna to scream, and bit her hard on her arm, feeling the need to suck hard.

Due to Larry's lack of strength, he felt dizzy, dropping the bottle and leaving Jenna screaming on the floor. Suddenly the door to the basement opened up, and several members came running down the floor. Gabriel and Arabella both showed up with shock in their eyes. Gabriel grabbed Jenna and cradled her in his arms.

"Gabriel," Arabella said. "You need to bring her to a doctor or have Amelia look at her."

Gabriel ran with his speed over to Amelia, knocking loudly on her door until she opened the door with a gasp. "What happened?" Amelia asked. Gabriel barged into her room with her in her arms. Arabella came into the room seconds later.

"I think Larry may have lured her down to the basement, Amelia. We need to finish the transition now. There will be no more tests on her being a shapeshifter. She will soon become one of us," Gabriel said.

Jenna's breathing got heavier and wispy. "Now Amelia," Gabriel snapped. Amelia slid open Gabriel's wrist and hovered it over Jenna. Jenna started gulping down the blood, occasionally choking and coughing it out. Then Gabriel sat Jenna up against the sofa, sitting next to her, and noticed that she was slowly turning into a beautiful, sculpted, and darkened shape shifter.

Gabriel sighed with fear while Arabella had tears falling down her cheeks. "This is too much," Gabriel whispered as he moved some strands of hair off Jenna's face. "We need to get rid of Larry once and for all. I am not waiting any longer for any planning. Tomorrow night, it will end."

Arabella and Amelia exchanged glances, nodding at each other. "Now we have a bigger problem. "What do we tell Jenna's parents?" Gabriel asked.

"I cannot handle this," Arabella said. "This is too much for me to handle. Amy is going to be heartbroken."

Amelia placed her hand on Arabella's shoulder. "We will figure this out," Amelia said. "Everything is going to be okay." Arabella walked back toward her sleeping quarter. "I think Jenna should rest on this sofa in my quarter, Gabriel. I will look after her. You need to get some sleep to finish off the job tomorrow." Gabriel nodded.

Back in the cell, Larry was slurping up the spilled blood from the concrete floor, feeling stronger and more alive than before.

Larry licked his lips as he looked around and saw the same rat approach him. He waited patiently for the rat to walk through the bars and get up closer to him until he snatched him and drained the rat. Larry let out a long sigh of relief as he felt like his old self again. He needed to find a way to escape. He knew he should not make much noise to draw attention to himself, but he had to find a way.

Larry was not certain of what time it was, but if Gabriel had to sleep, it was probably still sunny outside. He should not have bitten that girl. He should have used her to get him to escape. Larry sat back on the marble slap, trying to find any weak areas that he could break. The cell looked quite sturdy. There was probably only one way to escape. Wait for Gabriel to plan his death, and make a run for it.

Back at the apartment complex, Caleb was not able to sleep. No matter how comfortable and relaxed he felt, sleep would not take him. He decided to go to the living room and try to create a plan for helping Larry escape. He was going to show up at the castle and propose to Gabriel that he collaborate with him on keeping the humans distracted and see if Larry was able to make a run for it. Viviana woke up and heard Caleb talking to himself and writing on paper, which was quite loud for her ears.

Caleb heard footsteps approaching him and looked up. "Viviana, what are you doing up so early?" Caleb asked. Viviana looked at the table.

"I could ask you the same thing, Caleb. Is there a reason why you have the living room table covered in paper?"

Caleb smiled and beckoned for Viviana to look at his plan. Caleb explained the plan to her, causing her to chuckle.

"You are certain this plan will work?" Viviana asked. "I feel quite skeptical about it, but if you feel a certainty, make sure you come out alive and do not get yourself captured."

Caleb kept his focus on the paper and shrugged. "Nothing is ever certain, Viviana. Everyone can doubt their plans because we do not know what the future holds," Caleb said. "How did we ever end up in a situation like this?"

Viviana shrugged before she put her right arm around Caleb's shoulders. Caleb suddenly felt this weird feeling inside of him, turned to face Viviana, and kissed her lips softly.

Viviana flinched. "What was that?" Viviana asked. Viviana got to her feet, but she did not walk away. Viviana then leaned down and kissed Caleb back. Caleb then moved away.

"Viviana, I am so sorry. I should not have let my lust get to me like that. What would Larry have thought about that?" Caleb asked. Viviana leaned down, pinned Caleb to the couch, and added more passion to her kisses. Caleb did not resist.

Hours passed. Caleb checked the clock on the wall in the kitchen area, seeing that it was two o'clock in the morning. Caleb and Viviana had not slept that evening, but Viviana did return to her room.

Caleb suddenly felt anxious about what had happened with him and Viviana. He should never mention that to anyone, especially Viviana. Bianca would definitely rat them out, or at least use extortion to her advantage. Caleb then walked over to his bedroom and managed to fall asleep in a deep sleep. What felt like minutes were actually seven hours later. Caleb woke up from his slumber and saw that it was nine o'clock in the evening. Caleb left his bedroom and looked down at his clothes, which looked wrinkled.

Once Caleb arrived in the dining room, Viviana, Bianca, and the other members were hanging around, sharing blood packs with each other. Bianca gave Caleb a confused look. "Someone needed their sleep badly," Bianca said. Caleb nodded.

"Of course I did," Caleb said. "Sleep is important for us, especially since we will get our Larry back home."

"Okay. Viviana, did Caleb share his plan with you?" Bianca asked. Viviana looked over at Caleb sternly.

"Yes, he did, Bianca," Viviana said. "So, I think we will manage quite well this evening to get Larry back home safely. We may need to find a different blood source. Are any of you?" Viviana asked, looking around at everyone. "Are any of you familiar with the city and the blood bank areas?"

Nobody responded. "Okay. Well, I guess we should find some new blood sources. I know that Larry would be quite famished once he returns after being locked up for all this time," Viviana said. "If we were to find a new blood source, we should split up to avoid any law enforcement humans that wonder what three or four individuals are doing out so late. We do not look like we are partygoers, so we should try to avoid drawing attention to ourselves."

The other members nodded. "Okay," Caleb said. "We should avoid drawing too much attention to ourselves, especially since that one girl is probably one of us."

Viviana scoffed. "Larry just fed her some of his blood. Nothing new or bad will happen to that human girl. This was just to get a reaction from Gabriel and his family. Sometimes you need to create a thunderstorm to get a beautiful rainbow in the end," Viviana said.

Bianca and Caleb exchanged glances and smiled. "Okay," Bianca said. "I guess we should get ready for operation, save Larry."

Caleb got to his feet. "I think I will go out first to scout the area for new blood bank resources, and then I would suggest you ladies do the same in like an hour. If law enforcement does question you about being out too late, just tell them that you are on your way back home from a late party and ignore them. Good luck out there," Caleb said.

Bianca looked over at the other members, who did not look like the average human. "Well, perhaps Viviana and I will take the lead for now," Bianca said before she got to her feet to gussy herself up, as if she were to go to a party.

An hour later, Bianca and Viviana wore makeup, jewelry, and their best fancy clothes and walked outside of the apartment complex to look for their next blood source. They walked through the main streets and saw how closed-off and dark everything looked. They scouted a bit further. They saw the same hospital, with police officers hanging around. "Is there any way to try out a different city?" Viviana asked.

Bianca shrugged. "Okay. It is about midnight, so how far is it to the next alternative clinic? Would Caleb have already been there?" Bianca asked.

"Okay. We should go back the same way we came," Viviana said. As the two women walked back toward the same route they took, there was a car that approached them. Three men, two in the front and one in the back, rolled down their windows.

"Good evening, ladies," the male driver with brown hair and brown eyes with a tattoo on his face said. His friend, another brown-haired and brown-eyed man with an earring on his left side. The other man in the backseat with black hair and green eyes, with his hair gelled backwards, smiled at both Viviana and Bianca. "Need a ride?"

Bianca and Viviana exchanged glances and smiled. "That would be wonderful," Bianca said. Both Bianca and Viviana entered from each side of the car. "What are your names?" The driver asked. Both Bianca and Viviana chuckled.

"My, my, asking a lady about her name without introducing yourselves?" Bianca aked teasingly.

The three men chuckled. Viviana knew they were bad guys, but they did need a quicker way to find their blood supply. "So, where are you all headed?" Viviana asked. The driver ignored her question. Viviana looked over at Bianca, who looked back at her. "We need to get to a hospital. Could you drive us to another city?"

The man in between Viviana and Bianca looked at his friend behind the wheel and nodded. The driver took a sudden sharp turn to the right, locked all the doors, and started driving fast down a few alleyways. Bianca wrapped both her hands around the male passenger's neck in front of her. "Pull over, or your friend gets it," Bianca said, with her nails around the man's neck.

The driver suddenly pumped the breaks, causing everyone to nudge forward. "What are you?" The driver asked. The man in between undid his seatbelt and tried to lean forward until Viviana grabbed him, pulling him backward.

"Women you do not want to mess with," Vivana said. "We need you boys to drive us over to the next city and drop us off at any hospital or clinic."

The driver started to panic, but did as Viviana said. About an hour later, Viviana and Bianca were dropped off at a different hospital. Bianca and Viviana tried to get out, but due to childproof locks, they were unable to. Bianca then leaned over to the man next to her and dug her teeth into his neck, causing him to scream. The driver quickly got out and ran, as did the passenger friend of his. Viviana then managed to get into the driver's seat and undid the locks from the back.

The men ran off in different directions, leaving their friend with Bianca, in the backseat. "Well, that was something," Viviana said as she took the keys out of the ignition and opened the door. Then she opened the door to Bianca's side, letting her out. "What do we do?"

Bianca looked around, grabbed the man, and dragged him out. "We should let the nurses know that there is a monster out there. We, being two female good semaritans, would not be suspsected of such monstrous activity, Viviana," Bianca said. Both Bianca and Viviana carried the partially dead man into the clinic and placed him on the floor at the front desk. There was nobody around. "Okay. We should go looking for their blood section and try to gather as much as we can. Especially since we have a car at our disposal."

Viviana nodded and followed Bianca through the hospital. They walked over to the blood section, but to their disappointment, it has a special lock on it where doctors and nurses use their badges to get in. Both Bianca and Viviana sighed simultaneously. "Well, what do we do now?" Viviana asked. "It seems almost impossible to get blood right now, Bianca. This is making life a bit harder to handle."

Bianca looked around. "Well, I guess we will need to use our powers on a doctor to get us a badge," Bianca said. "Want to split up, or should we stick together?"

Viviana looked around. "Caleb did advise us to split up and decrease our chances of humans suspecting us of being shape shifters," Viviana said. "So, I will go down the left side while you go right."

Viviana walked over toward the left side and accidentally came across the main receptionist, seeing two doctors and the receptionist doing resuscitation on the man from the car. The man then suddenly gasped. Viviana quickly walked past them, avoided eye contact with the man, and headed down the hallway to find a different doctor. The hallway was empty. Some of the doors were open, and there were some closed doors with patients sleeping. She was able to hear their soft breathing.

Viviana never liked hospitals, but then again, she would never have to worry about going to hospitals again. She tried to find someone, just anyone to get a key card. There was a female doctor with her brown hair tightened in a bun, clean-cut nails, and a wedding ring on her left hand who came around a corner wearing a white doctor's coat and holding a clipboard in her hands. "Excuse me," Viviana said. The doctor looked up from the clipboard. "My friend needs help. She needs…" Viviana stopped in her mid-sentence to avoid asking for blood. "Um, sorry for bothering you."

Viviana turned around to find the two doctors carrying the injured man from the car. He looked at her and started to whimper. Vivina walked by the three men, headed toward the entrance of the hospital. She left the hospital and felt incredibly hungry. Bianca had her snack with the man, but she had not had anything since last evening. Suddenly, there was a whisling sound behind her. She turned around to find Bianca holding a keycard in her hands. Viviana smiled and followed her into the blood section.

After Bianca opened the door, she walked ahead, and they could smell the euphoric scent of donated blood. Viviana's mouth was watering. She opened up the first cabinet, found a blood pack, and drank down the entire pack in a matter of seconds. She let out a loud sigh. "Whoever donated this type of blood has perhaps the best kind, Bianca," Viviana said.

Bianca grabbed a plastic box and placed as much of the blood donations as possible, and she realized she needed to find a way to cover up the box to avoid the doctors and receptionists noticing what they were doing. Bianca looked around, but could not find anything. Viviana looked out through the window and saw the doctors approaching the blood bank. "Bianca, we best hide or run out of this place as fast as we can," Viviana said.

Bianca looked up and then at Viviana. "Okay, okay. Give me a moment," Bianca said as she felt herself panic. "Okay. Follow my lead." The door to the blood bank opened. Viviana hit behind the open door while Bianca remained in the middle of the room. "Evening boys, I must have gotten lost. I was looking for some feminine products, and I must have accidentally stumbled into this room and could not leave."

The two doctors exchanged awkward glances. "You need a card to get into the room," said a male doctor with brown hair and brown eyes, wearing a doctor's coat. "Who let you in?" Bianca sighed and nodded.

"The woman with the white coat and brown hair. She opened the door for me to enter," Bianca said.

The other doctor, with brown hair and brown eyes, kept his gaze on Bianca. She looked up at the second doctor and gave him her best seductive smile. "Thank you for helping me, doctors. I guess I can go now." Bianca winked at Viviana, who was behind the door, and left the room. The doctors closed the door behind them, following Bianca. Viviana quickly grabbed the plastic box of blood. It was a bit on the heavy side to fit in about fifty packs, but Vivaina managed to carry it outside. Bianca kept all eyes on her while Viviana left the hospital, carrying the box in her hands. The car was still there. "Well, thank you all for a lovely evening. I best get going."

Bianca blew them all a kiss and left the hospital. She got into the driver's seat and turned on the ignition with the keys that she kept with her, and they both drove back to the apartment complex. It was going five o'clock in the morning when they returned. Caleb had returned earlier and sat with Larry's friends in the living room. The door opened and closed. Caleb focused his attention on who was approaching the living room and saw Bianca still dressed up in her pretty clothes, helping Viviana carry the box into the living room. "We will be okay for a while, friends," Bianca said. Viviana nodded.

Back at the castle, Gabriel headed down to the basement, where there were no windows, and saw Larry looking better than before. "I normally go to sleep around this time, Larry, but you and me need to have a talk," Gabriel said.

"Well, Gabriel, I have nothing but time for you," Larry said teasingly. "I have nowhere to go."

Gabriel growled at Larry. "If you think I am a heartless monster for going after both you and Viviana, what you just did right now was probably one step above me, Larry. You really have done it this time," Gabriel snapped. Larry scoffed. "What are you going to do to me? Torture me and then kill me?" Larry asked.

"No," Gabriel said. "I am going to keep you confined to this cell and order all the other members, including Hildegard, to never allow your friends inside our castle. You will die of starvation."

Larry did not respond. "You will never see Viviana again, Larry, dear," Gabriel said. "You will not get a proper farewell or funeral planned either. Is that understood?"

Larry got to his feet and approached the bars. "You are quite sick and twisted, Gabriel Ambrose. As far as I am concerned, I am an angel as compared to you," Larry said.

Gabriel shook his head. "No," Gabriel said. "You are no angel. You are someone who is too sick to understand right from wrong. You are nothing but a dangerous animal that needs to be put down. I have atoned for my behavior in the past, Larry Harrison, but there will be no atonement coming from you ever again." Gabriel turned around to head back to the staircase.

"Your fate will soon be sealed, Gabriel Ambrose. Just because my friends are not allowed to enter your precious home does not mean you will survive it all. I may not survive that long in this cell, give or take a year, but Viviana and Caleb will soon save me and give me the strength I need, and you will be burned on a fire while Viviana and I read our vows to each other in front of your precious daughters," Larry said.

Gabriel turned around and barred his teeth. "Perhaps I should end you right now," Gabriel hissed. Larry chuckled.

"Okay, come and get me, big guy. I am just standing here waiting for you to stop beating around the bush and to finally take me down like you have before," Larry said.

Gabriel shook his head quickly and adjusted his stance. "My, I should not allow you to provoke me like this," Gabriel said with a chuckle and turned back around to walk towards the staircase to the main floor. Upon his arrival on the main floor, Amy stood at the top of the stairs with her arms crossed and a tear-stained face.

"Amy," Gabriel said with shock. "What are you still doing up at this hour, my dear?"

Amy looked at Gabriel. "How did it happen, Father?" Amy whispered. "I saw the bite mark on Jenna's arm when I went to find out where she was. Amelia is trying to keep her detained as much as possible, but how did it all happen?"

Gabriel sighed and nodded as he stepped foot on the main floor and closed the door behind him.

"Larry must have lured her down to the basement, Amy," Gabriel said. Gabriel went to wrap his arms around Amy, but she took a step back and shook her head.

"Amy, let me care for you. It is my fatherly duty to comfort you in a time of need."

Amy shook her head. "I feel dead inside, Father," Amy whispered. "I cannot feel or think anymore. What are we to do about us, her, her parents, everything?" Gabriel shushed Amy. "Please, Father, tell me."

"Go to bed, my dear Amy," Gabriel whispered. "Tomorrow we will take matters into our own hands and finish them forever."

The Challenge

Gabriel walked down to his sleeping quarter and saw Arabella preparing herself for a slumber. Arabella sat on the edge of the bed. "Gabriel, we need to end this. Either you allow Amy to drop the blade or swing the axe, or you go in for the final attack. Now that Larry is still detained in the dungeon, you must do something," Arabella said. "Plus, I think it is time that we go over to the human world, explain the situation to Jenna's parents about some kind of animal attack, or something like that, or you use your pursasive powers to distract the humans. Either way, something needs to happen."

Gabriel nodded. "Okay. I think we should first distract the humans, because I have been hearing sirens around our area. How about this? We go over to Jenna's house tomorrow evening, either you and I or my brothers and I, and we use our powers on the humans to take their minds off of the whole search party for that girl," Gabriel said.

Arabella shook her head with disgust. "I am so ashamed of our kind, Gabriel," Arabella whispered. "We are monsters in this world, even though most of us did not choose to be brought into this lifestyle."

Gabriel nodded. "I know, my love," Gabriel said as he put on his satin black robe. "That girl is going to need some time to adjust to this new life. I never wished this darkness upon anyone, Arabella. I know I was quite ruthless and reckless, especially toward you and your family. Why else do you think I would rather end myself than remain living in such guilt and shame?"

Arabella looked confused at Gabriel. "Are you being serious right now, Gabriel?" Arabella asked. "First, would you end my entire family and then end yourself? Oh, please," Arabella said.

Gabriel looked over at Arabella. "It was just a thought, my love," Gabriel said. "Well, I am quite exhausted from everything. Goodnight."

Arabella rolled her eyes, focusing back on her hair. "Goodnight," Arabella whispered. Gabriel got under his side of the covers and closed his eyes. He was not that tired, as he was waiting for Arabella to join him in bed. Instead, Arabella decided to walk over to the dungeon area. She snuck around the area and headed for the other side of the basement area. Gabriel got out of bed and put his robe and slippers on.

Gabriel followed Arabella over to where she was headed. Arabella was in the dungeon area and walked toward the cell where Larry was lying. "Arabella, what a surprise?" Larry said it in a singsong. "What brings you so late in the slumber to come to me?"

Arabella stood about ten feet away from the bars with her arms crossed. "Oh, dear, did I do something wrong?" Larry asked.

"What you did to that girl is disgusting," Arabella said. "You really messed up this time with exposing our kind to the human world."

Larry walked toward the bars, heard footsteps coming down the stairs, and smiled. "Arabella, have I ever told you how beautiful you look in your nightgown?" Larry asked. Arabella glared at Larry. "Well, if you would not mind, but I need to catch up on my sleep as well, sweetheart."

Larry walked back toward the marble slap and lay down on his back. "Sweet dreams," Larry whispered.

Arabella walked back toward the staircase and gasped when she saw Gabriel standing on the stairs. "Gabriel," Arabella whispered. "I…well," Arabella stuttered.

Gabriel shook his head. "Why, Arabella?" Gabriel asked. Arabella headed up toward the main floor. Gabriel did not nudge. "What were you hoping to achieve by going over to that creature?"

Arabella walked by him and ran up the stairs. Hildegard opened and closed the door. It was going on six o'clock in the morning. "Arabella, what were you hoping to achieve?" Gabriel asked. "Larry is not someone with whom you could have a regular talk, and he will understand your perception."

Arabella sighed. "I am so heartbroken by this new situation, Gabriel," Arabella said. "That poor girl. It made me think about my situation, Gabriel. Not being given a choice to join the shape-shifting world."

Gabriel sighed. "Everything will work out just fine, Arabella," Gabriel said. "Going to that creature this early in the morning is not the best way to handle our problem."

Arabella sighed. "I am scared, Gabriel," Arabella whispered. "I am scared about the future of our kind, but I am so angry that we are heading into some darker times."

Gabriel nodded. "You are quite strong, Arabella. Show how well you can handle this with grace and strength toward Amy and Ginger. Show them what it means to be a strong woman in our family. Remember, we grow and develop through the trials and tribulations, and we will overcome the biggest hurdle in our entire lives, Arabella. We will overcome everything, and you can decide what you want to do once Larry, Caleb, and the other ones are gone," Gabriel said.

Arabella nodded and smiled. "If you are confident enough to be certain that we will be okay, I will try my best to believe in it as well, Gabriel," Arabella said. Gabriel nodded. "Well, we should probably get back to our slumber," Gabriel said. Arabella nodded, and together, she and Gabriel headed toward their slumber.

As dusk approached, Amy walked over to Amelia's slumbering quarter, knocked on her door, and waited for Amelia to open the door for her. Amelia showed up with sleepy eyes. "Amy, what are you doing here so early? I could have slept for another hour or two," Amelia said.

"Where is Jenna?" Amy asked. "I must see her right now."

Amelia turned around and beckoned for Amy to enter her quarter. Jenna was on the sofa with a spare blanket and two pillows, sleeping peacefully. Amelia looked over at Amy. "She is doing fine, Amy. Give her some time to rest up for a bit longer. Soon, you will be able to see her and spend the evenings with her. Try to get some more sleep or get yourself a drink, Amy," Amelia said.

Amy nodded and walked back to the main floor. She felt this intense anger but knew that if she were to go down to Larry, nothing good would come of it. He would probably provoke her. Amy needed to speak to someone. She walked over to Bryan and Raymond's bedroom and gently knocked on their door. Bryan opened the door. "Amy?" Bryan asked. "What are you doing up so early?"

"Larry turned Jenna. We need to get rid of him," Amy said. "He needs to go." Bryan shook his head with disbelief. "Seriously? Okay. Give me a few minutes. I will wake up my brothers, and the six of us will take him down this evening."

Amy nodded before she headed back toward the staircase, walking toward the dining quarter to grab herself an unopened bottle of blood to chug it down. About an hour later, Bryan and his brothers were dressed and ready to take on Larry. Amy led the way toward the dungeon area, and they all saw Larry sitting up against the wall of the dungeon. Larry, it ends right now," Amy snapped. Boys, please break the lock and allow me to end him."

Joshua, Silas, and Xavier used their strength to break the lock on the cell. Raymond and Bryan opened the gate to the cell. Amy stood at the threshold of the cell, analyzing him. She walked toward him, grabbed him by the shoulders, and pushed him outside of the cell. Bryan and Raymond quickly grabbed him, while Silas grabbed his neck, forcing him to look up at Amy.

"Please, Amy," Larry begged. "I am actually the victim in this situation. It was your father who killed off my future. I am just the product or reaction of what he has done to me."

Amy shook her head, feeling empty and blank inside. "You went too far with going after my kin, Lawrence Harrison," Amy said. "Having Daniel killed off was wrong, but you went after an innocent young woman. A human who I saw as a sister. She was the only reason I felt safe and comfortable being me, and you had to break that part of me. For what reason, Larry? Because you hate my father so much."

"Amy!" Larry begged. "Please, we were never going to hurt her. I even told Caleb and the other ones that as well. She was only being used as a bargaining chip for your father. Amy, you are not like your father. You are not cruel. You are beautiful, strong, and smart, just like your mother. You take after her in many ways, Amy. Please, do not end me like this."

"Amy, when you are ready, do not let Larry get into your head right now. Do the right thing," Bryan said. Amy looked up at him.

"I never even harmed you myself," Larry said. "It was my parents who gave you that one drink, but I never would have harmed you in any way, Amy Rose Ambrose. You have to believe me."

Amy started to feel overwhelmed. She placed her hands on Larry's neck, but something inside of her caused her to stop. "I am no killer," Amy whispered. "I am not sure I can do this, Bryan."

Bryan clicked his tongue, shaking his head. "Fine, Joshua, I will allow you to do the honors," Bryan said. Joshua headed toward the spot Amy was standing on. Amy walked away. "This is so wrong, Bryan, boys," Amy said. "We are not the bad guys in this situation. I mean, if we were to release Larry, he would definitely return with vengeance, but for now, I do not think I can end anyone's life. Please excuse me," Amy said as she headed toward the staircase.

"What do we do, Bryan?" Joshua asked. "Do we finish him off, or do we save him for Gabriel?"

Bryan looked around. They were so close to ending their biggest problem, but that would mean that Viviana, Bianca, Caleb, and the other ones would plan their next attack on the family. Bryan did not want to be seen as the cause of the upcoming battle. Bryan pushed Larry back in the cage, but there was nothing to lock the cell up with. "Joshua, Raymond, could you both hold the bars together while I look for an alternative lock or cell to keep him confined in?" Bryan asked. Both the boys nodded.

Bryan saw different types of cells with cobwebs, dust, dead rats, and fecal matter, which looked horrific. Bryan saw another cell with a different lock. "This should work," Bryan said. Bryan headed back toward Larry's cell. "On the count of three, we open the bars and grab him. Silas and Xavier were standing several feet apart behind the three boys. "One, two, and three." The three boys released the bars and went to grab Larry. Larry dove and pushed Joshua aside, and then he punched Raymond so hard in the face, causing him to fall backwards. Silas and Xavier lunged at him, but he dodged both of them and ran up toward the main floor. Amy was in the dining quarter and heard the loud screaming and panting. She headed for the basement door. Larry came out running. Amy lunged at him, but he quickly ran ahead and managed to jump through one of the windows, causing the glass to shatter.

Gabriel and Arabella quickly ran up toward the main floor. "What happened?" Gabriel asked. Amy looked at the broken window. "Amy?"

"Larry managed to escape," Amy said.

"What?" Gabriel snapped. "How did he manage to escape from the dungeon, Amy? What were you doing down there?"

Amy broke down, crying out of anger and frustration. "I wanted to kill him myself, but I realized that I am not a killer, Father," Amy sobbed. Gabriel clicked his tongue and shook his head. "I am so sorry about everything."

"No, Amy," Gabriel said. "You never have to apologize to me. Ever." Gabriel wrapped his arms around Amy, holding her close. "I was hoping you would have, Amy, but I can understand that the timing was bad. Normally I would be angry at such situations, but I am glad that you were not harmed or dead either, Amy. Okay?"

Amy nodded as she used the back of her left hand to dry her eyes. "I just do not know what happened back there, Father. I was so close, but then he managed to slip through our hands," Amy said.

"Our hands? Who else was down there, Amy?" Gabriel asked. Amy exhaled.

"Bryan and his brothers," Amy said. Gabriel scrunched his brow.

"How did those five boys let one man go, Amy? Please tell me everything," Gabriel said.

One by one, Bryan and his brothers entered the main floor, rubbing their wounds with their hands. They saw Gabriel and froze with fear. "Bryan," Gabriel said. "What happened?"

Bryan sighed. "Well, Larry had overpowered us all, Gabriel," Bryan said. "We underestimated how strong he was, even though he had not fed for a long time."

Gabriel shook his head. "Please join me in the living quarter and tell me how it all happened. It is true that I wanted Amy to feel a sense of justice, but how did he overpower you all?"

Bryan looked at his brothers. "Feel free to join in, any of you, in this discussion," Bryan said. "Raymond and I had Larry pinned on his knees, and Larry must have used his manipulation powers or did something to cause Amy to lose interest in ending him. I looked around for a new lock since we broke the first one."

Gabriel checked his watch. "It is only eight o'clock in the morning. Why did you choose to attack him so early? We could have all gone down as a team to deal with him, Bryan," Gabriel said.

"Amy came over to me, Gabriel," Bryan said. "She had the look of anger and sadness. I knew I had to help her. I could not leave her standing in the hallway like that."

Gabriel looked over at Amy. "My dear child, what made you want to attack Larry so early?" Gabriel asked. Amy shrugged.

"I just cannot handle it anymore, Father," Amy said. "I saw Jenna sleeping on Amelia's sofa, and I saw how beautiful she looked. It broke my heart, Father." Gabriel nodded. "I understand, but did you have a strategy or a plan for going after Larry, Amy?"

Amy shook her head. "Amy," Gabriel said. "I will not go into a big lecture about this, but what you did was not that smart. You should have waited for us and told us about your plan. We could have ended our problem with Larry and our exposure to the human world. "Now we need to restrategize and reconstruct our plan to make sure it works once and for all. Okay, boys, go and get yourself a drink. I sure need one, myself."

Bryan and the other boys nodded. "We will talk again soon, Amy," Gabriel said. Arabella came back into the room.

"What is the plan?" Arabella asked. Gabriel gestured for her to enter the dining quarter.

"We need to inform all the other covens and let everyone know about what just happened. Perhaps everyone can come over, and we will have ourselves a final battle once and for all," Gabriel said.

Arabella nodded and grabbed herself a glass from the cupboard. "We really are heading into some darker times, Gabriel. Well, we shall see what Larry has planned for us."

Gabriel poured everyone a full glass of blood, then placed the bottle on the table and drank down his glass in a matter of minutes.

Larry ran through the woodsy park and, to his surprise, came across Viviana and Caleb, who were crouched down behind some shrubs. "Larry," Viviana whispered as she beckoned for him to come over to her. Larry ran over to Viviana and hugged her tightly.

"You are alive," Viviana whispered. "How was that even possible? I would have never thought Gabriel would have allowed you to leave like that."

Larry shook his head. "I managed to escape past those five monstrous boys," Larry panted. Caleb rose up and hugged Larry.

"You look quite ill, Larry," Caleb said with a chuckle. Larry playfully punched Caleb.

"I am quite thirsty and hungry," Larry said. The three of them headed back to the apartment complex. Once Larry stepped over the threshold, Bianca approached them with shock in her eyes. She ran over to Larry and wrapped her arms around him.

"Brother, dear," Bianca said. "You are home. How did you manage to leave that horrid place, Larry?"

"Give him some space, please," Caleb said as he led Larry into the kitchen to grab him a blood pack. He poured the contents of the pack into a glass and handed it to Larry. Larry swilled it down in a matter of seconds. "Another one?"

Larry nodded.

Caleb emptied another pack of blood and handed the glass back to Larry. "It is good to have you back home, Larry," Caleb said. Larry nodded after he swallowed the last sip.

"How have you all managed during my absence?" Larry asked. Caleb, Viviana, and Bianca exchanged glances.

"Quite well," Bianca said. "Well, there were just a few moments of getting into a serious situation with some law enforcement officials."

Larry looked over at Bianca. "What happened?" Larry asked. Bianca looked over at Caleb. "Ever since that human girl has been brought over here, the American law enforcement has contacted the Romanian law enforcement about the search for that girl, Jenna, was it?"

Larry nodded. "What specifically happened? Did they think any of you were Jenna?"

Bianca shook her head. "No, but they have law enforcement officials outside of hospitals in the evening times, as well," Bianca said. "I think they are catching onto the fact that there are mystical blood-drinking creatures in our world. Since Romania is sort of the story regarding Dracula, many humans are not suspecting that there are real vampires in this world, Larry."

Larry nodded. "We are no vampires, Bianca. How would they even know that we are connected to such stories? Blood donations are common in our world as well," Larry said.

"Not blood-drinking, Larry. The fact that we occasionally go out to the human world to get ourselves some blood packs does make us a potential target for vampirism," Bianca said. "We managed to score ourselves a lot of blood for a while, Larry. All we have to do is keep low for a while. I think you might want to sleep for about a week and consume some more blood since you did not look so good when you came in."

Larry nodded and walked over to the living room. "Greetings, friends," Larry said to his other shape-shifting friends. "I am back now, forever. I hope you all did not miss me too much. I will be asleep for a while since I barely got any sleep in that dungeon." The other members waved and nodded. "Okay. I hope you all are doing well, but I should get myself back into my comfortable bed. See you all around."

Back at the castle, Gabriel was not sure of a plan. He sat in his office chair, spinning his golden fountain pen in his hands, pondering how he was going to go about ending Larry and Caleb. He felt angry and disappointed in how reckless Amy was with her anger towards Larry. Had Amy just waited till everyone else woke up, and had she just taken her time to get justice for what happened to her friend, there would be no problems right now.

There was a knock on the door. "Enter," Gabriel said. Lucien came into the room and closed the door. Lucien sat down in a chair across from Gabriel. "Brother, is it true that Larry managed to escape the dungeon?" Lucien asked. Gabriel nodded.

"Yes, brother," Gabriel said as he kept his eyes focused on Lucien. "Amy decided to pursue him without letting me know and got Alistair and Darcia's sons to join in, causing Larry to escape. I know I should not be that mad at my daughter, but when such things happen without telling me about them and they result in a chaotic situation, I feel very disappointed, leaning towards anger when I have to witness such acts, brother."

Lucien nodded. "I understand that, Gabriel," Lucien said. "What are the plans regarding Larry and Caleb?"

Gabriel shrugged. "I need some time to construct a plan, brother. Right now, Larry is probably consuming a lot of iron products and resting up after being deprived of all that in the dungeon. He might need about a week or so to get his strength back up to his regular self. For now, I am too tired to even think about anything. What is going on with you and the other ones?" Gabriel asked.

"We were just wondering what you were up to. I mean, we were wondering how it all happened and why everything is a bit too quiet around here," Lucien said. "Well, if you want to give the others an update, just tell them that we should take it easy for a while and let Larry take the next step. That is what I just have to say right now."

Lucien nodded. "Okay. Well, enjoy the rest of your evening, I guess," Lucien said before he walked out of the office and headed for the living quarter. Gabriel remained in his office chair, staring above the closed door, wondering how he was going to take care of his problem. He could not blame his daughter for what had happened. He could not blame Bryan or the others, either. There was another knock on the door. Gabriel sighed. "Yes?" Gabriel asked. The door opened. Alsitair and Darcia both entered the room.

"My friends," Gabriel said, gesturing for both of them to sit. "What can I do for you this evening?"

"Bryan, Raymond, Joshua, Silas, and Xavier all feel bad for what happened in the dungeon, Gabriel," Alistair said. Gabriel shrugged.

"It could have happened to either one of us, Alistair," Gabriel said. "It could have even happened to me."

Darcia nodded. "What can we do to redeem ourselves, Gabriel?" Darcia asked. Gabriel shook his head.

"There is nothing to redeem. We just have to be prepared for what Larry has planned," Gabriel said as he focused his attention on the fountain pen in his hands. "Is everything okay with you, Gabriel? Your silence and demeanor tell us that you seem depressed. We will get rid of Larry and Caleb once and for all. We will live a happy and beautiful future while Amy and Ginger live their lives, and you will watch your grandchildren grow up to become whatever they choose to be. I know everything is going to be okay."

Gabriel smiled and nodded. "I hope so, Darcia," Gabriel said. "I really hope that the future will become brighter than it is now."

Alsitair put his right arm around Darcia. "Nobody ever has a beautiful story to tell in their lives. My story about how Alistair and I met was scary and wrong on so many levels, but we managed to find each other in the darkness. Probably how Arabella felt towards you," Darcia said.

Gabriel shrugged. "I hope so, Darcia," Gabriel said. "I know I did some horrible things to many humans, her family, even her, even Larry and Caleb, but I am also attoning for them in other ways as well. As long as I know what I did was wrong, I just wish the other ones, my children, could realize that I have changed. I wanted my daughters back. I would never have given up on them, no matter what. Had Arabella remained alive, holding and nursing our children, that would have resulted in a nicer and more beautiful moment than to lose my wife, give up my children, and allow them to return. Sometimes these make better stories about learning the most valuable lessons in life. The ones that had an easy life would not be able to show their next generation what suffering is about."

Alistair chuckled. "I know that all too well, Gabriel. I mean, after Amy and Ginger shifted around that fake wedding, I remember feeling the need to help them, even though I would have preferred to have left that moment up to you. My youth and shape-shifting days were not easy at all. What do you think about your past, Darcia?"

Darcia shrugged. "It started off decent until we met each other," Darcia said with a chuckle. "No, sorry, I cannot be saying such things. I know that when people have to face some hardships in life, they usually come out stronger and wiser than before. This does not apply to everything, since most of the humans we seduced ended up deceased. This does apply to us all, especially Amy and Ginger, who had to endure the last two years of their unknown situation in life and ended up becoming princesses of a shape-shifting family. I know Amy's children will probably have a safer and more relaxed life, but we all do need some time in our lives to coast rather than constantly racing around manically."

Gabriel and Alistair both nodded. "I agree," Alistair said. "I mean, I was hoping this Larry problem could have ended earlier, but sadly, we are just dealing with a detour and no setback. We just have to restrategize and reorganize our plan, and this time, it will work out better than before."

Darcia smiled and hugged Alistair. "You always know what to say to make the situation better," Darcia whispered. Alistair hugged her gently.

Gabriel watched those two together. "Well, I think I will see what the other ones are up to," Gabriel said before he left his office to head over to the living quarter.

Seventh Round

At the apartment complex, Larry lied in his bed, staring up at the ceiling, feeling comfortable and relaxed after those days of being stuck in a cold concrete cell. He loved the feeling of being under a warm blanket and feeling a sense of security again. He checked his watch. It was going on two o'clock in the morning, which meant that he would have another few hours before he would have to sleep, but he felt too exhausted to wait that long. Larry closed his eyes and fell into a deep slumber within a few minutes.

In his dream, he was back at the tavern. He saw Viviana in a wavy white gown, standing in the corner, looking shy at everyone. Larry remembered that it was that moment when he introduced himself. Suddenly, there was a different attractive young man with long black hair, wearing a suit, approaching Viviana. He took her by the hand and kissed it gently.

Viviana giggled and blushed at his sweet comments about her appearance and giggle. The man turned around, and it was Gabriel with red eyes, winking at him. Larry suddenly felt this intense anger boiling inside of him, approached Gabriel, and tapped him on the shoulder. Gabriel turned around.

"Can I help you?" Gabriel asked. Larry looked over at Viviana sternly.

"Is this man bothering you, sweetie?" Larry asked. Viviana shook her head.

Gabriel turned to face him, holding a translucent beverage in his hand. "Is everything okay with you, son?" Gabriel asked. Larry barred his teeth and growled. "Perhaps we should take this outside and away from the other ones," Gabriel said. He turned back to face Viviana. "I shall return shortly, my dear." Gabriel walked out of the tavern first, and Larry followed right closely behind him.

"What are you doing?" Larry snapped. "I had my eyes on that girl, and I saw you flirting with her."

Gabriel placed his hands on his hips, locking his eyes with Larry's. "It is a free country, son," Gabriel said. Larry raised his hand to want to hit him, but Gabriel quickly grabbed his hand, holding it tightly in his. "Violence is never the answer. If you want her so badly, go on inside and claim her."

Larry did not move. "Your hand is still on mine, sir," Larry said. Slowly, some of the humans were leaving the tavern, looking concerned over at both Larry and Gabriel. Gabriel released his grip on Larry and walked away. Larry did not move. He looked back inside to see if Viviana was around, but she was not anywhere to be seen.

Larry looked back in the direction where Gabriel walked and saw Gabriel and Viviana making out. Larry wanted to scream but was unable to, and he woke up screaming. Caleb came running in. "Larry! What happened?" Caleb screamed. Larry calmed himself down. "Larry, what is going on?"

Larry inhaled and exhaled. "Nothing, just a bad dream," Larry said. "About Gabriel."

Caleb sat down. "What of, Larry? What did Gabriel do? Did he try to annihilate you?" Caleb asked. Larry shook his head.

"I was back at the tavern, and I saw him making out with Viviana," Larry said. "Before I was kidnapped and held hostage, I had dreams about Gabriel. Why am I dreaming about him? Have you noticed anything, Caleb?"

Caleb remembered how he had nightmares about Gabriel, but that was only because he was putting his thoughts into Amy's children, causing them to overthink and go crazy. "Well, I think I can try to intervene in your dreams, Larry. I think Gabriel is trying to provoke you into a reaction. What is your plan for taking down Gabriel?" Caleb asked.

Larry shrugged. "I am not sure anymore, Caleb. I know how strong Gabriel is, and I know that he will not stop either. I am starting to feel the need to want to leave Roamnia for a while and go over to a country like Greenland, Norway, or a different country, Caleb. I am tired of going after Gabriel constantly, and perhaps we should take a break for a while," Larry said.

Caleb sat down on the edge of the bed. "Seriously, Larry? We are close to taking him down, and you want to stop now? Look, I can understand how scary and traumatizing it must have been in the dungeon, but you cannot give up right now, Larry. If you want to go on a little outing to a different environment for a bit, that might be good, but do not give up on your goal, Larry. It is at times like this that we must persevere and not give up, no matter how tall this mountain is. I have a good feeling that we will be able to overcome this obstacle and celebrate that wonderful moment for many years, Larry. Trust me," Caleb said.

Larry shrugged. "Perhaps you are right, Caleb," Larry said. "I think that dream of Gabriel kissing Viviana just caused me to lose faith in myself and make me want to run away, like I have done before. Now I do think we should restrategize on how we go about getting rid of Gabriel once and for all. I think I do want to take a break from this problem for a while and rejuvenate and reenergize my mind and body. If I were to face Gabriel right now, I think I would lose."

Caleb nodded. "Well, it is going on at seven o'clock in the morning. Try to get back to sleep when you can, Larry. You are in a safe and comfortable environment. Gabriel or his friends are nowhere to be seen. You are in your own bed. Did you want me to get you a blood pack?" Caleb asked. Larry looked around and nodded.

"That might help, Caleb," Larry said. Caleb got to his feet, headed over to the kitchen area, and came back moments later with a blood pack. Larry leaned against the bedpost and drank down the entire blood pack in a matter of seconds.

"Okay. Well, good luck falling asleep again, Larry," Caleb said before he left back to his bedroom. Larry placed the empty pack of blood on his nighttable and stared out at the wall across from him. He could not shake off that dream. His dreams always seemed unrealistic, which made it hard for him to occasionally differentiate reality from his dreams. He felt scared and intimidated when he was in the dungeon, which made him feel incredibly uneasy and angry inside. He was happy that he had the chance to escape the castle and run back home.

Larry looked at the curtains. It looked like there was an overcast. The sun would normally shine through his curtains, but this time, it looked quite dark and cloudy. Larry got out of bed, headed for the living room, and opened a part of the curtains to see the rain pouring down.

Larry admired the beauty of nature in many ways. He started to feel more at peace as he watched the rainfall on the concrete floor outside. He looked further down ahead of him, watching the humans looking out at the rain. There was suddenly a flash of lightning and a loud bang of thunder. Larry then closed the curtain and walked back to his bedroom, curled up in the covers, and closed his eyes. The tapping of the rain sounded rhythmic, which helped Larry fall asleep within a few minutes.

After the sun had set, Caleb opened Larry's bedroom gently to see how he was doing. Larry heard the creaking sound of the door and quickly sat up. "Sorry," Caleb whispered. "I had to know you were okay."

Caleb closed the door and walked back to the living room, where some of Larry's friends were sitting. "Larry is still asleep."

Larry came out a few minutes later in his pajamas and robe. "Caleb, please do not ever do that again. I really thought it was Gabriel, Bryan, or someone else that was planning their attack on me."

Caleb nodded. "I understand, Larry. Sorry for my intrusion," Caleb said. Larry nodded.

"So, where are Viviana and Bianca?" Larry asked. Caleb looked in the direction of their bedroom.

"Probably still asleep, Larry," Caleb said. "It is only about seven in the evening. After you were captured, most of us slept a lot. It was quite stressful, especially with all the humans running around with sirens.

"Right," Larry said. "Speaking of that, Caleb. Did you think to have Viviana use her powers on humans as a means of distracting them from our kind? She is quite powerful. If she was able to weaken Gabriel, Father and patriarch of our kind, she could have used her powers to tell all the law enforcement humans to divert their attention to going after Gabriel. She could have told them that Gabriel is a monster and the one going after blood banks. Have you not considered that plan?"

Caleb shrugged. "Not really, but that does sound like a good plan, Larry. We should have Viviana tell those humans that there is a monser killing humans and send them over to that castle. In modern days, what type of person still lives in a castle?" Caleb asked.

Larry nodded. "I will propose that idea to Viviana. Perhaps she can get rid of our problem once and for all," Larry said. Caleb smiled and nodded.

"Well, I hope that plan will work out, Larry," Caleb said. A bedroom door opened. There were footsteps coming down the stairs. Bianca came in her robe and slippers, yawning in her left hand.

"Evening everyone," Bianca said with her tousled hair, walking over to the kitchen. "How did you all sleep?"

"Quite well," Larry said. "I heard the rain. It sounded quite peaceful." Bianca returned with her blood pack and curled up on the sofa. "Is Viviana still asleep?" Bianca nodded.

"The poor girl was overly excited when you came back, Larry. She will probably rise in a bit. Why?" Bianca asked.

Caleb shrugged. "Larry and I might have a good plan for getting rid of Gabriel and his family forever," Caleb said. "We will wait for Viviana to come down to tell everyone about it."

Bianca sipped slowly and kept her eyes on both Caleb and Larry while they both smiled at her.

About an hour later, Viviana woke up and came down the stairs to get herself her evening drink. She walked into the kitchen and saw

Bianca putting glasses in the dishwasher. "Good evening, Viviana. Larry and Caleb want to talk to you," Bianca said.

"Oh? Of what?" Viviana asked. Bianca shrugged. "Whatever it is, I need to have my cup of blood first."

Bianca handed Viviana a blood pack and a glass. Viviana walked over to the dining room and sat down on one of the chairs. Caleb and Larry walked over to her and sat across from her. Viviana looked up at them, licking some of the blood off her fingers. "Bianca mentioned something about you needing to speak to me, boys?" Vivaiana asked.

Both Larry and Caleb nodded. "Yes," Larry said. "We think we may have a plan to weaken Gabriel and his family." Viviana focused her gaze on Larry. "We were hoping that you could use your magical powers to persuade the law enforcement humans that there are monsters living in that castle. With all the blood bottles in their cooler, they would most likely suspect them to be something other than humans, so perhaps they could do something to get rid of them somehow."

Viviana nodded in acknowledgement. "When did you figure out this plan, Larry?" Viviana asked.

"Before you woke up," Caleb said. "This way, the law enforcement humans would never suspect us of being shape shifters in their human world, and Gabriel would face a great deal of problems. What do you say?"

Viviana thought about it and rolled her eyes. "What if Gabriel were to reciprocate that plan?" Viviana asked. "What if Gabriel finds out and does the same to us?"

Caleb and Larry exchanged glances. "We will just have to cross that bridge when we get there.

Caleb cleared his throat. "After those agents came into the house, wondering if we were ending the lives of those humans, that really scared me," Caleb said.

Larry looked over at Caleb confusingly. "What? They have already scouted our area. How did you manage to get rid of them?" Larry asked.

Caleb sighed. "We did our best, but Bianca really put on a good show for them by seducing them," Caleb said. Viviana chuckled.

"I remember," Viviana said. "She was quite seductive in her nightwear and her way of talking to those humans."

Larry nodded. "Well, perhaps both women can use their magical ways of getting humans to ignore us forever. What do you say, Viviana?" Larry asked. Viviana shrugged. "I guess it is worth a try, but you should also ask Bianca about this plan as well. She also managed to help us score a lot of blood packs at this one hospital in a different city and managed to end one of the humans that had driven us to that hospital," Viviana said.

"What?" Caleb asked. "When did this happen?"

Viviana swallowed some of the blood and sighed. "When we had to look for a different blood source, that one hospital near us suspected humans drinking blood, so they hired some security outside of their clinic. Bianca and I managed to get a ride with these awful men, who thought we were vulnerable girls that they could take advantage of. Bianca tore into one of them, and the other two ran away," Vivivana said.

"What?" Larry snapped. "Now they know that we exist. What were you girls thinking?" Viviana sighed with annoyance. "Yes, are you going to say anything, or are you going to wait for me to pull the answer out of you? My goodness, Viviana. You may have ruined our chances of getting the upper hand again. Caleb, these girls have disrespected our kind. I am not sure if we should keep them around any longer. I will think about that option. Excuse me for a moment."

Viviana looked over at Caleb. "What does this mean for us, Caleb? We really did our best not to expose ourselves. I mean, their car is out in front of our home. We needed to find a way to get back home quickly. The fact that these men tried to kidnap us or go on an aggressive joyride caused us to defend ourselves," Viviana said. "Please talk to Larry about this. I do not want to end up getting hurt or, worse, die."

Caleb nodded. "I understand. I will talk to Larry about this and explain the situation from your perspective. Larry is probably still undergoing the transition to returning to his old self. Give me a moment, Viviana," Caleb said.

Viviana lost her appetite for the rest of her glass and walked over to the living room, extending the glass toward Bianca. "I lost my appetite, Bianca. Are you interested?" Viviana asked. Bianca took the glass.

"Sure, are you okay?" Bianca asked. Viviana nodded.

"Yes, but I may have told Larry about how we almost got kidnapped by those men," Viviana said. "Now he is wondering if we are too dangerous to be kept alive."

Bianca scrunched her brow. "Why? We did nothing wrong," Bianca said. Viviana nodded. "I know. Say, did you ever find those other two men, or even wondered if that wounded man that we took into the clinic talked about us being monsters?"

Bianca thought about it and raised her eyebrows. "Well, I am not entirely sure about that," Bianca said. "I do not think those doctors and nurses, or whoever was in there, would actually believe that man."

Viviana nodded. "I hope you are right, Bianca. Larry might consider us a threat and end our lives in a matter of seconds, or we would have to escape and hide out till the law enforcement humans are distracted by something else," Viviana said.

Bianca nodded. "Wonderful. As if this life could not get any worse. So, what is the plan for now? Did you find out what Larry and Caleb wanted from you?"

Viviana nodded. "Yes. They wanted me to use my powers to persuade the humans that Gabriel is the actual monster in that castle of his and how they are vampires and werewolves, or cannibals trying to end the lives of innocent humans," Viviana said.

Bianca giggled. "Seriously? Well, that might work. I mean, you managed to weaken Gabriel quite well."

Caleb and Larry both came into the living room. "Bianca, Viviana, may I have a word?" Larry asked. Both Viviana and Bianca followed Larry to the kitchen area. Caleb closed the door behind them. "What you both did was incredibly dangerous. I need you both to take me over to the clinic where those men ran off. Another dangerous fact is that their car is out in front of our home. They could have easily tracked us down. What the four of us are going to do is get rid of all the forms of evidence, and you, Viviana and Bianca, need to distract those humans and divert their attention away from us and towards Gabriel. Is that understood?"

Both Viviana and Bianca nodded. "Yes," Bianca said. Larry sighed with a bit of relief in his mind and looked at Viviana.

"Yes, Larry. We will make sure the humans have no idea of our existence. When did you want to leave?" Viviana asked. Larry checked his watch. It was going on midnight.

"We can leave in a few minutes. I will inform my friends about this situation and let them know that we will be gone for a while," Larry said before he headed for the living room. Viviana and Bianca both grabbed their jackets and waited for Larry to return. "Okay, where are the keys to that car?"

Bianca grabbed the keys from her jacket pocket and handed them to Larry. Larry opened the door and led the other three out of the apartment and into the car. Bianca sat in the front seat next to Larry, while Viviana and Caleb sat in the backseat. "Guide me over to that clinic, Bianca."

While Larry was driving, Bianca looked around but did not remember exactly where they were headed. She did not recognize the area, but she sort of knew where they had to go. Larry occasionally looked over at Bianca. "Are you going to give me directions, Bianca, or are you going to have me drive around like a maniac till we reach our destination?" Larry snapped.

Bianca looked around and shrugged. "It all happened too fast. My anger caused my mind to go blank with rage, and I could not help but attack the man in the passenger seat," Bianca said. Larry looked at her and shook his head.

"I cannot believe you both did that. I mean, what would our parents have thought of you doing this, Bianca?" Larry asked. "I will tell you to save you the trouble of thinking hard. They would have been incredibly disappointed in you, Bianca. As your brother,

I cannot help but feel angry towards you for having us go through this wild-goose chase because you were reckless."

Bianca sat in silence. "Well? Anything you want to say to me, Bianca, or will you just sit there passively in hopes that a miracle will take place and take care of all of our problems?" Larry snapped. Caleb sighed. "Caleb, is there something you want to add?" Caleb shook his head.

"I am sure the girls did not intentionally mean to do this, Larry. I think they already feel bad enough. Try to be easy on them. Once our problems are taken care of, we will laugh about this occurrence someday," Caleb said.

Suddenly, Larry pumped the car and turned around to face Caleb. "You want to walk, Caleb?" Larry asked. "Are you defending Bianca and Viviana's behavior for endangering us, Caleb? If the law enforcement already showed up at our house, that is only the first step before they return with actual evidence, such as this car." Larry slammed the wheel and let out a loud growling sound.

Larry then got out of the car and exhaled to get all the anger out of his body. Bianca turned around to face Caleb and Viviana. "What should we do?" Bianca whispered. Caleb looked outside and saw Larry pacing around angrily. "I am scared."

Caleb got out of the car. "Larry, try to keep as focused on our goal as possible right now. I am sure you are quite angry, but we need to get rid of the evidence before it is too late," Caleb said. Larry turned around with his black eyes and sharp teeth barred. "Larry, you need to calm yourself right now or go home. I will take the girls over to the hospital."

Larry walked around the car toward Caleb. "Will you now, Caleb? And then? You will leave the group and run off with the girls? Is that your master plan?" Larry asked. Caleb suddenly felt the need to defend himself and closed the car door. Caleb closed his eyes to inhale and exhale. Larry then relaxed himself, his eyes returning to normal, and he got back into the driver's seat. Caleb then got back into the backseat. Bianca tried her best to remember which way they drove, and about an hour later, they ended up driving toward the clinic.

"Caleb," Larry said. "Could you go inside and see if there is anything going on regarding the wounded man?" Caleb nodded and got out of the car. He walked toward the entrance of the clinic, walked through the spinning door, and headed toward the receptionist table. There was nobody around. Caleb looked around, and it looked quiet and bare. Caleb then walked toward the left hallway and looked around to see if there were any signs of wounded humans. It was a good thing that Caleb had already fed, because had he not, he would have probably caused a scene and caused the humans to suspect him of being a monster.

Caleb cleared his throat. "Hello?" Caleb asked. "Is anyone around here?" Caleb turned around to walk toward the receptionist's table. He realized that the coast was clear. He walked back to the spinning door until he heard a female voice. Caleb turned around. "English?" The woman wearing green scrubs approached him.

"Can I help you?" The woman asked. Caleb looked around and then at her. "We were looking for a man," Caleb said as he tried to describe what he looked like. The woman thought about it and nodded. "Ah, yes. He left yesterday. Are you family?" the woman asked. Caleb shrugged and nodded. The woman made a phone gesture with her hand. "Can you call him?"

Caleb shook his head. "No, but we wanted to make sure he was going to be okay," Caleb said. The woman nodded and smiled. "I guess I will leave now and see if I can find him back home. Have a good evening, madam." The woman waved to him and walked back to the receptionist desk. Caleb walked over to the car that Larry was in. Larry rolled down the window on his side.

"Well, how did it go?" Larry asked. Caleb looked around and saw how quiet it was. "The man got discharged yesterday, so I guess he is either in a transition phase or he managed to escape," Caleb said.

Larry sighed. "Great. This just went from a drizzle to rain showers, you guys," Larry said. "Unbelievable. Well, our next stop would be the police station." Larry drove over to the nearest police station, parked the car, and the four of them got out, walking toward the entrance. There was a button that they had to press and state through a call box what their purpose was for visiting the station.

"We must speak to someone about a monstrous household," Larry said. The bell chimed, and two sliding doors opened. The four of them walked through and had to wait for the doors to close before they could proceed past the second sliding door.

A male police officer with dark brown hair and brown eyes, wearing a uniform, approached them and gestured for them to join him in his office. The four of them followed the officer into his office and waited for him to close the door behind Caleb. The officer sat down in his chair, clicked on his mouse a few times, and turned to face Larry and the other three. "What can I do for you?" the officer asked with a strong Romanian accent.

Larry licked his lips nervously and cleared his throat. "We suspect that there might be a family that may have committed deaths on innocent humans," Larry said. The officer scrunched his brow, looking confused at Larry. "I know how weird this sounds, but we heard screaming coming from that castle. The main guy is named Gabriel Ambrose."

The officer looked over at the other three, who looked a bit nervous. He analyzed how pale they looked and sat back in his seat. "Aside from screaming, what other evidence do you have that would convince us to go over to Gabriel Ambrose?" the officer asked. Larry looked over at Caleb.

"Well, they have been going to hospitals to consume blood packs and lie about how they need transfusions. I mean, I have been reading in the paper recently how hospitals have security because of such suspicions," Caleb said.

The officer nodded. "You are certain that these people are killing people and drinking their blood?" The officer asked with a smile on his face. "Like vampires?" Larry clicked his tongue and sighed. "I know how weird this sounds, but you must believe us," Larry said with a raised voice. The officer looked over at Larry with slight irritation. "Please, just go over to them either tonight or tomorrow evening and see for yourself."

The officer leaned back again in his chair, shaking his head. "There have been talks about blood banks losing a lot of donations, but then again, we have not noticed any humans with their blood drained either. If you can provide me with any other evidence than that blood banks are losing their blood, I might reconsider this, but right now, I cannot create a file based on what you have told me about humans drinking blood," the officer said.

Larry nudged Viviana on the shoulder. Viviana inhaled and exhaled and looked at the officer. She used her seduction and persuasion magic on him. "Gabriel Amrbose is a shape shifter. He is a monster that hunts for humans and kills them. Gabriel is a threat to our environment, and he must be held accountable or even receive a death sentence for his crimes," Viviana said. The officer nodded mindlessly. "You will have a warrant prepared to place Gabriel under arrest and take him away from the castle to have him shot," Viviana said.

The officer nodded mindlessly some more. "Go and call for backup and go to this address," Viviana said. The officer nodded mindlessly, wrote down the address of the castle, and grabbed his microphone to call for backup. Viviana smiled and got to her feet. "Our job here is done. Come friends, let us return home," Viviana said with a chuckle. Larry left the room, laughing at the officer. Caleb then left the room. Bianca turned around and blew a kiss at the officer before she left the room.

"Well done, Viviana," Larry said as they headed back toward the car. They all got in and drove back to the apartment complex to celebrate this moment with several packs of blood.

Revenge

Back at the castle, Amy and Jenna were playing with her children, throwing plush balls back and forth, playing peek-a-boo, and other entertaining activities. Arabella was in their library, reading up on some of the histories of mystical creatures. Amelia was in her own quarter, reading up on the different potions and spells that could be helpful to counteract other powers. Gabriel decided to take a walk outside in the courtyard, looking at all the porcelain statues that he once had purchased all over the world. Despite being a shapeshifter, with his skills and powers, he was able to travel and enjoy the various beauties of the world.

He walked around, remembering what each statue represented and how he got it. Gabriel was always someone who, deep inside, knew that no matter how hard life was, he managed to find a silver lining in his troubles. Occasionally, he would look up at the sky and see the stars and planets. He might have done all of those horrible things of killing and acting ruthless, but he did get himself a family and many friends who respected him. Gabriel looked over at the different flowers, plants, and trees around the courtyard that had different names and meanings. He enjoyed the tiny moments of beauty in his life.

Regarding the fact that he gave up his children, he did suffer a lot in silence, knowing how foolish he was. He regretted many things he had done, but he also had to remind himself to put a lot of his past behind him and remember all of the positive things as well.

Ginger was in bed, reading up on the histories of the world. She decided to take a break from her reading and get herself a drink. She walked over to the dining quarter. She headed down the staircase and walked over to the dining quarter. She grabbed herself a new, unopened bottle and an empty glass. She placed both objects on the table, undid the screw of the bottle, and poured herself a nice, full cup of blood. What always gave Ginger a euphoric feeling was the first sip. She would moan and sigh with happiness. She decided to bring both the bottle and glass outside onto the patio until she realized her father was returning from his walk outside.

Ginger then decided to stay inside and sit down at the table. Gabriel entered the house and closed the sliding doors. "Ginger," Gabriel said in a surprised tone. Ginger smiled and nodded.

"Father," Ginger said in return. "How is the weather outside?" Gabriel nodded and smiled.

"Quiet and relaxed, my dear child," Gabriel said as he grabbed himself a glass and sat down adjacent to her. Ginger poured him a full cup. "What have you been doing with yourself?"

Ginger shrugged. "I was reading up on the various historical events in our world. It would be fun to have a discussion with you based on your live experience from the past," Ginger said. Gabriel smiled. "I am sure these historians are quite accurate in their explanations and definitions of what had happened, but perhaps you might have your own perception of them."

Gabriel listened attentively to Ginger. "Well, my ears are yours for now," Gabriel said.

As Gabriel and Ginger were discussing the history of their world, Bryan and his brothers were in his room, clicking through the different channels on the television. Just then, Joshua gasped, and his eyes turned dark. "Joshua," Bryan said. "Are you having another one of your visions?" Joshua was unresponsive. Raymond looked over at Bryan, who looked back at him.

"Perhaps he will tell us in a few seconds," Raymond said. Joshua returned moments later to his own self and sighed. Bryan waited for Joshua to speak. "Brothers," Joshua said. "We might be having company real soon. I think Gabriel might be dragged away by the police and sent off to get tortured, or even sentenced to death."

The other brothers exchanged worried glances with each other. Raymond cleared his throat. "Are you certain, brother?" Raymond asked. "Your visions do tend to change. When you mentioned that Caleb or Larry shifted into that human girl, it turned out to be quite the opposite. Perhaps Gabriel will just get rapped on the knuckles for being a loud neighbor or something. I cannot picture Gabriel, the strongest of us all, being dragged away by humans."

Joshua let out a loud exhale and leaned against the chair he was sitting in, closing his eyes. "We should mention this to Gabriel," Bryan said. "I mean, we should be prepared for any upcoming events that could result in some problems. Shall we?"

Joshua looked up at Bryan. "I never feel comfortable talking to Gabriel, you know. Could you perhaps do the talking for me, Bryan?" Joshua asked. Bryan shrugged.

"Sure, whatever. Gabriel and the other ones should know about your vision, Joshua," Bryan said.

The others nodded. "Okay," Silas said. "I will lead us over to the big man downstairs. Xavier and Raymond followed them downstairs. Joshua and Bryan brought up the rear, entering the dining quarter. "Gabriel, we have some news to share with you."

Xavier, Raymond, Joshua, and Bryan then joined Silas. Gabriel looked up at the five boys. "What is it this time?" Gabriel asked. Joshua started biting the side of his pinky nail and nudged Bryan to talk.

"Joshua had another vision of you being dragged away by law enforcement humans, Gabriel," Bryan said. "Of course this sounds quite weird and unrealistic, but that is what he just saw. We know that Joshua's visions do tend to change, so we are not that concerned about what may happen instead, but we need you to be on your guard."

Gabriel nodded and sighed. "Well, that is something I never thought would happen to me, but thank you, boys, Joshua, for letting me know. Yeah, I am not sure what to think or feel right now. Should I be worried, or is this just a fake plan to distract me?" Gabriel asked. The boys shrugged.

"No," Ginger said. "Father is too strong to be taken away by law enforcement. This makes absolutely no sense."

Gabriel smiled, placing his left hand on Ginger's. "Nothing bad is going to happen to me, sweet child," Gabriel said. "If the doorbell does ring, we will make sure that nobody answers it, and if they try to break through the door or windows, we will be prepared in our own way to take care of the situation."

Ginger started to feel afraid of the vision. She took Gabriel's hand in hers and refused to let go of it. "So, when will this vision take place, Joshua?" Gabriel asked. Joshua took his pinky out of his mouth.

"Soon," Joshua said. "My visions have no timeframe, so it is hard to see when they will happen."

Gabriel nodded. He slowly released his grasp from Ginger's hand. "My child, I would go to your mother and aunt and explain this new situation to them. I will notify my brothers of this potential vision," Gabriel said before he kissed Ginger on top of her head. He walked over to Lucien's bedroom and turned to the right, remembering the room Daniel used to sleep in. He opened the door gently and saw what his room looked like. Dark curtains, his bed, and a desk with pictures of him and the other three brothers, framed in gold. He looked at the pictures and felt sadness inside of him. How the constant fighting and conflicts with Larry stopped him from properly mourning the death of his brother.

Adrian came out of his room and found the door to Daniel's room open. He walked in and was surprised to find Gabriel sitting on Daniel's bed. "I have not had a moment since Daniel's death to mourn him. I think of him a lot, but I know I must be thinking about the future of our kind and lives, brother," Gabriel said while his gaze was focused on one of the pictures of all his brothers and him together. Adrian sat down next to him.

"As do I, brother. I mean, this whole conflict with Larry needs to be dealt with before one of us gets injured," Adrian said.

Gabriel scoffed. "Joshua, the son of Alistair and Darcia, saw a vision of me being taken away by law enforcement officials,"

Gabriel said with a chuckle, causing Adrian to chuckle. "Me, Gabriel Ambrose, head of shape shifters, will be taken down by humans. Oh please."

Adrian nodded. "Sounds like childish imagination, but then again, I do not want anything bad to happen to you either, brother," Adrians said.

Two more doors opened, and the other brothers, Lucien and Vladimir, both walked in to Daniel's old room. "What is this about humans coming after us again?" Lucien asked. Gabriel shrugged.

"Joshua's vision of me being taken away by humans. I would like to see them try," Gabriel said before he let out a hysterical laugh. Vladimir and Lucien both laughed with him. "Yep. These times are quite hard, but we will prevail, and we will have ourselves a celebratory bonfire after he dismantled the old chap," Gabriel said. "Well, now that we have ourselves a plan, we should probably get ready for any potential intruders. If the police show up, just invite them in and let them wander around before we snatch them one by one, or even better, use our powers to send them back to Larry."

The other men chuckled at Gabriel's plan. "It is like we are returning a broken product to the manufacturer, right, Gabriel?" Vladimir asked. "Perhaps we should then put them in a box with a bow on it." The other men, including Gabriel, laughed at that remark.

"I should inform Hildegard about these guys; please excuse me," Gabriel said before he placed the picture back on the table and walked over to Hildegard's bedroom. It was going on three o'clock in the morning, which meant that she would be asleep. This news was quite urgent. Gabriel gently opened Hildegard's door, snuck into her room, and placed his hands gently on Hildegard's shoulders, gently shaking her awake.

Hildegard moaned as she turned around and gasped when she saw Gabriel. She quickly turned on her nightlight. "Master Gabriel, what are you doing here?" Hildegard whispered. Gabriel placed his right index finger on his lips.

"We may be receiving unexpected company from Larry. If the doorbell rings, do not answer the door, and instead, find cops from another city; do you understand?" Gabriel asked.

Hildegard nodded. "Okay," Hildegard whispered. When she checked the time, she frowned.

"I know, Hildegard. The price of being with shape shifters. Different sleep schedules," Gabriel said with a chuckle before he left. Hildegard shook her head, turned around, and tried to go back to sleep. She was unable to, so she rose from her bedroom around five o'clock in the morning and saw the other members going over to their chambers.

Hildegard turned on the dishwasher from all the used glasses, wiped down the table and counters from any blood, and turned on the coffee machine to brew herself some. Then she waited for the newspaper to show up in the mailslot, around six o'clock, and read till it was time for her to run a few errands. She headed around eight o'clock to the car she normally drives and drove over to the nearest market.

When Hildegard returned to the castle, she placed the grocery bags and her purse on the table. The castle bell chimed. Hildegard remembered not to let anyone inside. She ignored the bell but forgot to call police from a different city. She put her groceries in the refrigerator and cabinets, and the bell chimed again. Hildegard started to get a headache from the lack of sleep and the chiming of the bell. Hildegard walked over to the front door and opened it by a few inches. There were ten officers standing in front of her. "Is Mr. Gabriel Ambrose around?" A male officer with brown hair and brown eyes, in uniform, asked.

Hildegard sighed and remembered that she should have called the police. "Um, no, he left on vacation," Hildegard said. "He lives here, but he is not here." The police officer repeated his question again. This time, two of the officers pushed open the door, causing Hildegard to fall backwards. The officers then entered the castle, leaving the door open and scouting out any areas where Gabriel might be.

Hildegard got to her feet but felt an intense, sharp pain in her right hip area, struggling to get to her purse so she could grab her phone. A police officer then snatched her purse and poured out the contents. "Where is Gabriel Ambrose?" asked a different officer. Hildegard shook her head.

"Away," Hildegard said. "Vacation." The officer looked back at the other male officers who were using their flashlights, trying to open closed doors that were locked.

Gabriel woke up from his slumber, hearing loud boots hitting the floor above him. Arabella then opened her eyes. "Gabriel, what is going on?" Arabella asked. Gabriel shook his head.

"I told Hildegard not to open the doors, Arabella," Gabriel whispered. "At least the doors to all our quarters are locked, so they cannot snoop around down here." Arabella sat up in bed, looking up at the ceiling.

Gabriel checked his watch and saw that it was going on eleven o'clock in the morning. "Well, hopefully they will leave in a bit, and if they were to return in the evening, we will use our powers on them all, Arabella," Gabriel said. Arabella nodded. About an hour later, the officers made a circle around Hildegard.

"There were four young people who complained about monsters eating humans in this castle," said one of the male officers with brown hair, a bit shorter than his colleagues.

Hildegard shrugged. "I do not know of such rumors, officers," Hildegard said. "Monsters do not exist." Another officer stepped forward, a young, handsome-looking man with black hair and black eyes.

"Where is Gabriel?" The man asked. Hildegard shook her head.

"Away on vacation. Please stop asking me about him. I am housesitting for him while he is gone. He locked up the rooms to prevent intruders or even me from snooping around his home. I cannot open up any doors for you to look for evidence of monsters," Hildegard said.

The same officer kneeled down in front of Hildegard. "When will Gabriel Ambrose return from vacation?" the officer asked.

Hildegard thought quickly about what kind of answer she should give.

"Next week," Hildegard said. "He left about a month ago, so I am just keeping everything clean and am temporarily living here to avoid house squatters, or whatever people call them. Now please leave; I need to take care of a few errands." The officers exchanged glances and left through the front door again. Hildegard walked over to the door and locked it this time. She walked back to the table to catch her breath and tried to relax her mind and body as much as possible.

After the sun had set, Gabriel quickly walked up to the main floor around nine o'clock in the evening to look for Hildegard. "Hildegard," Gabriel said as he found her getting ready for bed. "I heard what happened this morning. Could you tell me why you let those officers inside and did not do as I asked you to do?" Hildegard nodded. "I am sorry, Master Gabriel," Hildegard said. "Due to a lack of sleep and the start of a headache, I sort of forgot about the plan. I did not mention anything about you or the others, like we had agreed on, more or less, but you are right that I should have known better. They did eventually leave."

Gabriel nodded. "Okay, but you gave them a week to come and find me, so I need to create a new plan with my family on the best course of action, so we can continue living our lives without any interference from the outside world," Gabriel said. Hildegard nodded. Gabriel left back toward the main floor, watching the other members approaching the dining quarter.

Darcia and Alistair walked over to Gabriel. "What happened last morning?" Darcia asked. "Why were there police officers walking around?"

Gabriel held up his right hand. "Nothing but a minor mistake on Hildegard's part, but other than that, no harm. Your son had a vision of being taken away by humans, but I ordered Hildegard not to allow them to enter, but she did. They might return back in a week or so, until I metaphorically return from a vacation," Gabriel said with a chuckle.

Alistair looked at Gabriel with sympathy. "What is the plan now?" Alistair asked. Gabriel shrugged.

"When they return, we will make sure they get sent back to Larry's home and let them think they are the monsters in our world, so we can send humans back and forth," Gabriel said. Darcia sighed, shaking her head. "Everything is going to be okay. I am not worried at all about what could happen, so try to distract yourselves from what has happened. We will survive this situation, so you both can go on your little vacation once this is all over."

Darcia and Alistair both nodded. "Okay," Darcia said. "Oh man, that was quite something. I do not want to be dealing with that again." Gabriel smiled and walked over to get himself a glass from the cabinet. Alistair and Darcia both sat down next to each other at the table, holding each other's hands. "So, it was Joshua who had the vision, right?"

Gabriel nodded. "Yes," Gabriel said. "I was sitting here with my daughter, Ginger, till the boys came over to me, and Bryan explained the whole situation to me. I have been on this planet for many years and have gained plenty of experience from different people, so I can handle whatever is coming my way. I am glad you both and your sons stayed behind as support."

Alistair nodded and smiled. "Well, we could not separate Bryan from Amy for too long. I mean, those two really do love each other, and I would have hated to have kept him in a heartbreak state," Alistair said. Gabriel nodded.

"Bryan is also good with those children, so it all seems to work out quite well," Gabriel said.

There were slow footsteps walking down the stairs and walking over to the dining quarter. "Jenna," Darcia said. "What a surprise! Did you need anything, sweetie?"

Jenna looked over at them and stood by one of the chairs on the opposite side of Gabriel. "I would like to see if I can handle the sun, Gabriel," Jenna said. "I mean, I got an email from my parents on how they are looking forward to me returning to them. This is sort of making me nervous and anxious about the whole situation. I cannot be a shapeshifter. It seems so unrealistic and impossible that I will become one of you."

Gabriel looked over at Alistair and Darcia. "Well, I guess we can try that, but what if you get hurt?" Gabriel asked. "I know how difficult it is to process this whole situation, but you are probably in the transitioning phase, and if we were to release you back out into the human world, that will definitely cause a lot of problems, and it will all lead back to this castle. If the police have shown up, looking for me, the next time, it might end quite badly for all of us."

Jenna did not respond. "Has Amy mentioned anything about this process to you?" Gabriel asked. Jenna shrugged.

"Sort of, but then again, you are her father with more experience, so I trust you more with providing me with a good explanation and guidance, rather than letting me find out through various sources," Jenna said.

Gabriel nodded. "Fair enough. Well, we can try you out this morning, like in about eight hours, to see if you can handle going outside and walking in the sunlight," Gabriel said. Jenna nodded. "Okay, we will try that."

Jenna walked back toward the staircase and walked over to Amy's bedroom. She knocked on the door and opened it to find Amy putting her children in clean clothes. Arabella was on the floor.

"Oh, sorry about that," Jenna said. "I did not realize you had company. I can return later."

"Jenna, please join us. We just bathed these little ones, and we are going to put them down for their nap. Want to help?" Amy asked. Jenna smiled and nodded as she looked at the three children, who already had beautiful brown hair and one with reddish hair. "Huh, I never knew you had the red gene in you, Amy."

Amy smiled and nodded. "Probably from an ancestor," Amy said. Arabella nodded.

"From my side of the family. Sadly, most of them have passed on, but I used to have some family members with that color of hair," Arabella said. Jenna smiled and nodded.

As Amy, Jenna, and Arabella were tending to the children, Ginger walked over to Bryan's room and knocked on his door. Bryan answered the door. Ginger quickly walked past him. "Are these visions always accurate or not?" Ginger asked. Bryan shrugged. "I cannot bear the fact of seeing my father get hurt. I feel like I must do something."

Bryan looked over at his brothers, who were focused on Ginger. "Well, visions do tend to change. They are not always that accurate," Bryan said. Ginger nodded.

"When are they accurate? Could this moment actually be accurate?" Ginger asked. Bryan shrugged. "Perhaps, but as long as we are on top of our plan for handling any situation, we should be good."

Ginger nodded. "I really hope this big problem with Larry will end real soon. I cannot handle the stress and anxiety any longer, Bryan," Ginger said. "How do you all handle your problems?"

Nobody responded. Bryan chuckled. "Well, I normally either have myself a drink or I go out for a quick and speedy run, which would take me to another city or even a country if I was that upset about something," Bryan said.

The other boys scoffed. "Yeah, right," Silas said. "Another country?" Bryan turned around and scrunched his brow.

"Jealous?" Bryan asked. Silas then got to his feet and grabbed a pillow from the bed. "Oh dear, it looks like I might be challenged for a pillow fight."

Joshua and Xavier chuckled at that comment. Silas then threw a pillow at Bryan. Bryan caught the pillow, handing it to Ginger. "Perhaps she might need to vent her frustration," Bryan said. Ginger looked at the pillow and shook her head.

"I am good. I will see what my sister and her friend are up to," Ginger said before she walked out of the room. She heard the sound of them smacking each other with pillows, shaking her head in disbelief. She knocked on the door to Amy's bedroom and waited for Amy to respond.

"Yes?" Amy asked. Ginger walked into the room and found Amy, Jenna, and her mother sitting together, talking. "Ginger, come and join the party."

Ginger smiled, entered the room, and closed the door behind her.

"The boys next door are having themselves a pillow fight, but I am not up for such violence," Ginger said. Amy chuckled.

"I had a weird dream about humans walking around in our castle," Amy said. "Or was that real?"

Ginger looked at them all. "Joshua had a vision of our father being dragged away by humans," Ginger said. "There were police officers down here looking for him. Our doors were locked, so nobody could enter." Amy scrunched her brow.

"Seriously? When was I going to hear about this? What if I needed to get myself a drink from the dining quarter, and they would have spotted me?" Amy asked.

"Well, the vision took place two evenings ago, and we talked to some of our friends about these visions, and they are not always accurate, so we did not want to worry everyone," Ginger said.

Amy looked over at Arabella. "Did you know about this, mother?" Amy asked. Arabella nodded. "Why did you not mention this to me? I feel like I am being left out and potentially cast away by the whole family."

Arabella placed her right hand on Amy's shoulder. "It will be okay. Nothing bad is going to happen to any of us. Your father is quite capable of handling these situations, and we are also quite strong in our own ways. Nothing bad is going to happen. Okay?"

Amy sighed. "Where is Father anyway?" Amy asked. Ginger pointed at the bedroom door.

"Probably in the dining quarter," Ginger said. Amy got to her feet and walked over to the dining quarter. Gabriel looked up and smiled at Amy.

"Amy, what a pleasant surprise. How have you been, my child?" Gabriel asked. Amy shook her head.

"What is this about you getting taken away by humans? Why was I not told about this news? I heard people walking around our home, but I thought it was a dream," Amy said.

Gabriel sighed and gestured for Amy to sit. "Joshua's visions are not always accurate, so I did not want to cause too much unnecessary drama in our lives. Nothing bad is going to happen to me, you, or any one of us," Gabriel said. Amy sighed. "I need you to be there for your children, Amy. They need their mother. I can handle my own problems, but I need you to take care of them if anything were to happen to me. Please promise me that, Amy."

Amy rolled her eyes and nodded. "I appreciate that, my child. Did you want a drink?" Gabriel asked. Amy shrugged and nodded. Gabriel handed Amy a glass from the cupboard and poured her a full glass of blood.

Gabriel's Match

Back at the apartment complex, Larry waited patiently to hear the news regarding the exposure of shape shifters. He clicked through the channels, but nothing seemed to work. The doorbell rang. Caleb came into the living room. "Are you not going to answer that, Larry?" Caleb asked. Larry got to his feet and walked over to the front door. He peaked into the little hole and saw the police officers standing at the front door.

Larry opened the door. "Yes?" Larry asked. The same brown-haired police officer stepped forward. "Gabriel is on vacation. He will return in a week." Larry scrunched his brow.

"What?" Larry asked. "Seriously? How did you manage to allow them to deceive you like this?" The officer did not respond. "Gabriel is not on vacation. He is a shapeshifter who gets up in the evening. Why did you not show up around ten o'clock in the evening?" Again, the police officer did not respond. "Well, go back to his castle right now and show him the warrant for his arrest and his death sentence."

The police officer nodded and turned around to head back to the castle. Larry sighed with frustration. "I think we should make sure everything will work out this time, Caleb. Could you gather the rest of my team, and we will follow them over to the castle to make sure that Gabriel gets what he deserves?" Larry asked. Caleb assembled the other members. Viviana and Bianca walked over to Larry. "What is going on?" Viviana asked. "Are we seriously going to return to that castle?"

Larry nodded. "This is perhaps our only chance of getting rid of Gabriel forever," Larry said. "If the humans know of his existence, that will cause a lot of drama, which would also create chaos for the other coven members around the world. We will finally be able to regain our power, and never suffer under Gabriel's drama anymore."

Bianca looked confused at Larry. "Are you certain we are actually prepared for a final battle?" Bianca asked. "I mean, what if we expose ourselves by accident, brother dearest?"

Larry shook his head at Bianca. "It will not happen, sister, dearest. We will make sure we expose Gabriel for who he really is, get him shot several times, and perhaps even get him tortured and burned," Larry said. "Well, shall we?"

The other twenty members, including Caleb and Viviana, stood behind Bianca, watching Larry open the door and leave the apartment complex. The rest followed, and they walked toward the castle. Once they reached the castle from a distance of about ten yards, they saw the police officers stand in front of the castle and ring the doorbell. There was no response. Larry started to wonder if Gabriel was on vacation, but he quickly shook off that thought. No, Gabriel was probably hiding. He probably knew what was going to happen to him.

Larry led the other members around the area, keeping his focus on the front door. The police officers now started to bang on the front door, ordering Gabriel to open the door, or they would use force. Again, there was no response. Larry did not have much faith in humans doing his bidding, but he also never gave up on his goals either. The officers then grabbed their guns, pointing them in the direction of the front door and giving the final warning that they were going to shoot open the door. Suddenly, the door opened. The housekeeper showed up. Then Gabriel showed up from a distance, but he did not go into attack mode. He stood with poise and grace, greeting the officers.

Larry, with his sharp hearing, could hear the whole conversation. "Good evening, officers," Gabriel said. "What brings you over to my home?" The same officer Larry had spoken to earlier stepped forward.

"We have a warrant for your arrest, Gabriel Ambrose," the officer said, holding up a piece of paper. Gabriel smiled and nodded.

"I see. Well, I guess that there is probably no other way for me to get out of this one, but please, if you could enter my home for just a moment," Gabriel asked. The officer gave out a fearful vibe and swallowed nervously.

"I will not harm you at all, officer," Gabriel said in a soothing tone. "I just need to see what this document is about. Nothing more. Hildegard, dear, could you fetch our guest a nice cup of tea?" Hildegard nodded and walked over to the dining quarter to heat up some water. "Please." Gabriel gestured for the officer to enter. "The rest of you can wait here." The officer entered the castle and saw Gabriel close the door.

Gabriel walked ahead of the officer over to the dining quarter and sat down, watching Hildegard pour a cup of tea for the officer. The officer looked at the tea and placed the paper on the table. Gabriel grabbed the piece of paper and smiled at some of the words that were used in the document, such as monster, blood drinker, and terms like that. "So, what makes you think we are blood drinkers, officer?"

The officer pushed the cup of tea aside, analyzing Gabriel thoroughly. "There have been complaints that someone has been taking the blood donations from the hospitals, and we got a notice from someone who was quite worried about your existence, Mr. Lawrence Harrison," said the officer. Gabriel smiled and chuckled.

"Well, I have to be honest with you, officer," Gabriel said with his pursasion powers. "It is true that we have taken blood packs from the clinics, but we have a weak and near-dead family member who has some type of rare cancer in our home. She is too weak to even show up, and we were told by the doctors and nurses to treat her health problem at home rather than letting her stay at a hospital," Gabriel said.

Suddenly, Arabella and Amelia came into the dining quarter. Amelia got a slight makeover done on her face to make her look extra sick with white makeup and extra dark around her eyelids, putting in bloodshot red contacts to make her look ill. She had a thick bandage on her left arm to show where she was getting the transfusion inserted. "Oh dear," Gabriel said. "Honey, you should have let Amelia rest up from her treatment.

Arabella put on a sympathetic act. "I know, but she wanted to get some fresh air, and knowing that she sleeps during the day after her treatment, her clock has turned us all around, causing the rest of us to sleep during the day and stay up with her.

The officer looked at Amelia with fear. "Well, I think I will forget this warrant ever happened. I apologize for my intrusion into this home. I hope you will get well soon, madam," the officer said. Gabriel smiled and clasped his hands together.

"Thank you for such kind words," Gabriel said. Amelia gave a weak wave until her arm fell beside her. The officer grabbed his hat and the warrant and walked out of the castle.

Larry stood about ten feet away from the castle. "What happened in there?" Larry asked. "You were supposed to get him arrested. Why is he not with you?" The officer looked over at Larry.

"A woman is greatly ill inside that castle, Larry," the officer said. "There are no monsters in there."

Larry let out a loud shriek. "Yes, they are, officer!" Larry yelled. "Get back in there and get rid of them!" The other officers looked over at Larry and then at the other officer. "They are shape shifters that have been consuming blood. The fact that they have not killed off other humans is only to distract us from their real actions."

The door opened up again. Gabriel came outside. "Oh, by the way, Larry, do not ever try to one-up me. I am not an easy one to defeat," Gabriel said. Larry scoffed. "Go ahead, make a spectacle in front of the humans." Larry licked his dry lips and looked over at the officers. Viviana then used her powers on the officer. "Gabriel Ambrose needs to die," Viviana said. The other officers pointed their guns at Gabriel.

Amelia then came outside with Arabella, whispering a shield spell. The officers cocked their guns at Gabriel, aimed, and started shooting at him. The bullets only went about five feet until they fell to the ground. "Officers," Amelia said. "Your boy, Larry, is the actual killer. He is the one who has been stealing blood donations from the banks and blaming them on Gabriel. Go after him." The officers turned around and started shooting at Larry until one bullet grazed Viviana's shoulder, causing her to stumble backwards.

Amelia whispered another protection spell on them and the house. Larry let out a loud growling sound and ran ahead of his friends, over to Gabriel. His friends then ran after him, till they fell before them on the floor, writhing in pain. Viviana screamed from her wound and ran off, with Caleb running after her into the woods. Lucien, Vladimir, and Adrian then came over to the entrance. Bianca coughed from the sudden blow to her body and got to her feet. She pounced on Amelia, causing her to stumble. Arabella then tried to grab Bianca until Larry got to his feet, taking a few steps backwards.

"Brother!" Bianca shrieked. Larry looked over at Bianca and shook his head. "Perhaps you were right, sister, dear," Larry said. "Gabriel is far too strong for us." Larry did not move and waited for Arabella to push Bianca off of Amelia until another one of Larry's friends grabbed a knife from his pocket, stabbed Arabella in the back, between her rib blades, and ran off. Larry then took off running, leaving Bianca in the grasp of Amelia. Gabriel quickly grabbed and yanked the knife out of Arabella's back, causing her to scream, and quickly sliced open his left arm, feeding her his life source. The wound started to heal slowly, but Gabriel felt an intense need to want to end Larry.

"Amelia, please take Arabella inside and feed her a fresh bottle. Vladimir, please put the girl in our dungeon. Lucien and Adrian, follow me," Gabriel growled. Gabriel started to run, and he shifted himself into a wolf so he could get to Larry faster. Adrian and Lucien followed, and they shifted into wolves as well. Right before Larry could enter the house, Gabriel pounced on Larry, causing them both to spin in mid-air onto the concrete floor. Gabriel then used all of his might to rip off as much flesh as he could from Larry while Larry grabbed Gabriel by the head, pushing him away.

Some of the other members were inside the apartment complex with the door open, and some others came outside to see if Larry needed any backup. Lucien and Adrian returned to their human form, heading for the apartment complex and taking down the members who were trying to run away from them. Just then, there was a loud howl. Larry used his knife to stab Gabriel in the form of a wolf into his side, causing Gabriel to back away from him and taking out the knife.

Larry chuckled as blood trickled down his chin. "You are getting weaker, old man," Larry snapped. "I think I might be too strong for you." Gabriel placed his hand on the wound, licking his lips from the blood. Then some of the other members came out of the apartment complex: a girl with long brown hair and green eyes, a brown-haired boy with brown eyes, and a dark-toned man came over to Larry. Gabriel looked at the four individuals staring at him.

Moments later, Vladimir came over to the apartment complex in his human form and checked his watch. "We should probably return home, brother," Vladimir said. "We do not want to draw too much attention to ourselves either." Gabriel nodded. "Brother, please give me some of your life source; the wound is not healing so well."

Vladimir approached Gabriel and let Gabriel take a few sips from his neck. Larry could not help but chuckle and clap at Gabriel, even though he looked quite rough from Gabriel's attack. Adrian and Lucien came out with three of Larry's friends and used a lighter from Lucien's inner pocket to set them on fire. Larry looked over at them. "Where are the others?" Larry asked. The two men ignored him and walked down the stairs over to Gabriel, who started to heal from his wounds.

Gabriel turned around and suddenly saw Viviana standing at the top of the stairs, staring at him in shock. She tried to use her powers on him, but he did not seem to react to her. Gabriel then led the way back to the castle with his ripped suit and blood stains all over. "We should probably get home in a quicker way," Gabriel said before he shifted himself back into a wolf and ran back to the castle.

Upon his entrance into the castle, Gabriel headed over to Amelia's quarter to find Arabella on her sofa, looking tired. "Are you all right, Arabella?" Gabriel asked. Arabella nodded as she was taking more sips from a straw in a big glass with glass. Amelia looked up at Gabriel with shock.

"You look quite bad, Gabriel. Is Larry dead?" Amelia asked. Gabriel shook his head.

"No, but I do feel myself getting weaker every time I fight that man," Gabriel said. "I am really starting to feel weak and tired."

Amelia looked concerned at Gabriel. "Go to your quarter and get some sleep. Perhaps sleep for a few days to really rejuvinate your body and mind, Gabriel," Amelia said. "We have all been through a lot lately, and we all deserve some time to relax and rejuvenate from all of the conflicts we have been dealing with."

Gabriel nodded. "Well, thank you, Amelia, for everything you have done for us, especially me, and it is good to see that you are still alive, Arabella," Gabriel said before he left them. He walked over to the main floor to find his brothers waiting for him. "Brothers, how did it go with the other ones?"

Lucien and Adrian exchanged glances. "Better than what he had expected, brother, but we should have ended Larry right there. Amelia's protection spell on you would have helped you get rid of him forever," Lucien said. Gabriel shrugged.

"I am not sure how you all feel, but lately, I have been feeling more tired than before," Gabriel said.

The other brothers nodded. "Well, Bianca is in our dungeon, and this time we will not release her or bargain for her," Vladimir said. "Let Larry come over and see how far he can get with getting his sister back." Gabriel nodded.

"Okay. I think I deserve a week of good slumber. If I am not awake by tomorrow evening, I would like you three to take care of the castle and be the patrarichs of the castle till I am able to deal with more responsibilities," Gabriel said.

The other brothers nodded. "Okay. Well, enjoy the rest of your days for now," Gabriel said before he headed for his slumbering quarter. He locked the door from the inside and went off to a deep sleep.

Amy and Jenna came down the stairs around four o'clock, seeing Vladimir walking around, closing the curtains, and turning off all the lights.

"Vladimir," Amy said. "Where is my father? Did he get kidnapped?" Vladimir shook his head.

"No, Amy, but he will be sleeping for a few days. The battle from yesterday exhausted him, but it was also quite hard on the rest of us, including your mother. Amelia is helping her heal quite well," Vladimir said before he continued turning off the lights.

"What? My mother got injured? Where is she?" Amy asked. Vladimir turned to face her.

"She is with Amelia, but I would let your parents rest up so they can heal faster. Plus, we should all be going to sleep real soon." Vladimir said before he looked over at Jenna. "Are you able to walk out into the sunlight?"

Amy looked over at Jenna and then back at Vladimir. "What is he talking about, Jenna?" Amy asked.

"I am still wondering if I am actually one of you or if I am still human, Amy. My parents wrote to me. I do feel like going back home. I hope we can still be friends, but after what I have experienced in this place, there have been nothing but problems," Amy said. "Your father wanted to know if I could handle the sunlight."

Amy shook her head. "Please, Jenna, perhaps you are still in the transition phase. I cannot lose you right now," Amy said.

Vladimir stood a few feet away from Amy and Jenna. "It might be time to see if it is possible, Amy," Vladimir said. "I mean, it would have been better if your father and mother were here to witness this moment, but sadly, nothing is ever planned that well in advance. So, see if it is possible, Amy. I could stay to witness this moment instead, if you like."

Amy looked over at Vladimir in anger. "Why are you trying to push for this moment, Vladimir?" Amy asked. "What if she burns to a crisp?" Vladimir shrugged.

"Or," Vladimir said. "We could all go on a trip back to Oregon and persuade your parents that you have decided to study in Romania instead."

Amy clicked her tongue and shook her head. "I cannot think so well right now. Why must such decisions be so hard?" Amy asked. "I never wished for any of this to have happened. To me, to you, to Ginger, to anyone."

Vladimir nodded as he approached Amy. "Nobody ever gets to decide such things, Amy. Some of us are willing to become shape shifters while others are either forced, such as Larry and Caleb, or, sadly, Jenna," Vladimir said. "It is never fair for the ones who do not get to decide."

Amy felt defeated by his words and shook her head. "What time is it?" Amy asked. Vladimir checked his watch. "A bit over half past four, which means we should be getting ready for our slumber, Amy. If you need me to be here for Jenna, I will," Vladimir said.

Amy sighed. "Okay, whatever," Amy murmured. "I want to stay up as well and see what happens." Vladimir nodded.

"Remember not to go out too far into the sun, Amy. Let Jenna take her time," Vladimir said. "Oh, by the way, I would start off very easy and slow, and let your fingertips touch the sun first, Jenna. Then slowly extend your arms if it seems to go well, and then step out fully into the sun."

Jenna nodded, walked over to the sliding doors, and walked onto the patio. It was still dark. Amy stood next to Vladimir, watching Jenna from a distance. About an hour later, the sun started to rise slowly. Jenna felt her body shake and her mind panic. She had to remind herself that she was doing this to see if it was possible to return home. As the time was going onto six o'clock, Jenna held out her hand to the sun and let the sun touch her fingertips. Nothing happened. Amy looked confused at her and then at Vladimir, who kept his gaze focused on Jenna. Jenna then extended her arm. The sun did feel quite warm on her body, but nothing had happened. "Vladimir, what is going on?" Amy asked. Vladimir did not respond.

"She could be a daywalker, Amy," Vladimir said. "One of us who consumes blood but can withstand the sun."

Amy cleared her throat, which felt dry and scratchy. "Seriously? I thought those were just myths, Vladimir. How is this even possible?"

Vladimir shrugged. "I am not sure what to say, Amy. I never even knew shapeshifters existed until I met your father," Vladimir said. Jenna then walked slowly down the staircase over to the courtyard and felt the sun quite hot on her body, but she was not burning up. Jenna walked around in the sunlight, twirling around and skipping around the courtyard. Her throat felt dry, but she managed to survive the sun.

Jenna returned about a few minutes from the outdoors, through the sliding doors, closing them behind her, and pulling down the blinds to keep the sun out. Amy looked shocked and amazed at Jenna. "How did it go out there, Jenna?" Amy asked. Jenna turned around and looked a bit pink, but she had survived.

"Better than I had expected. Does this mean I get to go home?" Jenna asked. Amy looked over at Vladimir.

"I think we should make sure Gabriel is aware of this new situation, and if he gives his consent, I think you could return home, under a few conditions, of course," Vladimir said.

"What conditions?" Amy asked before Jenna could say anything. "She should be free and never feel obligated to return home."

"The conditions, Amy, are that she has to keep her new diet a secret from the human world and be very cautious, and the second condition is to keep the whole shape-shifting topic a secret from the humans," Vladimir said. Jenna nodded.

"We should wait till Gabriel is awake to tell him of this new existence. I am sorry to say this, Jenna, but you will have to wait a few days before you can return home. With this, I will bid you both a good slumber," Vladimir said before he headed for his own chamber.

Amy and Jenna stood in the dining quarter. "I wish this never happened to you, Jenna," Amy said. "I never wished this for you at all."

Jenna nodded in acknowledgment of Amy. "I know. I do not feel that angry, but only a bit sad and perhaps frustrated about this whole situation of shape shifters, consuming blood, and stuff like that. How did we even miss this in history classes, Amy? None of the historical topics ever covered the topic of shapeshifters. We have seen different movies about vampires, werewolves, Dracula, and other mystical creatures, but those were just fictional stories, Amy. How is this even possible?" Jenna asked.

Amy listened to Jenna, feeling sadness inside of her. "I am so sorry for everything, Jenna," Amy said as she wrapped her arms around her, holding her close to her. Jenna wrapped her arms around Amy, feeling tears fall down her cheeks. "I love you like a sister, Amy, and I wish we would have vacationed in a different way," Jenna said.

Amy choked on her words, feeling tears fall down her cheeks. "I know, Jenna," Amy whispered. "I wish this would have never happened to you." Jenna released her grip on Amy, placing her hands on Amy's shoulders.

"I promise that your family's secret will never be known in our world," Jenna said. Both Amy and Jenna then walked over to their own quarters. Amy could not sleep so well. She looked at the crib where her children were sleeping and smiled at how innocent they looked. She sat in her bed, staring out at the wall across from her, wondering what she should be doing. She wanted to go after Larry for what he had done to her family. Then she remembered that she had the opportunity to end his life, but she chose not to. Was she actually a killer, or did she have more empathy for humans? Would she have killed her foster parents?

While Amy was pondering the choices in her life, Caleb got into her mind.

Amy, if you have time, please meet me at the park after the sun has set. I must speak to you about a few things Amy heard in her head. She quickly shook her head, wondering if she was hallucinating. *We know Bianca is in the dungeon area. If she could return home safely, I promise to make sure that Larry never bothers you or your family again,* Amy heard in her head.

"Stop it," Amy snapped. "Get out of my mind and leave me alone forever." Then it went silent. What did Caleb mean by saying that Bianca was in the dungeon area? Is she there now? Amy grabbed her cotton robe and slippers and snuck down to the dungeon area. She stood by the door, opened it gently, and headed down the stairs toward the dungeon cage. She saw the one where Larry had been before was still empty until she heard a clicking sound next in a different cell. Bianca, with her black dilated eyes and sharp teeth, wearing a torn-up pair of jeans with a black crop top, and with her wavy brown hair all tangled up, growled at Amy.

"So Caleb was not lying," Amy said. "How did you end up here?" Amy asked.

The Plan

Bianca just glared at Amy, with her hands on the bars, yanking on them to be released. "Let me out," Bianca snapped. Amy did not respond. "I will end you first, Amy Ambrose."

"Oh yeah," Amy said in a provocative manner. "How will you be doing that? You are stuck in there." Bianca growled some more. "Look, I just had to make sure that Caleb was speaking the truth. I should get my rest upstairs, Bianca. Have a good night."

"Wait," Bianca said as her eyes returned to normal and she retracted her teeth. "I want to help end this whole conflict between your father and Larry. If I do, can I use that to bargain my way out of the dungeon?"

Amy did not respond and walked over to the staircase. "Larry plans to get rid of your children, Amy. I told him it was a bad idea, but if you will not let me out, I cannot stop him from going after Gabrielle, Maggie, and Nathaniel."

Amy walked over to the cell and barred her teeth. "You are never to mention those names ever again, Bianca," Amy snapped. Bianca chuckled at Amy's facial expression. "Or I can have my uncles end your life once they have risen. I am sure you probably have some good blood."

Bianca scoffed. "As if. My diet is not that good, like yours or your children's, Amy. We only drink donated blood, which does not always have a nice taste to it." Amy clicked her tongue, shaking her head. "So have we, Bianca. The only time I ever tasted a human was during my transitioning phase. After that, my father taught both Ginger and me to drink from the sources that our housekeeper purchased for us from blood banks and hospitals," Amy said.

"Look, me being in this cell is not going to give you any leverage on keeping you and your children safe, Amy. Larry will come for me, and even though most of his friends got killed by your uncles, there are more humans in this world to turn to," Bianca said. "If you release me, I will make sure your children remain safe and away from Larry's grasp."

Amy shook her head. "I already had a moment like this with your brother, Bianca, but I am not going to allow you to get me to release you. Have a nice stay," Amy said before she headed for the staircase.

"If your children ever wonder about who their actual father is, I am sure they will find out someday and probably hate you for lying to them, Amy. It is your choice, of course. Be honest, and see if they will understand and love you, or lie to them, and let them figure it out the hard way," Bianca said before she turned around and sat down on the ground amidst the dirt and filth of the unkept cell.

Amy turned around. "What makes you bring that up, Bianca? Has Caleb said anything about what he has been doing to them in their dreams?" Amy asked. Bianca made a zipper gesture on her lips with her fingers and shrugged. Amy then turned around to head up to the main floor. She walked over to the second staircase and sighed. She knew she had to find a way to protect her children from harm. Sending them off to the human world was not something she wanted to consider. When she approached her bedroom door, she opened it, walked back to her bed, and managed to fall asleep after another hour or so.

When dusk approached, Amy got out of bed, grabbed her robe and slippers, and decided to see how her father was doing. To her disappointment, when she tried to open the door to the basement, it was locked. "Your father needs his rest, Amy," Vladimir said as he walked past her. Amy followed Vladimir into the dining quarter.

"I need to speak to my father about what he is planning to do with Bianca in the dungeon," Amy said. Vladimir shrugged.

"For now, I would try to avoid going down there, because the last time you went down there with your friends, it did not end well for us," Vladimir said as he grabbed himself a glass from the cupboard and an opened bottle of blood from the cooler. "Did you want some?"

Amy looked at the bottle and shook her head. "I have no appetite right now, but I need to know what is going on. Who else would know about the plans, Vladimir?" Amy asked. Vladimir shook his head.

"Amy, dearest, try to distract yourself from that Bianca girl in the dungeon. I know how frustrating it is to be patient, but right now, there is not much we can do about this situation. Try to see what your sister, friend, or even children are doing," Vladimir said.

Amy sighed and turned around to walk toward the staircase to get herself dressed for the evening. She put on a pair of dark blue jeans, a light blue t-shirt, a red hoodie, and a pair of white tennis shoes. She walked over to Ginger's bedroom and gently opened the door. Ginger was still asleep. She decided to wait another hour or so until the rest of the members would wake up. Slowly, her children started to wake up and whimper for their mother. Amy approached the crib, picked up Gabrielle, and placed her on the ground. Then she grabbed Maggie, and then Nathaniel. She grabbed their sippy cups and handed them each their bottle, watching them hold their own in their hands.

"I need to see if there is a place I can keep you three at, like a deserted cabin or a protected room where nobody would be able to find you. If Larry's next move is to go after her children again, he might probably kill them, just to prove his point about how strong he is. Amy saw how fast her children were developing with their hair and their waddling, almost walking. Goodness, whatever she was feeding them had sped up some of their developments. Soon, they would be able to start talking in full sentences and then start building on their own future. Would she be able to allow her children that type of freedom? Was she supposed to keep them confined to her at all times?

Such decisions were always hard to even think about. Had Alistair and Darcia never taken her that one time, would she have remained human? What if she was never sent off to the human world with Ginger? Would she have turned out differently? Such questions were never answered by her father. Just letting her and her sister read journals and only talk briefly about meeting Larry in a tavern was not enough to keep her mind quiet about other questions. Amy started to feel depressed, wondering what her life could have been had she never been injected with Caleb's life force. Would she have had children with Bryan, or would she have preferred to be free from everyone and travel around the world?

After a while, there was a knock on the door. "Yes," Amy said as she turned to face the closed bedroom door. Bryan came into the room and closed it gently. "Good evening to you," Amy said.

"Good evening to you too, Amy," Bryan said. "How are the little ones?"

Amy looked at the children, admiring their skills and beauty. "Quite well, Bryan. They are growing up quite fast. It is so weird how they are over a year old and they are able to hold their own bottles," Amy said.

Bryan nodded and smiled. "With a mother like you, I would not be surprised," Bryan said. Amy smiled.

"What can I help you with?" Amy asked. Bryan shrugged.

"Not much, but I was wondering what the plans are for any upcoming battles," Bryan said.

"My uncle Vladimir told me not to think or do anything without talking to my father. Right now, my father wants to be left alone. He even locked the basement door, so he would not be disturbed," Amy said.

Bryan nodded. "I get it, so is your mother with him in the basement or is she sleeping elsewhere?" Bryan asked. Amy shrugged.

"Not sure, but I spoke to Bianca in the dungeon last morning, Byran. She told me that if I did not let her go, Larry would return and do something to my children," Amy said.

Bryan started to feel anger inside of him. "Did she say anything else?" Bryan asked. Amy shook her head.

"I mean, she could be bluffing, you know," Amy said. "He did manage to kidnap me and my children, but this time I will be prepared for any potential threats to my children, Bryan. I was wondering if you had any idea what I should be doing." Bryan shrugged. "Well, we should have a backup plan for your children's wellbeing, Amy. Right now, I cannot think of anything except for what I want to do to them," Bryan said.

Amy did not respond. She looked at her children, who had dropped their bottles on the ground, and started to crawl around the area. She could not help but love them. They may have some of Caleb's blood in them, but they also had hers. As far as Amy was concerned, they would never be angry with her for lying to them about Caleb, or at least tell them that Caleb had left them for another woman. Bryan looked over at Amy, watching her look at her children. "I can bring this up with my parents and brothers," Bryan said before he got to his feet. "I shall return real soon."

Amy waved at Bryan and looked back at her children. She wondered if they had any kind of power or gift they could use to protect themselves. Amy remembered that the only way she and Ginger were able to show their gifts and powers to their father was when he attacked them. That was not a nice memory to remember. The whole situation of wearing a suit to meet him and being lied to and deceived started to make her angry. She sighed and shook her head to distract herself.

Down in the dining quarter, Lucien and Adrian sat down with Vladimir, drinking some of the blood. "When did Gabriel say he was going to rise again?" Lucien asked. Vladimir shrugged.

"As far as I am concerned, he should rise whenever he feels it is right. Seeing him covered in those bite and scratch marks and looking like he was on the verge of collapsing made me think that he needs a break from the whole conflict. I wonder if we should actually go over to them now before they decide to rebuild their group again," Vladimir said. "Would that be wise?"

Lucien chuckled at that idea and shrugged. "Seriously? We just got through a bit of a battle last evening, brother. What makes you think I am physically and emotionally up for it?" Lucien asked. Adrian did not respond to Lucien. He looked over at Vladimir.

"Perhaps our brother is right, Lucien," Adrian said. "We should try to weaken his stance some more each time till he has nowhere to go."

Vladimir smiled at Adrian and then looked over at Lucien. "It is just a thought, brother," Vladimir said. "Perhaps Amelia, Alsitair, Darcia, and the other five boys could help us."

Lucien shook his head. "As interesting as that sounds, brother," Lucien said. "I am afraid we might be facing a problem or some sort of trap. Perhaps Larry would be waiting for us. Or. Perhaps he is waiting for us to leave, so he and Viviana can release that girl in the basement."

Adrian looked at Lucien. "What if Larry is mourning the loss of his friends and his sister and is too depressed to leave his home?" Adrian asked. Lucien looked over and shook his head. "I am afraid to decline this proposal, brothers. If you both want to go back to that place, go ahead, but I will stay here in case there are problems that our family can face. Larry returns for his sister, or that Bianca girl decides to try to escape. Enjoy the rest of your evening, brothers," Lucien said before he left for Gabriel's office to see what he could do for the time being. He opened up the laptop, pressed the on button, and remembered how he had struggled to work such a machine.

While Lucien was trying to figure out any news or plans regarding Gabriel, Amelia and Arabella were in Amelia's quarter. "What are you hoping to do after the whole Larry conflict is over, Amelia?" Arabella asked. Amelia shrugged.

"To be honest, after I became a shapeshifter, I became so confined and institutionalized that I have lost my human goals. I remember how I enjoyed drawing and dancing, but for many years, I have been focused on reading and concocting potions and serums for our family," Amelia said. "What about you?" Arabella shrugged. "I remember how I barely had any goals or ambitions in my life when I was growing up. After I met Gabriel, I did not do much except listen to him read poetry to me by fire or talk about the history of our world and how much it has changed. I hope that both Amy and Ginger will find their goals and ambitions back, Amelia. I do know how much they have suffered in this world," Arabella said.

Amelia nodded. "Would you spend more time with your grandchildren, Arabella?" Amelia asked. Arabella nodded and smiled.

"Of course I would. I would hope to guide and support them through their life's journey. Sweet Gabrielle with her reddish hair, then Maggie with her brown hair, and Nathaniel with his brown hair. They would be so attractive to the human world. I do wonder if Amy wants to present them to the human world or if she would prefer to keep them confined in this castle. As much as this castle has so much history, it also has a lot of darkness inside it," Arabella said.

Amelia nodded again. "I agree. I also wonder what Amy has planned for her children. She probably wants to keep them inside of this castle and help them transition into their true forms," Amelia said. Arabella nodded.

"I will ask Amy when I see her around the castle. What time is it anyway, Amelia?" Arabella asked. Amelia checked her watch.

"It is going on about eleven in the evening. Say, what will happen to that Jenna girl anyway? Did Gabriel say anything? Was she able to go outside into the sunlight yet?" Arabella shrugged.

"Even if Jenna could survive out in this world without drawing too much attention to her appearance, her taste for blood could be a problem," Amelia said. Arabella nodded. "Whatever, I should not be overthinking such thoughts." Arabella nodded.

"Well, I should see what the other ones are doing. Amelia, you should take a break from all of the hard work you have done for this family," Arabella said. "Come upstairs and join me for a drink. You deserve it."

Amelia smiled. "I agree," Amelia said. "Remember how you and I used to have our hunting moments and seduce the men at those clubs, parks, and practically everywhere? Many men found you quite attractive, and even the women admired your beauty with perhaps a hint of jealousy."

Arabella giggled and playfully punched Amelia. "So what you are saying is that I have lost those good looks after having my children?" Arabella asked. Amelia playfully punched Arabella back. Once they arrived on the main floor, they headed for the dining quarter. Lucien came out of the office and beckoned for both Amelia and Arabella to enter the office. Amelia looked over at the dining quarter.

"Can we get ourselves a drink first, Lucien?" Amelia asked. Lucien sighed and gestured for both women to get themselves a drink. "What did you need to speak with us about, Lucien?"

Lucien put his left index finger to his lips. "When you are ready, please join me in Gabriel's office," Lucien said before he headed back. Arabella and Amelia exchanged confused glances, grabbed themselves a glass, and poured themselves a full glass before they walked over to Gabriel's office. Lucien sat in Gabriel's chair with his fingers steepled beneath him. "Welcome! I have something I must share with you women, and I need your perception of what my brothers are potentially planning to do."

Amelia and Arabella both listened attentively. "They want to take you, Amelia, Darcia, and Alsitair back to Larry's home and attack him again," Lucien said. Amelia looked over at Arabella. "I know how weird this sounds, but I need you to help me persuade them not to do anything drastic. Would you actually agree with Vladimir, for example, that if we were to attack Larry right now, that it would be wise?"

Arabella shook her head. "Why now, Lucien?" Arabella asked. "I mean, he still has Viviana, but then again, she did get grazed by that bullet."

Lucien was deep in thought. "I mean, I am sure that Larry would not have a new group right now, so perhaps it is wise to go after them right now," Lucien said. "What do you think?"

Amelia sighed, shaking her head. "Again, I have asked this question many times, but how certain are you that it will work this time? It seems that no matter how hard we fight, we barely get to ending Larry, and then something bad happens, and he manages to escape or regenerate his broken body, like last time," Amelia said.

"Look at it from this angle, Amelia. Each time we fail, we do gain another advantage in finding out how to end his life quicker," Lucien said.

"The same goes for us too, Lucien," Amelia said. "I am sure he is also learning how to improve his fighting skills and strategy."

"I agree with you both," Arabella said. "I think we should get Vladimir and Adrian involved with our plans, as well."

"About that," Lucien said. "It might be best if you stayed here with your daughters. Your life is too precious for your children."

Arabella did not respond. Amelia shrugged and nodded. "I hate to agree with him, but he is right, Arabella. With Gabriel losing strength a lot, you need to stay back home," Amelia said.

Arabella sighed. "I understand that, but what would happen if you all lost this time? With Gabriel hybernating with the door locked, what am I supposed to do? Leave and run away with my children and grandchildren." Arabella asked.

Lucien looked over at Amelia. "Well, not exactly," Lucien said. "You yourself are a shape shifter as well. Amy and Ginger are both shape shifters, and as for your grandchildren, well, perhaps they might even have some type of skill or power that they still need to develop."

Arabella sighed some more. "I really hate this right now," Arabella said. "I hate the feeling of being left behind with uncertainty and fear."

Lucien nodded. "As do we, Arabella," Lucien said. "I do not want my brothers to get injured either. After Daniel's death, I caught Gabriel in his room the other evening, looking at a picture of us together. That was so hard on everyone, Arabella. This time, we will be the ones to fight and win, rather than joining Daniel."

Arabella sighed, shaking her head with anger. "Whatever you do, do not lose, or I am afraid I will have to leave Romania and perhaps move in with Logan and Audrey," Arabella said. Both Lucien and Amelia nodded.

As Lucien was preparing for their upcoming battle, Larry was dragging his friends out into their own separate graves, which eight of his friends, including Bianca, had helped him with. They set their bodies on fire before throwing them into the rectanular hole. "How did this all happen?" Larry asked as he was patting down one grave. "How did we end up losing so many members?"

Viviana looked over at him while holding the shovel in her left hand. "I have no words to describe what happened last evening, Larry, and I do not know how my powers to subdue Gabriel did not work either," Viviana said. Larry nodded.

"I have a question before I finish filling up the final grave," Larry said. "Should we reconsider going to a different country for a while?"

Viviana looked at Larry, and then at his friends, a young female teenager with long black hair wearing slacks, a dark male with jeans and a t-shirt, and, a short-haired blonde woman with jeans and a crop top, looked over at them. "Well, perhaps that might be a good idea," Viviana said. "I was considering a Scandinavian country, where it is mostly cold and dark."

Larry nodded. "Yeah, that might be something. First, we need to release my sister from their dungeon this time. Soon she and I can discuss our experiences of which cell looked more comfortable," Larry said with a chuckle. "I wonder how she is even doing. She is probably suffering, just like me."

Down in the dungeon, Bianca sat on the floor with her back against the concrete floor, getting more tired and weaker by the minute. If only there was something or someone that could help her escape. She looked around and saw nothing but dirt and cobwebs. "I guess the housekeeper does not think it is important to do a little cleaning in their dungeon area," Bianca said to herself.

Bianca just looked ahead of her and tried her best to keep as relaxed and calm as possible. The less time she spent overthinking about potential plans, the bigger the chance she had of surviving. She looked at her nails, which looked quite dirty but also razor-sharp. Then she remembered that Larry mentioned that girl, Jenna. Could she perhaps release her from the cell? What if she were to communicate with her in thought?

Jenna, are you still alive? If so, could you come over to the dungeon area and help me? Bianca thought. Perhaps it was pointless, because Jenna could not be a shape shifter, and she did not think that shape shifters could control humans either. She gave up that thought and pulled her knees closer to her chest, trying to keep as relaxed as possible.

Epilogue

Amy was in her bedroom when she heard a knock on her bedroom door. "Yes?" Amy asked. The door opened, and Arabella came into her room. "Mother, what brings you here?"

Arabella sighed. "While your father is resting up, your uncles and aunt, Darcia and Alsitair, with their sons, want to go over to Larry's home and see how far they can get with killing him off," Arabella said. Amy's eyes widened. "I know, but listen. I will stay here with your children and Ginger and make sure nothing bad happens to us. If we need to, we can relocate over to Australia and stay with Logan and Audrey for a while."

Amy sighed, feeling a sense of frustration. "I know how you are feeling right now, Amy, but if your relatives have a good chance of winning this battle, we should give them a chance," Arabella said. Ginger knocked on the open door. Both Arabella and Amy looked over.

"Is everything okay?" Ginger asked. "I am sensing something quite distressful." Amy looked back at her mother.

"Lucien believes it might be a good idea to have your extended relatives go after Larry one last time, my dear," Arabella said. Gabriel clicked her tongue, shaking her head.

"Why?" Ginger asked. "Why would they think that it would work out this time?" Arabella shook her head and shrugged.

"I know how you feel, Ginger," Arabella said. "When Lucien told me of this plan, I had a weird feeling that something bad was going to happen. I hope not, but I also do not trust these plans anymore."

"What about Bryan and his brothers, mother? Why must they join them? Where were Dante's children, Alarick's children, or even

Kristjan's children? They got to stay at home while their parents put their lives at risk. Do they not know how important Bryan is to the future of my children? Where is he anyway?" Amy asked.

Amy walked past Arabella and Ginger, walking over to Bryan and Raymond's bedroom knocking loudly. This time, Raymond opened the door. "Where is Bryan?" Amy asked. Bryan showed up at the door with a smile on his face.

"Amy, what is going on? You seem upset about something," Bryan said. Amy sighed, shaking her head.

"Are you seriously going to put your life at risk by taking down Larry, Bryan?" Amy asked. "What about my children? What about me? Does our love and future partnership not mean anything?"

Bryan sighed and gestured for Raymond to take a few steps back. "Amy, I know how bad this sounds, but if we can put an end to Larry, Caleb, Viviaan, or even Bianca, I want to get rid of them forever, so we can all live happily ever after. I cannot let my parents or brothers go out fighting while I remain here. I love you, Amy Ambrose, and once we are done forever, I hope we can perhaps take our final step, if you know what I mean," Bryan said.

"Marriage?" Amy asked. "Were you going to propose to me?" Bryan nodded as he patted his pocket.

"Where did I place that box?" Bryan asked as he looked around. Raymond pointed at his night table. There was a small black box on the table. Arabella and Ginger walked over to Bryan's room with surprised expressions.

Bryan got down on one knee. "I was going to save this moment for when we finish Larry off for good, but I guess we still have some time before we have to face the music, as they say," Bryan said with a chuckle. Bryan smiled and sighed. "Okay, here I go," Bryan said. He cleared his throat and let out another sigh. Arabella smirked at the whole preparation. "Amy Rose Ambrose, will you take this ring and marry me?" Bryan asked.

Suddenly Jenna came walking down the stairs, looked over, and then headed for the basement area. Jenna had black dilated eyes, sharp nails, and sharp teeth that were protracted. She headed down to the dungeon area and walked over to the cell where Bianca was sitting. "Oh goodness, I guess the mind communication worked," Bianca said. "Jenna, how good it is to see you again." Jenna did not respond. She just stood in front of Bianca's cell, staring at her. "Well, if you could be a dear and help me out of this cell, that would help me a lot."

Jenna shook her head. "It was your brother who started my process of becoming a shapeshifter. He was the one who had fed some of his life source to me," Jenna growled. Bianca suddenly felt scared. "Please, Jenna, I never would have thought that you would have ended up in this situation. Amy, for sure, but you, luring you over to Romania, please," Bianca begged.

Jenna brushed her long, sharp nails against the bars, causing a loud screeching sound. "Larry, please help me!" Bianca screamed, hoping Larry would be around to hear her. Jenna ripped off the slot from the cell, tossing it aside before she opened the cage door, and pounced on Bianca, causing her to scream loudly.

Amy looked over at where the screaming was coming from and ran over to Jenna's room. "Jenna!" Amy screamed. "Are you all right?"

Ginger and Arabella then followed up to Jenna's bedroom. Bryan remained in the same position. The bedroom door for Silas, Xavier, and Joshua opened.

"Bryan?" Joshua asked. "What are you doing?"

Bryan rose back up and closed the box. "I was hoping I would have gotten an answer from Amy after I had proposed to her, but I never heard a confirmation or a response from her," Bryan said. Raymond came over and put his right hand on Bryan's shoulder.

"You will," Raymond said. "We should find out what that screaming was about. Lucien, Vladimir, and Adrian then ran down to the basement and stood at a distance with shock on their faces.

"Jenna," Vladimir whispered. "What have you done?"

Jenna held Bianca like a ragdoll in her arms before she turned around to face them with blood covered around her mouth, dripping down her chin, and onto her pajama shirt.

"Bianca called to me, and I realized that me becoming this monster was all Larry's fault. He lured me over to his home, pretending to be Amy, and fed me some of his life source. I am not sure if I am a shape shifter or still in the transitioning phase, but I felt the need to end her life," Jenna said.

The door to the basement opened up, and there were loud and fast footsteps coming down the stairs. Amy gasped at the sight of Jenna. She broke down, crying. Arabella looked over at Jenna with shock while she placed her right hand on Amy's shoulder, holding her close. Bryan then came running down the stairs in shock.

"Jenna?" Bryan asked. "Are you one of us?"

Jenna shrugged. "I am not sure, but I heard Bianca's voice inside of mine and realized that Larry was the main cause of this new life," Jenna said. "I do not think I can return to my parents looking and acting like this."

"Okay," Lucien said. "Well, this could cause a big fight to break out, but we will be prepared for any upcoming fights."

Ginger looked at the drained body of Bianca. "She is still breathing, I think," Ginger said as she approached Bianca. She leaned down to Bianca's mouth and heard the sound of strained breathing coming from her mouth. "Jenna, I think we should put Bianca in a different cell before it is too late. Please hand me the body."

Jenna held Bianca's body out to Ginger and started walking toward the other group members who had their focus all on her.

"Jenna," Amy whispered. "Are you all right?"

Jenna looked over at Amy, still with her dilated eyes, and looked over at the other members. "What am I?" Jenna asked. "Is there a way to reverse it?"

Vladimir, Lucien, and Adrian exchanged glances, shaking their heads. "I am afraid not, dear Jenna," Lucien whispered. "Nobody ever transitions back to their human form."

Jenna could not help but break down, crying. Amy ran over to her, holding her in her arms. "Where is Amelia? Amy asked. "Please, see if she can help her." Lucien walked over to the staircase and headed up to the main floor to find Amelia standing at the top.

"There is no cure, Lucien," Amelia said in a monotone voice. "There never has been. Whatever we became is something out of the ordinary. Not everyone gets to have a good ending. Some of us or them, or whoever has suffered, have ended their own lives. Us? There is no way for us to escape our lot that easily."

Lucien nodded. "Did you want to come down and see the girl, Amelia?" Lucien asked. Amelia shrugged.

"Why? The thought of her suffering is too much to bear right now, and I am not sure if I can handle that. I tried helping her before this moment, but there was not much I could do for her. On a positive note, she has three different types of blood added to her own, Lucien. Larry, Gabriel's, and Bianca. She might become one of the strongest shape shifters in our lives," Amelia said.

Lucien could not help but smirk at Amelia's comment. "Well, I will tell Amy and Jenna the bad news. We shall talk soon," Lucien said before he walked back down the stairs and walked over to Amy and Jenna, explaining the situation. Amelia stayed behind on the top of the stairs and sghed.

"Poor child," Amelia said. "Nobody ever deserves to suffer like that. She was only used as a bargaining chip, and she ended up becoming one of us. She did not deserve that."

As Amy sat in the dungeon area, she realized that her children were awake and also quite vulnerable, especially since Bianca did mention that Larry would go after them. Amy quickly ran upstairs to her bedroom and panted when she reached her closed bedroom door. She opened the door gently and saw her children playing with their toys on the ground. Amy sighed with relief and closed the door again.

Suddenly, she heard a familiar voice inside her head again. *Amy, I must speak with you. Please meet me at the park where we have met before, I must speak with you.*

www.ingramcontent.com/pod-product-compliance
Lightning Source LLC
Chambersburg PA
CBHW040515170726
48295CB00012B/203